Fear Not

ANNE HOLT spent two years working for the Oslo Police Department before founding her own law firm and serving as Norway's Minister for Justice during 1996–1997. Her first book was published in 1993 and she has subsequently developed two series: the Hanne Wilhelmsen series and the Johanne Vik series. Both are published by Corvus.

ANNE HOLT
Fear Not

TRANSLATED BY MARLAINE DELARGY

CORVUS

First published in the English language in Great Britain in 2011
by Corvus, an imprint of Atlantic Books Ltd.

Originally published in Norwegian in 2009
by Piratforlaget AS, Postbooks 2318 Solli, 0201 Oslo.

Published by agreement with Salomonsson Agency.

This translation has been published with the financial support of NORLA.

1 3 5 7 9 10 8 6 4 2

A CIP catalogue record for this book is available from
the British Library.

Hardback ISBN: 978-1-84887-610-1
Trade paperback ISBN: 978-1-84887-611-8

Printed in Great Britain by the MPG Books Group

Corvus
An imprint of Atlantic Books Ltd
Ormond House
26-27 Boswell Street
London WC1N 3JZ

www.corvus-books.co.uk

To Ann-Marie,
for fifteen wonderful years
of love and collaboration

PART I

Christmas 2008

The Invisible Child

It was the twentieth night of December.

One of those Saturday nights that promise more than they can deliver had imperceptibly slipped into the last Sunday of Advent. People were still moving from bar to bar and from pub to pub as they cursed the heavy snow that had moved in across Oslo without warning just a few hours earlier. The temperature had then crept up to three degrees above zero, and all that remained of the festive atmosphere was grey slush on top of the mounds of snow, and lakes of dirty water as it melted.

A child was standing motionless in the middle of Stortingsgate.

She was barefoot.

'When the nights grow long,' she sang quietly, 'and the cold sets in ...'

Her nightdress was pale lemon with embroidered ladybirds on the yoke. The legs beneath the nightdress were as thin as chopsticks, and her feet seemed to be planted in the slush. The skinny, half-naked child was so out of place in the image of the city at night that no one had noticed her yet. The Christmas party season was approaching its climax, and everybody was preoccupied with their own affairs. A half-naked, singing child on one of the city streets in the middle of the night became completely invisible, just like in one of the books the little girl had at home, where exciting animals from Africa were cunningly hidden in drawings of Norwegian landscapes, concealed among bark and foliage, almost impossible to spot because they didn't belong there.

'... then the little mummy mouse says ...'

Everyone was out to have a good time, and a few actually were enjoying themselves. Outside Langgaard's jewellers a woman was leaning against the security grille over the window as she stared at her

8

own vomit. Undigested, deep red raspberry jam oozed among the remains of spare ribs and fried beef, slush and sand. A gang of young lads whooped at her and sang dirty songs from the other side of the street, their voices off-key. They were dragging a wasted mate with them past the National Theatre, ignoring the fact that he had lost a shoe. Outside every bar smokers stood huddled against the cold. A salty wind from the fjord blew along the streets, blending with the smell of tobacco smoke, alcohol and cheap perfume; the smell of a Norwegian city night just before Christmas.

But nobody noticed the girl singing so quietly on the street, right in the middle of two shining silver tramlines.

'And the mummy mouse ... and the mummy mouse ... and the mummy mouse ...'

She couldn't get any further.

The Number 19 tram set off from the stop further up towards the Palace. Like a sleigh as heavy as lead, full of people who didn't really know where they were going, it accelerated slowly down the gentle slope towards the Hotel Continental. Some people hardly even knew where they had been. They were asleep. Others were rambling about going on somewhere, having a few more drinks, chatting up a few more girls before it was too late. Others simply stared blankly out into the thick warmth that settled on the windows like a damp, grey veil.

A man by the entrance to the Theatre Café looked up from the expensive shoes he had chosen for the evening in the hope that the snow wouldn't come just yet. His feet were soaked, and the marks left by the road salt would be difficult to get rid of when his shoes had finally dried out.

He was the first to see the child.

His mouth opened to shout a warning. Before he had chance to take a breath, he was pushed hard in the back, and it was all he could do to stay on his feet.

'Kristiane! Kristiane!'

A woman in national costume stumbled in her full skirt. Instinctively she grabbed at the man with the ruined Enzo Poli shoes. He hadn't properly regained his balance, and both of them fell over.

'Kristiane,' the woman sobbed, trying to get up.

The warning bell on the tram was clanging frantically.

The driver, who was coming to the end of an exhausting double shift, had finally spotted the girl. There was a screech of metal on metal as he slammed the brakes on as hard as he could on the wet, icy rails.

'... and the little mummy mouse says to all her babies,' sang Kristiane.

The tram was only six metres away from her and travelling at the same speed when the mother finally managed to get to her feet. She hurled herself into the road with her skirt half ripped off, stumbled but managed to stay upright, and screamed again:

'Kristiane!'

Afterwards someone would say that the man who appeared from nowhere resembled Batman. In which case it was due to his wide coat. He was, in fact, both short and slightly overweight, and bald into the bargain. Since everyone's eyes were on the child and the despairing mother, no one really saw how the man darted in front of the screeching tram with surprising agility. Without slowing down he scooped up the child with one arm. He had just cleared the line when the tram slid over the almost invisible footprints left by the child and stopped. A torn-off scrap of the dark coat flapped gently in the breeze, caught on the tram's front bumper.

The city let out a sigh of relief.

No cars could be heard; screams and laughter died away. The bell on the tram stopped clanging. The tram driver sat motionless, his hands on his head and his eyes staring. Even the little girl's mother stood there frozen to the spot a metre or so away from her, her party outfit ruined, her arms dangling helplessly by her sides.

'... if nobody gets caught in the trap,' Kristiane continued to warble, without looking at the man carrying her.

Someone tentatively began to applaud. Others joined in. The applause grew, and it was as if the woman in national costume suddenly woke up.

'Sweetheart!' she screamed. She dashed up to her daughter, grabbed her and clutched her to her breast. 'You must never do anything like that again! You must promise me that you'll never, ever do anything like that again!'

Johanne Vik raised one arm without thinking and without slackening her grip on her child. The man's expression didn't change as her hand struck his cheek. Without paying any attention to the livid red marks left by her fingers, he gave a wry smile, inclined his head in a slow, deep, old-fashioned bow, then turned away and disappeared.

'... but steady as you go, soon everyone will be celebrating Christmas,' the child sang.

'Is it all right? Is everything OK?'

More and more people were pouring out of the Hotel Continental, all talking at the same time. Everyone realized that something had happened, but only a few knew what it was. Some were talking about someone being run over, others about an attempt to kidnap little Kristiane, the bride's sister's unusual child.

'Oh, sweetheart,' her mother wept. 'You mustn't do this kind of thing!'

'The lady was dead,' said Kristiane. 'I'm cold.'

'Of course you are!'

The mother set off towards the hotel, taking small, tentative steps to avoid slipping. The bride was standing in the doorway. Her strapless bodice was strewn with shimmering white sequins. Heavy silk fell in luxurious folds over her slender hips and down to her feet, where a pair of beaded shoes were still equally white and shimmering. The main focus of the evening was, as she should be, beautiful and perfectly made up, with her hair just as elegantly swept up as it had been when the reception started several hours earlier. The glow on the skin of her bare shoulders suggested she had been on her honeymoon in advance. She didn't even look cold.

'Are you OK?' she smiled, caressing her niece's cheek as her sister walked past.

'Auntie,' said Kristiane. 'Auntie Bride! You look so beautiful!'

'Which is more than you can say about your mother,' muttered the bride.

Only Kristiane heard her. Johanne didn't even glance at her sister. She hurried inside, into the warmth. She wanted to get to her room, crawl under the covers with her daughter, perhaps a bath, a hot bath. Her child was freezing cold and must be thawed out as soon as possible. She staggered across the floor, struggling to breathe. Even though Kristiane, who was almost fourteen, hardly weighed more than a ten-year-old, her mother was almost collapsing beneath her weight. In addition, her skirt was hanging down so much that she stood on it with every other step. Her hair, which she had wound around her head in a braid, had fallen down. The style had been Adam's suggestion, and she had been sufficiently stressed in the hours before the wedding to take his advice. Just a few minutes into the celebrations she had felt like Brünnhilde in a production from the interwar years.

A well-built man came running down the stairs.

'What's happened? What ... is she OK? Are you OK?'

Adam Stubo tried to stop his wife. She hissed at him through gritted teeth:

'Stupid idea! We're ten minutes from home by taxi. Ten minutes!'

'What's a stupid idea? What are we ... ? Let me carry her, Johanne. You're dress is torn and it would be ...'

'It's not a dress! It's a national costume! It's called a kirtle! And it was your idea! This ghastly hairstyle and this hotel and bringing Kristiane with us. She could have died!'

She was overcome by tears, and slowly let go of her daughter. The man with the strong arms gently took the child, and together they walked up the stairs. Neither of them said anything. Kristiane carried on singing in her thin, pure voice:

'Hey hop fallerallera, when Christmas comes let every child rejoice!'

*

'She's asleep, Johanne. The doctor said she was fine. There's no point in going home now. It's ...'

The man glanced over at the silent TV screen, where the hotel was still welcoming Mr & Mrs Stubo.

'Quarter past three. It's almost half past three in the morning, Johanne.'

'I want to go home.'

'But ...'

'We should never have agreed to this. Kristiane's too young ...'

'She's almost fourteen,' said Adam, rubbing his face. 'It's hardly irresponsible to let a fourteen-year-old come to her aunt's wedding. It was actually incredibly generous of your sister to pay for a suite and a babysitter.'

'Some babysitter!' She spat out the words in a mist of saliva.

'Albertine fell asleep,' Adam said wearily. 'She lay down on the sofa

12

when Kristiane finally went to sleep. What else was she supposed to do? That was why she was here, Johanne. Kristiane knows Albertine well. We can't expect her to do any more than she was asked to do. She brought Kristiane up here after dessert. This was an accident, a sheer accident. You have to accept that.'

'An accident? Is it an accident when a child like ... like Kristiane manages to get out through a locked door without anyone noticing? When the babysitter – who, incidentally, Kristiane knows so well that she still refers to her as 'the lady' – is sleeping so heavily that Kristiane thought she was *dead*? When the child starts wandering around a hotel full of people? People who were drunk! And then wanders out into the street in the middle of the night without proper clothes and without any shoes and without ...'

She put her hands to her face, sobbing. Adam got up from his chair and sat down heavily beside her on the bed.

'Can't we go to bed?' he said quietly. 'Things will seem so much better in the morning. I mean, it all worked out fine after all. Let's be grateful for that. Let's get some sleep.'

She didn't respond. Her hunched back trembled every time she breathed.

'Mummy?'

Johanne quickly wiped her face and turned to her daughter with a big smile.

'Yes, sweetheart?'

'Sometimes I'm completely invisible.'

From the corridor came the sound of giggling and laughter. Someone was shouting 'cheers!' and a male voice wanted to know where the ice machine was.

Johanne lay down cautiously on the bed. She slowly caressed the girl's thin, fair hair, and put her mouth close to Kristiane's ear.

'Not to me, Kristiane. You are never invisible to me.'

'Oh yes I am,' said Kristiane with a little laugh. 'To you, too. I am the invisible child.'

And before her mother had time to protest – as the town-hall clock proclaimed that yet another half-hour had passed on this twentieth day of December – Kristiane fell into a deep sleep.

A Room with a View

As the town-hall clock struck half past three, he decided that enough was enough.

He stood by the window, looking out at what there was to see.

Which wasn't a great deal.

Ten hours earlier heavy snow had fallen on Oslo, making the city clean and light. In the empty silence of his office he had immersed himself so deeply in his work that he hadn't noticed the change in the weather. The city lay dark and formless below him. Although it wasn't raining, the air was so damp that water was trickling down the window panes. Akershus Fortress was discernible only as a vague shadow on the other side of the harbour. The grey, indolent crests of the waves were the only indication that the black expanse between Rådhuskaia and Nesodden, all the way out to Hurumlandet, was actually made up of fjord and sea.

But the lights were beautiful, street lamps and lanterns transformed into shimmering little stars through the wet glass.

Everything lay ready on his desk.

The Christmas presents.

A Caribbean cruise for his brother and sister and their families. On one of the company's own ships, admittedly, but it was still a generous gift.

A piece of jewellery for his mother, who would turn sixty-nine on Christmas Eve; she never tired of diamonds.

A remote-controlled helicopter and a new snowboard for his son.

Nothing for Rolf, as they always agreed and invariably regretted.

And 20,000 kroner to charitable causes.

That was everything.

The personal gifts were quickly dealt with. It had taken less than half an hour with his regular jeweller in Amsterdam in November, a walk around a mall in Boston the same week, plus twenty minutes on the computer this evening to produce an attractive gift card for his brother and sister's families. There were plenty of tempting pictures of Martinique and Aruba on the shipping company's home pages. He was pleased with the result, and he managed to make it personal by lining up the entire family along the railing on board MS *Princess Ingrid Alexandra* at sunset.

It was the charitable donations that had taken time.

Marcus Koll Junior put his heart and soul into each donation. Dispensing generous gifts was his Christmas present to himself. It always did him good, and reminded him of his grandfather. The old man, who had been the closest thing to God that little Marcus could imagine, had once asked him the following question with a smile. A man helps ten other men who are in need, and takes the credit for doing so. A different man helps one other man in need, but keeps it to himself and gets no thanks for what he has done. Which of the two is the better person?

The ten-year-old replied that it was the first man, and had to defend his position. Marcus stuck to his guns for a long time: the intention of the donor was not the issue. It was the result that mattered. Helping ten people was better than helping one. The old man had stubbornly argued for the opposite point of view – until, at the age of fifteen, the boy changed his mind. Then his grandfather did the same. The argument continued until Marcus Koll Senior died at the age of ninety-three, leaving behind a well-organized life in a pale green folder with the logo of the Norwegian state railway on it. The documents showed that he had given away 20 per cent of everything he had earned throughout his adult life. Not 10 per cent, as was traditional within the labour movement, but 20. A fifth of his grandfather's earnings had been a gift to those worse off than himself.

Marcus looked through all the documents on the day his grandfather was buried. It was a journey in time through the darkest events of the twentieth century. He found receipts for deposits made to needy widows before the war and Jewish children after it. To refugees from Hungary in 1956. Save the Children had received a small amount each month since 1959, and his grandfather had made decent donations after most disasters from 1920 onwards: shipwrecks in the years between the wars, the famine in Biafra, right up to the tsunami in Southeast Asia. He died on New Year's Eve 2004, only five days after the tidal wave, but had managed to get to the post office in Tøyen in order to send 5,000 kroner to Médecins Sans Frontières.

As a train driver with a wife who stayed at home, five children and eventually fourteen grandchildren, it couldn't have been particularly easy to nibble away at his wage packet and later his pension, year after year. But he never took any credit for it. The money had been paid at different post offices, always far enough away from his apartment in Vålerenga so that he wouldn't be recognized. The name of the donor was always false, but the handwriting gave him away.

His grandfather hadn't helped one person, he had helped thousands.

Just like his grandson.

Marcus Koll Junior's contributions to charity and research were of quite a different order from those of the old man. As was to be expected. He earned more in just a few weeks than his grandfather had in his entire life. But he imagined the joy of giving was just the same for both of them, and that there was no real answer to his grandfather's riddle. Sharing what you had was not a question of being noble for either man. It was simply about being contented with one's own life. And just as his grandfather had allowed himself the small vanity of letting his grandson know what he had done, when it was all over and the discussion had literally died, Marcus Junior also kept a detailed record of his donations. They were made with great discretion, through various channels which made it impossible for the recipient to identify the real donor. The money was a gift from Marcus himself, not from one of his companies; it was declared and taxed before he passed it on via circuitous routes that only he knew about. And nobody would know, apart from the youngest Marcus Koll, eight years old in two months, who would find out one day, when he turned thirty-five, what his father had been doing every night up to the last Sunday in Advent.

It usually brought him a sense of calm; the calmness he needed.

His heart was beating too fast.

He walked back and forth across the room. It wasn't particularly large, and there was no evidence of the money generated behind the old oak desk. Marcus Koll's office was located on Aker Brygge, which had been an impressive address a couple of financial crises ago, but the area was no longer so desirable. Which suited Marcus very well.

He clutched his chest and tried to breathe slowly. His lungs had a will of their own, gasping for air much too quickly, his breathing much too shallow. It was as if he had been nailed to the floor. It was impossible to move: he was dying. His fingertips prickled. His lips were numb, and the stiffness in his mouth made his tongue feel huge and dry. He had to breathe through his nose, but his nose was blocked, he had stopped breathing, he would be dead in a few seconds.

He saw himself in a way that he had read about, a sensation he had experienced so many times before. He was standing outside his body, leaning slightly at an angle with something approaching a bird's-eye view, and he could see a stocky, 44-year-old man with bags under his eyes. He could smell his own fear.

A hot flush surged through his body, making it impossible for him to shake it off. He staggered over to the desk and grabbed a paper bag from the top drawer. He gathered the top loosely between his right thumb and forefinger, put the bag to his lips and breathed as deeply and evenly as he could.

The metallic taste didn't diminish.

He tossed the bag aside and rested his forehead against the window.

Not ill. He wasn't ill. His heart was OK, even though he had a stabbing pain beneath his left shoulder blade and in his arm – his left arm now that he thought about it. No, no pain.

Don't think about it.

Breathe.

His hands felt as if they were covered in tiny crawling insects and he didn't even dare to shake them off. His head felt light and alien, as if it didn't belong to him. His thoughts were whirling so fast that he couldn't catch them. Fragmented images and disjointed phrases kept spinning by on a carousel that made him sway. He tried to think of a recipe, a recipe for pizza, pizza with feta cheese and broccoli, an American pizza he had made thousands of times and could no longer remember.

Not ill. Not a brain haemorrhage. Not feeling sick. He was perfectly fine.

Perhaps it was cancer. He felt a stabbing pain in his right side, the side where his liver was, his pancreas, the side for cancer and disease and death.

Slowly he opened his eyes. A small part of his mind knew that he was fine. He must focus on that, not on forgotten recipes and death. The dampness on the window pane left its ice-cold impression on his forehead, and the tears began to flow.

It was becoming easier to breathe. His pulse, which had been pounding at his eardrums, against his breastbone, in the tips of his fingers and painfully hard in his groin, was slowing down.

Oslo still lay there on the other side of the window, outside this room with its view of the harbour, the fjord and the islands. Marcus Koll had just donated a fortune to charitable causes and he really wanted to feel the warmth that the last Sunday in Advent always gave him: the contented feeling of happiness because of Christmas, because of the gifts, because his son was looking forward to the holiday, because his mother was still alive, quarrelsome and impossible, because he had done the right thing, and because everything was as it should be. He wanted to think about his life which was not yet over, if he could just manage to calm his breathing.

Calm down. Just calm down.

He caught sight of someone out walking, one of the few people still wandering around down there on the quayside, apparently with no goal or purpose. It was almost five o'clock on Sunday morning. All the bars were closed. The man down below was alone. He was staggering from side to side, having difficulty staying upright on the slippery surface. Suddenly he took a couple of despairing steps off at an angle, grabbed hold of his hat as if it were a fixed point, and disappeared over the quayside.

Suddenly everything was different. His heart was beating normally once more. The pressure on his chest eased. Marcus Koll straightened his back and focused. It was as if his mucus membranes suddenly became slippery and smooth; his tongue shrank; his mouth was lubricated as it was meant to be. His thoughts gradually fell into line, one following the other in a logical sequence. He quickly worked out how long it would take him to get out of the office, down the stairs and over to the edge of the quayside. Before he had finished he could see people running to the scene. Five or six men, including a Securitas guard, yelling so loudly that he could hear them from where he was standing, five storeys above them and behind a triple-glazed window. The uniformed man was already clambering down the side of the quay.

Marcus Koll turned away and decided to go home.

Only now did he realize how tired he was.

If he hurried he might manage three hours' sleep before the boy demanded his attention. It was Sunday, after all, and it would soon be Christmas. Presumably some of the snow that had fallen yesterday would still be lying on the hills around the city. They could go out. Skiing, perhaps, if they went far enough into Marka.

The last thing Marcus Koll did before leaving was to open the little jar of white, oval tablets in the top drawer. They were probably past their best-before date. It was such a long time ago. He tipped one of them into the palm of his hand. A moment later he put it back, screwed on the lid and locked the drawer.

It was over. For now.

The sirens were already approaching.

*

'Are the police on their way? Is that them? Has someone called an ambulance? Those sirens are the police, for God's sake! Call an ambulance! Give me a hand here!'

The security guard had one arm over the edge of the quayside. One foot was resting on a slippery crossbar no more than half a metre above the surface of the water. The other was dangling back and forth in a desperate attempt to keep the heavy body balanced.

'Grab hold of me! Get hold of my jacket!'

A young lad lay down on his stomach in the slush and seized the guard's sleeves with both hands. His eyes were shining. He would be eighteen in a couple of months, but was blessed with dark stubble that made it possible for him to go from bar to bar all night without any questions being asked. He was broke, and had mostly stuck to finishing the dregs of other people's beer. Right now he felt stone-cold sober.

'That's not him,' he panted, getting a firmer grip. 'The guy who fell in is further out.'

'What? What the hell are you talking about?'

The guard stared at the body he was desperately trying to haul out of the water. He had a good grip on the collar, but the body inside the clothes was lifeless and as heavy as lead in the water, with the hood pulled up and fastened.

'Help,' someone yelled in the dark water further out. 'Help! I ...'

The cry died away.

The boy with the stubble let go of the guard.

'You'll have to hang on yourself!' he shouted. 'I'll get the other one!'

He stood up, kicked off his shoes, pulled off his padded jacket and dived into the dark water without hesitation. When he came up he was in the exact spot where he had seen the drunken man splashing around.

'Were there two of them? Did two people fall in? Did you see? Did anyone see?'

The guard was still hanging on with one arm over the quayside, bellowing. His other hand was clutching something that was definitely a body: a head facing away from him, two arms and a dark jacket. It was just so heavy. So bloody heavy. His arms were aching and he had no feeling in his fingers.

He didn't let go.

The young man who had just jumped in was gasping for air. The first paralyzing shock of the cold water had given way to an agonising pain so fierce that his lungs were threatening to go on strike. He was treading water so frenetically that half his body was above the surface. Beneath him he could see nothing but a dark, colourless depth of water.

'There!' shouted an out-of-breath police officer from the quay.

The boy turned around and made a grab. He couldn't actually see anything. It was more of a reflex action. His fingers closed around something and he pulled. The half-drowned drunk broke the surface of the water with a roar, as if he had already started screaming underwater. His rescuer had a firm hold on his hair. The drunk tried to wrench himself free and clamber on top of the younger man at the same time. Both of them disappeared. When they came up a few seconds later, the older man was lying on his back, his arms and legs outstretched on the water. He screamed with pain as his rescuer refused to let go of his hair, and, in fact, clutched it more tightly as he wound a rope four times around his other arm, without considering where it had come from.

'Have you got it?' shouted the police officer up above. 'Can you hold on?'

The boy tried to answer, but ended up with a mouthful of water. He managed to give a sign with the arm that was attached to the rope.

'Pull,' he groaned almost inaudibly, swallowing even more water.

Never in his life had he imagined that the cold could be so intense. The water seared its way into every pore. Needles of ice pierced him all over. His temples felt as if someone were trying to push them into his brain, and it seemed as if his sinuses were packed with ice. He could no longer feel his hands, and for one moment of pure, sheer terror he thought his testicles had disappeared. His crotch was on fire, a paradoxical warmth spreading from his balls and out into his thighs.

He was finding it more difficult to move. He knew his eyes were dead. Somebody must have unscrewed them. There was nothing but wetness, cold and darkness. It couldn't have been more than a minute since he dived in, but it occurred to him that this was the last thing he would ever experience, losing his balls in the depths of the December sea, because of some fucking idiot on Aker Brygge.

Suddenly he was out.

He was lying on the ground on a blanket that looked as if it were made of aluminium foil, and somebody was trying to remove his clothes.

He held on tight to his trousers.

'Take it easy,' said a police officer, presumably the same one that had thrown the rope. 'We need to get those wet clothes off. The paramedics will soon be here to look after you.'

'My balls,' whimpered the boy. 'And my fingers, they ...'

He turned away. Two police officers – the place was crawling with them now – were just laying a person down on the ground a few metres away. Streams of water poured from the figure as they struggled, but he didn't move. As soon as they had put him down, an ambulance driver came running over with a trolley. The older police officer pushed him away when he tried to help move the body again.

'He's dead. Look after the living.'

'Fuck,' groaned the boy. 'He's dead? He didn't make it?'

'He's not the one you saved,' the police officer said calmly, still struggling to undress the boy. 'I think it was too late for him. Your man is over there. The one who's put his hat back on.'

He grinned and shook his head. His movements were rapid, and soon the reckless young man realized his sexual organs were still intact. He gave in and allowed himself to be undressed. Three police officers were busy cordoning off the area with red-and-white tape, and one of them placed a tarpaulin over the body on the trolley.

'H-h-h-hey you there,' said the man in the hat, moving closer. 'W-w-w-w-were you trying to sc-sc-scalp me?'

He was still fully dressed. Someone had placed a woollen blanket around his shoulders. Not only were his teeth chattering, but his entire body was shaking, droplets of water cascading from the clumps of hair sticking out from beneath his sodden hat.

The boy on the ground didn't remember any hat.

'I s-s-s-s-saved my hat,' the other man grinned. 'I h-h-h-held on to it as hard as I could.'

'Shift yourself,' the police officer said wearily. 'Over there!'

He pointed to an ambulance parked at an angle on the quayside, casting its blue flashing light across the melee of uniformed figures.

'Who-who-who's that?' asked the man, completely unmoved as he gazed with interest at the lifeless form on the stretcher. 'I d-d-d-didn't s-s-s-see h-h-h-him in the wa-wa-water.'

'That's nothing to do with ... Arne! Arne, can you take this guy over to the ambulance? He's pushing his luck here.'

The shivering man was led away to the ambulance with a certain amount of brute force.

'He could at least have thanked you,' said the police officer, waving over one of the paramedics. 'It was pretty brave, jumping in like that. Not everybody would have had the courage. Over here!'

He stood up and placed his hand on the shoulder of a man in a high-visibility yellow uniform.

'Look after our hero,' he said with a smile. 'He needs warming up.'

'I'll just go and get another stretcher. Two seconds and ...'

The boy shook his head and tried to get to his feet. He was naked beneath a thick blanket, and without his even noticing somebody had pushed his feet into a pair of trainers that were far too big. The paramedic grabbed him under one arm as he swayed.

'I'm fine,' mumbled the boy, pulling the blanket more tightly around him. 'I'm just so fucking cold.'

'I think we'd be better with a stretcher,' the paramedic said doubtfully. 'It's just ...'

'No.'

The boy wobbled towards the ambulance. When he had almost reached the edge of the quay, he stopped for a moment. The salty gusts of wind blowing in from the fjord suddenly made him realize how close he had been to death. He was on the point of bursting into tears. Embarrassed, he pulled the blanket over his eyes. He had to take a little sidestep, and tripped over the edge of the blanket. In order to keep his balance, he grabbed hold of the nearest thing. It was the tarpaulin covering the body on the stretcher.

Things took a definite turn for the worse.

It couldn't have been more than five minutes since he came ambling along Aker Brygge, alone, fed up and with no money for a taxi home. During those paltry 300 seconds he had swum in icy water, been certain he was going to die, saved a man from drowning, been praised by the police and almost frozen to death. In that same period of time, two fully equipped ambulances and three police cars containing a total of six uniformed officers had arrived at the scene. Which was almost incomprehensible, given the brief time span. In addition, as soon as he was pulled up on to the quay and the police had taken responsibility for the lifeless body he had held in a grip of iron, the security guard had called in no less than five of his colleagues from the nearby office buildings.

In the midst of this chaotic crowd of uniformed men and one lone woman, some thirty members of the public were milling about, all in various states of intoxication and all paying little attention to the temporary police cordon. Those who were still around in the early hours of this Sunday morning were drawn to the dramatic scene like moths to a flame. And since no more than five minutes had passed since Aker Brygge had been more or less deserted, the police had yet to grasp the connection between the security guard, the young swimmer, the drunk in the hat and the dead body that two of them

had struggled to haul out of the water. The police had their proce-
dures, of course, but it was dark, it was chaos, and the most important
thing had been to get the drunk out of the water alive. For that reason,
and perhaps also because one of their own had managed to fall in
while they were heaving the body out, only two officers had taken a
closer look at the corpse. One of them, a young man, was bent over
and throwing up ten or fifteen metres beyond the cordon without
anyone even noticing.

The other had covered the body and was quietly explaining the
situation to a detective inspector when the young man with the
stubble lost his balance due to sheer exhaustion.

He fell backwards. His blanket started to slip off. For a little while
he was more preoccupied with not revealing his nakedness than
regaining his balance, so he grabbed hold of the tarpaulin with both
hands as he fell. It had got stuck on the far side of the trolley, which
started to tip over. For a moment it looked as if the weight of the
corpse would be enough to prevent total disaster, but the boy didn't
let go. He went down wearing nothing but the oversized trainers. The
back of his head struck the icy ground with an audible thud. The pain
made him cry out, then he lost consciousness for a couple of seconds.

When he came round, he noticed the smell first of all.

Something was lying on top of him, something that was suffocating
him, taking his breath away with the stench of rotten flesh and sewers.
Someone screamed and it occurred to him that he ought to open his
eyes. The corpse was lying in perfect symmetry with his own body, as
if in a kiss of death, and he found himself staring straight into the
opening in the hood.

There was something in there that from a purely logical point of
view had to be a head.

After all, it was inside the hood of a padded jacket.

In the police report which would be written some hours later it
would emerge that for the time being the police were assuming that
the body had been in the water for approximately one month. In the
same report they would stress the fact that in all probability it was the
clothes that were holding the body together, by and large. From a
purely clinical point of view the corpse would be described as 'badly
swollen, partly disintegrating', whereupon the writer of the report

briefly pointed out that it was impossible to establish with any certainty whether it had been a man or a woman. However, the clothes might possibly indicate the former.

The boy, who had spent the whole of Saturday night trailing round Oslo in his quest for girls and booze, and who had thrown himself fearlessly into the fjord in the middle of winter to save another person's life, passed out once more. This time he remained unconscious for a considerable period; he didn't come round until he was lying in a bed in the hospital at Ullevål, his mother sitting beside him. He started to cry as soon as he saw her. The poor lad sobbed like a child, clinging tightly to her warm, safe embrace as he tried to suppress the memory of the last thing he had seen before the blessed darkness had borne him away from the sea monster.

From a hole in the formless mass, right where there had once been an eye, a fish had suddenly poked its head out. A tiny shimmering silver fish, no bigger than an anchovy, with black eyes and quivering fins; they had stared at one another, the boy and the fish, until it suddenly flicked its body and fell from the dead head, straight into the boy's bellowing mouth.

On the Way to a Friend's House

'From now on we shall always have fish on Christmas Eve!'

Adam Stubo picked up the cod's head from his plate with his fingers before sucking out the eye and chewing thoughtfully. His mother-in-law, who was sitting opposite him at the oval dining table, pursed her lips and turned her head away, raising her eyebrows. Her husband had already had a little too much to drink. He pointed at his son-in-law with both his knife and fork.

'That's my boy! Real men eat every bit of the fish.'

'Actually,' his wife began, 'spare ribs on Christmas Eve has been a family tradition since—'

'I'm sorry, Mum.' Johanne put down her knife and fork. 'It was a mistake, OK? A stupid and completely insignificant mistake. Can't you just forget the spare ribs? The Middle East is in flames and we're in the middle of a major financial crisis and you're sitting here making a song and dance about the fact that Strøm-Larsen lost my sodding order. Everybody around this table likes cod, Mum, it's not such a bloody—'

'I hardly think it's necessary to use language like that, dear. And I have to say that in my personal experience I have never known Strøm-Larsen to forget one single thing. I've been shopping with this city's best butcher since before you were born, and I've—'

'Mum! Can't you just ... ?' Johanne closed her mouth, forced a smile and looked at her younger daughter Ragnhild. She was almost five, and was looking with curiosity at her father, who was eating the other eye.

'Is that good, Daddy?'

'Mmm ... strange and interesting and delicious.'

'What does it taste like?'

'It tastes like a fish's eye,' said Kristiane, hitting her plate rhythmically with her fork. 'Obviously. Fish's eye, high in the sky.'

'Don't do that,' her grandmother said gently. 'Be a good girl for Granny and stop making that noise.'

'Some people think fish is delicious,' said Ragnhild. 'And some fish think people are delicious. That's only fair. Sharks, for example. Do sharks celebrate Christmas Eve, Daddy? Do they have little girls for dinner before they open their presents?'

She laughed uproariously.

'It isn't only sharks that eat people,' said Kristiane.

As usual her little sister's sense of humour had completely passed her by. Miraculously, she seemed untouched by the events of Saturday, apart from the odd sniffle and a blocked nose. It was more difficult to say how the whole thing might have affected her mentally. So far she hadn't said a single word about any of it. The only minor change Johanne thought she perceived was that in the four days since her sister's wedding Kristiane repeated texts learned by heart for longer periods than usual. Characteristically, Adam was looking at things from a positive point of view: the child was also in a phase where she asked more questions, reasoned more. She was curious, not merely repetitive.

'Many species of fish have a varied diet,' she said slowly, her gaze fixed on some distant point. 'Under the right conditions they would feed extensively on human flesh, given the opportunity.'

'I think we could talk about something a little more pleasant,' said her grandmother. 'Now, what are you really, really hoping to find among your presents after dinner?'

'You know perfectly well, Granny. We gave you our lists ages ago. That dead man they pulled out of the harbour at the weekend, that night when Mummy got so cross with me because I—'

'Granny's right,' Johanne said quickly when Adam didn't notice the pleading look she had given him. 'It's Christmas Eve and I think we could talk about something—'

'He'd been in the water for a really, really long time,' said Kristiane, swallowing before she piled more food on to her fork. 'It was in the paper. That means you swell up. Like a great big balloon. This is because the human body is made of salt, and draws the water surrounding it.

This is called osmosis. When two fluids with different osmotic pressures, or salt balance, are separated by a thin membrane, for example the cell walls in a human being, the water seeps through in order to even out ...'

Her grandmother had turned noticeably paler. Her grandfather's mouth was hanging open, and he closed it with an audible smack.

'That kid,' he grinned. 'You're quite a girl, Kristiane.'

'Most impressive,' said Adam calmly, wiping his mouth with a large white serviette. 'But your grandmother and your mother are absolutely right. Death isn't exactly a topic—'

'Hang on, Adam,' his father-in-law broke in. 'Does that mean a human corpse swells up even more in fresh water than it does in the sea?'

'What's a corpse, Mummy?'

Ragnhild had picked up the cod's head from her father's plate. She slipped it over her nose, peering out through the empty eye sockets.

'Booooo!' she said, laughing. 'What's a corpse?'

'A corpse is a dead person,' said Kristiane. 'And when dead people are in the sea for a long time they get eaten. By crabs and fish.'

'And sharks,' her little sister interjected. 'Mostly sharks.'

'Had the corpse been eaten?' asked her grandfather with obvious interest. 'It didn't mention that in the paper. Is this one of your cases? Tell us all about it, Adam! As I understood from *Aftenposten* today, they still haven't identified the body.'

'No, it's a case for the Oslo police, and all I know is what's been in the paper. As you know I work for NCIS.' He gave his father-in-law a strained smile. 'We rarely help the Oslo police with anything other than technical matters. And circulating information on missing persons. International co-operation. That kind of thing. As I've told you several times in the past, in fact. Time for a change of subject, OK?'

Adam got up decisively and started clearing the table.

Silence fell. Only the sound of plates and cutlery being loaded into the dishwasher mingled with the muted voices of the Sølvguttene boys' choir on television in the apartment below. The remains of the fish made Johanne feel slightly sick as she scraped the plates into the bin.

As usual she had gone to buy the spare ribs at the last minute. When she got to the butcher's at ten o'clock that morning, they had already sold out. Nobody had any knowledge of the order she could swear she had phoned through two weeks earlier. The staff were full of apologies and expressed the greatest sympathy for the unfortunate situation that had arisen, but they had sold out of ribs. The owner couldn't help coming out with a faint reproach: Christmas dinner should be purchased in good time, well before Christmas Eve itself. The thought of serving her mother cheap ribs from Rimi or Maxi on Christmas Eve had seemed even more alien than the idea of serving cod.

'I should have bought that cheap pork from Rimi and sworn blind it came from Strøm-Larsen,' she whispered to Adam as she put the last plate in the dishwasher. 'She's hardly eaten a thing!'

'That's her loss,' he whispered back. 'Calm down.'

'Could we perhaps open a window?' her mother suddenly said in a loud voice. 'Of course, I'm not criticising the cod, it's tasty and nutritious, but, after all, the smell of freshly cooked spare ribs is the smell of Christmas itself.'

'Well, we'll soon have the smell of coffee,' Adam said cheerfully. 'We'll have coffee with the dessert, shall we?'

The choir had reached 'Härlig är jorden' in the apartment downstairs. Ragnhild joined in, and ran over to the TV to switch it on.

'No TV, Ragnhild!'

Johanne tried to smile as she looked across from the open-plan kitchen.

'We don't watch TV on Christmas Eve, you know that. And definitely not while we're eating.'

'Personally, I think it's an excellent idea,' her mother protested. 'After all, this meal is far too early in any case. It's so lovely to watch Sølvguttene first. Those wonderful voices bring so much of Christmas. Boy sopranos are the most beautiful sound I can think of. Come along, Ragnhild, Granny will help you find the right channel.'

A red wine glass fell on the kitchen floor with a crash.

'Nothing to worry about, everything's fine!' Adam shouted with a laugh.

Johanne dashed to the bathroom.

'The soul weighs twenty-one grams,' Kristiane announced.

'Does it indeed?'

Her grandfather filled his schnapps glass to the brim for the fifth time.

'Yes,' Kristiane said seriously. 'When you die, you become twenty-one grams lighter. You can't see it. Can't see can't be can't see can't be.'

'See it?'

'The soul. You can't see it leaving.'

'Kristiane,' Adam said from the kitchen. 'I really mean it this time. Enough. We are not having any more talk about death and destruction. Besides which, that stuff about the weight of the soul is just nonsense. There's no such thing as a soul in any case. It's just a religious concept. Would you like some tea and honey with your pudding?'

'Dam-di-rum-ram,' Kristiane said in a monotone.

'Oh no ...' Johanne was back from the bathroom. She crouched down beside her daughter. 'Look at me, Kristiane. Look at me.'

She gently cupped the girl's chin.

'Adam asked if you wanted tea with honey. Would you like that?'

'Dam-di-rum-ram.'

'I don't think it's a very good idea to give the child tea when she's in that ... state. Come to Granny and we'll listen to those clever boys. Come here, sweetheart.'

Adam was standing in the kitchen where his mother-in-law couldn't see him. He waved to Johanne, silently forming words with his lips: 'Take no notice. Pretend you can't hear her.'

'Dam-di-rum-ram,' said Kristiane.

'You can have whatever you want,' Johanne whispered. 'You can have the very thing you want most of all.'

She knew it didn't help at all. Kristiane made her own decisions about where she was. During the course of fourteen years with this child so close to her that she sometimes found it difficult to tell which was her and which was her daughter, she still had no idea what made her go from one state to the other. They had learned simple patterns, Johanne and Adam and Isak, Kristiane's father. Routines and habits; foods to be avoided and food that had a particular effect on her; drugs they had tried before agreeing they were unsuitable ... specific paths had been cleared that made life with Kristiane simpler.

But for the most part her daughter was in a world of her own, following her own map and making her own incomprehensible choices.

'Mummy loves you all the way to the stars and back,' Johanne whispered quietly, her lips tickling her daughter's ear and making Kristiane smile.

'Daddy's coming,' she said.

'Yes, Daddy will be here soon. When he's had dinner with Grandma and Granddad he's coming to see his little girl.'

Kristiane's face was completely expressionless. It looked as if her eyes were moving independently of one another, and it frightened Johanne. Usually they were just fixed on something no one else could see.

'The lady was—'

'Her name is Albertine,' Johanne interrupted. 'Albertine was asleep.'

'It was so cold. I couldn't find you, Mummy.'

'But I found you. In the end.'

Johanne was so focused on the child that she hadn't noticed her mother. She caught the scent first, a present from her sister that cost more than Johanne spent on cosmetics and personal hygiene in an entire year.

Go away, she tried to convey with every fibre of her being. She arched her back and made a tiny movement to the side, still crouching beside her daughter.

'Kristiane,' the child's grandmother said in her calm, firm voice. 'Come to Granny, please. First of all we are going to open the red present with the pink ribbon on it. It's for you. Inside is a box with a lid. When you open the box and lift the lid, you will find a microscope. Which is just what you wanted. Now take my hand ...'

Johanne was still sitting with her hands resting on Kristiane's narrow thighs.

'Microscope,' said Kristiane. 'From the Greek *micro*, small, and *skopein*, to look at.'

'Quite right,' said her grandmother. 'Come along.'

Sølvguttene were no longer singing. Ragnhild switched off the television, as did the neighbours down below. The aroma of coffee drifted from the kitchen, and the world outside was silent in the way it was only on this night of the year, when the churches had emptied, the

31

bells had fallen silent and no one was on the way to or from anything or anyone any longer.

Her grandmother's long, slender hand crept into Kristiane's.

'Granny,' the girl said with a smile. 'I want my microscope.'

But her eyes were fixed on Johanne. Her gaze was steady, and remained so until she went over to the sofa with her grandmother to open a Christmas present, the contents of which she already knew.

Johanne got stiffly to her feet and remained where she was.

An unaccustomed shiver of happiness ran through her body, only to disappear before she really had time to work out what it was.

*

For Eva Karin Lysgaard, happiness was a solid concept.

Happiness was her faith in Jesus Christ. Every day since she had met the Saviour while walking in the forest when she was sixteen she had experienced the joyous feeling of His presence. She spoke to Him often, and frequently received answers. Even in times of sorrow – and, of course, a woman of sixty had lived through such times – Jesus was with her, giving consolation and support and endless love.

It was almost eleven o'clock on the night of His birthday.

Eva Karin Lysgaard had an agreement with Jesus. A pact with her husband Erik and with her Lord. When life had been at its darkest for both her and Erik, they had found a way out of all their difficulties. It was not the simplest way. It had taken time to find it and it must always remain a matter between her, Erik and the Saviour.

Now she was here, on her way.

The rain blew in off Vågen, tasting of salt. Behind many of the windows in the picturesque development of small houses a soft light was still visible; Christmas Eve was not over for most people. She tripped on a paving stone as she turned the corner, but quickly regained her balance. Her glasses were wet and misted over, and it was difficult to see clearly. It didn't matter. This was her path, and she had walked this way so many times before.

Taken by surprise, she stopped for a moment.

She could hear footsteps behind her.

She had already been walking for over twenty minutes and hadn't seen another living soul apart from a stray cat and the sea birds, screaming so faintly above Vågen.

'Bishop Lysgaard?'

She turned towards the voice.

'Yes?' she said in an enquiring tone, and smiled.

There was something about his voice, something strange. Harsh, perhaps. Different, anyway.

'Who are you? Is there something I can help you with?'

When he struck her with the knife she realized she had been wrong. During the sixteen seconds it took her from the moment of realizing that she was going to die until she was no longer alive, she offered no resistance. She said nothing, and allowed herself to fall to the ground with the strange man leaning over her, the man with the knife; he was of no relevance to her. She was the one who had been wrong. During all these years, when she had thought Jesus was by her side in her vain belief that He had forgiven and accepted, she had been living a lie that was impossible to live with in the future. It was too big.

And at the moment of her death, when there was no longer anything to see and all perception of existence was gone, she wondered what He who has eternal life had been unable to accept. Had it been the lie or the sin?

It all came down to the same thing, she thought.

And died.

*

'Baby Jesus can't possibly be two thousand and eight years old,' said Ragnhild with a yawn. 'Nobody lives for ever!'

'No,' said Adam. 'He actually died when he was quite young. We celebrate Christmas because that's when he was born.'

'In that case we should have balloons. It's not a proper birthday without balloons. Do you think baby Jesus liked balloons?'

'I don't think they had balloons in those days. But it's time you got some sleep, my girl. It's almost one o'clock in the morning! It's already Christmas Day, in fact.'

'My personal best,' Ragnhild rejoiced. 'Is one o'clock later than eleven o'clock?'

Adam nodded and tucked her in for the fourth time in two hours.

'Time to sleep.'

'Why is one later than eleven when one is a little number and eleven is a big number? Can I stay up this late on New Year's Eve?'

'We'll see. Now go to sleep.'

He kissed her on the nose and headed for the door.

'Daddy ...'

'Go to sleep. Daddy's going to get cross if you don't try. Do you understand?'

He flicked the switch and the room was filled with a reddish glow from a string of small red hearts around one window.

'But Daddy, just one more thing.'

'What?'

'I think it's a bit stupid for Kristiane to have that microscope. She'll only break it.'

'Perhaps. But that was what she wanted.'

'Why didn't I get a micro—?'

'Ragnhild! I'm getting really cross now! Settle down at once ...'

The rustling of the duvet made him break off.

'Night night, Daddy. Love you.'

Adam smiled and pulled the door to.

'I love you, too. See you in the morning.'

He crept along the corridor. Kristiane had fallen asleep long ago, but the sound of a feather falling on the floor could wake her. As he passed her door he held his breath. Then he gave a start.

The telephone? At one o'clock on Christmas morning?

In two steps he had reached the living-room door in order to silence the ringing as quickly as possible. Fortunately, Johanne had got there before him. She was engaged in a quiet conversation next to the Christmas tree, which was looking somewhat the worse for wear after Jack – Kristiane's yellowy-brown dog – had gone berserk and knocked it over in a tangle of garlands and tree lights. Johanne's mother had wrapped up a bone and put it at the bottom of the pile of presents, so you could hardly blame the dog.

'Here he is,' Johanne said, handing Adam the phone.

She had the resigned expression that always felt like a punch in the stomach. He spread his arms apologetically before taking the phone.

'Stubo.'

Johanne wandered aimlessly around the room, picking up a toy here, a book there. Putting them down where they didn't belong. Moving a Christmas rose and spilling soil on the tablecloth. Then she ambled into the kitchen, but couldn't bring herself to start emptying the dishwasher in order to load it with the dirty dishes piled everywhere. She was exhausted, and decided to finish off the last drop of red wine left in the bottle her sister had given her for Christmas. According to her mother it had cost more than 3,000 kroner. Talk about casting pearls before swine. Johanne topped up her glass from a box of cheap Italian wine on the worktop.

'OK,' she heard Adam say. 'See you in the morning. Pick me up at six.'

He ended the call.

'Six,' Johanne groaned. 'When we have the chance of a lie-in for once?'

She took a swig of her wine and sat down on the sofa.

'We've had a really lovely evening,' said Adam, flopping down beside her. 'Your father was both pleasant and enervating, as usual. Your mother ... your mother ...'

'Was vile to me, kind to Ragnhild, good with Kristiane and patronizing to you. And utterly charming to Isak when he finally turned up. As usual. Who's dead?'

'What?'

'Work.'

Johanne nodded at the mobile on the coffee table.

'Oh. It's a difficult one.'

'When they ring you on Christmas Eve, I assume it's going to be difficult. What's it about?'

Adam took her glass and raised it to his lips with such fervour that he had a red moustache when he put it down. Then he hesitated, looked at his watch and hurried into the kitchen. Johanne heard him spitting into the sink.

'I might have to drive tomorrow,' he said, wiping his mouth with his sleeve as he came back. 'In which case I need to be able to think clearly.'

'You always think clearly, don't you?'

He smiled and sat down heavily by her side. The coffee table was still covered in wrapping paper, glasses, coffee cups and empty soft drinks bottles. With a degree of care you might not expect from such a big man, he slid his feet among the whole lot and crossed his legs.

'Eva Karin Lysgaard,' he said, sipping at a bottle of Farris mineral water he had brought from the kitchen. 'She's dead.'

'Eva Karin Lysgaard? The bishop? Bishop Lysgaard?'

He nodded.

'How? I mean, if they've called you it has to involve a crime? Has she been murdered? Has Bishop Lysgaard been murdered? How? And when?'

Adam had another drink and rubbed his face, as if that might sober him up.

'I don't know much at all. It must have happened just ...' He glanced at his watch. 'Just over two hours ago. Killed with a knife, that's all I know. Well, we can't say for certain that she was stabbed to death, but so far the cause of death appears to be a stab wound in the area of the heart. And she was murdered in the open air. Outdoors. I don't know much more. The Hordaland police wouldn't normally ask for our help in a case like this, at least not so soon. But this is going to ... Anyway, Sigmund Berli and I are going over there in the morning.'

Johanne sat up and put down her wine glass. After a while she pushed it resolutely further on to the table.

'Jesus,' was all she could think of to say.

They sat in silence. Johanne felt a cold draught on her skin, giving her goosebumps. Eva Karin Lysgaard. The well-known, gentle bishop of Bjørgvin. Murdered. On Christmas Eve. She tried to follow a train of thought through to the end, but her brain just wasn't working properly.

Only the previous Saturday – the day of that wretched wedding – there had been a profile of Bishop Lysgaard covering four pages of the *Dagbladet* supplement. Johanne hadn't had time to read a newspaper that day, but she bought it so that she could save the article for later. She still hadn't got round to reading it.

Suddenly she reached over the arm of the sofa and rummaged around in the magazine rack.

'Here,' she said, placing the newspaper on her knee. 'A BISHOP WITHOUT A WHIP.'

Adam put his arm around her and they both leaned over the article. The cover photo was a close-up of a woman growing old. Her eyes were almond-shaped, but sloped down slightly. This made her look sorrowful, even when she was smiling. The irises were dark brown, almost black, with strong, dark eyebrows and lashes that looked unusually long, in spite of the wrinkles surrounding her eyes.

'Quite good-looking,' Adam mumbled, wanting to turn the page.

'Not good-looking exactly. Special. Different. She looks just as nice as she seemed to be when ... when she was alive.'

Johanne stared and stared. Adam gave an enormous yawn.

'Sorry,' he said, shaking his head. 'But I think I'd better try and get some sleep. We really ought to tidy up before we go to bed, because otherwise you'll have to do it all tomorrow, and that might—'

'Outdoors,' said Johanne. 'Did you say she was killed outdoors? On Christmas Eve?'

'Yes. Miraculously it was a police patrol that found her. One of the few that were out tonight. She was lying on the street. From that point of view we have a major advantage. For once it seems as if the press haven't got wind of a murder within two minutes. And there won't be any papers tomorrow.'

'The Internet press is just as bad,' Johanne muttered, still gazing at the photo of the bishop of Bjørgvin. 'Worse, actually. And then there's the radio and the TV. With a case like this it doesn't make any difference if everybody's on holiday. Anyway, why are you involved? Surely the Bergen police are perfectly capable of handling something like this?'

Adam smiled.

NCIS certainly wasn't what it had been. From being a kind of elite group of investigators known as the Murder Squad almost fifty years ago, the National Criminal Investigation Service had gradually developed into a much larger organization with the highest level of competence in tactical and particularly technical investigation. Gradually, the organization was allocated more and more tasks of a significantly greater import, both nationally and internationally. To the public, they were mainly visible as a support network for the police service in major cases, particularly murders, right up to the turn of the millennium. But as times changed, so too did criminal activity.

In 2005 NCIS had effectively been scrapped in order to rise again as an organization called The National Unit for the Prevention of Organized and Other Serious Crime. The objections to the new name were vociferous. The acronym would have been TNUFPOOAOSC, which a number of people pointed out sounded like an onomatopoeic expression for vomiting. The members of the team won in the end, and NCIS was able to look forward to its golden jubilee in February 2009 under its old familiar name.

But the work they did had changed, and it remained that way in accordance with the name that had been rejected.

The police forces around the country had become bigger, stronger and much more competent. The great paradox when it came to combating crime was that an increase in the amount and professionalism of criminality led to a larger and more skilled police force. As more murder cases occurred in even the smaller police districts, the officers involved became more skilful. They could manage on their own. At least when it came to the tactical aspects of the investigation.

Adam put his mouth right next to Johanne's ear.

'Because I'm so good.'

She smiled in spite of herself.

'And besides, there's going to be a hell of a lot of fuss about this one,' he added with a yawn. 'I assume they're pretty worried over there. And if they want me, they can have me.'

He stood up and looked despondently around the room.

'Shall we tackle the worst of it?'

Johanne shook her head.

'What was she doing outside?' she said slowly.

'What?'

'What on earth was she doing out on the streets, so late on Christmas Eve?'

'No idea. On the way to a friend's, maybe.'

'But—'

'Johanne. It's late. I know virtually nothing about this case, apart from the fact that I have to set off for Bergen far too early in the morning. It's pointless to speculate based on the minimal information we have. You know that perfectly well. Let's tidy up and go to bed.'

'Bed,' said Johanne, getting to her feet.

She went into the kitchen, picked up a bottle of mineral water and decided to take the newspaper supplement to bed. She would deal with tomorrow when it arrived.

'What's wrong?' asked Adam when she suddenly stopped dead in the middle of the floor, seemingly incapable of moving one way or the other.

'I just felt so terribly ... sad.'

She looked up, her expression surprised.

'It's natural for you to feel sad,' said Adam, placing his hand on her cheek.

'Not really. I'm not usually affected ... I *don't allow myself* to be affected by your cases. But the bishop always seemed so ... so good, somehow.'

Adam smiled and kissed her gently.

'If there's one thing you and I both know,' he said, taking her hands, 'it's that good people are murdered too. Come on.'

It was a sleepless night. When the day finally claimed her, Johanne had read the article about Bishop Eva Karin Lysgaard so many times she knew it off by heart.

And it didn't help in the slightest.

A Man

Nothing helped.

Nothing would ever help. They had offered to stay with him, of course. As if they were what he needed. As if life would be bearable again for one moment if strangers sat with him, in her armchair, the shabby, yellow armchair at an angle in front of the TV, a half-finished piece of knitting in a basket beside it.

They had asked if he had someone.

Once upon a time he had someone. A few hours ago he had Eva Karin. All his life he had had Eva Karin, and now he had no one.

Your son, they reminded him. They asked about his son. Did he want to tell his son or should they take care of things? That was how she put it, the woman who sat down on Eva Karin's chair. Take care of things. As if it was a thing. As if there was anything else to take care of.

He felt no pain.

Pain was something that hurt. Pain hurt. All he could feel was the absence of existence. An empty space that made him look at his own hands as if they belonged to someone else. He clenched his right hand so tightly that the nails dug into his palm. There was no pain anywhere, no existence, just a huge, colourless nothingness where Eva Karin no longer existed. Even God had abandoned him, he realized now.

Time had stopped.

*

Her watch had stopped. She shook her wrist crossly and realized she was much later than she wanted to be. She had to get the children inside and in their best clothes without Kristiane playing up.

She went over to the window.

40

In the courtyard in front of the house, behind the fence on Hauges Vei, Ragnhild and Kristiane had scraped together enough rime frost to build the smallest snowman in the world. It was no more than ten centimetres high, but even from the second floor Johanne could see that it had been kitted out with a yellow oak-leaf hat and a mouth of tiny pebbles.

Johanne folded her arms and leaned on the window frame. As usual Ragnhild was directing operations and taking care of the construction. Kristiane was standing up straight, completely motionless. Although Johanne couldn't make out the words, she could hear Ragnhild chattering away as if addressing the most spellbound audience in the world.

Perhaps she was.

Johanne smiled as Ragnhild suddenly got up from her small work of art and began to sing with great enthusiasm. Now Johanne could hear her voice inside the apartment. *Å leva det er å elska* rang out over the neighbourhood. Wherever had she learned that particular hymn? At any rate, it had most likely been Kristiane's idea to sing it once the snowman was complete.

A figure caught Johanne's attention. It looked like a man, and she wasn't sure where he had come from. Nor did it seem as if he was sure where he was going. For some reason this made her uneasy. Of course, there were youngsters in the area who turned up out of nowhere from time to time, but if she saw adults walking the streets they were always heading somewhere with a purpose. She recognized most of them after living for so many years in this little side road.

The man was strolling along with his hands in his pockets. His hat was pulled down over his eyes and his tightly knotted scarf obscured the lower half of his face. But there was something about the way he walked that told her he wasn't all that young.

Johanne shook her right arm again. Her watch still wasn't working. It must be the battery. They were probably running late. She was about to turn away from the window when the man stopped by the bins.

By their bins.

Johanne felt the fear racing inside her, as always when she didn't have full control over Kristiane. For a moment she stood there, not knowing whether she should run downstairs or stay where she was and see what happened. Without making a conscious decision, she stayed where she was.

Perhaps he called out to them.

At any rate, both girls looked at him, and Ragnhild's gestures indicated that she was talking to him. He made some reply and waved her over. Neither of the girls went towards him. Instead, Ragnhild took a step back.

Johanne ran.

She raced through the apartment, out of the living room, along the hallway, out through the extension that had become the girls' playroom, she ran, half-stumbled down the stairs and hurtled out into the cold wearing neither shoes nor slippers.

'Kristiane!' she shouted, trying to inject a calm, everyday tone into her voice. 'Ragnhild! Are you there?'

As she came around the corner of the house she saw them.

Ragnhild was once again crouching down in front of the little snowman. Kristiane had spotted a bird or a plane. She was gazing up at the sky and without taking any notice of her mother she stuck out her tongue to catch the feather-light flakes that had begun to fall.

There was no sign of the man.

'Mummy,' Ragnhild said sternly. 'You are not allowed outside in your stocking feet!'

Johanne looked down at her feet.

'Goodness me,' she said with a smile. 'What a silly mummy you have!'

Ragnhild laughed and pointed at her with a toy spade.

Kristiane carried on catching snowflakes.

'Who was that man?' Johanne asked casually.

'What man?'

Ragnhild licked the snot trickling from her nose.

'The man who was talking to you. The man who—'

'Don't know him,' said Ragnhild. 'Look what a brilliant snowman we've made! And without any snow!'

'It's lovely. But now it's time to come in. We're going to a Christmas party, remember. What did he ask you?'

'Dam-di-rum-ram,' said Kristiane, smiling up at the sky.

'Nothing,' said Ragnhild. 'Are we going to a party? Is Daddy coming?'

'No, he's in Bergen, isn't he? But that man must have said something. I mean, I saw him—'

'He just asked if we'd had a nice Christmas,' said Ragnhild. 'Aren't your feet cold, Mummy?'

'Yes, they are. Come along, both of you. Time to go inside.'

Amazingly, Kristiane started to walk. Johanne took Ragnhild by the hand and followed her.

'And what did you tell him?'

'I said it was absolutely the best Christmas ever – with bells on!'

'Did he want ... did he try to get you to go over to him?'

They reached the gravel path and walked along by the building towards the stairs. Kristiane was talking to herself, but seemed happy and contented.

'Yeees ...'

Ragnhild was taking her time.

'But we know we mustn't go up to strangers. Or go off with them or anything like that.'

'Quite right. Good girl.'

Johanne's toes felt as if they were about to drop off with the cold. She pulled a face as she left the gravel and put her foot on the ice-cold stone staircase.

'He asked if I'd got any nice Christmas presents,' Kristiane said suddenly as she opened the outside door, which had blown shut behind Johanne. 'Just me, not Ragnhild.'

'Oh? And how do you know he was only asking you?'

'Because he said so. He said—'

All three of them stopped. Kristiane had that strange look on her face, as if it were turned inward, as if she were searching an archive inside her head.

'*What are you doing out here, girls? Did you have a nice Christmas? And what about you, Kristiane, did you get anything nice?*'

Her voice was expressionless, and was followed by complete silence.

'I see,' said Johanne, forcing a smile. 'That was nice of him. And now we need to put on our best clothes as quickly as we can. We're going to see Grandma and Grandpa, Kristiane. Daddy will soon be here to pick us up.'

'Oh ...'

Ragnhild immediately sat down and started whining.

'Why does Kristiane get to have her daddy when I can't have mine?'

'Your daddy has to work, I told you that. And you always have a lovely time when we go to see Kristiane's grandma and grandad.'

'Don't want to. *Don't want to!*'

The child pulled back and started to slide down the stairs head first, her arms stretched out in front of her as if she were swimming. Johanne grabbed her arm and pulled her up, slightly more firmly than she had intended. Ragnhild let out a howl.

The only explanation Johanne could cope with was that Kristiane must have remembered wrongly.

'I want my own daddy!' Ragnhild screamed, trying to twist free of her mother's grasp. 'Daddy! *My daddy!* Not Kristiane's stupid daddy!'

'We do not say that kind of thing in our family,' Johanne hissed, nudging Kristiane in through the door while dragging the little one behind her. 'Do you understand?'

Ragnhild immediately stopped crying, stunned by her mother's fury. She started laughing instead.

But Johanne had only one thought in her head: Kristiane never, ever remembered wrongly.

*

'We all make mistakes. Don't get so cross about it.'

Marcus Koll Junior smiled at his son, who was studying the instructions.

'Come over here and we can work it out together.'

The boy sulked for a little while, but eventually stomped over and threw the little booklet on the coffee table. The helicopter was still on the dining table, only half-completed.

'Rolf promised to help me,' the boy said, pushing out his lower lip.

'You know what Rolf's clients can be like.'

'They're rich, stupid and they have ugly dogs.'

His father tried to hide a smile.

'Yes, well. When an English bulldog decides that her puppies are coming out on Christmas Day, then out they have to come. Ugly or not.'

'Rolf says that bulldogs have been totally overbred. That they can't even feed properly. Shouldn't be allowed. Animal cruelty.'

'I couldn't agree more. Now, let's have a look at this!'

He picked up the booklet and leafed through it as he walked over to the imposing dining table. He had had the instructions translated by an authorized technical translator in order to make it easier for the boy to build the helicopter. The model in front of him was so big that he now regretted his purchase. Even if the boy had an unusual talent for mechanics, this was a little over the top. The man in the shop in Boston had stressed that the toy wasn't suitable for children under the age of sixteen, not least because it weighed almost a kilo and would constitute a risk to anyone around it the moment it rose in the air.

'Hm,' said his father, scratching his stubble. 'I don't really get it.'

'It's the rotor blades that are the problem,' said the boy. 'Look here, Dad!'

The eager fingers tried to put the blades together, but something wasn't right. The boy soon gave up and put down the pieces with a groan. His father ruffled his hair.

'A bit more patience, little Marcus. Patience! That's what you should have got for Christmas.'

'I've told you, don't call me that. And I'm not doing anything wrong, there's something the matter with the instructions.'

Marcus Koll pulled out a chair, sat down and took his glasses out of his breast pocket. The boy sat down beside him, keen to help. The blonde, curly hair tickled Marcus's face as his son leaned over the manual. A faint smell of soap and ginger biscuits made him smile, and he had to stop himself from hugging the boy, holding him close, feeling the glorious warmth of the son he had managed to have in spite of everything and everyone.

'You're the best thing in my life,' he said slowly.

'Yeah, yeah. What does this mean? *Insert the longest batten through the unhooked ring at the bottom of rotor blade four.* I mean, there is only one batten! So why does it say the longest? And where's the stupid ring?'

The December sun filled the room with a calm, white light. Outside it was cold and clear. The trees were completely covered with crystals of rime frost, as if they had been sprayed for Christmas. Through the white branches beyond the window he could see the Oslo fjord far below, grey-blue and still, with no sign of life. The crackling of the open fire blended with the snores of two English setters, curled up together in a big basket by the door. The smell of turkey was beginning to drift in from the kitchen, a tradition Rolf had insisted on when he eventually allowed himself to be persuaded to move in five years ago.

Marcus Koll Junior lived his life in a cliché, and he loved it.

When his father died nine years ago, just before Marcus Junior turned thirty-five, he had at first refused to accept his inheritance. Georg Koll had given his son nothing but a good name. That name was his grandfather's, and it had enabled him to pretend that his father didn't exist when he was a boy and couldn't understand why Daddy couldn't come and see him at the weekend now and again. When he was just twelve years old he began to realize that his mother didn't even receive the maintenance to which she was entitled for him and his two younger siblings. When he turned fifteen he resolved never again to speak to the man responsible for his existence. His father had wasted his opportunity. That was the year Marcus received 100 kroner in a card on his birthday, sent through the post and with five words in handwriting he knew wasn't his father's. He became a grown man when he put the money in the envelope and sent the whole lot back.

Severing all contact was surprisingly easy. They saw each other so rarely that the two or three visits per year were easy to avoid. Emotionally, he had chosen a different father: Marcus Koll Senior. When he was able to grasp the fact that his real father simply didn't want to be a father and would never change, he felt relieved. Liberated. Free to move on to something better.

And he didn't want his inheritance. Which was considerable.

Georg Koll had made a lot of money in property in the sixties and seventies. The majority of his fortune had been moved to other, much safer arenas in plenty of time before the crash in the housing market during the last financial crisis of the twentieth century. When it came to looking after his money he more than made up for his great inadequacies as a father and provider. Unlike others, he had used the yuppie era to secure his investments rather than risking them for short-term gain.

When Georg Koll died he left behind a medium-sized cruise-ship company, six centrally located and extremely well-maintained properties, plus a skilfully compiled share portfolio which had provided the majority of his very respectable income for the past five years. Death had obviously surprised him. He was only fifty-eight years old, slim and apparently fit when he had a massive heart attack on his way home from the office one day in late August. Since he hadn't remarried, and no will was found, his entire estate went to Marcus Koll, his sister Anine and his younger brother Mathias.

Marcus wanted no part of it.

When he was fifteen years old he had returned his father's blood money, and when he was twenty he had received a reply. His father had heard that his son was a homosexual. Marcus had glanced through the letter and realized all too quickly what his father wanted. For one thing, he expressly dissociated himself from Marcus's lifestyle, which was a not uncommon attitude in 1984. What was worse was that his father, who had never been well in with any God, went on to paint a picture of Marcus's future along the lines of the blackest descriptions of Sodom and Gomorrah. He also reminded him of a new and dangerous plague from America, which affected only homosexual men. It led to an agonizing death, complete with boils, like the Black Death itself. Of course, Georg Koll didn't believe this was a punishment from any higher power. No, this was Nature herself taking revenge. This fatal disease was a manifestation of natural selection; in a couple of generations people like him would have been eradicated. Unless he changed his ways. Life as a homosexual meant a life without a family, without security, without ties, obligations and the happiness that came with being a good member of society and someone who made a real contribution. Until his son realized this and could guarantee that he had seen the error of his ways, he was disinherited.

Since the obligatory bequest to his own children was a mere bagatelle in comparison to Georg Koll's entire fortune, there was a reality behind this threat. It made no difference whatsoever to Marcus. He burned the letter and tried to forget the whole thing. And when the estate was divided up fifteen years later, in 1999, it turned out that his father, convinced of his own immortality, had omitted to make a will.

Marcus stuck stubbornly to his guns. He still wanted nothing to do with his father's money.

He gave in only when his grandfather, who never mentioned Georg either, managed to convince Marcus that he was the only one of the three siblings capable of managing the family fortune in a professional way. His brother was a teacher, his sister an assistant in a bookshop. Marcus himself was an economist, and when both siblings insisted that the best thing would be to set up a new company with the combined assets of their father's estate, with all three of them as joint owners and Marcus as director and administrator, he allowed himself to be persuaded.

'Just look at it as a bloody good joke,' Mathias had said with a grin. 'The bastard did Mum and us out of money all his life, and now we can live very well on the proceeds he worked so hard to keep from us.'

It was ironic, Marcus had gradually come to accept. A splendid irony.

'Dad,' little Marcus said impatiently. 'What does that say? What does it mean?'

His father smiled absently and dragged his gaze away from the ridge, the fjord and the white sky. He was feeling hungry.

'Right,' he said, fixing a tiny screw in place. 'There, that's the rotor finished. Then we do this ... Do you want to do it?'

The boy nodded, and slotted in the four blades.

'We did it, Dad! We did it! Can we go outside and fly it? Can we do it now?'

He picked up the remote control in one hand and the finished helicopter in the other, tentatively, as if he didn't quite trust it not to fall apart.

'It's too cold. Much too cold. As I said yesterday, it could be weeks before we can take it outside.'

'But Dad ...'

'You promised, Marcus. You promised not to go on about it. Why don't you ring Rolf instead and ask if he's coming home for our special lunch?'

The boy hesitated for a moment before putting everything down without a word. Suddenly he brightened up with a smile.

'Granny and the others are here!' he shouted, running out of the room.

The door slammed behind him. The sound rang in Marcus's ears until once again only the faint snoring of the oblivious dogs and the crackling of the fire filled the enormous room. Marcus's gaze rested on the fire, then swept around the room.

He really did live in a cliché.

The house in Åsen.

It was large, but set back from the road so that only the top floor was visible to passers-by. When he bought the house he had decided to remove the ridiculous wooden panelling on the outside, along with the turf roof and the portico in front of the garage, which bore the legend *Home Sweet Home*, roughly carved and with a dragon's head at either end. Just when he was about to tackle the panelling, Rolf had entered his and young Marcus's lives. Rolf had laughed until he cried when he saw the house in all its glory for the first time, and he refused to move in unless Marcus promised to keep the more eccentric and what one might call rustic elements.

'We're an extended family with a twist,' Rolf would laugh.

A little bit richer than most, Marcus thought, but he said nothing.

Rolf wasn't thinking about the money. He was thinking about their family life, with little Marcus and a wide circle of aunts and uncles and cousins, his grandmother and friends who came and went and were almost always at the house in Åsen; he was thinking about the dogs and the annual hunting trip in the autumn with friends, old friends, boys Marcus had grown up with and never lost contact with. Rolf always laughed so heartily at the happy, ordinary, trivial life they led.

Rolf was always so happy.

Everything had turned out the way Marcus had hoped.

He had even managed to use his father's money for something good. His father had consigned him to oblivion and regarded him as a lost soul. By condemning his son's future, Georg Koll had paradoxically given him a new one. The first, wild years lay behind him, and Marcus had managed to avoid the disease that had brutally taken so many of those he knew, in pain and embarrassment and often loneliness. He was deeply grateful for this, and when he burned the letter from his father he resolved that Georg Koll would be wrong. Utterly and emphatically wrong. Marcus would be what his father had never been: a man.

'Dad!'

The boy came running into the room, his arms flung wide.

'They're all coming! Rolf said the bulldog had three puppies and everything was fine and he's on his way home and he's looking forward to—'

'Good, good.' Marcus laughed and got up to accompany the boy into the hallway. He could hear several cars in the courtyard; the guests were arriving.

He stopped in the doorway for a moment and looked around.

The doubt which had tormented and nagged him for several weeks had finally gone. He had a sharp instinct, and had made a fortune by following it. In the early summer of 2007 he had spent weeks fighting a strong urge to sell up and get out of the stock market. He had sat up night after night with analyses and reports, but the only sign he could see that something was wrong was the stagnation of the US property market. When the first downgrading of bonds linked to the unsafe sub-prime loans came later that summer, he made his decision overnight. Over a period of three months he cashed in more than a billion in US shares at a significant profit. A few months later he would wake in the middle of the night out of sheer relief. His fortune remained in the bank until interest rates began to fall.

Marcus Koll was now buying properties at a time when everything was cheap. When he sold them in a few years, the profit would be formidable.

He had to protect himself and his family. He had a right to do so. It was his duty.

Georg Koll had reached out from beyond the grave to try to destroy Marcus's life once again, and he simply could not be allowed to do that.

*

'May I?'

Adam Stubo nodded in the direction of a yellow armchair in front of the television. Erik Lysgaard showed no sign of reacting. He just sat there in a matching chair in a darker colour, staring straight ahead, his hands resting in his lap.

Only then did Adam notice the knitting and the long, almost invisible grey hairs stuck to the antimacassar on the back of the armchair. He pulled out a dining chair and sat on that instead.

He was breathing heavily. A slight hangover had been plaguing him since he got up at half past five, and he was thirsty. The flight from Gardermoen to Bergen had been anything but pleasant. True, the plane was almost empty, since there weren't many people desperate to get from Oslo to Bergen at 7.25 on Christmas morning, but the turbulence had been a problem and he had had far too little sleep.

'This is not a formal interview,' he said, unable to come up with anything better. 'We can do that later, down at the police station. When you're ...'

When you're feeling better, he was about to say before he stopped himself.

The room was light and pleasant. It was neither modern nor old-fashioned. Some of the furniture was clearly well used, like the two wing-backed armchairs in front of the TV. The dining room also looked as if it had been furnished with items that had been inherited. The sofa, however, around the corner in the L-shaped living room, was deep and cream-coloured, with bright cushions. Adam had seen exactly the same one in a Bohus brochure that Kristiane absolutely insisted on reading in bed. Along one wall were bookshelves built around the window, full of titles indicating that the Lysgaards had a wide range of interests and a good knowledge of languages. A large volume with Cyrillic letters on the cover lay on the small table between the armchairs. The pictures hanging on the walls were so close together that it was difficult to get an impression of each individual work. The only one that immediately caught his attention was a copy of Henrik Sørensen's *Kristus*, a blonde Messiah figure with his arms open wide. Actually, perhaps it wasn't a copy. It looked genuine, and could be one of the artist's many sketches for the original, which was in Lillestrøm Church.

The most striking item was a large Nativity crib on the sideboard. It had to be more than a metre wide and perhaps half a metre deep and tall. It was contained in a box with a glass front, like a tableau. The baby Jesus lay on a bed of straw among angels and little shepherds, sheep and the three wise men. A bulb shone inside the simple stable, so cleverly hidden that it looked as if Jesus had a halo.

'It's from Salzburg,' said Erik Lysgaard, so unexpectedly that Adam jumped.

Then he fell silent again.

'I didn't mean to stare,' said Adam, venturing a smile. 'But it really is quite ... enchanting.'

The widower looked up for the first time.

'That's what Eva Karin says. Enchanting, that's what she always says about that crib.'

He made a small snorting sound as if he were trying to stop himself from crying. Adam edged his chair a little closer.

'During the next few days,' he said quietly, pausing to think for a moment. 'During the next few days many people will tell you they know how you're feeling. But very few actually do. Even if most people of our age ...'

Adam had to be ten years younger than Erik Lysgaard.

'... have experienced the loss of someone close, it's completely different when a crime is involved. Not only has the person been snatched away all of a sudden, but you're left with so many questions. A crime of this kind ...'

I have no idea what kind of crime this is, he thought as he kept talking. Strictly speaking, nothing had been established so far.

'... is a violation of far more people than the victim. It can squeeze the strength out of anyone. It's—'

'Excuse me.'

Erik's son Lukas Lysgaard opened his mouth for the first time since he had shown Adam into the living room. He seemed tired and looked as if he had been crying, but was quite composed. So far he had stood in silence by the far window looking out over the garden. Now he frowned and moved a little closer.

'I don't really think my father needs consolation. Not from you, anyway, with respect. We would prefer to be alone. When we agreed to this interview ...'

He quickly corrected himself.

'... to this conversation, which is *not* an interview, it was, of course, because we would like to help the police as much as we can. Given the circumstances. As you know I am willing to be interviewed by the police as soon as you wish, but when it comes to my father ...'

Erik Lysgaard straightened up noticeably in his armchair. He stretched his back, blinked hard and raised his chin.

'What is it you want to know?' he asked, looking Adam straight in the eye.

Idiot, Adam thought about himself.

'I'm sorry,' he said. 'Of course I should have left you both in peace. It's just that ... For once we haven't got the media hot on our heels. For once it's possible to get a little ahead of the pack out there.'

He jerked his thumb over his shoulder as if there were already a horde of journalists on the front step.

'But I should have known better. I'll leave you alone today. Of course.'

He stood up and took his coat from the back of one of the dining chairs. Erik Lysgaard looked at him in surprise, his mouth half-open and a furrow in his forehead, just above the thick glasses with their heavy, black frames.

'Haven't you got any questions?' he asked, his tone gentle.

'Yes. Countless questions. But as I said, they can wait. Could I possibly use your bathroom before I leave?'

He directed this request to Lukas.

'Along the hallway. Second on the left,' he mumbled.

Adam nodded briefly to Erik Lysgaard and headed for the door. Halfway across the room he turned back.

Hesitated.

'Just one thing,' he said, scratching his cheek. 'Could I ask why Bishop Lysgaard was out on her own at eleven o'clock on Christmas Eve?'

An odd silence filled the room.

Lukas looked at his father, but there wasn't really any kind of enquiry in his eyes. Just a wary, expressionless look, as if he either knew the answer or thought the question was of no interest. Erik Lysgaard, however, placed his hands on the arms of the chair, leaned back and took a deep breath before looking Adam in the eye once more.

'That's nothing to do with you.'

'What?' Somewhat inappropriately, Adam started to laugh. 'What did you say?'

'I said that's nothing to do with you.'

'Right. Well, I think we'll have to ...'

Silence fell once more.

'We can talk about this later,' he added eventually, raising a hand in Erik's direction as he left the room.

The surprising and absurd answer had made him forget for a moment how much he needed the bathroom. As he closed the door behind him he could feel that it was urgent.

Along the hallway, second on the right.

He mumbled to himself, placed his hand on the knob and opened the door.

A bedroom. Not large, maybe ten square metres. Rectangular, with the window on the short wall facing the door. Under the window stood a neatly made single bed with lilac bed linen. On the pillow lay a folded item of clothing. A nightdress, Adam assumed, inhaling deeply through his nose.

Definitely not a guest room.

The sweet smell of sleep mingled with a faint, almost imperceptible perfume.

It wasn't possible to open the door fully, it bumped against a cupboard on the other side.

He ought to close the door and find the toilet.

There was no desk in the little room, just a fairly large bedside table with a pile of books and a lamp beneath a shelf containing four framed family portraits. He recognized Erik and Lukas straight away, plus an old black-and-white photograph which presumably showed the little family many years ago, when Lukas was small, on a boat in the summer.

On the wall between the cupboard and the bed there was a painting in strong shades of red, and a number of clothes hung on the back of a wooden chair at the foot of the bed. The curtains were thick, dark, and closed.

That was it.

'Excuse me! Not in there!'

Adam stepped back into the hallway. Lukas Lysgaard came quickly towards him, hands spread wide. 'What are you doing? Snooping around the house? Who gave you permission to ... ?'

'Along the hallway, second on the right, you said! I just wanted to—'

'Second on the *left*. Here!'

Lukas pointed crossly at the door opposite.

'Oh, sorry. I didn't mean to—'

'Could you get a move on, please? I'd like to be alone with my father.'

Lukas Lysgaard must be around thirty-five. A man with an ordinary appearance and unusually broad shoulders. His hair was dark with deep waves, and his eyes were presumably blue. It was difficult to tell; they were narrow and hidden behind glasses reflecting the glow of the ceiling light.

'My mother had problems sleeping sometimes,' he said as Adam opened the correct door. 'When that happened she liked to read. She didn't want to disturb my father, so ...' He nodded towards the small bedroom.

'I understand,' said Adam, smiling before he went into the toilet.

He took his time. He would give a great deal to have another look in that bedroom. It annoyed him that he hadn't been more alert. Noticed more. For example, he couldn't remember what kind of clothes had been hanging over the chair: dressy clothes for Christmas Eve, or ordinary everyday clothes. Nor had he noticed the titles of the books on the bedside table. There was no reason to assume that anyone in this family had anything whatsoever to do with the murder of a wife and mother who was obviously loved. But Adam Stubo knew better than most that the solution to a murder was usually to be found with the victim. It could be something the family knew nothing about. Or it could be a detail, something neither the victim nor anyone else had picked up.

But it could be important all the same.

At any rate, one thing was certain, he thought as he zipped up his trousers and flushed the toilet. Eva Karin Lysgaard must have had serious problems when it came to sleeping if she sought refuge in that little bedroom every time she had a bad night. A better explanation was that husband and wife slept in separate rooms.

He washed his hands, dried them thoroughly and went back into the hallway.

Lukas Lysgaard was waiting for him. Without a word he opened the front door.

'No doubt you'll be in touch,' he said, without offering his hand.

'Of course.'

Adam pulled on his coat and stepped into the small porch. He was about to say Merry Christmas, but stopped himself just in time.

The Stranger

'All the best!'

Detective Inspector Silje Sørensen ran up the steps, waving goodbye to a colleague who had stopped for a chat after leaving the police headquarters, which was now virtually empty. All the public departments were closed apart from the main desk, where a yawning officer had nodded to her through the glass wall as she dashed in through the entrance to Grønlandsleiret 44.

'I've got the kids in the car!' she shouted by way of explanation. 'Just going to fetch my skis, I left them in the office and ...'

Silje Sørensen ran up to her floor. She was out of breath as she rounded the corner and set off along the corridor, then slowed down as she approached the door of her office. She fumbled with her keys. They were ice cold after lying in the car for a whole day. Besides which she had far too many keys on the bunch; she had no idea what half of them were for. Eventually, she found the right one and unlocked the door.

Once upon a time the architect had won an award for this building. It was hard to understand why. Once you were inside the narrow entrance, you were fooled into thinking that light and space were key. The vast foyer extended several floors up, surrounded by galleries in an angular horseshoe formation. The offices, however, were little cubes linked to long, claustrophobic corridors. Silje always felt it was cramped and stuffy, however much she opened the windows.

From the outside, police headquarters looked as if it had not withstood the changing seasons well, but simply clung on at an odd angle to the hill between Oslo's main prison and Grønland Church. During her fifteen years with the police service, Silje Sørensen had seen the community, the state and optimistic city enthusiasts slowly attempt to upgrade the area. But the beautiful Middelalder Park lay much too far away to cast its glow over the battered building housing police headquarters. The Opera House was no more than a slanting white roof, just visible from her office beyond seedy areas beneath a lid of exhaust fumes.

She would have liked to open the window, but she didn't have much time.

Her eyes swept over the desk. She was pedantically tidy when it came to her office, unlike every other area of her life. The overfilled in-tray at the edge of the desk had pricked her conscience when she left on the Friday before Christmas. Her out-tray was empty, and she shuddered at the thought of the stress that was waiting for her on the first day back after the holiday.

In the middle of the desk lay a file she didn't recognize. She leaned over and read the yellow Post-it note stuck to the front.

DI Sørensen
Enclosed please find documentation relating to
Hawre Ghani, presumed date of birth
16.12.1991. Please contact me asap.
DCI Harald Bull tel 937✱✱✱✱✱ / 231✱✱✱✱✱

The kids would be bad-tempered and impossible if she was away too long. On the other hand, they were sitting quietly, each with their Nintendo DS when she left them in the back of the car, illegally parked and with the engine running. They had received the games yesterday and were still fascinated by something new, so she thought she might be OK for a while.

She sat down, still wearing her coat, and opened the file.

The first thing she saw was a photograph. It was black and white and grainy, with pronounced shadows. It looked like an enlargement of a picture from some kind of ID document, but didn't exactly fulfil the new criteria for passport photographs. The boy – because this was definitely a boy rather than a grown man – had his eyes half-closed. His mouth was open. Sometimes people who had been taken into custody pulled faces when they had their photo taken in order to make themselves unrecognizable. For some reason she didn't think this boy had been playing up. It struck her that the picture had been taken in a rush, and that the photographer simply couldn't be bothered to take another one.

Hawre Ghani was of no significance.

He hadn't been important enough.

The photograph moved her.

The boy's lips were shining, as if he had licked them. There was something childish and vulnerable about the full upper lip with its pronounced Cupid's bow. The skin around his eyes was smooth, and there was no sign of stubble on his cheeks. The shadow of a moustache beneath a nose that was so large it almost obscured the rest of his face was the only indication that this was a boy well on his way through puberty. In general there was something youthfully disproportionate about the face. Something puppyish. A quick calculation told her that Hawre Ghani had just turned seventeen.

As she looked through the papers she realized he hadn't, in fact, lived long enough to do so.

Despite the fact that Silje Sørensen had worked in the violent crime and sexual offences unit for many years, and had seen more than she could have ever imagined when she was a young police cadet, the next picture came as a shock. Something that must be a face lay inside a hood made of dark fabric. All the features had been smoothed out, the skin was discoloured and badly swollen. One eye socket was distended and empty, the other barely visible. The corpse's upper lip was partially missing in a ragged tear, revealing four white teeth and one made of silver. At least she assumed it was silver; in the photograph it was more like a black, illogical contrast to the rest of the chalk-white teeth.

She moved on quickly.

The penultimate sheet in the thin file was a report written by an officer from the immigration squad. She had never heard of him. The report was dated 23 December 2008.

Two days ago.

```
I was at police headquarters this morning in
order to transfer two illegal immigrants to the
detention centre in Trandum. During the arrest I
```

happened to hear two colleagues discussing an unidentified body which had been found in the harbour early on Sunday 20 December. One of them mentioned that the corpse, which had partially disintegrated, had a silver tooth in the upper jaw. I reacted immediately, because for the past six weeks I have been trying without success to track down Hawre Ghani, a Kurdish asylum seeker below the age of consent, in connection with his application to remain in Norway. During a fight between gangs in Oslo City in September (see my report number 98*****37/08), the right front tooth in Hawre Ghani's upper jaw was knocked out. He was brought in after this incident, and I accompanied him to the dentist's the following day. He requested a silver tooth instead of a porcelain crown, and as far as I am aware this was arranged in collaboration with social services, the asylum seekers' council and the aforementioned dentist.

Since no registered enquiries have come to light regarding a missing person who might correspond to the body found in the harbour, I would suggest that the officer leading the investigation should contact the dentist, Dag Brå, Tåsensenteret, tel. 2229****, in order to compare the dead man's teeth with his X-rays / records.

Silje Sørensen turned to the final page in the file. It was a copy of a handwritten document addressed to Harald Bull.

Hi Harald!
Due to the Christmas holiday I ran a quick and highly unscientific check today, Christmas Eve, based on the tip from the immigration squad. Dag Brå agreed to meet me at his surgery this morning. I showed him some pictures of the deceased's teeth which I took myself (I took a few shots on Aker Brygge on Sunday morning, not brilliant quality but worth a try). He compared these with his own

notes and X-rays, and we can assume until further notice that the deceased probably is the underage Kurdish asylum seeker as indicated. All documents have been copied to forensics. I presume that a formal identification will take place immediately after New Year – or perhaps between Christmas and New Year if the gods are on our side. I'll write a report as soon as I'm back in the office. But now I need a HOLIDAY!

Merry Christmas!
Bengt

P.S. I spoke to forensics yesterday. There are indications that the deceased was killed using something resembling a garrotte. The guy I spoke to said it was a miracle the head was still attached. Perhaps we should consider sending the case over to the violent crimes squad straight away.
B

Silje Sørensen closed the file and leaned back in her chair. She was sweating. The good mood she had been in on her way to work had been swept away, and she wished she had left the damned file alone.

Now she felt a strong urge to open it again, just to look at the young man: this rootless, homeless Kurdish boy without any parents, with his silver tooth and smooth cheeks. Regardless of how many times she came across these children – and God knows it happened all too often – she just couldn't distance herself. Sometimes in the evenings, when she looked in on her own two sons who had now decided they were too old for goodnight kisses, but who still couldn't get to sleep until she had tucked them in, she experienced something that resembled guilt.

Perhaps even shame.

The sound of a car horn shattered the silence, making her heart miss a beat. She opened the window and looked down at the turning area in front of the entrance and the main desk.

'Mum! Mum, will you be much longer?'

Her youngest son was hanging out of the car window, yelling. Silje immediately felt cross. Quickly she placed Hawre Ghani's file on top of her in tray, pulled off the Post-it note with Harald Bull's number and tucked it in her pocket.

As she locked the door behind her and ran towards the foyer in the hope of reaching the car in time to stop her son sounding the horn again, she had completely forgotten why she had gone to the office early on the afternoon of Christmas Day on the way to dinner with her in-laws.

The skis.

They were still behind the door of her office. By the time she eventually remembered them, it was too late.

*

It wasn't too late yet, the duty editor established. The bulletin was going out in two minutes, but since this was anything but a lead story, they could easily put together a short item from the studio with a picture of the Bishop towards the end of the broadcast. He quickly rattled off a message to the producer.

'Get something written for Christian right away,' he ordered the young temp. 'Just a short piece. And double check with NTB that it's correct, of course. We can do without announcing someone has died when they haven't, even on a slow news day.'

'What's going on here?' said Mark Holden, one of NRK's heavyweights on home affairs. 'Who's died?'

He grabbed the piece of paper from the temp, read it in one and a half seconds and shoved it back in the young woman's hand. She didn't really have time to realize he'd taken it.

'Tragic,' said Mark Holden, without a scrap of empathy. 'She can't have been all that old. Sixty? Sixty-two? What did she die of?'

'It doesn't say,' the news editor replied absently. 'I hadn't heard she was ill. But right now I need to concentrate on this broadcast. If you could ...'

He waved away the much older reporter, his gaze fixed on one of the many monitors in the large room. The brief news headlines were shown, with all the captions as agreed. The presenters were more smartly dressed than usual, in honour of Christmas.

The editor leaned back in his chair and put his feet up on the desk.

'Are you still here?' he said to the young woman. 'The idea is to put out the item today, not next week.'

Only now did he notice that her eyes were about to brim over with tears. Her hand was shaking. She took a quick breath and forced a smile.

'Of course,' she said. 'I'll do it right away.'

'Did you know her?' There was still no warmth in Mark Holden's voice, just a deeply rooted curiosity and almost automatic desire to ask everybody questions about everything.

'Yes. She and her husband are friends of my parents. But it's also the fact that she ...'

Her voice broke.

'She's ... she was very popular after all,' said the news editor gently. He chewed on his pencil and lowered his feet to the floor. 'Give that to me,' he said, holding out his hand for the small piece of paper. 'I'll write the piece, and you can start putting together an item with archive pictures for the nine o'clock bulletin. A minute, something like that. OK?'

The young woman nodded.

'The Bishop of Bjørgvin, Eva Karin Lysgaard, passed away suddenly on Christmas Eve, at the age of sixty-two.' The editor spoke the words out loud as his fingers flew over the keys. *'Bishop Lysgaard was born in Bergen and was a student priest in the town before later becoming a prison chaplain. For many years she was the pastor of Tjenvoll parish in Stavanger. In 2001 she was anointed bishop, and has become well known as ...'*

He hesitated, smacked his lips then suddenly continued.

'... a mediator within the church, particularly between the two sides in the controversial debate on homosexuality. Eva Karin Lysgaard was a popular figure in her home town, something that was particularly evident when she held a service at Brann Stadium after Brann won their first league title in forty-four years in 2007. Bishop Lysgaard is survived by her husband, one son and three grandchildren.'

'Is it absolutely necessary to mention that business with the football match?' asked Mark Holden. 'Not entirely appropriate in the circumstances, is it?'

'I think it is,' said the editor, sending the text to the producer with one click. 'It's fine. But listen ...'

Mark Holden was scrabbling around in a huge bowl of sweets.

'Mmm?'

'What does a person die of at that age?'

'You've got to be joking. Anything, of course. I haven't a clue. It's odd that it doesn't say anything about it. No "after a long illness" or something like that. A stroke, I suppose. A heart attack. Something.'

'She was only sixty-two ...'

'So what? People die much younger than that. Personally, I give thanks for every single day on earth. As long as I can have some chocolate now and again.'

Mark Holden couldn't find anything he liked. Next to the bowl lay three rejected liquorice sweets and two coconut chocolates.

'You've taken all the best ones,' he mumbled sourly.

The editor didn't reply. He was deep in thought, and bit on his pencil so hard that it broke. His eyes were fixed on the monitor in front of him, although he didn't really seem to be following what was going on.

'Beate!' he suddenly shouted to the young temp. 'Beate, come over here!'

She hesitated for a moment, then got up from her desk and did as he said.

'When you've finished your little piece,' he said, pointing the broken pencil at her, 'I want you to make a few phone calls, OK? Find out what she died of. I can smell ...'

His nose twitched like a rabbit's.

'... a story. Maybe.'

'Phone people after the programme? That late on Christmas Day?'

The editor sighed loudly. 'Do you want to be a journalist or not? Come on. Get going.'

Beate Krohn's face was expressionless.

'You said your parents knew her,' the editor insisted. 'So give them a call! Ring whoever you damn well like, but find out what the bishop died of, OK?'

'OK,' mumbled the young woman, dreading it already.

*

Johanne never really dreaded doing anything. It was just so difficult to get going. Since she took her doctorate in criminology in the spring of 2000, she had completed two new projects. After submitting her

63

thesis on 'Sexualized violence, a comparative study of conditions during childhood and early experience among sexual and financial offenders' she was awarded a grant which enabled her to write an almost equally comprehensive study of miscarriages of justice in Norway. Ragnhild came along towards the end of this project. She and Adam agreed that Johanne would stay at home with their daughter for two years, but before her maternity leave was over she had made a start on her latest project: a study of underage prostitutes, their background, circumstances and chances of rehabilitation.

Last summer she had been given a piece of work to do for the National Police Directorate.

Ingelin Killengreen herself had contacted Johanne. The Commissioner had obviously been given clear political directives on the issue of putting hate crime on the agenda.

The problem was that this particular type of criminal activity hardly existed at all.

Well, of course it did.

But not when it came to figures. Not statistically speaking. Working in tandem with the Oslo police force, the National Police Directorate had already started mapping all reports made during 2007 where the motive for the crime could be linked to race, ethnicity, religion or sexual orientation. The final report was just around the corner and Johanne had already seen most of the material.

The number of crimes was small, and dwindling.

During 2007 in the whole of Norway 399 cases of hate-motivated crime were registered. Of this number more than 35 per cent were simply the result of an incorrect code being entered in the police register. In other words, just over 250 cases could be classified as hate crime.

For an entire year, in a country with a population of almost five million. Compared with the total number of reported crimes, 256 cases was too small a number to be of any interest.

But it was, at least to politicians. Since just one hate crime was one too many; since the hidden statistics for hate crime must be significant; and since the Red-Green coalition government wanted to enter the election in autumn 2009 with a trump card up its sleeve when it came to minority groups that sounded off whenever a homosexual was assaulted in the street or a synagogue was sprayed with graffiti. That's why Johanne had been asked to undertake a closer study of the phenomenon.

The task was formulated so vaguely that she had spent the entire autumn defining her parameters and limiting the work that lay ahead. She had also started collecting the relatively comprehensive quantities of data available from other countries. Mainly the United States, but also several European countries had been cataloguing and to some extent working on this particular form of law breaking for quite some time. The material was growing, and she still didn't really have a proper grasp of what she was going to do and where she wanted to go.

Then came the financial crisis.

And all those billions in public money.

Certain branches of Norwegian research were drowned in funds. Since the police were included in the many initiatives aimed at keeping the wheels moving and preventing economic collapse, Johanne found herself with four times as much money at her disposal as a few weeks before. This opened up new opportunities, including the possibility of hiring younger researchers and scientific assistants. At the same time, this extra money created fresh problems. She had been on the point of finalizing a framework for her project, and now she had to start all over again.

It was hard work, and it was always difficult to get going. But she was looking forward to it.

It was evening. Kristiane had been unusually co-operative while they were visiting Isak's parents, and Ragnhild had cheered up as soon as the children each received a big bag of Christmas sweets. As Kristiane was staying with her paternal grandparents so that she could spend the next three days with her father, Ragnhild had also insisted on staying. As usual, Isak had smiled broadly and said that was fine. Presumably he had realized the same thing as Adam and Johanne quite some time ago: Kristiane was calmer, slept better and was more cheerful when Ragnhild was around.

The building was quiet. The neighbours downstairs must have gone away. When Johanne got home at about eight o'clock, the ground floor was in darkness. In her own apartment she went from room to room, switching on all the lights. She left all the doors open;

the dog liked to wander around if he wasn't shut in Kristiane's room at night. The soft pattering of his paws and the cheerful thud every time Jack settled down on the floor always made her feel slightly less lonely on the rare occasions when she actually was alone. Eventually she took her laptop into the living room, sat down on the sofa and sipped a glass of wine as she surfed the net, without concentrating on anything in particular. She was looking for some kind of Scrabble game when the phone rang.

'Hi, it's me.'

It was a long time since she had been so pleased to hear his voice.

'Hi darling. How's it going up there?'

Adam laughed.

'Well, basically I've trodden on the toes of the Bergen police; I called to see the widower just a few hours after he'd been told that his wife was dead. I've already fallen out with his son, I think, and on top of all that I've eaten so much for dinner that I feel ill.'

Johanne laughed too.

'That doesn't sound good. Where are you staying?'

'At the SAS Hotel on Bryggen. Nice room. They moved me to a suite when they found out where I was from. It's not exactly packed out here at Christmas.'

'So did they know why you were there?'

'No. It's a miracle. It's almost exactly twenty-four hours since Bishop Lysgaard was murdered, and so far not a single bloody journalist has got wind of it. All that Christmas food must have finished them off.'

'Or the schnapps. Or maybe it's just that the Bergen police are better at keeping quiet than their colleagues in Oslo. By the way, I've just been watching the evening news. They had a little piece about the case, but they more or less just said she was dead.'

On the other end of the line she could hear noises that indicated Adam was taking off his tie. She suddenly felt quite emotional. She knew him so well she could hear something like that on the phone.

'Hang on,' he said. 'I'm just going to take off my shoes and this damned noose around my neck. That's better. What kind of a day have you had? Was it horrible having to do all that clearing up with the kids around? You must be worn out. I'm sorry I—'

'It was fine. As you know I can get by perfectly well without one night's sleep. The kids played in the garden for a couple of hours and I just ...'

She had managed to push away the thought of the strange man for the entire afternoon and evening. Now a feeling of unease stabbed through her, and she fell silent.

'Hello? Johanne?'

'Yes, I'm here.'

'Is something wrong? Johanne?'

Adam would simply dismiss it. He would sigh his weary sigh and tell her not to be so worried about the children all the time. Adam would have very little understanding of the fact that Johanne had discovered that a complete stranger knew the name of her elder daughter. Besides which, the man had been so well wrapped up in his overcoat, hat and scarf that Adam would maintain it could have been a neighbour if she told him about the incident; and that horrible little coldness would come between them and make it more difficult for her to get to sleep later, alone, with no other sounds around her apart from Jack's snuffling and constant farting.

'No, no,' she said, trying to make her voice smile. 'Except that you're not here, of course. Ragnhild wanted to stay over with Isak's parents.'

'That's good. Isak really is generous. He puts—'

'As if you weren't every bit as kind to his daughter! As if—'

'Calm down, Johanne! That wasn't what I meant. I'm glad you all had a nice evening, and that you've got some time for yourself. That certainly doesn't happen very often.'

She moved the laptop on to the coffee table and drew the blanket more tightly around her.

'You're right,' she said, this time with a genuine smile. 'It's actually really nice to be all on my own. Apart from Jack, of course. By the way, there must be something wrong with his food. He's farting like mad.'

Adam laughed. 'What are you up to?'

'Doing a little bit of work. Surfing the net a little bit. Drinking a little drop of wine. Missing you.'

'That all sounds good. Apart from the work – it's Christmas Day! I'm just about to go to bed. I'm worn out. Tomorrow I'm hoping to interview the Bishop's son. God knows how that will go – he's already taken a dislike to me.'

'I'm sure he hasn't. Everybody likes you. And because you are the very best detective in the whole wide world, I'm sure it'll be fine.'

Adam laughed again.

'You mustn't keep saying that to the kids! Just before Christmas when we were queuing at the checkout in Maxi, Ragnhild suddenly stood up in the shopping trolley and announced at the top of her voice that her daddy was the very, very, very best – I think she must have said "very" ten times – detective in the world. Embarrassing. People laughed.'

'But she's right,' said Johanne with a smile. 'You're the best in the world at most things.'

'Idiot. Night-night.'

'Night-night, my love.'

Adam's voice disappeared. Johanne stared at the telephone for a while, as if she was hoping he might still be there and would reassure her that the man by the fence posed no threat. Then she got up slowly, put down the phone and went over to the window. The new moon was suspended at an angle above the apartment block next door. There was still frost on the ground. The cold had sunk its teeth into Oslo, but the sky was clear, day after day, and all week there had been the most breathtaking sunsets. The few sparse snowflakes that had fallen during the afternoon covered the garden like a thin film. The sky was clear once again, it was dark, and after a while Johanne felt ready for bed.

*

A woman stared out of a window, not knowing if she would ever sleep again. Perhaps she was already sleeping. Everything was strange and unreal, like a dream. She had been born in this house, in this room, she had always lived here and looked out of this leaded window, a cross dividing the view into four different parts of the world, as her father had told her when she was little and believed every word he said. Now everything was twisted and distorted. She was used to the rain against the window pane. It often rained, almost all the time. It was raining in Bergen and she wept and didn't know what she was seeing. Life had been chopped into pieces. The view from the little house was no longer hers.

She had waited for twenty-four hours – a long night and an even longer day – in a state of not knowing which she could do nothing about. Just as her life had followed a course that had been determined by circumstances beyond her control, so these endless hours of waiting had been something she just had to suffer. There had been no way out, not until the woman on TV had told her what she had, in fact, already known when she woke up in the armchair in front of the screen exactly twenty-four hours earlier, with a fear that grasped her by the throat and made her hands shake.

Because she had waited before.

She had waited all her life, and she had got used to it.

This time everything was different. She had felt a confirmation of something that couldn't be true – shouldn't be true – and yet she still knew, because she had lived like this for such a long time, utterly, utterly alone.

The doorbell rang, so late and so unexpectedly that the woman gave a little scream.

She opened the door and recognized him. It was an eternity since they had last met, but the eyes were the same. He was weeping, like her, and asked if he could come in. She didn't want him to. He wasn't the one she wanted to see. She didn't want to see anyone.

When she let him in and closed the door behind him, she asked God to let her wake up.

Please, please God. Please be kind to me.

Let me wake up now.

*

'Surely nobody's awake at this time of night?'

Beate Krohn looked at the news editor with a resigned expression. It was almost midnight. They were alone in the news office among silent, flickering monitors and the quiet hum of computers and the ventilation system. Here and there someone had hung up the odd Christmas decoration: a strand of red tinsel, a garland of little Norwegian flags. In one corner stood a sparse Christmas tree with a crooked star on top. Most of the chocolates and biscuits that had been provided as a consolation for those who had to work over Christmas had been eaten. Sheets of paper and old newspapers were strewn all over the place.

'What about your parents?'

He just wouldn't give up. He had lit a cigarette – such a blatant breach of the rules that she was quite impressed in spite of herself.

'They'll be asleep, too,' she said. 'Besides which, I'd frighten the life out of them if I rang this late. We have rules about that kind of thing in our family. Not before seven thirty in the morning, and not after ten at night. Unless somebody's died.'

'But somebody *has* died!'

'Not like that. I mean—'

He interrupted her with a deep drag on his cigarette and an impatient wave of his hand.

'Let me show you how it's done,' he grinned, the cigarette clamped between his teeth. 'Watch and learn.'

His fingers flew over his mobile before he put it to his ear.

'Hello Jonas, it's Sølve.'

Silence for three seconds.

'Sølve Borre. At NRK. Where are you?'

Beate Krohn had once read that the most common opening remark in the entire world when it came to mobile phone conversations was 'Where are you?' After that she had sworn never to ask the question herself.

'Listen, Jonas. Bishop Lysgaard died last night, as you've no doubt heard. The thing is—'

He had obviously been interrupted, and took the opportunity to have another deep drag on his cigarette.

'Sure. Sure. But the thing is, I just wanted to check what she died of. Just to satisfy my curiosity. I've got one of those feelings, you know ...'

Pause.

'But can't you give one of them a ring? There must be somebody there who owes you a favour. Can't you—?'

Once again he was interrupted. By now the cloud of smoke surrounding him was so dense Beate was afraid it would set off the alarm. She took a step back to avoid getting the smell in her clothes.

'Nice one, Jonas! Nice one. Give me a ring later. Doesn't matter what time it is!' He ended the call. 'There you go,' he said, his fingers moving over the keys. 'Come here and I'll teach you something. Look at these messages.'

Beate leaned hesitantly over his shoulder and read the message saying that Bishop Lysgaard was dead. It hadn't changed since she last saw it.

'Notice anything odd?' asked the editor.

'No.'

She coughed discreetly and turned away.

'I don't know how many messages like that I've read in my life,' he said, completely unmoved. 'But it has to be a lot. By and large, they're all exactly the same. The tone is slightly formal, and they don't really say much. But they almost always say more than the fact that the person concerned is dead. "So-and-so passed away unexpectedly at home." "So-and-so passed away after a short illness." "So-and-so died in a car accident in Drammen last night." That kind of thing.'

His fingers drew so many quotation marks in the air that ash went all over the keyboard. It was already so worn that the letters were barely visible.

'But this one,' he said, pointing at the display. 'This one just says "Bishop Eva Karin Lysgaard died yesterday evening. She was sixty-two years old ..." And so on and so on, blah blah blah.'

'That doesn't necessarily mean anything,' she said firmly.

'Oh no,' said the news editor, still smiling broadly. 'Probably not. But it needs checking. How do you think a guy like me became a journalist at NRK before I was twenty-one, with no training?'

He pointed meaningfully at his nose.

'I've got it, that's how.'

The telephone rang. Beate Krohn stared at it in surprise, as if the editor had just shown her a conjuring trick.

'Sølve Borre,' he yapped, dropping his cigarette stub into a mineral water bottle. 'Right. Exactly.'

He sat in silence for a few seconds. The mischievous expression disappeared. His eyes narrowed. He reached for a pen and made a few illegible notes in the margin of a newspaper.

'Thanks,' he said eventually. 'Thank you, Jonas. I owe you big time, OK?'

He sat staring at his phone for a moment. Suddenly he looked up, completely transformed.

'Bishop Lysgaard was murdered,' he said slowly. 'She was fucking murdered on Christmas Eve.'

'How ... ?' Beate Krohn began, sinking down on to a chair. 'How do you know ... ? Who was that you were talking to?'

The chief news editor leaned back in his chair and looked her straight in the eye.

'I hope you've learned something tonight,' he said quietly. 'And the most important thing of all is this: you're nothing as a journalist without good sources. Work long and hard to cultivate them, and never, ever give them away. Never.'

Beate Krohn struggled in vain to control her blushes.

'And now,' said the editor with a disarming smile as he lit yet another cigarette, 'now we're really going to hit the phones. Time to start waking people up!'

Small Keys, Big Rooms

'**G**ood grief,' said Adam Stubo, stopping dead in the doorway. 'Did I wake you up?'

Lukas Lysgaard blinked and shook his head.

'No,' he mumbled. 'Or rather, yes. I hardly slept last night, so I sat down here and ...'

He raised his head, smiling wanly. Adam hardly recognized him. The broad shoulders were drooping. His hair was getting greasy, and he had dark, puffy bags around his eyes. A blood vessel had burst in his left eye, staining it bright red.

'That's understandable,' said Adam, pulling out a chair on the opposite side of the table.

Lukas Lysgaard shrugged his shoulders. Adam didn't really know whether it meant he didn't care whether Adam understood or not, or if it was a kind of apology for the fact that he had fallen asleep.

'The wolves are out,' Adam said as he sat down. 'After all, it was only a matter of time before the press found out.'

The other man nodded.

'Have they been after you already?' Adam asked, glancing at the clock which showed that it was a few minutes after half past eight.

The man nodded dully.

'Anyway, I'm very grateful to you for coming in,' said Adam, gesturing with one hand. 'I see my colleague has taken care of the formalities. Has anyone offered you something to drink? Coffee? Water?'

'No thanks. Why are you actually here?'

'Me?'

'Yes.'

'What do you mean?'

Lukas leaned forward, resting his elbows on the desk.

'You work for NCIS.'

Adam nodded.

'NCIS is no longer what it was.'

'No.'

Adam couldn't understand what the man was getting at.

'As far as I understand it, NCIS exists primarily to combat organized crime. Do you think it was the Mafia that killed my mother?'

'No, no, no!'

For a brief moment Adam thought the man was serious. A humourless, almost imperceptible smile made him change his mind.

'The very best resources have been allocated to this enquiry,' he said, pouring himself a coffee from a Thermos. 'Including me. How's your father?'

No reply.

'My intention is to give you some information to begin with,' said Adam, pushing a thin file across the desk.

Lukas Lysgaard showed no sign of wanting to open it.

'Your mother died of a stab wound. To the heart. This means that she died very quickly.'

Adam watched the other man's face, looking for any indication that he ought to break off.

'She had no other injuries apart from a few grazes, which in all probability are due to the fall itself. Therefore it seems likely that she did not offer any form of resistance.'

'She was ...' Lukas raised a clenched fist to his mouth and coughed. 'She was sixty-two years old. You can hardly expect her to put up much resistance when some man attacked her.' He coughed again, then quickly added: 'Or woman. I assume that happens from time to time.'

'Absolutely.' Adam nodded and stroked his cheek, wondering whether he ought to take back the untouched file. The silence between them went on for just a little bit too long. It became embarrassing, and Adam realized that Lukas Lysgaard's fairly unfriendly attitude had hardly changed over the past twenty-four hours. He was staring at the desk with his arms folded.

'My wife is a criminologist,' Adam said suddenly. 'And a lawyer. And she's studied psychology as well.'

Lukas at least looked up, a furrow of surprise creasing his brow.

'She's quite a lot younger than me,' Adam added.

Neither the most reluctant witness nor the most hostile thug could manage to remain unmoved when Adam started talking about his family for no particular reason. It seemed so unprofessional that the person being interviewed was annoyed, surprised, or quite simply interested.

'She sometimes says ...' Adam picked up his cup and took a slow, noisy slurp. 'She would rather her nearest and dearest died after a long, painful illness than as the victim of a crime, however quick it might be.'

As he spoke he felt the usual pang of conscience as he misrepresented Johanne, saddling her with views she didn't hold. It disappeared when he saw Lukas's reaction.

'What does she mean ... ? What do you mean by that? It's terrible to wish something like that on someone you love, and—'

'It is, isn't it? I agree with you. But what she means is that the family of someone who has been the victim of a crime is subjected to a detailed investigation, and that can be a terrible strain. When someone dies of other causes, then ...'

Adam held up his hands, palms facing outwards.

'... then it's all over. The family is overwhelmed with sympathy, and no one asks questions. Quite the reverse, my wife stubbornly maintains. A death from natural causes has the effect of laying to rest any secrets the family might have. However, when the deceased is the victim of a crime ...'

He shook his head ruefully and stuck an imaginary key in an imaginary keyhole.

'Everything has to be brought out into the open. That's what she means. Not that I agree with her, as I said, but she is right to a certain extent. Don't you think?'

Lukas peered at him without giving any indication of whether he agreed or not. Adam held his gaze.

'I assume,' Lukas said suddenly, leaning across the desk, 'that what you're trying to tell me is that there are secrets in my family that could explain why my mother was stabbed and murdered out in the street!' His voice cracked at the end of the sentence. 'That she's the guilty party, somehow! That my mother, the kindest, most thoughtful ...'

His voice broke and he started to cry. Adam sat motionless with the coffee cup in his right hand and a pen balanced between the index and middle fingers of his left hand.

'I don't think my mother had any secrets,' said Lukas in despair, rubbing his eyes with the back of his hand. 'Not my mother. Not her.'

Still Adam said nothing.

'My mother and father loved each other more than anything in the world,' Lukas went on. 'They've had their disagreements, just like everyone else, but they've been married since they were nineteen. That's ...' He sobbed as he worked it out. 'That's more than forty years! They've been married for more than forty years, and you come along claiming there are all these secrets between them! It's ... it's ...'

Adam made a few brief notes on the pad in front of him, then pushed it away so that it fell on the floor. When he picked it up, he put it back on the table face down.

'You've got a nerve,' Lukas said harshly. 'Insinuating that my mother—'

'I apologize if that's the way you see it,' Adam said. 'That wasn't my intention. But it's very interesting that you immediately defend your parents' marriage when I talk in completely general terms about the fact that everyone has experiences they don't want to share with other people. Something they've done. Something they haven't done. Something that might have made them enemies. Something that has harmed others. Of course, that doesn't necessarily mean that ...'

He let the sentence dangle in the air in the hope that it was sufficiently vague.

'My parents don't have any enemies,' said Lukas, clearly making an effort to pull himself together. 'On the contrary, my mother was regarded as a mediator, an advocate of reconciliation. Both in her profession and in her private life. She never said anything to me about anyone wanting to kill her. That's just ...'

He swallowed and ran his fingers through his hair over and over again.

'As for my father ...'

He was finding it difficult to breathe.

'My father has always been in my mother's shadow.'

His voice altered as he slowly exhaled. Suddenly he seemed resigned. It was as if he was actually talking to himself.

'I mean, that's obvious. My mother with her career, and my father who never got any further than his degree. I don't suppose he wanted to ...'

He broke off again.

'How did they meet?' Adam asked gently.

'At school. They were in the same class.'

'High-school sweethearts,' said Adam with a little smile.

'Yes. My mother was saved when she was sixteen. She came from a perfectly ordinary working-class family. My grandfather worked at BMW.'

'In Germany?'

Adam leafed through the file in front of him, looking somewhat surprised.

'No. Bergen Mechanical Workshop. He was a member of the Norwegian Communist Party and a wholehearted atheist. My mother was the first member of the family to go to the grammar school. It was difficult for my grandfather to see his daughter reading theology, but at the same time he was incredibly ... proud of her. Unfortunately, he didn't live long enough to see her become a bishop. That would have ...'

He shrugged his shoulders.

'My father, on the other hand, came from a totally academic environment. His father was a professor of history, at the University of Oslo first of all. They moved to Bergen when my father was around eight years old. His mother was a lecturer. In those days it was quite unusual for women to ...'

Once again he broke off.

'But you know that,' he added, eventually.

Adam waited.

'In many ways my father is regarded as ... how shall I put it? A weak person?'

He sobbed out loud as he said it, and the tears began to flow again.

'Which he most definitely isn't. He's a wonderful father. Clever and well-read. Very thoughtful. But he just couldn't ... do everything ... become the kind of person who ... The thing is, his parents had great hopes for him. They expected a great deal of him.'

He sobbed and wiped his mouth.

'My father is more of a thinker than my mother was. In religious terms he's ... stricter, in some ways. He's absolutely fascinated by Catholicism. If it hadn't been for my mother's position I think he would have converted a long time ago. Last autumn my mother attended an ecumenical conference in Boston, and my father went with her. He visited every single Catholic church in the city.'

Lukas hesitated for a moment.

'He's also more strict with himself than my mother was. I don't think he's ever really got over the fact that his parents were disappointed in him. He's their only child.'

He added this final comment with an expression that suggested it explained most things.

'So are you, I notice.' Adam looked at his papers again, turned over his pad and quickly scribbled down a couple of sentences.

'Yes.'

'You're ... twenty-nine years old?'

Adam was surprised when he saw Lukas's date of birth in the file. The previous day he had assumed the bishop's son was well into his thirties.

'Yes.'

'So your parents had been married for fourteen years when you were born.'

'They studied for a long time. Well, my mother did, anyway.'

'And they never had any more children?'

'Not that I know of.'

The acidic alertness was back.

Adam smiled disarmingly and quickly asked: 'When you say they loved each other more than anything in the world, what are you basing that on?'

Lukas looked stunned.

'What am I ... ? What do you mean?' Without waiting for an answer he went on. 'They showed it a hundred times a day! The way they spoke to one another, the experiences they shared, everything ... for God's sake, what kind of a question is that?'

His expression was almost frightening, with the blood-red eye wide open. Suddenly he stiffened, holding his breath.

'Is something wrong?' Adam asked after a few seconds. 'Mr Lysgaard! What's the matter?'

Slowly the man expelled the air from his lungs.

'Migraine,' he said quietly. 'I've just started to get visual disturbance.' He spoke in a monotone, and was blinking rapidly. 'One half is shimmering ...' He held up one hand, forming a barrier between his right and left eye.

'It means that in exactly twenty-five minutes I will get a headache so severe that it's indescribable. I have to get home.'

He stood up so quickly that his chair fell over. For a moment he lost his balance and steadied himself against the wall. Adam looked at his watch. He had allocated the entire day to this interview, which had hardly begun. Although he had already learned enough to give him something to think about, it was difficult to hide his irritation at this interruption. But that was of no consequence. Lukas Lysgaard was already lost to this world.

'I'll drive you home,' he said quietly. 'Is there anything else I can do for you?'

'No. Home. Now.'

Adam fetched Lukas's coat from a hook on the wall. The man showed no sign of wanting to put it on. He simply took it and dragged it along behind him as he headed for the door. Adam moved quickly and got there first.

'I can see you're not well,' he said, his hand resting on the door handle. 'We will, of course, postpone the rest of this interview until a more suitable time. Unfortunately, however, there is one question I do have to ask. You heard it yesterday, in fact.'

Lukas Lysgaard's expression remained unchanged. It almost seemed as if he was no longer aware that Adam was in the room.

'What was your mother doing out walking on Christmas Eve?'

Lukas raised his head. He looked Adam straight in the eye, licked his lips and swallowed audibly. It was clearly taking a huge amount of effort to steel himself against the pain he knew would come.

'I don't know,' he said. 'I have no idea why my mother was out so late.'

'Did she usually go out in the evening? Just before bedtime? I mean, was it normal for her to ...'

Lukas was still holding his gaze.

'I have to get home,' he said hoarsely. 'No. I have no idea where my mother was going or what she was doing. Take me home. Please.'

You're lying, Adam thought as he opened the door. I can see that you're lying.

'I'm telling the truth,' said Lukas Lysgaard, wobbling into the corridor.

*

'You couldn't tell a lie if you were being paid for it,' Lina Skytter said with a laugh as she tucked her legs up on the sofa.

'Leave it out,' said Johanne, surprised that she felt slightly insulted. 'I'm actually a specialist in lies!'

'Other people's lies, yes. Not your own. If you'd bought spare ribs at Rimi and told your mother they were from Strøm-Larsen, your nose would have grown from here to Sognsvann. Just as well you went for cod instead.'

'My mother didn't think so,' Johanne mumbled into her wine glass.

'Give over,' said Lina. 'Your mum's lovely. Good with the kids and really kind. She's just a little ... emotionally incontinent, that's all. It's as if whatever's on her mind has to come out of her mouth right away, kind of. Forget it. Cheers!'

Johanne raised her glass and tucked her feet underneath her. Her best and oldest friend had turned up just an hour ago, with two bottles of wine and three DVDs. Johanne had felt slightly irritated for a few minutes; she had actually been looking forward to an evening on her own with the computer. But now they were sitting at either end of the big sofa, and Johanne couldn't remember when she had last felt so relaxed.

'God, I'm so tired.' She smiled and gave an enormous yawn. 'I don't notice it until I relax.'

'You have to stay awake. We're going to watch ...' Lina shuffled through the pile of films on the coffee table. '... *What Happens in Vegas* first. Ashton Kutcher is just gorgeous. And no critical comments. We're just going to have a nice time.'

She kicked out at Johanne, who shook her head, her expression resigned.

'How much time do you actually waste on stuff like this?' she asked.

'Don't be so bloody tight-arsed. You like it, too.'

'Well, can I at least watch the news first? Just so that we have some kind of basis in reality before we dive into a vat of syrup?'

Lina laughed and raised her glass in agreement.

Johanne switched on the TV and just caught the last few seconds of the opening headlines. The top story was as she expected: *Bishop Eva Karin Lysgaard murdered in the street – the police have no leads so far.*

'What?' said Lina, her mouth falling open as she sat up straight on the sofa. 'Murdered? But how the hell ... ?'

She put her feet on the floor, put down her glass and leaned forward, her elbows resting on her knees.

'It's been all over the net and on the radio all day,' Johanne said, turning up the sound. 'Where have you been?'

Christian Borch was wearing a dark suit and a serious expression.

'The police have today confirmed that the bishop of Bjørgvin, Eva Karin Lysgaard, was murdered on the evening of the twenty-fourth of December. Yesterday it was announced that Bishop Lysgaard had died, but the circumstances surrounding her death were not made public until this morning.'

The picture changed from the studio to a rain-soaked Bergen, where a reporter gave a summary of the case, which was basically two minutes about nothing.

'Is that why Adam's away?' Lina asked, turning to Johanne.

She nodded.

'As far as we are aware, the police have no leads regarding the identity of the killer at this stage.'

'Which means they have lots of leads,' said Johanne. 'But they have no idea what to do with them.'

Lina shushed her. They sat in silence and watched the entire item, which lasted almost twelve minutes. This was not only because the Christmas period was somewhat short on news as usual; this was something very special. You could see it in everyone who was interviewed – the police, church officials, politicians and ordinary people on the street, everyone was moved in a way that Norwegians didn't normally show in public. Many had difficulty speaking. Some burst into tears while being interviewed.

'It's almost like when King Olav died,' said Lina, switching off the TV.

'Hmm. He died of old age, in his own bed.'

'I know, but the atmosphere is kind of the same. Who in the world would want to kill a woman like that? I mean, she was so ... kind, somehow. So good!'

Johanne recalled that she had reacted in exactly the same way almost two days ago. Not only had Eva Karin Lysgaard seemed to be a good person, she was also clearly blessed with a talent for diplomacy. In theological terms she was right in the middle of the fragmented landscape that comprised the Church of Norway. She was neither radical nor conservative. On the question of homosexuality, which had raged within the church for many years – constantly moving Norway closer to a non-denominational constitution – she had been the principal architect of the fragile peace agreement. There would be room for both points of view. Bishop Lysgaard had nothing against marrying homosexuals. At the same time, she had defended the right of her opponents to refuse to do so. Bishop Lysgaard stood out as an open, tolerant person, a typical representative of a broad and popular state church. Which, in fact, she was not. On the contrary, she had strong, fundamental misgivings when it came to the unsatisfactory self-regulation within the church, and never missed an opportunity to put forward her opinion.

Always pleasant. Always calm, with a subtle smile that smoothed the edges of the odd sharp word that might slip out on those rare occasions when Eva Karin Lysgaard became too involved.

As a rule, this concerned the issue of abortion.

Eva Karin Lysgaard held extreme views in only one area: she was against abortion. Totally and completely and in all circumstances. Not even after a rape or when the mother's life might be in danger could she countenance interference to put an end to a life that had been created. For Bishop Lysgaard, God's creation was sacrosanct. His ways were unfathomable, and a fertilized egg had the right to life, because God willed it so.

Strangely enough she was respected for her views, in a country where the debate on abortion had actually ended in 1978. The small minority that had continued to oppose the law legalizing abortion were largely regarded as ridiculously conservative and – at least in the eyes of the general public – fairly extreme. Even the feminists toned things down when they were in a debate with Eva Karin Lysgaard. By sticking so firmly to her principles, she distanced herself from the idea that the issue of abortion was anything to do with women's liberation.

For her, abortion was a question of the sanctity of life, and nothing to do with gender.

'I wonder what happened to her out there in the forest?' Johanne said suddenly.

'The forest? I thought she was murdered on the street?'

'I don't mean the murder, I meant that time ... there was a profile of her in the Saturday supplement last week, did you see it?'

Lina shook her head and topped up her glass.

'We were up at the cottage over the weekend. We did lots of skiing, but didn't read a single newspaper.'

You never do anyway, wherever you are, thought Johanne, smiling as she went on.

'She said she met God in the forest when she was sixteen. Something special happened, but she didn't say what it was.'

'Isn't it Jesus they usually meet?'

'What?'

'I thought when somebody was saved they said they "met Jesus".'

'God or Jesus,' Johanne muttered. 'Same thing.'

She got up quickly and went into the bedroom. She came back with the supplement, and turned to the interview as she sat down again.

'Here,' she said, taking a deep breath.

'*I was in a very difficult situation. We human beings often find ourselves in this position when we are teenagers. Things become too big for us. And that's what happened to me. Then I met Jesus.*'

'Ha!' Lina exclaimed. 'I was right!'

'Shut up. *What actually happened?* That's the journalist asking.'

Johanne glanced quickly at Lina over the top of her glasses and went on:

'*That's a matter between me and God, the Bishop says with a smile, revealing dimples deep enough to hide in. We all have our secret rooms. That's the way it should be. That's the way it will always be.*'

She slowly folded up the magazine.

'And now I want to watch a film,' said Lina.

'*We all have our secret rooms*,' Johanne repeated, gazing at the close-up of Eva Karin Lysgaard on the cover.

'Not me,' Lina said breezily. 'Shall we watch *What Happens in Vegas*, or would you rather go straight for *The Devil Wears Prada*? I haven't actually seen it yet, and I can watch Meryl Streep in anything.'

'I'm sure even you have a couple of rooms with secrets in them, Lina.' Johanne took off her glasses and rubbed her eyes, then added: 'It's just that you've lost the keys.'

'Could be,' Lina said amiably. 'But what you don't know can't hurt you, as they say.'

'You're completely wrong there,' said Johanne, pointing half-heartedly at *The Devil Wears Prada*. 'It's actually what we don't know that *does* hurt us.'

Vanity Fair

The worst thing of all would have been not knowing, thought Niclas Winter. He had lived on the verge of financial collapse for so long that the certain knowledge his buyer was no longer interested had once again made him drink a little too much, a little too often. Not to mention all the other stuff he took to keep his nerves under control. In actual fact he had knocked all that crap on the head long ago. It dulled his senses and made him lazy. And listless. Unproductive.

Not the way he wanted to be.

When the financial crisis hit the whole world in the autumn of 2008, it didn't have the same effect in Norway as in many other countries. With billions in the bank, the Red-Green coalition government introduced the sort of expensive counter-measures that few could have imagined a few months earlier. Norway had been pumping money out of the North Sea for so long that it seemed more or less fireproof after the financial collapse in the United States. The property market in Norway, which for some time had been over-inflated and overactive, did indeed hit rock bottom in the early autumn. But it had already recovered – or there were signs of life, at least. The number of bankruptcies had rocketed in recent months, but many people regarded this as a healthy cleansing process, stripping away the companies that were never really viable. Unemployment was growing in the building industry, which was naturally taken very seriously. However, it was an industry that relied largely on an imported workforce. Poles, Swedes and workers from the Baltic states had one especially attractive quality: they were happy to go back home when there wasn't any work – at least, those who hadn't actually realized that they could pick up plenty of money through the Norwegian social security system. There were also enough economists who, quietly and in private, regarded an unemployment rate of around 40 per cent as good for the flexibility of the total labour market.

On the whole, Norway plc was moving forward; things may have changed, but at least the global financial crisis had not been a major catastrophe for the country and its people. They were still buying food; they still needed clothes for themselves and their children; they treated themselves to a bottle of wine at the weekend as usual and they were still going to the cinema just as often as before.

It was the luxury goods that were no longer attracting a significant number of buyers.

And, for some reason, art was regarded as a luxury.

Niclas Winter tore the foil off the bottle of champagne he had bought the day his mother died. He tried to remember if he had ever purchased such a bottle before. As he fumbled with the wire around the cork, he decided this was the first time. He had certainly drunk his fair share of the noble French wine, particularly in recent years, but always at others' expense.

The champagne foamed up and he laughed to himself as he poured the bubbling, gently fizzing drink into a plastic glass on the edge of his overfilled desk. He put the bottle down on the floor to be on the safe side and raised the glass to his lips.

The studio, which measured almost 300 square metres and had originally been a warehouse, was flooded with daylight. To an outsider the room would have given an impression of total chaos, with light coming in from above and from the huge bay windows in the wall facing south-east. Niclas Winter, however, was in complete control of everything. There were welding torches and soldering irons, computers and old toilets, cables from the North Sea and half a wrecked car; the studio would be a paradise for any eleven-year-old. Not that such a person would ever have been allowed through the door. Niclas Winter, installation artist, suffered from three phobias: large birds, earthworms and children. It had been difficult enough to get through his own childhood, and he couldn't cope with being reminded of it by seeing children playing and shouting and having fun. The fact that the studio lay just 200 metres from a school was a tragedy that he had somehow learned to live with. In every other way the location was perfect; the rent was low, and most of the kids kept out of the way once he put a BEWARE OF THE DOG sign with a picture of a Dobermann on the door.

The room was a slight rectangle, sixteen by eighteen metres. Everything was gathered along the walls, a frame of scrap and other necessities surrounding a large space in the middle. This was always clean and empty, apart from the installation Niclas Winter was working on at the time. Along one of the shorter walls stood installations which were more or less finished, but which he had not yet shown to anyone.

He sipped the champagne, which was too sweet and not cold enough.

This was the best thing he had done.

The piece was entitled *I was thinking of something blue and maybe grey, darling* and had actually been bought by StatoilHydro.

A monolith of shop window dummies rose up in the centre of the art work. They were wound around each other as in the original in Vigeland Park, but because the dummies were so rigid apart from their knees, elbows, hips and shoulders, the six-metre-high installation was positively spiky. Heads on almost broken necks, stiff, dead fingers and feet with painted nails stuck out on all sides. A thin, shimmering length of silver barbed wire was wound around the whole thing. Real silver, of course; the barbed wire alone had cost a small fortune. On closer inspection you could see that the naked, lifeless dummies were wearing expensive watches on their wrists, and almost every one was adorned with a necklace. The dummies had been literally sexless when he bought them. Only the broad shoulders and lack of breasts distinguished the men from the women, as well as a small, undefined bulge at the crotch. Niclas Winter had come to their rescue. He had bought so many dildos in a porn shop that they had given him a considerable discount, and he had mounted them on the castrated dummies. The dildos were marketed as being 'natural', which Niclas Winter knew was nonsense. They were colossal. He sprayed them in fluorescent colours, making them even more striking.

'Perfect,' he murmured to himself, emptying his glass in one swig.

He took a few steps back and shook his head.

His last exhibition had been an enormous success. Three outdoor installations had stood on Rådhuskaia for four weeks. People were enthusiastic. So were the critics. He sold the lot. For the first time in his life, he was almost debt-free. And best of all, StatoilHydro, who had already bought *Vanity Fair, reconstruction*, ordered *I was thinking ... on the basis of a sketch. The price was two million. He had been paid half a million in advance, but he had already spent that money and considerably more on materials.

Then the bastards changed their minds.

He hadn't much of a clue about contracts, and when he went to see a solicitor with the letter which had arrived in October, beside himself with rage, he realized it was time to get himself an agent. StatoilHydro were, in fact, perfectly within their rights. The contract had a cancellation clause. Niclas Winter had hardly even glanced through the document before signing it, dizzy with joy.

In the current financial climate, they wrote apologetically. *An unfortunate side-effect on employees and owners,* they babbled on. *Moderation. A certain level of restraint with regard to unnecessary outlay.*

Blah, blah, blah. Fuck.

The bloody letter arrived four days before his mother died.

As he sat with her during those last hours – more for appearance's sake than because he actually felt any sorrow – everything changed. Niclas Winter walked out of his dead mother's room at the Lovisenberg Hospice with a smile on his lips, fresh hope and a riddle to solve.

And he had done it.

It had taken time, of course. His mother had been so vague that it had taken him several weeks to find the right office. He had got too stressed and made a couple of mistakes along the way. But now he had done it. The appointment had been made for the first working day after the New Year, and the man he was going to meet would make Niclas Winter a very rich man.

He poured himself more champagne and drank.

The tiny, tiny feeling of intoxication did him good, and his piece was finished. If StatoilHydro didn't have the sense to take the opportunity, there would be other buyers. With the money that was due to come to him he could accept the offer of an exhibition in New York in the autumn. He could give up all those other jobs that sucked the energy and creativity out of him. And he would finally give up the drugs. And the booze. He would work all day long, with no worries.

Niclas Winter was almost happy.

He thought he heard a noise. An almost imperceptible click.

He half-turned. The door was locked, and there was no one there. He drank a little more. A cat on the roof, perhaps. He looked up.

Someone grabbed hold of him. He understood nothing as someone's hands pulled at his face, forcing his mouth open. When the syringe was pushed into his left cheek, he was surprised more than afraid. The needle caught his tongue, and the pain as it touched the sensitive mucus membrane was so agonizing that he cried out at last. A man was still standing behind him, gripping his hands. An intense heat spread from his mouth at lightning speed, and it was difficult to breathe. The stranger caught him as he fell. Niclas Winter smiled and tried to blink away the film that was covering his eyes like oil. He couldn't get any air. His lungs were no longer working.

He was hardly even aware of his left sleeve being pushed up.

The second needle ate its way into the blue vein in the crook of his arm.

It was 27 December 2008, and the time was thirty-three minutes past midnight. When Niclas Winter died, thirty-two years old and on the verge of an international breakthrough as an artist, he was still smiling in surprise.

*

Ragnhild Vik Stubo was laughing her biggest laugh. Johanne smiled back, picked up the dice and threw them again.

'You're not very good at Yahtzee, Mummy.'

'Unlucky at games, lucky in love. I'll just have to console myself with that.'

The dice landed, showing two ones, a three, a four and a five. Johanne hesitated for a moment before leaving the ones and taking her final throw.

The telephone rang.

'No cheating while I'm gone,' she ordered, pretending to sound severe as she got up.

Her mobile was in the kitchen. She pressed the green icon.

'Johanne Vik,' she said tersely.

'Hi, it's me.'

She felt a stab of irritation at the fact that Isak never introduced himself. It should be Adam's privilege to take it for granted that she would immediately recognize his voice. After all, it was more than ten years since she and Isak had split up. True, he was the father of her eldest daughter, and it was lucky for all of them that they got on. However, he wasn't a close family member any more, even if he behaved like one.

'Hi,' she said dryly. 'Thanks for driving Ragnhild home yesterday. How's Kristiane?'

'Well, that's why I'm ringing. Now, you're not to ... you must promise not to be ...'

Johanne could feel the skin between her shoulder blades contracting.

'What?' she said when he hesitated.

'Well ... I'm at Sandvika Storsenter. I wanted to exchange some Christmas presents and so ... Kristiane and I ... The problem is ... It won't help at all if you get angry.'

Johanne tried to swallow.

'What's happened to Kristiane?' she said, forcing herself to sound calm.

From the living room she could hear Ragnhild throwing the dice over and over again.

'She's disappeared. Well, not disappeared. But I ... I can't find her. I was just going to—'

'You've *lost Kristiane? In Sandvika Storsenter?*'

She could see the vast shopping centre in her mind's eye; it was the biggest in Scandinavia, with three floors, more than a hundred shops and so many exits that the very thought made her dizzy. She leaned on the kitchen worktop for support.

'Just calm down, Johanne. I've spoken to the management and they're looking for her. Have you any idea how many kids get lost in here every day? Loads! She'll be wandering around on her own in some shop. I'm only ringing to ask if there are any shops in here that she's particularly fond of ...'

'*For fuck's sake, you've lost my child!*' Johanne yelled, without giving

Ragnhild a thought. The girl started to cry, and Johanne tried to console her from a distance while she carried on talking.

'She's our child,' said Isak at the other end. 'And she isn't—'

'It's all right, Ragnhild. Mummy was just a little bit worried. Hang on a minute and I'll be there.'

The child was inconsolable. She howled and threw the dice on the floor.

'I don't want to be lost, Mummy!'

'Try that teddy bear shop,' Johanne hissed down the phone. 'The one where you can make your own bear. It's at the end of the walkway leading from the old part of the centre to the new part.'

'Mummy, Mummy! *Who's lost me?*'

'Hush, sweetheart. Mummy will be there in a minute. Nobody has lost you, you know that. *I'm coming!*'

The last comment was snapped furiously down the phone: 'Keep your mobile on. I can be there in twenty minutes. Call me straight away if anything happens.'

Johanne ended the call, shoved the phone in her back pocket, ran into the living room, scooped up her youngest daughter and comforted her as best she could, while racing through the apartment towards the stairs leading to the outside door.

'Nobody's going to lose you, you know that. There's nothing to be upset about. Mummy's here now.'

'Why did you say somebody had lost me?'

Ragnhild was snuffling, but at least she had calmed down slightly.

'You misunderstood, sweetheart. That kind of thing happens.'

She slowed down as she reached the staircase, and walked calmly.

'We're going for a little drive. To Sandvika Storsenter.'

'Storvik Sandsenter,' said Ragnhild, smiling through her tears.

'That's right.'

'What are you going to buy me?'

'I'm not going to buy you anything, sweetheart. We're just going to ... we're just going to pick up Kristiane.'

'Kristiane's coming back tomorrow,' the child protested. 'Tonight you and me are going to watch a film with popcorn on the sofa, on our own.'

'Put your boots on. Quickly, please.'

Her heart was fluttering. She gasped for breath and pulled on her jacket as she forced herself to smile.

'We'll take your jacket with us. Off we go.'

'I want my hat! And gloves! It's cold outside, Mummy!'

'Right, there you go,' said Johanne, grabbing something that was lying on the shelf. 'You can put them on in the car.'

Without even locking the outside door she grabbed her daughter's hand and ran down the steps and across the gravel to the car, which fortunately was parked just in front of the building.

'You're hurting me,' Ragnhild protested. 'Mummy, you're squeezing my hand too hard!'

Johanne felt dizzy. She recognized the fear from the very first time she held Kristiane in her arms. Perfect, said the midwife. Healthy and beautiful, said Isak. But Johanne knew better. She looked down at her daughter, just thirty minutes old, so silent and with something in her that was blowing her to pieces.

'Jump in,' she said just a little too sharply, opening the back door. 'I'll fasten your belt.'

Her mobile rang. At first she couldn't remember where she had put it, and started patting her jacket pockets.

'Your bottom's ringing,' said Ragnhild, clambering into the car.

'Yes, yes,' Johanne said breathlessly into her phone when she had managed to get it out of her back pocket.

'I've found her,' Isak said from a long way off. 'She was in the teddy bear shop, just as you thought, and she's absolutely fine. A man was looking after her, and they were actually standing chatting to each other when I got there.'

Johanne leaned against the car, trying to slow her breathing. An immense feeling of relief that Kristiane was safe was overshadowed all too quickly by what Isak had said.

'What man?'

'What man? I ring up to tell you that Kristiane is perfectly safe, just as I thought, and you start going on about—'

'Are you aware that shopping centres are an absolute El Dorado for paedophiles?'

Her words turned to grey clouds of vapour in the ice-cold air.

'Mummy, aren't you going to fasten my belt?'

'Just a minute, sweetheart. What kind of—?'

'No, Johanne, that's enough! I'm not having this!'

Isak Aanonsen rarely became angry.

Even when Johanne got up from the sofa late one night an eternity ago and explained that she didn't think their marriage could be saved, and that she'd already obtained the necessary forms to draw a line under it, Isak had tried to be positive. He just sat there for a while, alone in the living room, as Johanne went to bed in tears. An hour later he had knocked on the bedroom door, having already accepted the fact that they were no longer each other's most intimate confidant. Kristiane was the most important person in all this, he said. Kristiane would always be the most important thing for both of them, and he really wanted them to agree on the practical arrangements regarding their daughter before they tried to sleep. By the time dawn broke they had come to an agreement. Since then he had loyally adhered to it. And she could count on the fingers of one hand the number of times over the years he had shown even the slightest hint of irritation.

But now he was furious.

'This is just hysteria! The man who was talking to Kristiane was a perfectly ordinary guy who had obviously noticed what kind of ... what kind of child she is. He was very kind, and Kristiane smiled and waved to him as we left. She's standing here now and ...'

Johanne could hear Kristiane's usual dam-di-rum-ram in the background. She started to cry. Silently, so that she wouldn't upset Ragnhild any more than she already had.

'I'm sorry,' she whispered into the phone. 'I'm sorry, Isak. I mean it. I was just really, really scared.'

'I think we both were,' he said after a moment's hesitation, his voice back to normal. 'But everything's worked out fine. I assume you'd prefer it if I brought her straight home today? What do you think?'

'Thank you. Thank you so much, Isak. It would be wonderful to have her back home.'

'I'll make up my time with her another weekend or something.'

'Perhaps you could stay as well,' Johanne heard herself saying.

'Stay over with you? Great!'

In her mind's eye she could see a glint in those dark blue eyes that narrowed to slits in his always unshaven face when he smiled that crooked, sweet smile that she had once been so in love with.

'I'll be there in half an hour,' he said. 'Do you want me to pick up any shopping while we're here?'

'No thanks. Just bring yourselves. Just come.'

She ended the call, overwhelmed by an immense weariness. She rested her arms on the roof of the car. The metal was so cold that her skin contracted. Perhaps she could tell Isak about the man in the garden on Christmas Day. If she explained that her fear hadn't come from nowhere, that she had a good reason to be anxious, that the man had known Kristiane's name although neither of the children knew him, if she ...

No.

Slowly she straightened up and dried her tears with the back of her hand.

'Out you come,' she said, bending down to Ragnhild with a smile. 'We're not going to Sandvika after all. Isak and Kristiane are coming here instead.'

'But we were going to watch a film and pretend we were at the cinema!' Ragnhild complained loudly. 'Just you and me!'

'Well, we can do that with the others. It'll be brilliant. Come on, out you get.'

Raghnild slid reluctantly from her child seat and climbed out of the car. As they walked back across the gravel, she suddenly stopped and put her hands on her hips.

'Mummy,' she said severely. 'First of all we were in a big hurry to get to Storvika Sandsenter. Now we're going back inside. We were going to pretend we were at the cinema, just you and me, and now suddenly Isak and Kristiane are coming. Daddy's quite right.'

'About what?' said Johanne with a smile, stroking her youngest daughter's hair.

'Sometimes you just can't make up your mind. But you're still the best mummy in the world. The very best supermummy in the whole wide world, with bells on.'

*

Detective Inspector Silje Sørensen of the violent crime division in Oslo had drunk two cups of hot chocolate with whipped cream and was feeling sick.

The photographs in front of her didn't help.

This year Christmas Eve had fallen on a weekday, which was perfect for those who wanted to have the longest possible time off work. The twenty-third of December, when some people also held celebrations, was on a Tuesday, so most people had also taken the Monday off, even though it was a normal working day, and stayed away on Tuesday. Christmas Day and Boxing Day were bank holidays anyway, and today, the day after Boxing Day, it was Saturday, and therefore a working day for those within the public sector, but for the less conscientious Christmas 2008 was an opportunity to take two weeks off work, since there was no point in going in when New Year's Eve and New Year's Day fell in the middle of the following week.

Norway was working at a quarter speed, but not Silje Sørensen.

The sight of her full in-tray had put her in a foul mood. In the end it was easy to convince the family it would be best for all of them if she put in an extra day at work.

Or perhaps it was the thought of Hawre Ghani that distracted her, whatever she tried to do.

She flicked quickly through the photographs of the body, took out the picture of the boy when he was alive, plus a new document, and closed the file.

On the afternoon of Christmas Day she had phoned DCI Harald Bull, as he had requested. He wasn't all that interested in discussing work in the middle of the holiday. When he wrote 'as soon as possible', he meant 5 January. Despite the fact that the overtime budget had been blown long ago, they agreed to give DC Knut Bork the job of checking the Kurdish asylum seeker's background. Bork was young, single and ambitious, and Silje Sørensen was impressed by the report he had completed that morning and left in her office.

She glanced through the pages.

Hawre Ghani had come to Norway eighteen months ago, allegedly at the age of fifteen. No parents. Since he had no ID papers, the Norwegian authorities quickly became suspicious of his age.

Despite doubts about the boy's date of birth, he was placed in an asylum centre in Ringebu. There were several others like him in the centre, asylum seekers who were alone and under the age of eighteen. He ran away after three days. Since then he had been more or less permanently on the run, apart from a few days in custody every time the street-smart youngster wasn't quite smart enough.

A year ago he turned to prostitution.

According to the report he sold himself at a high price, often to just about anybody. On at least one occasion Hawre Ghani had robbed a punter, something which had been discovered by chance. He had stolen a pair of Nike Shocks from Sportshuset in Storo. A security guard had overpowered him, got him down on the floor and sat on him until the police arrived three quarters of an hour later. When he was searched they found a beige Mont Blanc wallet containing credit cards, papers and receipts bearing the name of a well-known male sports journalist. He wasn't interested in pressing charges, DC Bork's report stated matter-of-factly, but several colleagues who had some knowledge of prostitution were able to confirm that both the boy and the robbery victim were known to them.

On one occasion an attempt had been made to link Hawre up with a Kurd from northern Iraq who had a temporary residence permit, but without any right to bring in his family. The man, who had been allowed to stay on in Norway for more than ten years and spoke fluent Norwegian, had been working part-time as a youth leader in Gamlebyn. So far his projects working with difficult refugee children had been very successful. Things didn't go so well with Hawre. After three weeks the boy had persuaded four mates from the club to help him break into some basement offices; they also tried to empty an ATM with a crowbar, and stole and smashed up a four-year-old Audi TT.

Silje Sørensen stared at the picture of the immature young man with the big nose. His lips looked as if they belonged to a ten-year-old. His skin was smooth.

Perhaps she was naive.

Of course she was naive, even after all these years in the force, where her illusions burst like bubbles as she rose through the ranks.

But this boy *was* young. Of course it was impossible to say whether he was fifteen or seventeen, but the photograph had been taken after his arrival in Norway, and she could swear that at that point it would be quite some time before he came of age.

However, that didn't matter now.

Slowly she put the photograph down right on the edge of the desk. It would stay there until she had solved this case. If it was true that someone had taken Hawre Ghani's life – as the information gathered so far indicated – then she was going to find out who that person was.

Hawre Ghani was dead, and nobody had bothered about him while he was alive.

But at least someone was going to bother about his death.

*

'Don't bother about me,' said Adam Stubo, waving the man away. 'I've already had three cups of coffee today, and any more would do me no good at all.'

Lukas Lysgaard shrugged his shoulders and sat down on one of the yellow wing chairs. His father's. Adam still thought it best not to sit on Eva Karin's, and pulled out the same dining chair as before.

'Have you got any further?' asked Lukas, his voice suggesting a lack of interest.

'How's the headache?' said Adam.

The young man shrugged his shoulders again, then scratched his hair and screwed up his eyes.

'Better now. It comes and goes.'

'That's the way it is with migraine, or so I've heard.'

A grandfather clock slowly struck twice. Adam withstood the temptation to check the time against his own watch; he was sure it was after two. He felt a slight draught on the back of his neck, as if a window was open. There was a smell of bacon, and something else he couldn't identify.

'Not much new information to report, I'm afraid.'

He leaned forward on his chair and rested his elbows on his knees.

'Quite a lot of material has been sent away for more detailed analysis. It seems highly likely that we will find biological traces at the scene of the crime. Since it was the police who actually found her, and very soon after the murder took place as far as we can tell, we hope we've secured the evidence to the best of our ability.'

'But you don't know who did it?'

Adam realized he was raising his eyebrows.

'No, of course not. We still have to—'

'The newspapers are saying it was random violence. They say they have sources inside the police who claim they're hunting a lunatic. One of those "ticking time bombs"—'

His fingers drew quotation marks in the air.

'—that the psychiatrists let out far too soon. Could be an asylum seeker. Or a Somali. That type.'

'It is, of course, possible that we're looking for someone who is mentally ill. Anything is possible. But at this stage of the investigation it's important not to get locked in to one particular theory.'

'But if that patrol was on the scene so quickly, the killer can't have got far. I read in the paper today that it was only five or ten minutes from the time she died until she was found. There can't be that many people to choose from on Christmas Eve. People who are out so late at night, I mean.'

He clearly regretted his words as soon as they were out of his mouth, and grabbed a glass containing yellow liquid, which Adam assumed was orange juice.

'No,' Adam said. 'Your mother, for example.'

'Listen to me,' said Lukas, emptying the glass before he went on. 'I understand your point of view, obviously. I'd give anything in the world to know what my mother was doing out so late on Christmas Eve. But I don't know, OK? I don't know! We – my wife and I and our three children – spend alternate Christmases with her parents and with mine. This year my in-laws came to us. My mother and father were alone. I've asked my father – of course I have, God knows ...'

He pulled a face.

'I've asked him, and he refuses to give me an answer.'

'I understand,' Adam said kindly. 'I do understand. That's why I'd like to ask you a few questions about this particular issue.'

Lukas spread his hands in a gesture of resignation. 'Carry on.'

'Did your mother enjoy walking?'

'What?'

'Did she like going for walks?'

'Doesn't everybody like ... ? Yes. Yes, I suppose she did.'

'At night? I mean, lots of people are in the habit of going out for a breath of fresh air before they go to bed. Perhaps your mother liked to do that?'

For the first time since Adam met Lukas Lysgaard three days ago, the man actually seemed to be giving a question some thought.

'The thing is, it's many years since I lived at home,' he said eventually. 'I had ... We had our children when we were only twenty, my wife and I. We got married the same summer we finished our education, and ...'

He fell silent and a smile passed fleetingly over his tear-stained face.

'That was early,' said Adam. 'I didn't think that kind of thing happened these days.'

'My mother and father – particularly my father – were dead against the idea of us moving in together without being married. As we were convinced that ... But you asked if my mother was in the habit of going out at night.'

Adam gave a small nod and took his notepad out of his breast pocket as discreetly as he could.

'She was, actually. At least when I lived at home. When she was a priest she often visited her parishioners outside normal working hours. She was the kind of priest who made a point of going to see people, my mother. She sometimes went out in the evening and didn't get back until after I'd gone to sleep. But I've never known her visit anyone on Christmas Eve.'

He shrugged his shoulders.

'It was actually very good of her to visit people who needed her at night. She was afraid of the dark.'

'Afraid of the dark?' Adam repeated. 'Right. But she liked going out for walks at night? Here in Bergen, I mean. After you moved back?'

'No ... Well ... When my mother was appointed bishop I was an adult. I'm not sure she did that many home visits these days. As a bishop, I mean.'

He sighed heavily and picked up the glass. When he discovered it was empty he sat there twirling it around in his hands. His left knee was shaking as if he had some kind of nervous tic.

'To be honest, when I was young I didn't know what they did in the evenings. Hadn't a clue.'

This time the smile was genuine.

'I suppose I was like most teenagers. Tested the boundaries. Even had girlfriends. I've never really thought about it, but maybe my mother was in the habit of going for a walk a little while before bedtime. In Stavanger as well. But when I'm here with my family, of course she doesn't go out.'

'You live in Os, don't you?'

'Yes. It's only about half an hour from here. Except at rush hour. Then it can take for ever. But we often come to see them. And they come to us. But she never goes for any of those late-night walks when they visit us or when we're here, so—'

'Sorry to interrupt, but do you stay the night? When you come here?'

'From time to time. Not usually. The children often stay over, of course. Mum and Dad are so good with them. We always stay over on Christmas Eve or other special occasions. We like to have a drink then.'

'Your parents aren't teetotal?'

'Oh no. Not at all.'

'What do you mean by "not at all"?'

'What? What do I mean? They like a glass of red wine with their meal. My father likes a whisky on special occasions. They're perfectly normal people, in other words.'

'Did your mother ever drink before she went off on one of her walks?'

Lukas Lysgaard sighed demonstratively.

'Listen to me,' he said crossly. 'I'm telling you I'm not sure. In some ways I have a feeling that my mother liked to go for a walk at night. But at the same time I know she was afraid of the dark. Really afraid of the dark. Everybody teased her about her phobia, because she of all people should have felt secure in the presence of God. And His presence is with us all the time ...'

He made his last comment with a small grimace as he leaned back in the chair and put down the empty glass.

'Could I have a look around?' Adam asked.

'Er ... yes ... I mean no ... My father is with my family, and I don't think it's appropriate for you to be poking around among his things when he hasn't given his permission.'

'I won't poke around,' Adam smiled, holding up his hands. 'Definitely not. I just want to take a superficial look. As I've mentioned several times already, it's important for me to gain the clearest possible impression of the victims in the cases I investigate. That's why I'm here. In Bergen, I mean. I want to try and get a clearer picture of your mother. Seeing her home helps a little. That should be OK, shouldn't it?'

Once again Lukas shrugged his shoulders. Adam took this as a sign of agreement, and stood up. As he slipped his notepad in his pocket, he asked Lukas to show him around. 'So that I don't make a fool of myself,' he said with a smile. 'Like last time.'

The house on Nubbebakken was old but well maintained. The staircase leading to the upper floor was surprisingly narrow and unpre-possessing compared with the rest of the house. Lukas led the way, warning Adam about a projection from the ceiling.

'This is their bedroom,' he said, opening a door. He stood there with his hand resting on the handle, partly blocking the opening. Adam got the message, and simple leaned in to take a look.

A double bed, neatly made.

The quilt was made up of different coloured pieces of fabric, and lit up the large and fairly empty room. There were piles of books on the bedside table, and a folded newspaper on the floor by the side of the bed nearest the door. *Bergens Tidende*, as far as Adam could make out. A large painting hung on the wall directly opposite the bed: abstract patterns in blue and lilac. Behind the door – so that Adam was only able to see it in the mirror between the large windows – stood a capacious wardrobe.

'Thank you,' he said, stepping back.

Apart from the main bedroom, the upper floor consisted of a recently renovated bathroom, two fairly anonymous bedrooms, one of which had been Lukas's when he was a boy, and a large study where the couple each had a substantial desk. Adam was itching to get a closer look at the papers on the desks. However, he could tell that Lukas was running out of patience, so he nodded in the direction of the staircase instead. On the way they passed a narrow door with a wrought-iron key in the lock; he presumed it led up to an attic.

'Why do they live here?' Adam asked on the way downstairs.

'What?'

'Why don't they live in the bishop's residence? As far as I know, the diocese of Bjørgvin has a bishop's residence that was designed by an architect.'

'This is my father's childhood home. They wanted to live here when we came back to Bergen. When my mother became bishop, my father insisted on moving here. I think he only agreed on that condition – to my mother becoming bishop, I mean.'

They had reached the long hallway outside the living room.

'But isn't it a statutory requirement?' Adam asked. 'As far as I know, the bishop has an obligation to—'

'Listen,' said Lukas, rubbing the top of his nose between his thumb and index finger. 'There was a lot of fuss about getting permission, but I don't really know. I'm very, very tired. Could you ask someone else?'

'OK,' Adam said quickly. 'I'll leave you in peace. 'I just need to take a look in here.'

He pointed to the little bedroom he had found by mistake a couple of days earlier.

'Carry on,' Lukas mumbled, gesturing towards the door with his hand outstretched.

Only when he walked into the room did it strike Adam that Lukas hadn't stood in his way. Quite the reverse – the bishop's son had gone back into the living room, leaving Adam alone. He glanced around quickly.

The curtains were open, and the stuffy smell of sleep was less noticeable. The room was cooler than he remembered, and the clothes that had been hanging on the back of the chair were gone.

Otherwise everything seemed the same.

He bent down to read the titles of the books in a small pile on the bedside table. A thick biography of Jens Christian Hauge, the war hero; a crime novel by Unni Lundell, and an old, worn, leather-bound copy of Knut Hamsun's *Growth of the Soil*.

Adam stood motionless, all his senses alert. She had spent her nights in this room, he was sure of it. He carefully opened the wardrobe door.

Dresses and skirts hung alongside ironed shirts and blouses in one half; the other was divided into shelves. A shelf for underwear and a shelf for tights and stockings. A shelf for trousers and a shelf for belts and evening bags. And a shelf down at the bottom for everything that didn't have a shelf of its own.

You don't keep your everyday clothes in a guest room, thought Adam, silently closing the door.

A sense of revulsion rose within him, as it often did when he surfed into other people's lives on the wave following a tragedy.

'Have you nearly finished?' Lukas shouted.

'Absolutely,' said Adam, scanning the room for one last time before returning to the hallway. 'Thank you.'

At the front door he turned and held out his hand.

'I wonder when it will pass,' said Lukas, without taking it. 'All this bad stuff.'

'It never passes,' said Adam, letting his hand fall. 'Not completely.'

Lukas Lysgaard let out a sob.

'I lost my first wife and my grown-up daughter,' Adam said quietly. 'More than ten years ago. A ridiculous, banal accident at home. I didn't think it was possible for anything to hurt so much.'

Lukas's face changed. The hostile, reserved expression disappeared, and he put his hands to the back of his neck in a despairing gesture.

'I'm sorry,' he whispered. 'Forgive me. To lose a child ... And here am I ...'

'You have nothing to apologize for,' said Adam. 'Grief is not relative. Your grief is deep enough in itself. In time you'll learn to live with it. There are brighter days ahead, Lukas. Life has a blessed tendency to heal itself.'

'Yes, but I mean she was only my mother. You lost—'

'I still wake up sometimes in the middle of the night, thinking that Elisabeth and Trine are still alive. It takes a second or two for me to realize where I am in terms of time. And the grief I feel at that moment is exactly the same as the day they died. But it doesn't last as long, of course. Half an hour later I am able to sleep, the best and most secure sleep of all.' He gave a faint smile. 'But now I must go.'

The raw cold struck him as he walked out on to the low stone steps. The rain came lashing at him from the side, and he turned up his collar as he headed for the gate without looking back.

The only thought he could cope with was that one of the photographs on the shelf in the so-called guest room had disappeared. On

Christmas Day there had been four photographs there. Now there were only three. One of Lukas as a child, on Erik's knee. One of the whole family on a boat. The third was a photograph of a very young, serious Erik Lysgaard in his student cap. The tassel resting on his shoulder. The cap at an angle, as it should be.

When Adam opened the gate, pulling a face at the screeching of the hinge, he wondered if it had been stupid not to ask Lukas what had happened to the fourth photograph.

On the other hand, he probably wouldn't have got an answer.

At least not one he would have believed.

*

The idea that anyone could believe such stories was completely incomprehensible.

Johanne was sitting with her laptop on her knee, surfing aimlessly. She had visited both the *New York Times* and the *Washington Post*, but was finding it difficult to concentrate. At least the web pages of *The National Enquirer* were entertaining.

Ragnhild was already fast asleep, and Isak was putting Kristiane to bed. Although she didn't really like it, she caught herself hoping he would stay. In order to shake off the thought, she checked her e-mail. There were three new messages in her inbox, two of which were irritating adverts; one was for a slimming product made from krill and bears' claws. There was also a message from someone whose name didn't ring a bell at first, until she trawled her memory.

Karen Ann Winslow.

Johanne remembered Karen Winslow. They had studied together in Boston, two marriages and an eternity ago. At that time Johanne still thought she was going to be a psychologist, and didn't know that she was going to ditch her prestigious education in favour of an FBI course that would almost cost her her life.

She opened the message which came from a private address, and didn't say anything about where Karen was working.

Dear Johanne – remember me? Long time no see! We had some great days back at school and I've thought about you now and then. How are you? Married? Kids? Can't wait to hear.

I googled your name and found this address – hope it's correct.

Listen, I'm going to a wedding in Norway on January 10th. A dear friend of mine is marrying a Norwegian cardiologist. The wedding is taking place in a small town called Lillesand, not far from Oslo. Are you still living there?

Johanne realized that Karen's American idea of what constituted 'not far' would encounter the grim reality of the winding, lethal E18 to Sørlandet.

I'll have to go without my husband and three children (two daughters and a son, gorgeous kids!) due to other family activities. I arrive in Oslo three days before the wedding, and would be absolutely thrilled to meet you. Any chance? We have SO much catching up to do. Please get in touch as soon as possible. I'll be staying at the Grand Hotel, by the way, in the center of Oslo.

Lots of love,
Karen

At least she was right about the location of the hotel, thought Johanne as she closed the message, launched Google and typed Karen's full name in the search box.

Two hundred and six hits.

There were obviously at least two Americans with the same name, because a lot of the articles were about a seventy-three-year-old writer of children's books. As far as Johanne remembered, Karen was due to start studying law the same summer that she herself had gone to Quantico. If she knew Karen as well as she thought, she would have passed her exams with flying colours. Many of the hits concerned a lawyer working for an Alabama-based firm called the American Poverty Law Center (APLC). This Karen Ann Winslow – who, a quick glance at several articles confirmed, was the same age as Johanne – had among other things led a campaign against the state of Mississippi to close the huge prison for underage criminals after serious breaches of the most basic rights for children had been proved.

When Johanne looked at their website, she remembered that she had been there before. APLC was one of the leading firms in the United States when it came to prosecuting hate crimes. Apart from offering free support to needy victims – mostly African-Americans – it pursued wide-ranging campaigns on behalf of those who were poor and without means. It was also behind an impressive information service aimed at mapping hate groups all over the huge continent of America.

Johanne clicked around the packed home page. There were no pictures of the employees. For safety reasons, she assumed. However, after reading for ten minutes she was convinced that Karen Ann Winslow, the lawyer at APLC, was identical with her old friend.

'Perfect,' she murmured.

'I agree,' said Isak, flopping down in the armchair opposite the sofa where Johanne was sitting. 'Both the kids are asleep, and if you don't mind I'll take a look in your fridge and see what I can put together.'

Johanne didn't even look up from her laptop. She had clicked her way back to Outlook.

'Carry on,' she said. 'Those sausages weren't exactly filling.'

Dear Karen,
Thanks so much for your message. Of course I want to see you! I live in Oslo and you're more than welcome to stay with us for a couple of days. Have to warn you, though, I'm blessed with two daughters who are more than a handful!

Her fingers flew over the keys. She wasn't even thinking. It was as if there were a direct line between her hands and everything she had experienced in the past seventeen years. It was as if nothing needed to be amended or considered, as if she didn't have to work anything out, she simply told her story. She wrote about the children, about Adam, about her job. Karen Winslow was far away on the other side of the ocean – her old college friend didn't know anyone here and there was no need to consider anyone's feelings. Johanne wrote about life as a researcher, about her projects, about her fear of not being a good enough mother to a daughter that no one but Johanne understood. She didn't understand Kristiane either, if she was honest. She wrote without any inhibitions to a woman with whom she had once been young and free.

It felt almost like making a confession.

'Voilà,' said Isak, putting a large plate down in front of her. 'Spaghetti carbonara with a tiny, tiny variation. You didn't have any bacon, so I had to use ham. You didn't have any eggs, so I made a little sauce with some blue cheese I found. You didn't even have any spaghetti, so it's tagliatelle instead. And then there's loads and loads of finely chopped sautéed garlic on top. Not exactly carbonara, I have to say.'

Johanne sniffed the air. 'Smells fantastic,' she said absently. 'There's wine in the corner cupboard if you want to open a bottle. I'll have mineral water. Could you possibly bring me one?'

She was staring at the screen, distractedly chewing her lower lip.

Resolutely, she highlighted the entire text apart from the first three lines and pressed DELETE before finishing off the brief sentence that remained:

Let me know the details of your stay as soon as possible. I'm really looking forward to seeing you, Karen. Really!
All the best,
Johanne

'Who are you so busy writing to?' asked Isak, putting his feet up on the table and balancing the plate on his stomach as he started shovelling down his food.

His table manners had always annoyed her.

He didn't have any.

He grabbed his glass, which was full to the brim, and slurped down the red wine with his mouth full of food.

'You eat like a pig, Isak.'

'Who are you writing to?'

'A friend,' she said tersely. 'A really old friend.'

Then she closed the laptop, pushed it away and bent over her plate. The food tasted as good as it smelled. They sat there without speaking to each other until the meal was over.

*

The glass was empty.

Whisky and soda was Marcus's weakness.

Hardly anyone of his own generation was familiar with the concept, and his friends wrinkled their noses in disgust when he mixed enormously expensive whisky and soda in a tall glass. It was his grandfather's standard drink, every Saturday at eight o'clock in the evening after his weekly bath and hair wash. Marcus Junior had been given his first one the day he was confirmed. It tasted bitter, but he swallowed it. Real men drank whisky and soda, in his grandfather's opinion, and since then this particular drink had become Marcus's trademark.

He thought about mixing another, but decided against it.

Rolf was out. A dressage horse was experiencing some pain in its left foreleg, and with a purchase price of one and a half million kroner, the owner wasn't all that keen on waiting until the surgery reopened on 7 January. Rolf's opening hours were at best a guideline, at worst completely misleading. At least twice a week someone rang him during the evening and he had to go out.

Little Marcus was asleep. The dogs had settled, and the house was quiet. He tried to switch on the TV. A vague feeling of unease made it difficult for him to decide whether to go to bed or watch some kind of TV series. *Cold Case*, perhaps. Something like that. Anything that could take his mind off things.

The set was dead. He banged the remote against his thigh and tried again. Nothing happened. The batteries, no doubt. Marcus Koll yawned and decided to go to bed. Check his e-mail, brush his teeth and go to bed.

He padded out of the room, across the hallway and into his study. The computer was on. There was nothing of interest in his inbox. Idly he clicked on the national daily newspaper. Nothing of interest there either. He scrolled down the page.

CONTROVERSIAL ARTIST FOUND DEAD.

The headline flickered past.

His index finger stopped scrolling. He moved back up the page.

CONTROVERSIAL ARTIST FOUND DEAD.

His heart started pounding. He felt light-headed.

Not again. Not another attack.

It wasn't panic this time.

He felt strong. His mind was clear. Slowly he began to read.

When he had finished he logged off and shut down the computer. He took a little screwdriver out of the desk drawer. Then he crouched down on the floor, undid four screws, took off the cover and carefully removed the hard drive. From another drawer he took out another hard drive. It was easy to insert. He put the cover back on, screwed it in place and put the screwdriver away. Finally he pushed the computer back under the desk.

He took the loose hard drive with him when he left the room.

He was wide awake.

*

The woman standing in the arrivals hall at Gardermoen was surprised at how wide awake she felt. It had been a long drive, and she had slept badly for a couple of nights. For the last few kilometres before she reached the airport she had been afraid of falling asleep at the wheel. But now it seemed as if the same anxiety that had kept her awake at night was back.

For the hundredth time she looked at her watch.

The plane had definitely been delayed, according to the arrivals board. Flight SK1442 from Copenhagen was due at 21.50, but hadn't landed until forty minutes later. That was now more than three quarters of an hour ago.

She paced up and down in front of the entrance to customs control. The airport was quiet, almost deserted so late on a Saturday evening between Christmas and New Year. The chairs were empty outside the small cafeteria where she had bought a cup of coffee and a slice of inedible lukewarm pizza. But she couldn't calm herself enough to sit down.

She usually liked airports. When she was younger, in the days when the largest Norwegian airport was actually in Denmark and little Fornebu was the biggest in the country, she sometimes drove out there on Sundays just to watch. The planes. The people. The groups of self-assured pilots and the smiling women who were still called air stewardesses and were stunningly beautiful; she could sit for hours drinking tea from her Thermos and making up stories about all the people coming and going. Airports gave her a feeling of curiosity, expectation and homesickness.

But now she was anxious, verging on irritated.

It was a long time since anyone had come through customs.

When she turned back to look at the arrivals board, she saw that it no longer said BAGS ON BELT after SK1442. She knew what that meant, but refused to accept it. Not yet.

Marianne would have let her know if anything had happened.

Sent a message. Called. She would have been in touch.

The journey from Sydney took over thirty hours, with landings in Tokyo and Copenhagen. Obviously something could have happened. In Tokyo. In Sydney, perhaps. Or in Copenhagen, for that matter.

Marianne would have let her know.

Fear sank its teeth into the back of her neck. She made a sudden decision and rushed over to the corridor leading from customs control. It probably wasn't advisable to flout the rule forbidding anyone from going further down the corridor. For all she knew, the security measures adopted by the airline industry after 9/11 might mean the customs officers had orders to shoot to kill.

'Hello?' she called out, poking her head around the wall. 'Is anyone there?'

No response.

'Hello?' she called again, a little louder this time.

A man wearing the uniform of the customs service came over from the opposite wall, five metres away.

'You can't go in that way!'

'No, I know. I was just wondering ... I'm waiting for someone on the flight from Copenhagen. The one that landed an hour ago. SK1442. But she hasn't turned up. I just wondered if you could ... ? Could you possibly be kind enough to check if there are any passengers left in there?'

For a moment it looked as if he might say no. It wasn't his job to run errands for the general public. Then he changed his mind for some reason, shrugged his shoulders and gave a little smile.

'I don't think there's anyone there. Just a minute.'

He disappeared.

Maybe her mobile needed recharging. Of course, she thought,

breathing a little more easily. God knows it could be difficult finding a payphone these days. And if you found one, you didn't have any change. Most took cards, of course, but when she thought about it, there must be something wrong with Marianne's mobile.

'Empty. Silent as the grave.' The customs officer had his hands in his pockets. 'We're waiting for two or three more flights tonight, but at the moment there's no one there. And the luggage carousel for the Copenhagen flight is empty.'

He took his hands out of his pockets and made an apologetic gesture.

'Thanks,' she said. 'Thank you for your help.'

She moved away and set off towards the escalator leading up to the departures hall. Took out her mobile. No messages. No missed calls. Once again she tried to ring Marianne, but it went straight to voice-mail. Her legs started to move of their own accord. The escalator was going too slowly, so she ran up it. At the top, she stopped dead.

She had never seen the departures hall so empty and quiet.

Only a few check-in desks were staffed, the operators looking bored. A couple of them were reading newspapers. At the southern end she could hear the hum of a cleaning machine gliding slowly across the floor, a dark-skinned man at the controls. Only one security post was open, and she couldn't see anyone there. It was like a scene from a film, a Doomsday film. Gardermoen should be full of life, exhausting and unfriendly, teeming with countless travellers and employees who never did more than they absolutely had to.

Her heart was in her mouth as she headed resolutely for the Scandinavian Airlines desk on the other side of the hall. There was no one there either. She swallowed several times and wiped the cold sweat from her forehead with her sleeve.

A well-built woman emerged from the back room.

'Can I help you?'

'Yes, I'm here to meet ...'

The woman sat down behind the barrier. She logged on to her computer without looking up.

'I've come to pick up a friend who should have been on the plane from Copenhagen.'

'Hasn't he turned up?'

'She. It's a she. Marianne Kleive.'

The woman behind the desk looked up in some confusion before she managed to rearrange her expression and went back to concentrating on her keyboard.

'I understand,' she said. 'Quite.'

'But she didn't turn up. She's been in Australia, and the flight was supposed to land in Tokyo and Copenhagen en route. I wonder if you could check whether she was on board?'

'I can't, unfortunately. I'm not allowed to give out that kind of information.'

Perhaps it was the threatening emptiness of the gigantic hall. Perhaps it was the sleepless nights or the inexplicable unease that had haunted her all week. Or it could have been the fact that she knew, deep down inside, she had every reason to despair. Whatever the cause, the woman in the red anorak started to cry in public for the first time in her adult life.

Slowly, silently, the tears ran down her cheeks, through the dimples on either side of her mouth that were so deep they were visible even now, and continued over her pointed chin. Slowly the big fat drops landed on the pale wood of the desk.

'Are you crying?'

The Scandinavian Airlines clerk suddenly looked more sympathetic.

The woman in the red anorak didn't reply.

'Listen,' said the clerk, lowering her voice. 'It's late. You must be tired. There's no one here and ...' She gave a quick sideways glance at the door leading to the back room. 'Which flight did you say?'

The woman placed a folded piece of paper on the desk.

'A copy of the itinerary,' she whispered, wiping her face with the backs of her hands.

She couldn't see the screen from where she was standing. Instead she fixed her gaze on the other woman's eyes. They flicked up and down between the keys and the screen. Suddenly the furrow above her eyes became more pronounced.

'She had a ticket,' she said eventually. 'But she wasn't on the plane. She ...' The keys rattled beneath her dancing fingers. 'Marianne Kleive had a ticket, but she never checked in.'

'In Copenhagen?'

'No. In Sydney.'

It didn't make sense. It was impossible. Marianne would never, ever have failed to get in touch if something had prevented her from coming home. It was more than thirty hours since the plane had left Australian soil, and in that time Marianne would definitely have found a phone. A computer with Internet access. Something, and none of this made any sense at all.

'Just a moment,' said the clerk, picking up the copy of the itinerary again.

The woman in the anorak was forty-three years old and her name was Synnøve. The name suited her perfectly. Her blonde hair was braided, her face completely free of make-up, and she could easily be taken for ten years younger. She had been 140 metres from the top of Mount Everest when she was forced to turn back, and she had sailed around the world. She had encountered pirates off the Canary Islands and had been a hair's breadth from drowning in a diving accident in Stord. Synnøve Hessel was a woman who could think quickly and constructively, and who had saved both her own life and the lives of others on several occasions with her quick thinking.

Now everything stood still. Utterly, utterly still.

'I'm sorry,' the woman behind the desk whispered. 'Marianne Kleive had a ticket to Sydney last Sunday. But this shows ...'

The other woman's expression stabbed her like a knife.

'I'm sorry,' she said anyway. 'She didn't actually travel. Marianne Kleive never used her ticket. At least not for the return journey to Sydney. Of course, she could have gone somewhere else. With a different ticket, I mean.'

Without saying thank you for the kind and highly irregular service, without saying anything at all, without even picking up the copy of the itinerary which had not been followed, Synnøve Hessel turned away from the information desk and began to run through the deserted departure hall.

She had no idea where she was going.

The Beloved Son

As she stood there with her hand resting on the door handle, Trude Hansen no longer remembered where she was going. She swayed and realized she had already got hold of enough to see her through until tomorrow. The relief was so great that her knees gave way, and she had to lean on the wall when she let go of the door handle.

It still smelled vile in here.

She must do something about it.

Soon, she thought, staggering into the small room. In the alcove a sleeping bag lay on top of an unmade bed. At the bottom of the sleeping bag lay a red toilet bag with a picture of Hello Kitty on it. Someone had given the cat fangs and a patch over one eye. With hands that somehow didn't want to obey her she eventually managed to pull out the bag and unzip it.

Everything was there.

Untouched. Three fixes.

Just like countless times before, she was intending to take the whole lot at once. Routinely, dully, she considered the chances that it would all be over if she took an overdose on purpose. She always started thinking along these lines on those rare occasions when she had enough heroin even to contemplate suicide, and it was equally inevitable that she would always reject the idea. She probably wouldn't die. And when she came round, she would have nothing left.

The thought of running out of drugs was worse than the thought of going on living.

She took the toilet bag and staggered the few steps over to a green sofa against the other wall. It was covered with empty beer bottles from yesterday. Someone had dropped a cigarette on one of the cushions during the night, and she stood for a while looking at the big brown circle with a black hole in the middle.

Above the sofa hung a confirmation photo of Runar.

She grabbed it and threw it among the beer bottles.

Runar stared at her from the large picture in its gold frame. His hair was cut in a mullet, and he'd had a perm. His suit was powder blue. The narrow tie was pink. He had looked so smart, she remembered. He was her big brother, and the most stylish person in the entire church that day. Later, when the ceremony was finally over and her mother really wanted to get away before any of the other parents started asking about the party, he had picked up his sister and carried her in one arm all the way to the bus stop. Even though she was nine years old and much too fat.

They had eaten chicken wings.

Mum, Runar and Trude.

Runar hadn't received a single present, because all the money had gone on his new suit, his hairstyle and the photographer. But they had eaten chicken wings and chips and Runar had been allowed a beer to go with it. He had smiled. She had laughed. Mum had smelled clean and wonderful.

Slowly she took out the spoon and the Bunsen burner Runar had given her. Soon she would feel better. Very soon. If only her hands would obey her a little better.

Her dull brain tried to work out how long it was since Runar died. Nineteen plus nineteen? No. Wrong. From the nineteenth to the nineteenth was thirty-one days. Or thirty. She couldn't remember how many days there were in November. Nor how many days had passed since then. She couldn't even remember what day it was today.

The only thing she knew for sure was that Runar died on 19 November.

She had been at home. He was supposed to come. Runar had promised to come. He was just going to get some money. Score some heroin. Get everything she needed. Runar was going to help his little sister, just like he always did.

He was late. He was so fucking late. Then the cops came.

They came here. Rang the bell, at some ridiculous hour of the morning. When she opened the door they told her Runar had been robbed in Sofienberg Park that night. He had severe head injuries when he was found, and was probably already dead. Someone had called an ambulance, and he was pronounced dead when he arrived at the hospital.

The policewoman was serious, and might possibly have tried to console her.

She didn't remember anything apart from a piece of paper in her hand. The address and phone number of a funeral director. Five days later she had woken up so late in the day she realized she wasn't going to make it to the funeral.

Since then the cops had done fuck all.

Nobody had been caught.

She hadn't heard anything.

As the syringe emptied into a vein at the back of her knee, the blissful warmth spread so quickly that she gasped out loud. Slowly she sank back on the green sofa. She wrapped her stick-thin arms around the photo of Runar. Her last conscious thought before everything became warm clouds of nothingness was that her big brother had given her the last three chicken wings on the day he was confirmed and Mum gave him a beer for the first time.

The cops didn't care about people like Runar.

People like her and Runar.

*

'Do you care about this at all?'

For the first time in more than three quarters of an hour, Synnøve Hessel was on the point of losing control. She leaned towards the police officer, both hands gripping the edge of the table as if she were afraid she might hit him otherwise.

'Of course,' he said without looking at her. 'But as I'm sure you understand, we have to ask questions. If you had any idea how many people just leave their normal everyday lives without—'

'Marianne hasn't left! *When will you understand that she had absolutely no reason to leave?*'

The police officer sighed. He leafed through the papers in front of him, then glanced at his watch. The small interview room was becoming unbearably warm. An air-conditioning unit hummed in the ceiling, but there must be something wrong with the thermostat. Synnøve Hessel took off her knitted sweater and flapped her shirt in an attempt to cool down. A damp oval stain was visible between her breasts, and she could feel the sweat trickling down from under her arms. She decided to ignore it. The police officer smelled worse than she did.

At Gardermoen police station they had at least been friendly. Almost kind, in spite of the fact that all they could do was direct her to a normal police station. They had sympathized, of course, and made her a cup of coffee. An older uniformed female officer had tried to console her with the one thing everyone else seemed to know: people go missing all the time. But, sooner or later, they turn up again.

Later was too late for Synnøve Hessel.

The journey home to Sandefjord that same night had been an ordeal.

'Let's sum up what we have,' suggested the police officer, finishing off a bottle of cola.

Synnøve Hessel didn't reply. They had already summed things up twice, and it hadn't brought the man any closer to a realistic understanding of the situation.

'After all, you are ...'

He adjusted his glasses and read:

'... a documentary film-maker.'

'Producer,' she corrected him.

'Exactly. So you know better than most people what reality looks like.'

'We were supposed to be summing things up.'

'Yes. So. Marianne Kleive was supposed to be going to Wollogo ... Wollongo—'

'Wollongong. A town not far from Sydney. She was going to visit a relative. Celebrate Christmas there.'

'Hell of a short stay for such a long journey.'

'What?'

'I just mean,' the man said deliberately, 'that if I was going all the way to Australia, I'd stay longer than barely a week.'

'I don't really see what that's got to do with anything.'

'Don't say that. Don't say that. Anyway, she left Sandefjord on Saturday 19 December on the train that leaves at—'

'Twelve thirty-eight.'

'Mm. And she was going to meet a friend in Oslo ...'

'Which she did. I checked.'

'Then she spent the night in a hotel before catching the flight to Copenhagen at nine thirty.'

'And she never arrived there.'

'She didn't arrive in Copenhagen?'

'She didn't arrive at Gardermoen. At least, it's possible that she did arrive there, of course, but she wasn't on the flight to Copenhagen. Which naturally means that she didn't fly on to Tokyo or Sydney either.'

The police officer didn't pick up on her sarcasm. He scratched his crotch without embarrassment. Picked up the cola bottle and put it down when he realized it was empty.

'Why didn't you find out about this until last night? Hasn't she got a mobile, this ... your girlfriend?'

'She is not my girlfriend. She is the person I love. The fact is that she's my wife. My spouse, if you like.'

The man's sour expression showed very clearly that he didn't like it at all.

'And as I have already explained several times,' said Synnøve, leaning towards him with her mobile in her hand, 'I received three messages over the course of the week. Everything indicated that Marianne was actually in Australia.'

'But you haven't spoken to one another?'

'No. As I said, I tried to ring a couple of times late on Sunday, but I couldn't get through. Last night I tried at least ten times. It goes straight to voicemail, so I assume the battery is dead.'

'Could I have a look at the messages?'

Synnøve brought them up and passed him the phone.

'Everything OK. Excitting country. Marianne.'

The man couldn't even read fluently, but made a big thing of the fact that 'exciting' was spelt incorrectly.

'Not particularly ...' he went on, trying to find the right word before he read the next message. 'Not particularly romantic. *Having a good time. Marianne.'*

He looked at her over the top of his glasses. The chewing tobacco had formed black crusts at the corners of his mouth, and he constantly sprayed tiny grains into the air.

'Are you two usually so ... concise?'

For the first time, Synnøve was lost for words. She didn't know what to say. She knew the question was justified, because it was precisely the unusual brevity, the impersonality in the messages that had made her uneasy. She hadn't given much thought to the first one, which had arrived on the Monday. Marianne might have been in a hurry. Perhaps her great aunt was very demanding. As far as she knew, there could be thousands of reasons why a message didn't arrive or was very brief. On Christmas Eve the message she received said only *Merry Christmas*, which hurt Synnøve deeply. The last message, saying that Marianne was having a good time, neither more nor less, had kept her awake for two nights.

'No,' she said, when the pause began to get embarrassing. 'That's why I don't think she wrote them. She would never have misspelt "exciting".'

The police officer's eyes widened so dramatically that he looked like a clown at some ghastly children's party. Tufts of hair stuck out behind his ears, his mouth was red and moist and his nose resembled an almost round potato.

'So now we have a theeeeeory,' he said, stretching the *e* for as long as he could. 'Someone has stolen Marianne's mobile and sent the messages in her place!'

'That's not what I'm saying,' she protested, although that was exactly what she was saying. 'Don't you understand that ... that if Marianne has been the victim of a crime and someone ...'

Crime.

'... and someone wanted to make it more difficult to discover—'

'Discover?'

'Yes. That she'd disappeared, I mean. Or that she's ...'

For the second time in twenty-four hours she was close to bursting into tears with someone else looking on.

There was a knock at the door.

'Kvam! They're looking for you on the desk.'

A uniformed man smiled and came into the room. He placed a hand on his somewhat smelly colleague's shoulder and waved towards the door.

'I think it's urgent.'

'I'm in the middle of—'

'I can take over.'

Detective Inspector Kvam got to his feet with a sour expression. He started gathering up the papers in front of him.

'You can leave all that. I'll finish off here. A missing person, isn't it?'

Kvam shrugged his shoulders, gave a farewell nod and headed for the door. It slammed shut behind him.

'Synnøve Hessel,' said the new officer. 'It's been a while.'

She half stood up and took the outstretched hand.

'Kjetil? Kjetil ... Berggren?'

'The one and only! I saw you in here and I was a bit ...'

He held out his hand and wiggled it back and forth.

'... concerned when I saw that Ola Kvam was dealing with the report. He isn't ... he's actually retired, but over Christmas we bring in a few people to cover ... Anyway. You know. We all have our own way of doing things. I came as soon as I'd finished what I had to do.'

Kjetil Berggren had been a year below her in school. She wouldn't really have remembered him at all if he hadn't been the school athletics champion. He set a record for the 3,000 metres in Bugårds Park in the very first heat, and was a member of the national junior team before he gained a place at the Police Training Academy straight from high school.

He still looked as if he could run away from just about anybody.

'I have actually followed your career!' He grinned, putting his hands behind his neck and leaning back, tipping his chair. 'Great programmes. Especially that one you did in—'

'You have to help me, Kjetil!'

She thought his pupils grew smaller. Perhaps it was because the sun was suddenly in his eyes as he allowed the chair to drop back, and leaned towards her.

'That's why I'm here. We. The police. To protect and serve, as they say.'

He tried another smile, but she didn't respond to that one either.

'I'm absolutely, totally convinced that something terrible has happened to my partner.'

Kjetil Berggren slowly gathered up the papers in front of him and placed them in a folder, which he pushed to the left on the large desk between them.

'You'd better tell me everything,' he said. 'From the beginning.'

*

He had understood his father in the beginning.

When the police rang the doorbell of the house in Os on Christmas Eve just as everyone was about to go to bed, Lukas Lysgaard's first thought was for his father. His mother was dead, said the police officer, who seemed genuinely upset at having to deliver the tragic news. They had brought the priest – his mother's closest colleague – from Fana, but the poor man was in such a state that he just sat in the car while the police took on the heavy burden of telling Lukas Lysgaard that his mother had been murdered three hours earlier.

Lukas had immediately thought about his father.

About his mother, too, of course. He loved his mother. A paralysing grief began to drain away his strength as soon as he grasped what they were telling him. But it was his father that worried him.

Erik Lysgaard was a mild man. Some people found him awkward, while others appreciated his gentle, reserved nature. He didn't make much of an impact outside the family. Or inside it, come to that. He spoke little, but listened all the more. That was why Erik Lysgaard was a man who improved on closer acquaintance. He had his own friends, of course, some childhood friends and a couple of colleagues from the school where he had worked until his back became so twisted that he was granted early retirement on the grounds of ill health.

But above all he was his wife's spouse.

He's nothing alone, was the thought that struck Lukas when he was told that his mother was dead. *My father is nothing without my mother*.

And in the beginning he had understood him.

That night, that holy, terrible night that Lukas would never forget as long as he lived, the police had driven him to Nubbebakken. The older of the two officers had asked if they wanted company until daylight.

Neither Lukas nor his father wanted anyone there.

His father had shrivelled up into something that was hard to recognize. He was so thin and bent that he hardly even cast a shadow when

121

he opened the door to his son, and without a word turned his back on him and went back into the living room.

The way he cried was terrifying. He cried for a long time, almost silently, then he would emit a low, long-drawn-out howl, without any tears, an animalistic pain that frightened Lukas. He felt more helpless than he had expected, particularly when his father refused all physical contact. Nor did he want to talk. As the day gradually came, a dark Christmas morning heavy with rain, Erik had finally agreed to try and get some sleep. Even then he refused to let his son help him, despite the fact that every single night for more than ten years Eva Karin had taken off her husband's socks and helped him into bed, then rubbed his bad back with a home-made ointment sent by a faithful parishioner from their years in Stavanger.

But Lukas had understood him.

Now it was starting to get rather wearing.

It was five days since the murder, and nothing had changed. His father had literally eaten nothing during those five days. He was quite prepared to drink water – lots of water – and a couple of cups of coffee with sugar and milk in the afternoon. Lukas brought him to his own house in the hope that the grandchildren would at least arouse some spark of life in the old man, but Erik still refused to eat. The visit had been a complete disaster. The children were scared stiff at the sight of their grandfather crying in such a peculiar way, and the eldest, at eight years old, already had his hands full trying to deal with the knowledge that Grandma was never, ever coming back.

'This won't do, Dad.'

Lukas pulled a footstool over to his father's armchair and sat down on it.

'We need to think about the funeral. You have to eat. You're a shadow of yourself, Dad, and we can't go on like this.'

'We can't have the funeral until the police give their permission,' said his father.

Even his voice was thinner.

'No, but we need to do some planning.'

'You can do that.'

'That wouldn't be right, Dad. We have to do it together.'

Silence.

The old grandfather clock had stopped. Erik Lysgaard had given up winding the heavy brass weights below the clock face each night before he went to bed. He no longer needed to hear the passing of time.

Dust motes drifted in the light from the window.

'You have to eat, Dad.'

Erik raised his head, and for the first time since Eva Karin's death he gently took his son's hands between his own.

'No. *You* have to eat. You have to go on living.'

'Dad, you—'

'You were our beloved son, Lukas. Never has a child been more welcome than you.'

Lukas swallowed and smiled.

'That's what all parents say. I say the same thing to my own children.'

'But there's so much you don't know.'

Even though the noise of the city was out there, it seemed unable to penetrate the dead house on Nubbebakken. Lukas couldn't even hear his own heart beating.

'What do you mean?'

'There's so much that disappears with a person. Everything disappeared with Eva Karin. That's the way it has to be.'

'I have a right to know, Dad. If there's something about Mum's life, about both your lives, that—'

His father's dry laugh frightened him. 'All you need to know is that you were a much-loved child. You have always been the great love of your mother's life, and mine.'

'Have been?'

'Your mother is dead,' his father said harshly. 'I'm unlikely to live much longer.'

Lukas quickly took his hands away and straightened his back.

'Pull yourself together,' he said. 'It's high time you pulled yourself together.'

He stood up and started pacing the floor.

'This has to stop. Now. *Right now! Do you hear me, Dad?*'

His father barely reacted to this violent outburst. He simply sat there, as he had sat in the same chair with the same blank expression for five days, more or less.

'I won't put up with it!' Lukas yelled. '*Mum won't put up with it!*'

He grabbed a porcelain ornament from the little table next to the television. Two swans in a delicate heart: a wedding present from Eva Karin's parents. It had survived eight house moves, and had been one of his mother's most cherished possessions. Lukas seized the swans by the throat with both hands and smashed them against his thigh, causing himself considerable pain. The ornament shattered. The sharp surfaces cut into his palms. When he hurled the pieces on the floor, blood spattered the carpet.

'You are not allowed to die! You are not allowed to fucking die!'

That was all it needed.

Lukas Lysgaard had never – not even during his rebellious youth – dared to swear in front of his parents. Now his father got to his feet more quickly than anyone would have thought possible. He reached his son in three strides. He raised his arm. His fist stopped no more than a centimetre from his son's jaw. Then he stood there, frozen, as if in some absurd tableau, taller now and broader. It was from him that Lukas had inherited his broad shoulders, and it was as if they had suddenly fallen into place. His whole body grew bigger. Lukas held his breath, cowering from his father's gaze, as if he were a child again. Obstinate and young and Daddy's little boy.

'Why did Mum go out?' he whispered.

Erik let his hand drop.

'That's a matter between Eva Karin and me.'

'I think I know.'

'Look at me.'

Lukas was examining his own palms. There was a deep gash at the base of both thumbs. Blood was still dripping on to the carpet.

'Look at me,' Erik repeated.

When Lukas still couldn't manage to look up, he felt his father's hand on his unshaven cheek. Eventually he raised his head.

'You know nothing,' Erik said.

Yes I do, thought Lukas. Perhaps I've always known. For a long time, anyway.

'You know absolutely nothing,' Erik said again.

They were standing so close that their breath caressed each other's faces in small puffs. And just as bad thoughts turn to solid secrets when they are never shared with anyone, so both of them were absolutely certain about something they thought the other didn't know. They just stood there, each embarrassed in their own way, with nothing to say to one another.

*

'I'm embarrassed to admit it, Synnøve, but we usually take a back seat when it comes to this kind of case.'

Kjetil Berggren had at least managed to lower the temperature in the small interview room. He was sitting with his shirt sleeves rolled up, flouting the regulations, absent-mindedly drumming a pencil against his thigh.

She had told him everything, hiding nothing. The fact that she had made Marianne's disappearance less and less suspicious with every word was something she hadn't fully grasped until now.

'I see,' she said feebly.

'For example, you haven't even spoken to her parents yet.'

'Marianne hasn't been in contact with them since we moved in together!'

'I understand,' he said, running his hand over his short hair. 'I agree with you in principle that there is reason for concern. It's just that ...'

He was noticeably less favourably disposed than he had been when he rescued her from Ola Kvam ninety minutes earlier. He was more restless, and hadn't written a single thing down in more than half an hour.

'Yes, but I think you have to check with close family first. As far as I understand it, you've hardly been in touch with anyone.'

The enervating drumming against the thigh increased.

'Not even her parents,' he repeated.

As if the parents of a forty-year-old woman would have the answer to everything.

'They didn't come to our wedding,' Synnøve said wearily. 'How in the world could they possibly know anything about Marianne now?'

'But she was supposed to be visiting her mother's aunt, wasn't she? Perhaps her mother—'

'That great-aunt popped up out of nowhere. Listen to me, Kjetil. Marianne hasn't spoken to her parents since a terrible confrontation more than thirteen years ago. It was to do with me, of course. She's kept in touch with her brother, but only very sporadically. Both sets of grandparents are dead, and her father is an only child. Her mother keeps her own siblings in an iron grip. In other words, Marianne has virtually no family. And then, last autumn, a letter arrived from this relative. She emigrated before Marianne was born, and has been ... persona non grata as far as the family is concerned. Bohemian. Married an African-American in the early sixties when that kind of thing wasn't exactly popular with the posh families of Sandefjord. Then she got divorced and moved to Australia. She ...'

Synnøve broke off.

'Why am I sitting here giving you a load of totally irrelevant information about an eccentric and remarkable old lady who suddenly discovers that her niece has a daughter who is as excluded from the family as she is? I mean, the whole point is that Marianne never got to her!'

As she waved her arms she knocked over a full cup of coffee. She swore as the hot liquid ran down on to her thigh; she leapt up from her chair, and before she knew it, Kjetil Berggren was standing next to her with an empty water bottle.

'Did that help? Shall I pour on more cold?'

'No thanks,' she mumbled. 'It's fine. Thanks.'

He went to fetch some paper towels from a dispenser next to a small sink in the corner.

'And then there's the fact that she'd gone off before,' he said with his back to her.

Synnøve leaned back on the uncomfortable chair.

'She didn't go off. She finished with me. That's something completely different.'

'Here.' He gave her a thick bundle of paper towels.

'You said she was away for two weeks,' he said. 'Without getting in touch. The last time, I mean. I think you can see that this has a certain significance, Synnøve. The fact that this girl ... that Marianne disappeared only three years ago after a huge row and went to France without even telling you she was going abroad. We have to take that kind of thing into account when we're deciding whether to put resources into—'

'But we hadn't had a row this time. We hadn't argued at all.'

Instead of returning to his seat opposite her, he hitched his bottom on to the desk, resting one foot on the chair beside her. Presumably this was intended as a friendly gesture.

'I look like a wreck,' she said, moving away. 'And I stink like a horse. Sorry.'

'Synnøve,' he said calmly, seemingly unaware that she was absolutely right. His hand was warm as he placed it on her shoulder.

'I'll see what I can do, of course. You've reported Marianne's disappearance, and I've accepted it. That's a start, at least. But unfortunately I can't guarantee that we'll put much into this in the way of resources. Not for a while, anyway. In the meantime there are some things that you can do yourself.'

She stood up, mainly to break the physical contact, which felt unexpectedly unpleasant. When she reached for her sweater, Kjetil jumped down from the desk.

'Make some calls,' he said. 'You've got lots of friends. If there's any suggestion of ... infidelity ...'

Fortunately her sweater was over her head at the time. The blush spread quickly. She fumbled with the sweater until she regained control.

'... then there's usually someone within a circle of friends who knows about it.'

'I understand,' she said curtly.

'And if you have a joint bank account, you could check if she's withdrawn any money, and if so, where? I'll ring you in a couple of days to see how it's going. Or I'll call round. Do you still live in the old place on Hystadsveien?'

'*We* live on Hystadsveien. Marianne and I.'

The moment she said it, she was sure it was a lie.

'Apart from the fact that Marianne is dead,' she said harshly, grabbing her anorak and heading for the door. 'Thank you, Kjetil. Thanks for fucking nothing!'

She slammed the door behind her so hard that it almost came off its hinges.

Night Before a Dark Morning

Rolf was incapable of closing a car door in a civilized manner. He slammed it so hard that Marcus Koll could hear it in the living room, even though the car was inside the large garage. Rolf always blamed the fact that he had driven old bangers all his life. He still hadn't got used to German cars that cost more than a million. Not to mention Italian cars worth twice as much.

Marcus irritably swatted at an overwintering fly. It was big and listless, but it was still alive when Rolf came in.

'What on earth are you doing?'

Marcus was on his knees on the dining table, flapping his arms around.

'A fly,' he mumbled. 'Can't you be a bit more careful with our cars?'

'A fly? At this time of year? Sure.'

Three rapid steps and he slapped his hand down on the table.

'Got it,' he said mildly. 'By the way, shouldn't this table be laid by now?'

Marcus shuffled down. He felt stiff and had to put one knee on a chair to help him. Just like every New Year's Eve for the past nine years, he had begun the day swearing that he was going to start exercising. Tomorrow. This was his most important resolution, and this time he was going to stick to it. There was a fully equipped gym in the cellar. He hardly knew what it looked like.

'Mum will be here soon.'

'Your mother?' Rolf said. 'You've asked Elsa to come and do the table for a party she isn't even invited to?'

Marcus gave a resigned sigh. 'It was Mum who wanted to have little Marcus stay over at her house tonight. Celebrate the New Year together, just the two of them. It'll be more fun for both of them this way.'

'That's fine, but surely there's absolutely no reason why she should waste the morning coming over here to lay the table? Ring her right now and tell her I'll do it. By the way, what's this?'

Rolf was holding out a small square metal box.

'It's a hard drive,' said Marcus, his tone casual.

'Right. And what's it doing in the boot of the Maserati?'

'That's my car. How many times have I told you I'd prefer it if you used one of the others? You're the worst driver in the world and—'

'What's the matter with you?' Rolf smiled and leaned forward to kiss him.

Marcus turned away, glancing, without interest, at the hard drive.

'It's broken,' he said. 'I've put a new one in. That one can be thrown away.'

'OK, I'll chuck it,' said Rolf, shrugging his shoulders. 'And I think you ought to get yourself in a better mood before our guests arrive.'

He still had the hard drive in his hand when he left the room. It was all Marcus could do not to run after him; he wanted to destroy and throw away the bloody thing himself.

It wasn't really a problem, he thought as he tried to keep his pulse rate down. It had only been a safety measure. Which probably wasn't necessary. Not necessary at all. His pulse rate increased and he tried to concentrate on something completely different.

The menu, for example.

The fact that Rolf had found the hard drive was of no significance.

He couldn't remember a thing about the menu.

Forget the hard drive. *Forget it. It's not important.*

'Did you ring Elsa?'

Rolf was back with his arms full of cloths, serviettes and candles.

'Marcus, are you ... Marcus!'

Rolf dropped the whole lot on the floor. 'Are you ill? Marcus!'

'I'm OK,' said Marcus. 'I just felt a bit dizzy. It's gone now. Calm down.'

Rolf gently stroked his back. Because he was almost a head taller than Marcus, he had to lean forward in order to meet his downcast eyes.

'Is it ... ? Are you ... ? Was it one of those panic attacks again?'

'No, no.' Marcus smiled. 'That was years ago. You cured me, I told you that.'

It was difficult to make his dry, numb tongue work. His hands were clammy with cold sweat and he put them in his pockets.

'Would you like a glass of water? Shall I bring you some water, Marcus?'

'Thank you. That would be kind. A little drink of water and I'll be right as rain.'

Rolf disappeared. Marcus was alone.

If only he hadn't been so alone. If only he had spoken to Rolf from the start. They could have found a solution. Together they could have worked out what was the best thing to do; together they could do anything.

Suddenly he inhaled sharply through his nose. He straightened his back, moved his tongue around to get the saliva going and slapped both his cheeks. There was nothing to be afraid of. He decided once again.

There was nothing to worry about.

He had found a short item about Niclas Winter in *Dagens Naeringsliv* after Christmas. Reading between the lines, it seemed the man had died of an overdose. Of course that sort of thing was never stated directly, at least not so soon after the event. The artist's death was ascribed to his unorthodox lifestyle, as the writer so tactfully put it. The battle for the rights to his unsold works of art was already under way. They were worth more since the death of their creator; three gallery owners and an exhibition organizer estimated that their value had more than doubled in a week. The article was more interesting than its position in the paper suggested. No doubt more information would be forthcoming.

Niclas Winter had died of an overdose and Marcus Koll Junior had nothing to fear. He held on to that thought and focused on it until Rolf came hurrying back with a glass of water. The ice cubes clinked as he emptied the glass in one.

'Thanks,' he said. 'I'm fine now.'

I have nothing to fear, he thought, and started to lay the table. A red cloth, red serviettes with a silver border, red and green candles in silver-plated glass holders. Niclas Winter had only himself to blame, he told himself firmly. He shouldn't have taken that overdose.

His death has nothing to do with me.

He almost believed it himself.

*

Trude Hansen was fairly sure it was New Year's Eve.

The tiny apartment was still a chaotic mess of leftover food, empty bottles and dirty clothes. There were bits of aluminium foil all over the place, and in one corner a pizza box had been used as a litter tray by the terrified animal that was now sitting yowling on the windowsill.

'There now, Puss-cat! There's my little Puss-cat! Come to Mummy.'

The animal hissed and arched its back.

'You mustn't be cross with Mummy!'

Her voice was fragile and high. She couldn't remember if Puss-cat had been fed. Not today, anyway. Maybe not yesterday. No, not yesterday, because she'd been so furious that the fucking animal had pissed on the pizza.

'Shoo! Shoo!'

Trude waved her arms at the cat, which shot across to the sofa like a furry rocket, where it started kneading the cushions with its sharp claws.

It must be New Year's Eve, Trude thought.

She tried to open the window. It was stuck, and she broke a nail in the attempt. In the end it flew open, suddenly and with a crash. Ice-cold air poured into the musty room, and Trude leaned right out.

She could see rockets above the area to the east, the old buildings that blocked her view of Sofienberg Park. Red and green spheres of light fell slowly to the ground, and sparkling fountains rose towards the sky. The smell of gunpowder had already begun to spread through the streets. She loved the smell of fireworks. Fortunately there was always someone who couldn't wait until midnight.

She had only one fix left. She had saved it for the evening; the day had been bearable, thanks to a bottle of vodka someone had forgotten about under the bed.

It was difficult to tell how late it was.

As she was closing the window, Puss-cat slipped out. The cat moved quickly along the narrow window ledge before sitting down a metre away, miaowing.

'Come back, Puss-cat. Come to Mummy.'

Puss-cat was having a wash. Slowly and thoroughly she dragged her tongue over her fur. Rhythmically, after every fourth lick, she rubbed her paw over her ear.

'Puss-cat,' Trude snivelled as firmly as she could, stretching out to reach her. 'Come back here at once!'

She could feel that she was no longer in contact with the floor. If she held on to the windowsill between the two bottom panes in the old-fashioned window, divided into four, she might be able to stretch her other arm out far enough to grab the cat by the scruff of the neck. Her fingers clutched the wood. The bitter wind blew over her bare forearms, and her teeth were chattering.

'Puss-cat,' she said one last time before she overbalanced and fell.

As she lived three floors up and hit the asphalt with her head and her left shoulder first, she died instantly. A man was standing at his window having a cigarette on the opposite side of the street, so the police were called immediately. And because the man was able to tell them what had happened, and the door to Trude's empty flat was locked with a security chain from the inside, there was no reason to investigate the matter further. An accident, nothing more. A tragic accident.

On 31 December 2008, one and a half hours before a new year was due to be celebrated, there was no one in the whole world to give Runar Hansen a thought. He had been murdered in a park on 19 November that same year, aged forty-one. After his sister's death he wasn't even a vague, drug-addled memory.

Nor did anyone care about Puss-cat on the window ledge.

*

Synnøve Hessel was stroking the immensely fat cat. It settled down on her knee, its purr a low-frequency hum as it breathed in and out. There was something calming about the sound and the cat's affection as it butted her hands with its head as soon as she stopped stroking it.

'I'm so pleased to be here,' she said.

'No problem,' said the woman sitting at the other end of the sofa with a bottle of beer in her hand. 'I wasn't exactly in the mood for a celebration either.'

The apartment was even more elegant than Marianne's description the very last time she spoke to Synnøve on the telephone. Marianne had spent the afternoon of Saturday 19 December with Tuva on Grefsenkollveien. It had been eight o'clock in the evening, and Marianne had seemed so excited about the long journey. Synnøve had tried to hide her disappointment over the fact that they wouldn't be celebrating Christmas together, but with limited success. A sharp, chilly tone had come between them before the conversation ended.

It struck her that the end of their conversation was the reason why Marianne's text messages had been so short and impersonal. The first one, anyway.

'So you've checked whether she arrived at the hotel?' Tuva asked for the third time in less than an hour.

'Yes. She arrived, checked in, and the bill has been paid. That's where the trail ends.' Synnøve shuddered and pushed the cat on to the floor. 'That's where the trail ends,' she repeated with a grimace. 'Sounds like something out of a crime novel.'

The room was not large, but the view from the big windows gave the apartment a feeling of exclusiveness. All the furniture faced the spacious balcony, and from where she was sitting Synnøve could look out over the whole of Oslo. She stood up.

'Shall we go for a walk?' asked Tuva.

'What, now? An hour before midnight?'

Synnøve was standing by the window. The old apartment blocks had looked terrible from the outside. A gigantic piece of Lego standing on end, slotted into the side of a hill the same height as the building. Only when she walked into the room on the eleventh floor did she understand her friend's childish delight over the new apartment.

Synnøve had never seen Oslo looking so beautiful.

Lights were twinkling everywhere. The city lay before her like a Christmas decoration, a gift from the gods, surrounded by dark ridges and black water. Fireworks exploded against the sky with increasing frequency. Synnøve and Tuva had front-row seats for the show that would start in an hour.

'All right then,' she said, shrugging her shoulders.

Five minutes later they were on their way up Grefsenåsen, the cold biting into their faces. They had dressed warmly, unlike all the people tripping to and from festivities in party clothes and indoor shoes. A gang of boys aged about twelve or thirteen were amusing themselves by throwing firecrackers into a group of young women, who were screaming and jumping around on their stilettos. An elderly man came walking along the pavement with an old, overweight Labrador. He gave the boys a good telling-off; they swore and whooped and ran off down the hill laughing, before disappearing into a closed-up building site by clambering over a three-metre fence.

'It's very strange that she hasn't withdrawn any money,' puffed Tuva. 'Are you absolutely sure about that?'

Synnøve slowed down. She often forgot that she was fitter than most people.

'The only thing I've been able to check is our joint account. Marianne also has a card for a deposit account that only she has access to. I'll have to get the bloody police to ask the bank.'

She stopped.

There's no point, she thought.

They were standing at a fork in the road. Tuva pointed upwards, where a deserted track wound its way up towards the top of Grefsenkollen. Synnøve didn't move.

'It's just that I'm so sure she's dead,' she whispered.

Ice-cold tears poured down her face.

'You can't know that,' Tuva protested. 'I mean, she's only been gone a week! I remember the state you were in when she just took off for France and didn't get in touch for ages. Marianne is so—'

'Dead!' Synnøve screamed. 'Don't you start as well! Everything was different then. She didn't want anything to do with me! That's not how it is now. Can't you just … ?'

Tuva put her arm around her.

'Sorry. I'm just trying to cheer you up. Maybe we shouldn't talk about it.'

'Of course we should talk about it!'

Synnøve started to walk. Fast. She increased her speed with every step. Tuva scurried along after her.

'What else would we talk about?' Synnøve yelled. 'The weather? I want to talk about that idiotic fucking great-aunt who didn't even tell anyone that Marianne hadn't turned up. I want to talk about—'

'Have you called her?'

Tuva started jogging to keep up.

'Yes. She just wants to talk to Marianne's mother, which I can understand perfectly. But the old woman must be ...'

She stopped dead. There was an elk standing in the middle of the track.

'... bloody stupid,' she snapped. 'I asked her—'

'Sssh!'

The elk was no more than twenty or twenty-five metres away from them. The air around its muzzle turned grey as it breathed. Synnøve could see that it was a cow, and she glanced cautiously into the forest on either side of the track in case there was a calf nearby. She couldn't see one, but that didn't necessarily mean the female was alone.

'She's just on her guard,' Synnøve whispered. 'Don't move.'

The elk stared at them for almost thirty seconds. She held her head high, ears pricked forward. Tuva hardly dared breathe.

'I've never seen a live elk before,' she whispered, almost inaudibly.

That shows how little time you spend outdoors, Synnøve thought, then she suddenly bellowed and waved her arms. The elk gave a start, turned away and disappeared among the trees with long, graceful strides.

'Wow,' said Tuva.

'That aunt of Marianne's must be an idiot,' Synnøve said, setting off along the track once more. 'I asked her why she hadn't let me know, and she said she didn't know what my surname was.'

'Well, that's actually a good reason,' called Tuva, who was on the point of abandoning her attempts to keep up. 'Wait for me! Don't go so fast!'

Synnøve stopped. 'Number one,' she said, taking off her glove and holding up a finger, 'Marianne had written and told her that I make documentaries. And number two, she had told her my name was Synnøve. Number three ...'

Three fingers were spread in the air.

'The woman must have access to the fucking Internet somewhere. All she has to do is Google Synnøve plus "documentary", and she's bound to find out who I am.'

Tuva nodded, although the idea had never occurred to her.

They carried on walking in silence. Behind them the fireworks were increasing in intensity. As they passed the entrance to Trollvann, Tuva started to wonder how much further she could go. She was gasping for breath, and all she really wanted to do was turn back rather than stagger on.

They had arrived. Soft light shone out from every window of the restaurant at the top of Grefsenkollen. The car park was full of vehicles which would presumably remain there well into the following day. As Tuva and Synnøve moved closer, a large group of people in party clothes spilled out of the main entrance. Most stopped on the wide steps as they raised their glasses of champagne and exclaimed at the view. Three men had their arms full of rockets, and stumbled off around the corner to let them off in the car park.

'Here,' Tuva panted, moving over to the fence surrounding the terrace at the bottom of the steps. 'It's actually nicer here than back at my place.'

Out in the fjord the boats began to sound their sirens. Behind Tuva and Synnøve the guests were shrieking with delight at the fireworks, at the party, at the new, empty year ahead of them. The entire sky was lit up, fireworks crackling and sparkling, whistling and squealing, howling and banging in front of them and overhead.

'Happy New Year,' Tuva said tentatively, slipping an arm around her.

Synnøve didn't reply. She leaned against the fence and looked out over Oslo. 2009 was only a few seconds old, and if the emotions she was feeling were representative of the new year, the next twelve months were going to be appalling.

What she didn't know, of course, was that Marianne Kleive was exactly 8,100 metres from the spot where she was standing. If she had known, it is unlikely that it would have made her any happier.

For the first time in her life, Synnøve Hessel cried her way into a new year.

*

Erik Lysgaard had promised Lukas that he wouldn't cry.

'Dad! Dad!'

Erik gave a start. At first he had refused to go home with his son. It was only when Lukas threatened to bring the whole family to Nubbebakken and organize some kind of party for the children that he had agreed to come. He had promised not to cry. He hadn't promised to talk.

The children had finally fallen asleep. Astrid, Lukas's wife, was standing in the doorway in her dressing gown. She gave her father-in-law a wan smile and raised a hand in a limp goodnight. The evening had been something of a trial.

Lukas, in blue and white striped pyjamas and with shabby slippers on his bare feet, crouched down next to his father's chair, but didn't touch him.

'Were you asleep?'

'I think I was. I must have nodded off while you were getting ready for bed.'

'It's time you went to bed as well, Dad. I've sorted out the guest room for you.'

'I'd rather sit here, Lukas.'

'That's not on, Dad. You need to go to bed.'

'Actually, I can make my own decisions. I'm perfectly fine sitting here.'

Lukas got up.

'You're behaving as if you're the only one who's grieving,' he said wearily. 'I don't recognize you, Dad. You're ... you're just completely self-centred. You don't even notice that I'm struggling, you don't notice that the kids are missing their grandma, you don't notice that—'

'Of course I do. I notice all of it. I just can't do anything about it.'

Lukas trudged around the room in the semi-darkness. Blew out a candle in the window. Picked up a teddy bear from the floor and placed it on the bookcase. Bit his nails. Outside everything was silent. From the bathroom he could hear Astrid flushing the toilet, then the faint creak as she closed the bedroom door behind her.

'Why didn't you lie?' he asked all of a sudden.

His father looked up.

'Lie?'

'Why didn't you just make up a story about why Mum was out walking? Why didn't you say she wanted some fresh air or something? That you'd had a row. Anything. Why did you tell the police it was nothing to do with them?'

'Because it's true. If I'd made something up it would have been a lie. I don't lie. It's important to me that I don't lie. You of all people should know that.'

'But clamming up completely is OK?'

Lukas threw his arms wide in a gesture of resignation.

'Daddy, why ... ?'

He stopped himself when his father looked him straight in the eye with something that resembled a smile in his expression.

'You haven't called me daddy since you were ten,' he said.

'I have to ask you about something.'

'You won't get an answer. You must have realized that by now. I'm not going to tell why your mother was out—'

'Not that,' Lukas said quickly. 'It's something else.'

His father said nothing, but at least he was maintaining eye contact.

'I've always had a kind of feeling,' Lukas began tentatively, 'that I was sharing Mum with someone else.'

'We shared your mother with Jesus.'

'That's not what I mean.'

He stood there at a loss for a moment, then sat down on the sofa. It was so deep that leaning forward was uncomfortable. At the same time, he was too tense to lean back against the cushions. In the end he got up again.

'Have I got a sister or brother somewhere?'

The expression which suddenly came over his father's face frightened him. Erik's eyes darkened. His mouth grew strained, surrounded by coarse, deep lines. His eyebrows contracted. His hands, which had been resting on his knee, clenched so tightly that his knuckles turned white.

'I hadn't expected that from you,' he said, his voice unrecognizable.

'But I ... Did you and Mum, or just Mum ... ? I mean ... you've always been together, and this business with Jesus in the forest—'

'Hold your tongue!'

His father stood up. This time he didn't raise his hand; he simply stood there, his eyes flashing and his lower lip trembling almost imperceptibly.

'Ask yourself,' he said, his tone icy. 'Ask yourself if Eva Karin – your mother, my wife – has a child she refuses to acknowledge.'

'I'm asking you, Dad! And I'm not necessarily saying that she didn't want to acknowledge ...'

His father started to walk away. 'I'm going to bed,' he said, but turned abruptly when he reached the door. 'And I am never, ever going to answer that kind of question. Ask yourself, Lukas. *Ask yourself!*'

Lukas was left alone in the room.

'I'm asking you,' he whispered. 'I'm asking you, Dad.'

If his father had just said yes. *Couldn't you just have said yes and made my life infinitely easier?*

It was impossible to go to bed. He knew he wouldn't be able to sleep. He had asked a question and expected an answer. Hoped for an answer. Everything would fall into place if his father had just confirmed that there was a child out there. An older child, older than Lukas, an explanation for everything.

But his father had refused.

Is it because you don't want to lie, Dad?

Lukas lay down on the sofa without taking off his slippers. He pulled a woollen blanket over him, right up to his chin, the way his mother used to tuck him in when he was little. He lay there without sleeping until the morning came, a pitch-black start to the new year.

PART II

January 2009

Persecuted

I don't know if I'm doing the right thing in telling you this. We haven't actually found any signs of a break-in, and the Head doesn't want to involve the police. It's just that I—'

'Could you just ... ?' Johanne began, and cleared her throat. 'Could you just go through all that again?'

She tried to find a position where she could sit still.

'Well ...'

Live Smith, Director of Studies, ran her fingers through her thick grey hair. She had seemed pensive when she met Johanne in the corridor and asked her to come into the office. Now it was as if she regretted her action, and would prefer to forget the whole thing.

'Because we're a special school,' she said hesitantly, 'we hold a considerable amount of detailed information about every child. As you know, our pupils have widely differing forms of functional disability, and in order to maximize the education we are able to offer each individual child, we—'

'I know what this school is and what it's able to offer,' Johanne said. 'My daughter is a pupil here.'

Her voice sounded unfamiliar. Hard and expressionless. She coughed and had to pick up the glass of water, even though her hands were shaking.

'Is everything all right?'

Live Smith was looking at the water trickling down Johanne's sweater.

'Just a bit of a dry throat. I think I might be catching a cold. Can we get on?'

She forced a smile and made a circular motion with her hand. Live

142

Smith adjusted her jacket, tucked her hair behind her ears and sounded offended when she spoke.

'You were the one who wanted me to start from the beginning.'

'Sorry. Could you possibly—?'

'OK. The short version is that when I came in last Friday to get things ready for the new term, I had the feeling that someone had been here.'

Her hand swept around the room. It was a spacious office with filing cabinets along one wall and a door leading into a smaller room. The other walls were covered in children's drawings in IKEA frames. The curtains were bright red with yellow spots and fluttered gently in the warm air from the radiator under the window.

'I just had a funny feeling. There was a different ... smell in here, perhaps. No, that's wrong. It was more like a different atmosphere, somehow.'

She seemed embarrassed, and smiled before quickly adding: 'You know.'

Johanne knew.

'Not that I believe in the supernatural,' said Live Smith with a disarming smile. 'But I'm sure you recognize the feeling that—'

'There's nothing supernatural about it,' Johanne broke in. 'On the contrary, it's one of our most finely tuned capabilities. The subconscious notices things that we can't quite manage to bring to the surface. Something might have been moved. As you say, an almost imperceptible smell might linger. The more we have lived, the more capable our accumulated experience is of telling us more than we are able to define on a first impression. Some people are better than others at understanding what they feel.'

She finally managed to get some water down.

'Sometimes they refer to themselves as clairvoyant,' she added.

The sarcasm made her pulse slow down.

'And then there was the file,' said Live Smith.

Once again that smile behind every sentence, as if she were trying to make herself insignificant. Not really worth bothering about. Not to be taken all that seriously. Under normal circumstances, Johanne would have found this feminine display unbelievably irritating, but right now it took all of her strength to keep her voice steady.

'Kristiane's file,' she nodded.

'Yes, it's ...'

Live Smith stopped herself in the middle of a breath as if she were searching for the least dangerous word. Disappeared? Lost? Stolen?

'Perhaps it's just been mislaid,' she said eventually.

Her expression said something completely different.

'How did you find out it was missing?'

'I wanted another file from the same drawer, and I discovered it wasn't locked. The drawer, I mean. It hadn't been broken open or anything like that. It just wasn't locked. I was annoyed with myself, because as far as I can remember I was the last one to lock up before Christmas. We have very strict rules when it comes to storing information about our pupils. Partly because the files contain sensitive medical information, and I ...'

This time the smile was followed by a slight shrug.

Johanne said nothing.

'Since there was no sign of a break-in on the door or the cupboards and drawers, I assumed it was down to my own carelessness. But just to be on the safe side I checked that everything was where it should be. And it was. Apart from ...'

'Apart from Kristiane's file.'

Exactly.

Johanne felt an almost irresistible urge to wipe that smile off her face.

'Why don't you want to report it to the police?'

'The Head doesn't think it can have been a break-in. Nothing has been damaged. There are no marks on the doors, at least not that we can see. Nothing has been stolen. Not that there's much of value in this room, apart from the computer perhaps.'

She laughed this time, a high, strained little laugh.

And what about my child? thought Johanne. Kristiane's life, all the investigations, diagnoses and non-diagnoses, the medication and the mistakes, her progress and her setbacks, the whole of Kristiane's existence lay documented in a file that had been gathered together over years of trust, and now it was gone.

'I would say the children's files are worth a little bit more than your computer,' said Johanne.

144

At last the smile took a break.

'Of course,' said Live Smith. 'And that's why I thought I ought to speak to you. But perhaps the Head is right. This was an error on my part. I'm sure the file will turn up later today. I just thought that since I had that feeling, and since you actually work for the police—'

'I don't work for the police. I'm employed by the university.'

'Oh yes. It's your husband who's in the police, isn't it? Kristiane's father.'

Johanne didn't have the strength to correct her again. Instead she got to her feet. Glanced at the archive room in the back.

'You were quite right to let me know,' she said. 'Could I have a look at the cupboard?'

'The cabinet?'

'Yes, if that's what you call it.'

'It's really only the Head and I who ... As I said, we have very strict rules about—'

'I only want to look. I won't touch a single file!'

The Director of Studies got up. Without a word she went over to the door, picked out the right key from a huge bunch, and unlocked it. Her hand fumbled around to the left of the door frame. A bright fluorescent strip light crackled and flashed before eventually settling down to an even, high-frequency hum.

'It's that one,' she said, pointing.

Cabinets lined two of the walls from floor to ceiling. Grey, enamelled metal cabinets with doors. Johanne looked at the one Live Smith had pointed out. The lock appeared to be intact. She leaned closer, peering over the top of her glasses.

'There's a little scratch here,' she said after a few seconds. 'Is that new?'

'A scratch? Let me see.'

Together they studied the lock.

'I can't see anything,' said Live Smith.

'Here,' said Johanne, pointing with a pen. 'At a slight angle just here. Can you see it?'

Live Smith leaned forward. As she peered at the lock her top lip was drawn up, making her look like an eager mouse.

'No ...'

145

'Yes.'

'Well, I can't see anything.'

Johanne sighed and straightened up.

'Could you open it, please?'

This time Live Smith obliged without further discussion. The big bunch of keys rattled once more, and after a few seconds she had the door open. Inside the cabinet was divided into six drawers, each with their own lock and key.

'Kristiane's file was in this one,' she said, pointing at the top drawer.

With the best will in the world, Johanne couldn't spot any signs of a break-in. She examined the little keyhole from every possible angle. The cabinet was certainly old, with a number of scratches on the metal surface. But the lock appeared to be untouched.

'Thanks,' she mumbled.

Live Smith closed the cabinet and locked up after them.

'There,' she said with relief when everything was secure. 'I really do apologize for raising the alarm with no reason.'

'Not at all,' said Johanne, forcing a smile in response. 'As you said, it's better to be safe than sorry. Thank you.'

She was already over by the door. Only now did it occur to her that she was still wearing her outdoor clothes. She was hot, almost sweating.

'Ring me if it turns up,' she said.

'*When* it turns up,' said the Director of Studies. 'Of course I will. I'd also like to say what a pleasure it is to see the progress Kristiane is making.'

It was as if the middle-aged woman underwent a complete personality change. Gone were the artificial smiles. Her hands, which had been constantly fiddling with her hair and nervously pushing it behind her ears, lay motionless on her knee when she sat down. Johanne remained standing.

'She's a fascinating girl,' Live Smith went on. 'But then we have so many pupils like that here! What makes Kristiane special is the unpredictability of her predictability. I've had many autistic children here, but—'

'Kristiane is not autistic,' Johanne said quickly.

Live Smith shrugged her shoulders. But she wasn't smiling.

'Autistic, Asperger's, or perhaps just ... special. It doesn't really matter all that much what you prefer to call it. What I mean is that it's a pleasure to have her here. She has a wonderful ability to learn, not just to study. She can ask the most remarkable questions, which, if you look at them on her terms, can be strikingly logical.'

This time the smile was genuine. She even laughed out loud, a happy, trilling laugh that was new to Johanne. Given that she knew so little about the family, she knew Kristiane extremely well.

'But you know all that. I just want you to understand that it isn't only the teachers who work most closely with Kristiane who have grown fond of her. We all care about her, and learn something new from her every day.'

Johanne tugged at her scarf and licked her lips, which tasted salty.

'Thank you,' she said calmly.

'I'm the one who should be thanking you. I have the best job in the world, and it's children like your daughter who make me grateful for every single day in this school. So many of our children come up against limitations everywhere. It can mean three steps forward and two steps back. But not with Kristiane.'

'I have to go,' said Johanne.

'Of course. Can you find your own way out?'

Johanne nodded and opened the door. As she let it swing shut behind her, she was aware of the smell of soap in her nostrils. She hurried down the long corridor, the heels of her ankle boots clicking on the newly polished linoleum. When she finally reached the large glass doors at the main entrance, she couldn't get them open quickly enough.

The winter cold hit her, making it easier to breathe. She slowed down and stuck her hands in her coat pockets. As usual, Kristiane had insisted that they park a few hundred metres from the school so that they could then take the same circuitous route as always.

The weather had finally turned. A long spell of cold without snow had made the ground hard, ready to receive the dry fluffy flakes that were now drifting down over eastern Norway. The ski runs crossing the green lungs which the capital city still felt it could afford to maintain had been crowded with youngsters and parents with small children over the last few days of the Christmas holiday. Fresh, powdery snow covered the slopes every day. Adults and children armed with spades and shovels were busy on frozen football pitches. It wasn't just that the city was lighter now that it was dressed in white, it was as if its inhabitants gave a collective sigh of relief at the fact that nature had declared herself back to normal. For this season, at least.

Johanne knotted her scarf more tightly against the snowfall, and tried to think rationally.

The file had probably just been misplaced.

She just couldn't quite manage to believe that.

'Fuck,' she muttered. 'Fuck, fuck, fuck.'

She couldn't work out why she was so upset. True, she was more or less constantly worried about Kristiane, but this was ridiculous.

Misplaced, Live Smith had said.

Johanne increased her pace.

A new, frightening anxiety had sunk its claws into her. It had started with the man by the fence. The man they didn't recognize, but who called Kristiane by her name. The only unusual thing about the permanent feeling of unease that had tormented her since then was that she was dealing with it alone. Isak treated Kristiane as if she were robust and normal, and always laughed away any worries. Adam had always comforted Johanne in the past, at least when she was feeling particularly low. But now he no longer had the same patience. His resigned expression as soon as she hinted that all was not as it should be with her daughter made her keep quiet more and more often. She tried to calm down, telling herself that she had read too much. All the knowledge she had acquired over the years with Kristiane had become a burden. While Ragnhild knew that strangers could be dangerous, Kristiane was often completely unsuspecting. She might allow just about anybody to take her away.

Sexual predators.

Organ thieves.

She mustn't think like that. Kristiane was always, always supervised.

She had almost reached the car. It couldn't be more than an hour since she parked, but the car was snowed in. Not only that, a snow-plough had driven past and left a metre-high pile of snow between the old Golf and a narrow, one-way street.

Johanne stopped. There was no spade in the car. She had left her gloves in Live Smith's office.

For the first time she dared to follow the thought to its conclusion: someone was watching them.

Not them.

Kristiane.

The Vik-Stubo family had never had curtains in the living room. It didn't bother them that people could look in from the street, and the room felt lighter for it. However, she had recently begun to imagine something hanging there, something not too heavy. Something to stop passers-by from looking in. The people she didn't know, but who were out there. The rational part of her brain knew that a man by a garden fence, a friendly man in a toy shop and a missing file didn't exactly constitute stalking. But her gut feeling said something completely different.

Angrily, she started sweeping the snow off her car with her bare hands. Her fingers quickly grew stiff with cold, but she didn't stop until the car was completely clear. Then she started kicking away the compacted pile left by the snowplough. Her toes were sore and her ankles ached by the time she finally decided it would be possible for her to get the car out.

She flopped down on the driver's seat, stuck the key in the ignition and turned it. She pulled out much too quickly into the road, driving over all the snow she hadn't cleared away. She skidded and shot off, travelling at twice the speed limit. At the first junction she realized what she was doing, and slammed the brakes on just in time to avoid a collision with a lorry coming from the right.

She sat there leaning forward, her hands resting on the wheel. The adrenaline made her brain crystal-clear. She could plainly see how absurd it was to think anyone would be interested in watching a fourteen-year-old girl from Tåsen.

As soon as she put the car back in gear once more, she felt less worried.

*

'You mustn't worry because there isn't enough to do,' the secretary said sweetly, handing Kristen Faber a file. 'If a client doesn't turn up, it gives you time to do so many other things. Tidying your desk, for example. It's rather a mess in there.'

The solicitor grabbed the file and opened it as he headed for the door of his office. A miasma of sweat, aftershave and neat alcohol lingered in the air around the secretary's desk. She opened a drawer and took out an air-freshener spray. Soon the smell of last night's boozing mingled with the intense perfume of lily of the valley. She sniffed the air and pulled a face before putting away the aerosol.

'Hasn't he even called?' shouted Kristen Faber, before a coughing fit saved her the trouble of replying. Instead she got to her feet, picked up a steaming cup of coffee from a low filing cabinet behind her and followed him into his office.

'No,' she said when he had finished spitting phlegm into an overflowing waste-paper basket. 'I expect something came up. Here. Drink this.'

As Kristen Faber took the cup, he almost spilled the coffee.

'This fear of flying is too bloody much,' he muttered. 'Had to drink all the way back from fucking Barbados.'

The secretary, a slim, pleasant woman in her sixties, could well imagine that there had been a great deal of fucking in Barbados. She also knew he hadn't restricted his drinking to the duration of the flight.

She had worked for Kristen Faber for almost nine years. Just the two of them, plus one part-timer. On paper they shared the offices with three other solicitors, but the way the rooms were divided meant she could go for days without seeing the others. Faber's office had its own entrance, reception and toilet. As his office was quite spacious, she rarely had to organize coffee and mineral water in the large conference room they all shared.

Twice a year, in July and at Christmas, Kristen Faber took a holiday. Along with a group from his university years – all men, all divorced and well off – he travelled to luxury destinations in order to behave as if he were still twenty-five. Apart from his financial position, of course. He came back in the same state every time. It took him a week to get back to normal, but then he didn't touch a drop until it was time for the next trip with the lads. The secretary assumed he suffered from a particular type of alcoholism. But she could live with it.

'Was the flight on time?' she asked, mainly for something to say.

'No. We landed at Gardermoen two hours ago, and if it hadn't been for this appointment I would have gone home to have a shower and change my clothes. Fuck.' He sipped at the black coffee. 'Could I have a drop more, please? And I think you could postpone my two o'clock. I have to ...'

He raised his arm and sniffed at his armpit. Salty sweat rings were clearly visible against the dark fabric of his suit. He recoiled.

'Pooh! I have to go home!'

'As you wish,' said the secretary with a smile. 'You have a client at three o'clock as well. Will you be back by then?'

'Yes.' He glanced at his watch and hesitated briefly. 'I'll tell you what. Postpone my two o'clock until half past, and then the three o'clock can wait a little while.'

She fetched the coffee pot and put down a little dish of chocolates. He was already busy leafing through some papers, and didn't say thank you.

'Bloody man,' he mumbled, glancing over the documents in the thin file. 'He was adamant he needed to see me as soon as I got back.'

The secretary didn't reply, and went back to her own office.

This headache was killing him. He stuck his thumb in one eye and his index finger in the other. The pressure didn't help at all. Nor did the coffee; the combination of caffeine and alcohol was giving him palpitations.

The tray containing ongoing cases was overflowing. When he put the latest file on top, it slid off and fell on the floor. He got up crossly and retrieved it. He thought for a moment, opened a drawer and slipped the file inside. Then he closed the drawer and left the room.

'Shall I ring this ... ?' The secretary was looking at the diary over her half-moon glasses. 'Niclas Winter,' she went on. 'To arrange another appointment, I mean. As you say, he did make an enormous fuss and—'

'No. Wait until he rings us. I've got enough to do this week. If he can't even be bothered to cancel, then tough.'

He picked up the large suitcase which he had thrown down when he arrived, and disappeared without closing the door behind him. He hadn't asked his secretary one single question about how her

Christmas had been, visiting her children and grandchildren in Thailand. She sat there listening to his footsteps on the stairs. The suitcase bumped on every step. It sounded as if he had three legs and a limp.

Then, at last, there was silence.

*

The heavy snow muffled every sound. It was as if the peace of Christmas still lay over the area. Rolf Slettan had chosen to walk home from work, even though it took an hour and a half to get from the veterinary surgery on Skøyen to the house on Holmenkollen Ridge. The pavements were almost a metre deep in soft snow, and for the last two kilometres he had been forced to walk in the narrow track left in the middle of the road by the snowplough. The few cars that came slithering along from time to time forced him to clamber up on to the still-white mounds of snow at either side. He was breathing heavily, and soaked in sweat. Even so, he began to run when he reached the final stretch.

From a distance the house looked like a scene from a film about the Nazis. The white cap of snow hung down over the edges of the portico, partly hiding the rough-hewn text: *Home Sweet Home.* Thick drifts surrounded the courtyard, which would need clearing again in a few hours.

He stopped in the turning area outside the portico. Marcus probably wasn't home yet. A layer of virgin snow some ten centimetres deep revealed that no one had come or gone for quite some time. Little Marcus had gone home with a classmate, and wouldn't be back until about eight o'clock. The house was dark and silent, but several wrought-iron exterior lights provided a welcoming glow, making the snow sparkle. The turf roof was buried in snow. The dragons sticking out their tongues looked as if they might take off at any moment on their new white wings.

He was brushing the snow off his trouser legs when a tyre track caught his attention. A car had turned in and swung in a wide circle in front of the portico. It couldn't have been long ago. Crouching down, he could still make out the tyre pattern. Someone had probably pulled in to give way to oncoming traffic, he thought. As he stood up he followed the marks down the drive and back to the road.

Strange.

He took a couple of steps – carefully, so as not to destroy the tracks. They quickly became less distinct. After another half-metre, they had almost completely disappeared. There was only the vaguest hint of a track leading all the way to the road.

Rolf turned and followed the tracks in the opposite direction, where they were just as clear as in the middle. With a sense of unease that he couldn't really explain, he went back to the point where the tracks began, followed them carefully into the small courtyard and beyond until they blended with other tracks on the road. There was no snow piled up between the street and the house; Rolf and Marcus employed a company to clear the snow, and someone came along with a tractor twice a day. They must have come just after the snowplough.

He didn't really understand what he was looking for. Suddenly he realized that the car must have stopped. It had been snowing for a long time, but the car must still have stood there for quite a while. The difference in the depth of the tracks was striking. He could tell from the width that it was a car, or at least not a lorry or anything bigger. It must have come from down below, pulled in and stayed there for a while. As it waited the snow had come whirling in behind the back wheels, but the tracks weren't covered by quite as much snow where they were sheltered by the car.

Suddenly an engine started. He looked up and turned to face the slope just in time to see a car pulling away from the side of the road further up, from the bus stop right by the bend curving towards the east. The whirling snow and the gathering dusk made it impossible for him to read the number plate. Instinctively, he began to run. Before he had covered the fifty metres, the car had disappeared. Everything was silent once more. He could hear nothing but his own breathing as he crouched down to examine the tracks. Feather-light snowflakes danced in the air, covering a pattern he thought he recognized. Quickly he took out his mobile phone. It was so dark that the camera flash went off automatically.

'Shit,' he muttered, and ran back with the phone in his hand.

The quiet side road that wound its way upwards wasn't a natural through route. The gardens were large, and the expensive houses were spread out and sheltered from onlookers. Recently there had been a wave of break-ins around the area. Three of their neighbours had lost everything while they were away over Christmas, despite burglar alarms and a security company. The police believed they were dealing with professional thieves. Four weeks ago the family down at the bottom of the street had been the victims of a robbery. Three men had broken in during the night and taken the man of the house hostage. His nineteen-year-old son had been forced to drive to Majorstua with them in order to empty the family's accounts with the four debit cards and three credit cards the attackers had got hold of by threatening the family and firing a shot at an expensive work of art.

The tracks by the portico were still quite clear. Rolf tried to hold his mobile at the same distance from the ground as he took another picture. He could upload them on to the computer and enlarge the pictures in order to compare them. As he was putting the phone in his pocket, he caught sight of a cigarette butt. It must have been covered by the snow, but had now become visible in one of his footprints. He bent down and scraped gently at the impression left by his boot. Another butt appeared. And another. When he examined the first one in the dim light of a street lamp, it told him nothing. He couldn't even read the brand.

Three cigarettes. Rolf had given up smoking many years ago, but still remembered that it took about seven minutes to smoke a ciga- rette. Seven times three was twenty-one. If the driver had been chain-smoking, the car had been here for almost half an hour.

The police thought the burglars might be from Eastern Europe. In the newspaper they had said that people should keep their eyes open; this gang or gangs clearly undertook a considerable amount of prelim- inary investigation before they struck. The cigarette butts could be valuable evidence.

He carefully placed them in one of the black bags he kept in the pockets of all his jackets for picking up dog shit. Then he put the bag in his pocket and set off towards the house. He would ring the police immediately.

*

The answerphone cut out, but she had no idea why. Perhaps one of the children had pressed some button or other. At any rate, she hadn't heard the whole of Adam's message. When she heard footsteps on the stairs she stiffened, before a familiar voice called: 'It's me. I'm home.'

'So I see,' she said with a smile, stroking his cheek as he kissed her gently. 'Weren't you going back to Bergen?'

'Yes. I've already been there. But as there a number of things I can work on just as easily from Oslo, I caught an afternoon flight home. I'll stay here for this week, I think.'

'Excellent! Are you hungry?'

'I've eaten. Didn't you get my message?'

'No, there's something wrong with the phone.'

Adam pulled off his tie, after fumbling with the knot for so long that Johanne offered to help.

'The person who invented this ridiculous item of clothing should be shot,' he muttered. 'What on earth is all this?'

He frowned at the piles of documents and books, journals and loose sheets of paper lying around her on the sofa and almost covering the coffee table completely. Johanne was sitting cross-legged in the middle of it all with her reading glasses perched on her nose and a large glass of steaming hot tea in her hand.

'I'm getting into hatred,' she smiled. 'I'm reading about hatred.'

'Good God,' he groaned. 'As if I don't get enough of that kind of thing at work. What are you drinking?'

'Tea. Two parts Lady Grey and one part Chinese Pu-erh. There's more in the Thermos in the kitchen if you'd like some.'

He took off his shoes and went to fetch a cup.

Johanne closed her eyes. The inexplicable anxiety and unease were still there, but spending a chaotic afternoon with the children had helped. Ragnhild, who would be five on 21 January and hardly talked about anything else, had arranged a practice birthday for all her dolls and teddy bears. During dinner Johanne and Kristiane had acquired hats, made from Ragnhild's knickers covered in Hannah Montana stickers. Kristiane had given a long lecture about the movement of the planets around the sun, concluding with the announcement that she was going to be an astronaut when she grew up. Since Kristiane's perception of time could be difficult to understand, and as she rarely showed any interest in things that might happen more than a couple of days in the future, Johanne had delightedly dug out all the books from her own childhood, when she had had exactly the same dream.

When the children were in bed, her unease had come back. In order to keep it in check, she had decided to work.

'Tell me all about it,' said Adam, flopping down into an armchair.

He held the cup of tea up to his face, letting the steam cover his skin like a moist film.

'About what?'

'About hatred.'

'I should think you know more about it than I do.'

'Don't joke. I'm interested. What are you up to?'

He took a sip from his cup. The blend of tea was fresh and light, with a slightly acidic scent.

'I was thinking,' she said slowly, then paused. 'I was thinking of approaching the concept of hatred from the outside. From the inside, too, of course, but in order to say anything meaningful about hate crime I think we have to delve deeply into the concept itself. With all this money that's suddenly raining down on us ...'

She looked up as if it really was.

'... I can bring in that girl I mentioned, for example.'

'Girl?'

'Charlotte Holm. She specializes in the history of ideas. She's the one I told you about, the one who wrote ... this.'

She glanced around quickly before picking up a booklet.

'*Love and Hatred: A Conceptual Historical Analysis,*' Adam read slowly.

'Exciting,' she said, tossing the booklet aside. 'I've spoken to her, and she's probably going to start working with me in February.'

'So how many of you will that make?' asked Adam with a frown, as if the thought of a bunch of researchers using taxpayers' money to immerse themselves in hatred made him deeply sceptical.

'Four. Probably. It'll be cool. I've always worked alone, more or less. And this ...'

She picked up a piece of paper in one hand and waved the other hand at the rest of the papers surrounding her.

'This is all legal hatred. Verbal hatred that is protected by the concept of freedom of speech. Since malicious comments against minorities correspond to a significant extent with what is clearly hate crime, I think it's interesting to see how it all hangs together. Where the boundaries are.'

'What boundaries?'

'The boundaries for what is covered by freedom of speech.'

'But isn't that almost everything?'

'Unfortunately, yes.'

'Unfortunately? Surely we should thank God for the fact that we can say more or less anything we like in this country!'

'Of course. But listen ...'

She tucked her feet underneath her. He looked at her. When he got home he had just wanted to fall into bed, even though it wasn't even ten o'clock. He was still tired after a day that had been much too long and not particularly productive, but he no longer had any desire to sleep. Over the years he and Johanne had fallen into a pattern where most of their life together revolved around his work, her concerns and the children. When he saw her like this, sitting amidst a sea of paper without even mentioning the children, he remembered in a flash what it had been like to be intensely in love with her.

'Freedom of speech goes a long way,' she said, searching for an article among the chaos. 'As it should. But as you know, it has some limitations. The most interesting comes under paragraph 135a in the penal code. I don't want to bore you with too much legal stuff, but I just want to—'

'You never bore me. Never.'

'I'm sure I do.'

'Not at the moment, anyway.'

A fleeting smile, and she went on. 'A few people have been convicted for overstepping the law. Very few. The issue – or perhaps I should say the question of priorities – relates to freedom of speech. And judging by everything I have here ...'

She waved her hands wearily before she found the book she was looking for.

'... then freedom of speech rules. End of story.'

'Well, isn't that obvious?' said Adam. 'Fortunately. We're a modern society, after all.'

'I don't know about modern. I've ploughed through everything these homophobic idiots have said recently—'

'I'm not sure your conclusions are entirely scientific.'

She allowed herself to be interrupted. Sighed and put her hands behind her neck.

'I'm not feeling particularly scientific at the moment. I'm tired. Worn out. In order for something to be classified as hate crime, it isn't enough for the perpetrator to hate the victim as an individual. The hatred must be directed at the victim as the representative of a group. And if there's one thing I have difficulty in grasping, it's the idea of hatred against groups in a society like Norway. In Gaza, yes. In Kabul, yes. But here? In safe, social democratic Norway?'

She took a mouthful of tea and held it there for a few seconds before swallowing.

'First of all I spent two months going through public pronounce-ments about Muslims, blacks and other ethnic and cultural minorities. What I found was generalization of the worst kind. It's "they" and "we" right down the line.'

She drew quotation marks in the air with her fingers.

'In the end I felt sick. I felt sick, Adam! I don't know how an ordi-nary Norwegian Muslim mother or father can sleep at night. How they feel each night when they put their children to bed and settle them down and read to them, knowing how much crap people are saying and writing and thinking and feeling about them ...'

Her eyes narrowed and she took off her glasses.

'It's as if everything is allowed these days, somehow. And of course most things should be. Political freedom of speech in Norway is getting close to the absolute. But this culture of expressing opinions ...'

She breathed on the lenses and rubbed them with her shirt sleeve.

'Sorry,' she said, with a strained smile. 'It's just that I'd be so scared if I belonged to a distrusted minority and had children.'

Adam laughed. 'I'm sure you could teach them a lot in that partic-ular respect,' he said. 'On the subject of worrying about children, I mean. But ...'

He stood up and pushed his tea cup to the other side of the table. He quickly swept aside the papers closest to Johanne on the sofa, and sat down beside her. Put his arm around her. Kissed her hair, which smelled of pancakes.

'But what's this got to do with hate crime?' he asked. 'I mean, we're agreed that this isn't a criminal issue, but is protected by the law governing freedom of speech.'

'It's ...'

She searched for the right words.

'Since the substance in what is said,' she began again, before breaking off once more. 'Since the content of what is written and said corresponds exactly with ... with what the others claim, those who attack, those who kill ... then in my opinion ...'

She lifted the glass without drinking.

'If we're going to succeed in saying anything meaningful about hate crimes, then we have to know what triggers them. And I don't mean just the traditional explanations about the conditions in which a person grew up, experiences of loss, a history of conflict, the allocation of resources, religious opposition and so on. We have to know what ... *triggers* them. I want to investigate whether there's a connection between statements that could be regarded as full of hatred, but entirely legal, on the one hand, and hate-filled illegal crime on the other.'

'You mean whether the former facilitates the latter?'

'Among other things.'

'But isn't that obvious? Even though we can't ban such statements because of it?'

'We can't actually make that assumption. The connection, I mean. It has to be investigated.'

'Daddy! *Daddy!*'

Adam shot up. Johanne closed her eyes and prayed for all she was worth that Kristiane wouldn't wake up. All she could hear was Adam's calm, quiet voice interspersed with Ragnhild's sleepy fretfulness. Then everything went quiet again. The neighbours down below must have already gone to bed. Earlier that evening the noise of some film that was clearly action-packed had got on her nerves; it had sounded as if she were actually in the line of fire.

'She's fine,' Adam said, flopping down on the sofa beside her. 'Probably just a dream. She wasn't really awake. Now, where were we?'

159

'I don't know,' she said wearily. 'I don't actually know.'

'I thought you were pleased about this project.'

She laid her hand on his stomach and crept into his embrace.

'I am,' she murmured. 'But I've had an overdose of hatred at the moment. I haven't even asked you how your day went.'

'Please don't.'

She could feel him slowly beginning to relax under her weight. His breathing became deeper, and she fell into the same rhythm. She could tell his belt was too tight from the roll of flesh bulging over the waistband of his trousers.

'What do you think about some curtains, Adam?'

'Hm?'

'Curtains,' she repeated. 'Here in the living room. I just think the windows seem so big and dark in the winter.'

'As long as I don't have to choose them, go and buy them or hang them up.'

'OK.'

They ought to get up. She ought to tidy all these papers. If the girls got up first tomorrow morning, as they usually did, things would be even more chaotic than they already were.

'You smell so good,' she whispered.

'Everything about me is good,' he said sleepily, and in his voice there was a feeling of security she hadn't felt for a long time. 'Besides which I am the best detective in the whole wide world.'

*

'Police! Stop! *Stop, I said!*'

A young lad had just tumbled out of a dark green Volvo XC90. The number plates were so dirty they were illegible, despite the fact that the rest of the vehicle was quite clean. The oldest trick in the book, thought DC Knut Bork as he jumped out of the unmarked police car and set off in pursuit.

'Stop that car!' he yelled to his colleague, who was already striding across the carriageway.

For precisely five days it had been illegal to pay for sex in Norway. The new law had been passed by Stortinget without too much fuss, despite the fact that there was much to suggest that the new regulations would cause a significant setback for the sex industry. Open street prostitution had gone into hiding, presumably to wait and see what happened. However, there were still plenty of whores of both sexes in Oslo, and the punters hadn't stayed away either. Everything was just a little bit trickier for them all. Perhaps that was the idea.

The boy was unsteady on his feet, but fast. However, it took Bork only fifty metres to catch up with him.

The punter in the expensive car was terrified. He was about thirty-five and had tried to cover up two child seats in the back of the car with an old blanket. His designer jeans were still open at the fly when the driver's door was yanked open. He stepped out on to the pavement as requested, and began to cry.

'For fuck's sake,' yelled the boy on the other side of the street. 'You're killing me!'

'No, I'm not,' said DC Bork. 'And if you're a good boy I won't need to use the handcuffs, will I? OK? They're not particularly comfortable, so if I were you ...'

He could feel that the boy was reluctantly beginning to resign himself to the situation. The skinny body gradually relaxed. Bork slowly loosened his grip, and when the boy turned around he seemed younger than he had from a distance. His face was childish and his features soft, although he weighed no more than sixty kilos. A cold sore extended from his top lip right up into his left nostril, which was distended with scabs and pus. Bork felt sick, and was tempted to let the boy run away.

'I haven't fucking done anything!' He wiped his nose with the sleeve of his padded jacket. 'It's not illegal to sell yourself. It's that bastard who should go to jail!'

'He'll probably be fined. But since you're our witness, that means we need to talk to you as well. Let's go over to our car. Come on. What's your name?'

The boy didn't reply. He stubbornly refused to budge when Knut Bork indicated they should move.

'Right,' said Bork. 'There are two ways of doing this. There's the nice, easy way, and then there's the way that isn't cool at all. Not for either of us. But it's your choice.'

No response.

'What's your name?'

Still nothing.

'OK,' said Knut Bork, getting out the handcuffs. 'Hands behind your back, please.'

'Martin. Martin Setre.'

'Martin,' Bork repeated, putting away the handcuffs. 'Have you any form of ID on you?'

A slight shake of the head and a shrug.

'How old are you?'

'Eighteen.'

Knut Bork grinned.

'Seventeen,' said Martin Setre. 'Almost. Almost seventeen.'

The punter's sobs grew louder. It was nearly one o'clock in the morning, and there was very little traffic. They could hear the rattle of a tram from Prinsens Gate, and a taxi hooted angrily at the two badly parked cars as it whizzed past on the hunt for passengers, its FOR HIRE sign illuminated. The Christmas party season and the financial crisis had strangled the city's night life in January, and the streets were more or less deserted.

'Knut,' his colleague shouted. 'I think you should come over here for a minute.'

'Come on,' said Knut Bork, grabbing the boy by the upper arm, which was so thin he could easily get his hand around it.

The boy reluctantly went with him.

'I think we need to take this guy in,' said his colleague as they drew closer. 'Look what we've got here!'

Bork peered into the car.

Between the seats the central console was open. Under the armrest, in the space meant for sweets and snacks, lay a bulging bag that only just fitted. Knut Bork pulled on a pair of plastic gloves and opened one corner.

'Well, well,' he said, smacking his lips appreciatively. 'Well I never. Hash, I presume?'

The question was unnecessary, and went unanswered. Bork weighed the bag in his hand; he seemed to be thinking.

'Exactly half a kilo,' he said eventually. 'Not bad.'

'It's not mine,' sobbed the man. 'It's his!'

He pointed at Martin.

'What?' howled the boy. 'Thanks for fucking nothing! I asked him for five grams for the job, and look what I got!'

He unzipped his jacket and fumbled for something in the inside pocket. Eventually he managed to get hold of something between his index and middle fingers and pulled it out.

'Three grams max,' he said, dangling the little ball wrapped in cling film in front of his face. 'Max! As if I'd have got out of the car if that big bag was mine! As if I wouldn't have taken it with me if it belonged to me! Are you fucking crazy?'

'There's something in what he says, don't you think?'

The punter sobbed as Bork place a hand on his shoulder, demanding an answer.

'Please! You can't lock me up! I'll do anything, I can't ... You can have whatever you—'

'Hang on, hang on,' warned Knut Bork, holding up a hand. 'Don't go making things worse for yourself. Let's just calm down and—'

'Can I go now?' said Martin in a thin voice. 'I mean, it's not me you want. They'll just send me to social services and it'll mean a load of paperwork for you and—'

'I thought you said you were an adult. Come on.'

A night bus came along. It had to zigzag between the two cars, each blocking one side of the carriageway. There was just one nocturnal passenger looking down with curiosity at the four men before the bus roared away and it was possible to talk once again.

'My car,' the man sobbed as he was led to the police car. 'My wife needs it tomorrow morning! She has to take the kids to nursery!'

'Let me put it this way,' said Knut Bork as he helped the man into the back seat. 'Your wife has far bigger problems than the fact that she hasn't got transport tomorrow morning.'

Street Boy

The problem was that so many people had started to complain about the bad air. Quite frankly, there was a horrible smell. The receptionist had his hands full moving guests around as they came back from their allocated rooms and announced that they were uninhabitable. The strange thing was that it wasn't just one particular area of the hotel. On the contrary, the complaints were coming from one room here, another there, and in the end he had run out of patience. Given the number of rooms that could no longer be used, the hotel was seriously overbooked.

The Hotel Continental in Oslo was a proud establishment that most definitely did not tolerate an unpleasant smell in its rooms.

Fritiof Hansen, the operations manager, had been trying to track down the problem for more than fifty minutes. He had begun with the first room that had been rejected by an irate Frenchman threatening to move to the Grand. A disgusting, sweetish smell assailed his nostrils as he opened the door. There was nothing to explain the stench as far as Fritiof Hansen could see. The bathroom was freshly cleaned. All the drawers were empty, apart from the obligatory copy of the New Testament and brochures about Oslo's nightlife and the entertainment available. He did find a dirty cotton-wool ball under the bed, and, rather embarrassingly, a used condom behind one of the legs. But nothing that smelled. Nor were there any places in the room where the smell was stronger, as far as he could tell. And as soon as he stepped into the corridor, he was surrounded once more by the scent of luxury and carpet cleaner. In the room next door, all was as it should be. When he opened a door further along the corridor, the stench was there again.

It just didn't make any sense.

He was now standing down in the foyer, legs apart and hands behind his back as he stuck his nose in the air and sniffed. Admittedly, Fritiof Hansen was a man of sixty-three with a reduced sense of smell after smoking twenty cigarettes a day for forty years. But he had stopped smoking three years ago, and his senses of taste and smell had both improved.

'Edvard,' he said, holding out his hand to a bellboy who was staggering past with a bag under his arm and a suitcase in each hand. 'Is there a funny smell just here?'

'No,' gasped Edvard without stopping. 'But it stinks down in the cellar!'

'Right ...'

Fritiof Hansen clicked his heels like a soldier before brushing an imaginary speck of dust from his uniform. It was green, freshly ironed and with razor-sharp creases. His black shoes had been polished until they shone. His identity card with its magnetic strip dangled from an extendable cord clipped to his belt; combined with the carefully chosen code 1111, it gave him access to every room in the building. When he set off, his bearing was erect and military.

The cellar of the Continental was a confusing labyrinth, but not to Fritiof Hansen. For more than sixteen years he had taken care of small details and major issues at the hotel. When he was given the title of operations manager the previous year, he realized it was just a way of recognizing his loyalty. He wasn't really the manager of anything. Before he got the job at the Continental, he had packed paper clips in a protected workshop in Groruddalen. He proved himself to be unusually handy, and became a kind of informal caretaker there, until his boss had recommended him for a job at the Continental. Fritiof Hansen had turned up for the interview freshly shaven, wearing neat overalls and carrying his toolbox. He got the job, and since then he hadn't missed a single day's work.

He didn't like the cellar.

The complex machinery down here was maintained by a team of specialists. Fritiof Hansen might occasionally change a light bulb or fix a door that had got stuck, but the hotel used external companies for renovations and maintenance. And for the air-conditioning system. The module that collected fresh air from outside was located on the roof and in its own area on the top floor. The plant itself was in the cellar. Over the years it had been augmented in a way that made it into two independent appliances. During the latest phase of modernization it had been recommended that the whole thing be renewed, but this proved too expensive, so a compromise was reached between the hotel and the suppliers: a new, smaller plant was installed to ease the load on the old one. Fritiof Hansen could hear the low, monotone hum before he reached the inner corridor where the locked doors to the machine room were located.

As he walked down the stairs, he wrinkled his nose. It didn't smell quite the same as the polluted rooms, but here, too, a strange, sweetish smell found its way into his nostrils, combined with damp and dust and the distinctive mustiness of old buildings.

Fritiof Hansen didn't believe in ghosts. He believed in his brother and in Arbeiderpartiet and the hotel management, who had promised him a job here for as long as he could stand on his own two legs. Over the years he had also begun to believe in himself. Ghosts were invisible. Anything you couldn't see didn't exist. And yet he always felt that strange sense of unease as he set off down the long, dark corridors lined with doors leading to rooms which concealed things he recognized, but often didn't understand.

At the point where the corridor bore to the left, the smell grew stronger. He was getting close to the air-conditioning plants which were in two rooms next door to each other. With each step he took, the unpleasant feeling grew. Perhaps he should go and fetch someone. Edvard was a good lad who was always ready to stop for a chat when he had time.

But Edvard was just a bellboy. Fritiof Hansen was operations manager, with a badge on his chest and the code for every room in the entire building. This was his job, and the receptionist had told him he had an hour to sort out what was going on before the management called in professional help.

As if he wasn't a professional.

Despite the fact that most things in the cellar were old, the door was locked with a modern card reader. He swiped his card and keyed in the code as steadily as he could.

He opened the door.

The stench hit him with such force that he took a couple of steps backwards. He cupped his hands over his nose before hesitantly moving forward.

He stopped in the doorway of the dark room. His free hand groped for the light switch. When he found it he was almost dazzled by the fluorescent tube which suddenly drenched the room in an unpleasant blue light.

Four metres away, half-hidden behind some kind of machinery that could have been for just about anything, he could see a pair of legs from the knees down. It was difficult to tell whether they belonged to a woman or a man.

Fritiof Hansen had a set evening ritual. Every weekday at 9.35 p.m. he watched *CSI* on TVNorge. A beer, a small packet of crisps and *Crime Scene Investigation* before bed. He liked both the Miami and New York versions, but it was Gil Grissom in the original version from Las Vegas who was Fritiof Hansen's favourite. But Grissom was about to be replaced by that black guy, and Fritiof wasn't at all sure if he'd bother watching it any more.

Grissom was the best.

Gil Grissom wouldn't like it if an operations manager at a respectable hotel walked into a crime scene, destroying a whole lot of microscopic evidence that might be there. Fritiof Hansen was quite convinced this was a crime scene. At any rate, the person over by the wall was definitely dead. He remembered an episode where Grissom had established the time of death by studying the development of fly larvae on a pig's carcass. It had been bad enough on television.

'Dead as a doornail,' he muttered, mainly to convince himself. 'It stinks of death in here.'

Slowly he moved back and closed the door. He checked the lock had clicked into place and set off towards the stairs. Before he got around the corner where the corridor led off at an angle of ninety degrees, he had broken into a run.

*

'I was actually thinking about letting him go. But then we found the hash. I needed to interview him properly, and then it struck me that ...'

DC Knut Bork handed over a report to Silje Sørensen as they walked across the blue zone in the police station. She stopped as she glanced through the document.

On closer investigation, Martin Setre had turned out to be fifteen years and eleven months old. He had spent the first part of his life with his biological parents. He was already perceived as an unlucky child during his time at nursery. Broken bones. Bruises. Admittedly, he was clumsy at nursery too, but most of his injuries were sustained at home. There was the suggestion of ADHD when a pre-school teacher asked for the boy to be checked out. Before this process could begin, the family had moved. Martin started school in a small community in Østfold. After only six months he was admitted to hospital with stomach pains, which no one could get to the bottom of. During the spring term in his first year the family moved again, after one of the teachers called round unannounced and found the boy locked in a bike shed, his clothing completely inadequate. The teacher informed the authorities, but before the case reached the top of the pile, the family had moved yet again. Martin's life continued in this way until he was admitted to Ullevål Hospital at the age of eleven with a fractured skull. Fortunately, they had managed to save his life, but actually giving him any kind of life proved more difficult. Since then the boy had been in and out of various institutions and foster homes. The last time he had run away was at Christmas, from a residential youth care unit where he had been placed by the court.

The case against his parents was dropped due to lack of evidence.

'Ffksk,' mumbled Silje, looking up again.

'What?'

'For fuck's sake,' she clarified.

'You could say that,' agreed Knut Bork, leading her to an interview room. 'He's in here.'

He took out a key and inserted it in the lock.

'We're not really allowed to lock him in,' he said, his voice subdued. 'At least not without supervision. But this kid would have been long gone if I'd left the door open for one second. He tried to do a runner three times while we were bringing him in from the unit.'

'Has he been there since last Monday?'

'Yes, under supervision. He hasn't been alone for more than five minutes.'

The door opened.

Martin Setre didn't even look up. He was rocking back and forth on a chair, one foot on the table. The dark boot lay in a small lake of melted snow. The back of the chair was rhythmically hitting the wall, and had already started to leave a mark.

'Pack that in,' said Knut Bork. 'Right now. This is DI Silje Sørensen. She wants to talk to you.'

The boy still didn't look up. His fingers were playing with a snuff tin, but it didn't look as if he had anything under his lip. However, the herpes infection was considerably worse.

'Hi,' said Silje, moving so that she was opposite him. 'You can say hello to me if you like.'

She sat down.

'I understand,' she said, and started to laugh.

This time the boy did look up, but without meeting her eyes.

'What the fuck are you laughing at?'

'Not at you. At Knut here.'

She nodded in the direction of her younger colleague, who raised his eyebrows as high as he could before adopting the same indifferent expression once again. He had turned the chair around and was leaning over the back with his arms folded, a thin investigation file dangling from one hand.

'You see,' said Silje, 'when he showed me your papers we made a bet. I bet 100 kronor that you would be rocking back and forward on the chair, fiddling with a snuff tin, and that you'd refuse to speak. Then I bet another hundred that you wouldn't look me in the eye for the first quarter of an hour. It looks as though I'm going to be rich. That's why I'm laughing.'

She laughed again.

The boy took his foot off the table, let the legs of the chair crash to the floor and stared her straight in the eye.

'It hasn't been quarter of an hour yet,' he said. 'You lost.'

'Only partly. It's 1-1 between Knut and me. What the score will be between you and me remains to be seen.'

A faint knock on the door made the boy glance in that direction.

'Come in,' Knut Bork called loudly, and the door opened.

A woman in her thirties blundered in, heavily overweight and panting, with layers of flapping clothes.

'Sorry I'm a few minutes late,' she said. 'Busy day. I'm Andrea Solli, the social worker.'

She addressed her last remark to Martin and held out her hand. He responded hesitantly with a limp handshake. He didn't get up.

'Well, that's the formalities out of the way,' said Andrea Solli, sitting down on the remaining chair.

The boy closed his eyes and pretended to yawn. Andrea Solli was Number 62 in the series of social workers, experts, solicitors and lay judges who had played some part in Martin's life. The very first one had got him to talk. He had told her everything, concluding with an account of how his father had smashed his head against a toilet until he no longer knew whether he was alive or not.

She had said she believed him, and that everything would be all right.

Nothing had ever been all right, and a long time ago he had stopped believing a single word they said.

'So you were brought in three days ago,' said Silje Sørensen. 'For possession of three and a half grams of hash, it says here. To be perfectly honest, I'm not remotely interested in that. Nor am I particularly interested in your career as a prostitute. Except for ...'

Knut Bork handed her a document from his file.

'... this. It's a report from when you were brought in on 21 November last year.'

'What? Are you going to start poking around in ancient history?'

Martin squirmed on his chair.

'It's six weeks ago, Martin. The police don't really regard that as ancient history. But actually, it's not you I'm interested in this time.'

The boy was leaning forward, batting the snuff tin between his hands across the surface of the desk like an ice-hockey puck.

'It's Hawre. Hawre Ghani. You know him, don't you?'

The puck was travelling faster between his hands.

'Come on, Martin. You were brought in together. It's clear from the report that you knew one another. I just want—'

'Haven't seen Hawre for ages,' the boy said sullenly.

'No. I believe you.'

'Don't know anything about Hawre,' Martin muttered.

'Were you friends?'

The boy pulled a face.

'Does that mean yes or no?'

'It's not exactly easy to make friends when you live like I do. I mean, you never get to live in the same place for longer than a few weeks!'

'You're the one who takes off,' the social worker interrupted. 'I realize it's very difficult for you, but it's not easy to create—'

'You can sort all that out later,' Silje broke in. 'I'm asking you again, Martin. Did you know Hawre well?'

He carried on playing table hockey without answering.

'You're blushing. Were you together?'

'What?'

The sore in his nose had started to bleed. A thin trickle of red zigzagged down the crusty yellow scab covering the area between his left nostril and his upper lip.

'Me and ... Hawre? He isn't even gay, not really. He just needs the money!'

'But you are?'

'What?'

'Gay.'

'You've no fucking right to ask me that.'

A siren started howling in the courtyard at the back. Two magpies were sitting on the window ledge outside, staring at them with coal-black eyes and taking no notice of the noise.

Martin's eyes narrowed, and his hands finally stopped moving.

'But since you ask, the answer is yes. It's nothing to be ashamed of.'

Defiance shone from every inch of his tense body, and this time he was the one holding her gaze.

'I couldn't agree more,' said Silje.

If the boy had been ten kilos heavier, and if the sore on his face had healed, he might have been quite good-looking. Unfortunately his teeth were bad, which was rare for Norwegian children in 2009. When he spoke she could see a grey film of tartar, which still didn't hide a couple of botched fillings in his front teeth. But his eyes were large and blue, and the long eyelashes curled upwards like a small child's.

'Can't you get rid of them?' he said.

'Who?'

Martin pointed at the woman and Knut Bork.

'I'm quite happy to leave,' said Bork. 'But the social worker has to stay. We're not allowed to question you unless somebody from social services is present.'

Without any further discussion he got to his feet. He placed the file next to the report in front of Silje Sørensen, and pushed his chair under the table.

'Ring me when you've finished,' he said. 'I'll be in my office.'

As the door closed behind him, Martin stared nastily at Andrea Solli.

'I don't need any help from social services,' he said. 'You can go as well.'

Silje got in first.

'Out of the question,' she said firmly. 'Forget it. Tell me about you and Hawre instead.'

Martin had started to lick the sore. The blood from his nose turned pink as it mixed with his saliva, and suddenly a piece of the scab came away.

'Fuck,' he yelled, grabbing at his mouth.

Blood was pouring down his face, and Andrea Solli dug out a bundle of Kleenex from her capacious handbag. Martin took three and pressed them against the sore.

'Me and Hawre weren't together,' he said, sounding agitated and revealing that his voice hadn't completely broken yet. 'We were just mates.'

'Mates usually have some idea where their mates are,' said Silje.

The boy didn't reply. His eyes were wet, but Silje didn't know if it was because of the turn the conversation had taken or his sore lip. She wasn't sure how to proceed. To gain time she opened a half-litre bottle of mineral water and poured three glasses without asking if anyone would like some.

'Hawre's dead,' she said.

At that moment the magpies took off from the window ledge, shouting hoarsely as they disappeared into the darkness over the city. It had stopped snowing at last. It was quarter past four in the afternoon. From the corridor they could hear the rapid footsteps of people hurrying to get home.

'That's what I thought,' whispered Martin.

He dropped the blood-stained tissues on the floor, put his arms on the table and hid his face.

'That's what I thought,' he sobbed again.

'When did you last see him, Martin?'

Silje Sørensen really wanted to put her arms around him. Hold him. Comfort him, as if there were any way of comforting a boy who wasn't even sixteen years old and had lost any chance of a decent life long ago.

'When did you last see him?' she repeated.

'I don't remember,' he wept.

'This is really important, Martin. Hawre was murdered.'

The sobs broke off. 'Murdered?'

His voice sounded half-suffocated as he lay slumped over the table.

'Yes. And that's why it's really, really important that you try to remember.'

'Do you think I murdered Hawre?'

He wasn't even angry. Or accusing. Martin Setre simply took it for granted that everybody assumed he was guilty of everything.

'No, absolutely not. I don't believe for one moment that you murdered your friend.'

'Good,' he snivelled, slowly sitting up.

Andrea Solli pointed at the Kleenex. He didn't touch them.

'Because I wouldn't do that!'

'Can you try to remember when you last saw him? We can start from 21 November. When you were brought in together. It was a Friday. Can you remember anything about that day?'

He nodded, almost imperceptibly.

'You were taken into care and driven to the residential unit, it says here. Hawre, on the other hand, managed to do a runner during the journey. Did you see him after that?'

'Yes ...'

He really looked as if he was thinking hard. A deep furrow appeared at the top of his nose.

'I cleared off the following day. We met up ... on the Sunday. And on ...'

For the first time he picked up the glass of mineral water.

'Can I have a Coke instead?' he mumbled.

'Of course. Here.'

Silje passed him a bottle. He opened it and drank, not bothering with a glass. A grimace of pain passed over his face as the neck of the bottle caught the sore, which was still bleeding.

'We met on the Sunday. I'm quite sure about that, because ...'

He suddenly stopped speaking.

'Because ... ?' said Silje.

'I'm not saying.'

'You have to understand that—'

'I'm not saying anything about that night, OK? It's not important, anyway, because I saw Hawre the following day.'

'Right,' said Silje, bringing up the calendar on her mobile. 'So that would be ... Monday 24 November?'

'I don't know what the fucking date was, but it was the Monday after we were brought in. We were going to ...'

Finally he picked up a tissue and dabbed cautiously at his mouth. Tears still lingered on his eyelashes. He was no longer crying, but his whole body seemed more exhausted than ever, if that were possible.

'We were just going to pick up a couple of blokes, turn a couple of tricks. Then we were going to go and see a film. We needed the money.'

Silje Sørensen had a pen and paper in front of her. So far she hadn't written a single word. Now she cautiously picked up the pen, but didn't touch the paper.

'What film were you going to see?' she asked, adding quickly: 'Just so I can check the date.'

'*Man of War.*'

She smiled.

'Come on, Martin. *Man of War* had its premiere just before Christmas.'

'OK, OK. I don't remember. It's true. I don't fucking remember what we were going to see, because we never went in the end.'

'So what did you do?'

'We decided to ... we ... we needed some cash. We went down to the central station.'

He caught her eye again, as if seeking confirmation that she understood what he meant. She gave a slight nod, which he interpreted as a yes.

'There were loads of people there. It was packed.'

'What time of day was this?'

'Dunno – afternoon, maybe. Not very late, anyway. We were going to go to the pictures later. We hung out where we usually hang out ...'

'And where's that?'

'By the entrance from Jernbanetorget.'

'And then?'

'Nobody came.'

'Nobody? But you said it was—'

'Nobody we were looking for. Nobody who ...'

He was playing with the snuff tin again. She noticed that his fingers were unusually long and slender, almost feminine.

'So we decided to go Oslo City, the shopping centre. But just when we got outside some guy came up and started talking to us in English. Well, American really. I'm not sure. American, I think.'

'I see. And what did he want?'

'The usual,' Martin said defiantly. 'But he couldn't like just say it straight out. He didn't sort of use the normal ... He was creepy. There was something about him.'

'Like what?'

'I don't really know. But I didn't want to go with him. He was ...'

The pause grew so long that Silje asked a question: 'Do you remember what he looked like?'

'Old. Expensive clothes. Quite fat.'

'What do you mean by old?'

'At least forty. Disgusting. Asking and digging, kind of. I don't like old men. Twenty-five is OK. Not much older, anyway. But Hawre needed the money more than me, so he went off with this guy.' He stared at the Coke bottle. 'He was wearing the kind of clothes that show how rich you are. Know what I mean?'

Silje knew exactly what he meant. She was the wealthiest DI in the country, having inherited a fortune when she turned eighteen. It didn't really make any difference to her. When she applied to the police training academy she deliberately moved downmarket. But now she was so used to it that she bought her clothes at H&M. But she knew just what he meant, and nodded.

'And then?'

He looked up. His eyes frightened her; his despair over his friend's death had turned into sheer apathy. He shrugged his shoulders and mumbled something she couldn't catch.

'What?'

'I don't remember much more about that day.'

'But you haven't seen Hawre since then.'

His tongue couldn't stay away from the sore. Instead of answering, he shook his head.

The preliminary post-mortem report showed that Hawre Ghani probably died between the 18th and 25th of November. Martin Setre had seen Hawre on 24 November when he went off with an unknown sex client.

'You have to help me,' said Silje.

He remained silent.

'I need a drawing of the man Hawre went with,' she said. 'Can you help me with that?'

'OK,' he said eventually. 'If I can have something to eat first.'

'Of course you can. What would you like?'

For the first time she saw the hint of a smile on his damaged face.

'Steak and onions and loads of fried potatoes,' he said. 'I'm starving.'

*

Adam Stubo tried to drown out the rumbling of his stomach by coughing. Only an hour ago he had eaten an apple and a banana, but his belly already felt empty. On New Year's Eve he had stepped on the bathroom scales for the first time in two years. The number shining up at him from the display had three figures, and it frightened him. Since there was no space for exercise in his packed agenda, he needed to cut down on food. He had secretly joined an Internet diet club, which immediately and mercilessly informed him that his daily intake was over 4,000 calories. Getting it down to 1,800 was sheer hell.

He still had three chocolate bars in the drawer of his desk. He opened it and looked at the striped wrappers. It wouldn't be the end of the world if he had half a piece. Admittedly, he had looked up the number of calories in chocolate on the Internet calculator the other day, and had resolved never to touch the bloody stuff again. But he was so hungry that he wasn't thinking clearly.

The telephone rang.

'Adam Stubo,' he said more pleasantly than usual, deeply grateful for the interruption.

'It's Sigmund.'

Sigmund Berli had been Adam's friend and closest colleague for almost ten years. He was far from the sharpest knife in the drawer, but he worked hard and was totally loyal. Sigmund voted for Fremskrittspartiet, supported Vålerenga and ate ready meals seven days a week since splitting up with his wife about a year ago. What little free time he had he devoted to his two sons, whom he adored. Sigmund Berli was Adam's anchor in the sea of humanity, and he was grateful for precisely that. With increasing frequency he would find himself sitting through a dinner with Johanne's friends and colleagues from the university without saying a word. Telling them anything about how real life was lived in this country was usually pointless. He preferred Sigmund Berli and his broad generalizations; at least they were based on a life lived among ordinary people.

'We've found a bloody great pile of poison-pen letters,' said Sigmund.

'Are you still in Bergen?'

'Yes. In a safe in the Bishop's office.'

'You're in a safe in the Bishop's office?'

'Ha bloody ha. The letters. There was a safe in her office that we only found out about a few days ago. The secretary had a code, but it turned out to be wrong. So we got somebody from the firm who supplied the safe to come out and look at it. And there was a pile of shit in there, if I can put it that way.'

'What's it about?'

'Guess.'

'No games, Sigmund.'

'The usual homophobic crap.' Adam could clearly hear that Sigmund was smiling at the other end of the phone. 'What else?'

'Are we talking about e-mails?' Adam asked. 'Or ordinary letters? Anonymous?'

'A bit of both. Most are print-outs of e-mails, and the majority are anonymous, but there's the odd one that uses their full name. It's mostly complete garbage, Adam. Filth, no more and no less. And do you know what I've never understood?'

Quite a lot, Adam thought.

'Why anyone gets so worked up about what people do in bed. My boy's ice-hockey trainer is gay. Terrific bloke. Tough and masculine with the lads, but incredibly nice. Comes to every training session, unlike that idiot they had before, even though he had a wife and four kids. Some of the other parents started complaining when this bloke came out in the paper, but you should have seen old Sigmund go!'

His laughter crackled down the phone.

'I showed them what was what, and no mistake! You can't compare an ordinary gay bloke with a bloody paedophile. He's a friend for life now. We've had a beer together a few times, and he's sound. Fantastic on the ice, too. Used to be in the national junior team until it all got too much. Bunch of homophobes, that's what they are.'

Adam listened with mounting surprise. His eyes were still fixed on the striped chocolate bars.

'What are you doing with the letters?' he said absently.

Sigmund was munching on something.

'Sorry,' he said. 'Just had to get something inside me. They have top-notch cinnamon buns here in Bergen.'

The drawer containing the chocolate bars slammed shut before Sigmund continued.

'We've got one of the IT guys working on her computer. Looking for the addresses and so on. And, of course, the letters will be examined as well. I wonder why she saved them all? Nothing was ever reported.'

'Most people in the public eye get that kind of thing all the time. At least if they have controversial opinions. Not many make a fuss about it. After all, it can just make things worse. Johanne's working on a project that—'

'And how is my favourite girl?' Sigmund interrupted.

Adam's colleague had been steadfastly in love with Johanne for several years, and that clearly hadn't changed. It normally blossomed only in the form of sheer delight every time he saw or spoke to her. After a few drinks he might come out with clumsy compliments and the odd unwelcome fumble. On one occasion Johanne had slapped him hard across the face when he had grabbed her breast after getting roaring drunk on his hosts' cognac. For some bizarre reason she still seemed to like him, somehow.

'Fine,' said Adam. 'Call round some time.'

'Great! What about this weekend? That would fit in really well—'

'Ring me when you've got something new,' Adam broke in. 'Got to go. Bye.'

Just as he was about to end the call he heard Sigmund's electronically distorted voice: 'Hang on! Don't go.'

Adam put the phone to his ear again.

'What is it?'

'I just wanted to say that not all the letters are about gay stuff.'

'No?'

'Some are about abortion.'

'Abortion?'

'Yes, the Bishop was pretty fanatical about it, you know.'

'But what are they writing? And more to the point, who's writing?'

Sigmund had finally finished eating.

'It's all a bit of a mixture. Anyway, those letters aren't as aggressive. More kind of bitter. There's one from a woman who wishes she'd never been born. Her mother was raped, and because she was so young at the time, she didn't dare say anything until it was too late. Everything went wrong for the kid from the day she was born.'

'Hm. A person who complains to the Bishop about the fact that she actually exists?'

'Yep.'

'But what did she actually want?'

'She wanted to try to convince the Bishop that abortion can be justified. Something along those lines. I don't really know. A lot of the letters are from total nut jobs, Adam. I agree with you – I don't think we should take too much notice of them. But since we haven't got much else to go on, we need to have a closer look at them. Are you coming up here soon?'

Adam clamped the phone between his head and shoulder. Opened the drawer, grabbed one of the chocolate bars and tore off the wrapper.

'Not until next week, probably. But we'll talk before then. Bye.'

He put down the phone and broke the bar into four pieces. Slowly he began to eat. He let every piece lie on his tongue for ages, sucking rather than chewing. When he had finished one piece, he picked up the next. It took him five minutes to enjoy every last bit, and he finished off by licking his fingers clean.

His mood improved. His blood sugar rose and he felt clear-headed. When he realized a few seconds later that he had just consumed 216 empty calories he was so upset that he grabbed his coat and switched off the light. It was Wednesday 7 January, and seven days on starvation rations was enough for this time.

He would allow himself a decent dinner, anyway.

Rage

At around dinner time on 9 January the doorbell rang at a grey-painted house on Hystadveien in Sandefjord.

Synnøve Hessel was lying on the sofa. She was in a state somewhere between sleep and reality, in a haze of melancholy dreams. She couldn't sleep at night. The darkest hours felt both interminable and wasted. She couldn't search for Marianne when everyone else was asleep and everything was closed, but at the same time it was impossible to get any rest. The days just got worse and worse. From time to time she dozed off, as she had now.

There wasn't much else to do.

Their joint bank account hadn't been touched. Synnøve hadn't yet managed to gain access to Marianne's account. She had contacted every hospital in Norway, but without success. There were no more friends to ring. Even the most casual acquaintances and distant relatives had been asked if they had heard anything from Marianne since 19 December. Two days ago Synnøve had gathered her courage and finally phoned her in-laws. The last time she heard from them had been a terrible letter they had sent when it became clear that Marianne was going to leave her husband to move in with a woman. The call had been a waste of time. As soon as Marianne's mother had realized who was calling she launched into a venomous, two-minute tirade before slamming the phone down. Synnøve didn't even have time to tell her why she was calling.

And Marianne was still missing.

Synnøve had hardly eaten for a week and a half. She had spent the days after Marianne's disappearance searching for her. At night she went for long, long walks with the dogs. Now she didn't even have the energy for that. For the last two days they had had to make do with the dog run in the garden. Yesterday evening she had forgotten to feed them. When she suddenly remembered, it was two o'clock in the morning. Her tears had frightened the alpha male, who had whimpered and paced around, demanding lots of attention before he was prepared to touch his food. In the end Synnøve had crawled into one of the kennels and fallen asleep there with Kaja in her arms. She had woken up stiff with cold half an hour later.

The doorbell rang again.

Synnøve didn't move. She didn't want visitors. A lot of people had tried, but not many had got past the door.

Ding-dong.

And again.

She got up awkwardly from the sofa and folded the woollen blanket. She massaged her stiff neck as she shuffled towards the door, ready to convince yet another friend that she wanted to be alone.

When she opened the door and saw Kjetil Berggren standing there, she felt dizzy with relief. They had found Marianne, she realized, and Kjetil had come here to give her the good news. It had all been a terrible misunderstanding, but Marianne would soon be home and everything would be just like before.

Kjetil Berggren's expression was so serious. Synnøve took a step backwards into the hallway. The front door opened wider. There was a woman standing behind him. She was probably around fifty, and was wearing a winter coat. Around her neck, where everyone else would have had a scarf to keep out the bitter January cold, she was wearing a priest's collar.

The pastor was just as serious as the police officer.

Synnøve took another step back before sinking to her knees and covering her face with her hands. Her nails dug into her skin, making blood-red stripes on both cheeks. She was howling, a constant, desperate lament that was like nothing Kjetil Berggren had ever heard before. Only when Synnøve started banging her head on the stone floor did he try to lift her up. She hit out at him, and sank down once more.

And all the time that dreadful howling.

The intense sound of pain made the dogs in the backyard answer her. Six huskies howled like the wolves they almost were. The desolate chorus rose up to the low clouds, and could be heard all the way to Framnes on the other side of the grey, deserted, wintry fjord.

*

A siren sliced through the steady hum of the traffic as they stopped for a red light at a junction. In the rear-view mirror Lukas could see a blue flashing light, and he tried to manoeuvre the car closer to the pavement without encroaching on the pedestrian zone. The ambulance, travelling far too fast, came up on the outside of the queue and almost ran over an old man who walked straight in front of Lukas's big BMW X5. He was obviously deaf.

'That was close,' Lukas said to his father, staring at the bewildered pedestrian until the cars behind him started sounding their horns.

Erik Lysgaard didn't reply. He was sitting in the passenger seat, as silent as always. His clothes were now clearly too big. The seat belt made him look flat and skinny. His hair stuck out from his scalp in miserable, downy clumps, and he looked ten years older than he was. Lukas had had to remind his father to have a shower that morning; a sour smell had emanated from his body the previous evening when he reluctantly allowed himself to be hugged.

Nothing had changed.

Once more Lukas had insisted on taking his father back to his home in Os. Once more Erik had protested, and, as before, Lukas had eventually won. The sight of their grandfather had frightened the children yet again, and a couple of times Astrid had been on the point of losing her composure.

'We need to make some plans,' said Lukas. 'The police say we can hold the funeral next week. It'll have to be quite a big occasion. There were so many people who were fond of Mum.'

Erik sat in silence, his face expressionless.

'Dad, you need to make some decisions.'

'You can sort it all out,' said his father. 'I don't care.'

Lukas reached out and turned off the radio. He was gripping the wheel so tightly that his knuckles turned white, and the speed at which he travelled along the last section of Årstadsveien would have cost him his licence had there been a camera. The tyres screeched as he turned left into Nubbebakken, crossing the oncoming traffic before slamming on the brakes.

'Dad,' he said, almost in a whisper. 'Why has one of the photos disappeared?'

For the first time in the entire journey his father looked at him.

'Photos?'

'The photos in Mum's room.'

Erik turned away again.

'I want to go home.'

'There have always been four photographs on that shelf. They were there when I was at the house the day after Mum was murdered. I remember, because that detective went in there by mistake. One of the photographs isn't there any more. Why not?'

'I want to go home.'

'I'll take you home. But I want an answer, Dad!'

Lukas banged his fist on the wheel. Pain shot up his arm, and he swore silently.

'Take me home,' said Erik. 'Now.'

The coldness in his father's voice made Lukas keep quiet. He put the car into gear. His hands were shaking and he felt almost as upset as when the police came to tell him that his mother was dead. When they pulled into the small area behind the open gate of his father's house a few minutes later, he could clearly see the beautiful woman in the missing photograph in his mind's eye. She was dark, and although the picture was black and white, he thought she had blue eyes. Just like Lukas. Her nose was straight and slender, like his, and her smile clearly showed that one front tooth lay slightly on top of the other.

Just like his own teeth.

Not enough of her clothing was visible to enable him to guess when the photo was taken. He hadn't seen it until he was a teenager. Now that he had children of his own and had become aware of how observant children are, he had worked out that it couldn't have been on display when he was younger. Once he had asked who she was. His mother had smiled and stroked his cheek and replied: 'A friend you don't know.'

Lukas stopped the car and got out to help his father into the house.

They didn't exchange a word, and avoided looking at one another.

When the door closed behind Erik, Lukas got back in the car. He sat there for a long time as the wet snow obscured the windscreen and the temperature inside the car dropped.

His mother's friend looked an awful lot like him.

*

'She looks just like you! The spitting image!'

Karen Winslow laughed as she took the photograph of Ragnhild. She held it at an angle to avoid the reflection of the overhead lights, and shook her head. Ragnhild was lying in the bath with shampoo in her hair and a giant rubber duck on her tummy. It looked as if she was being attacked by a bright yellow monster.

'So she's the youngest,' she said, handing back the photograph. 'Have you got a picture of the older one?'

The photograph had been taken the previous Christmas.

Kristiane was sitting on the steps in front of the house on Hauges Vei, her expression serious. For once she was looking straight into the camera, and had just taken off her hat. Her thin hair was sticking out in all directions with static electricity, and the background light from the pane of glass in the door made it look as if she had a halo.

'Wow,' said Karen. 'What a beautiful child! How old is she? Nine? Ten?'

'Nearly fourteen,' said Johanne. 'It's just that she's not quite like other children.'

It was surprisingly easy to say.

'What's wrong with her?'

'Who knows?' said Johanne. 'Kristiane was born with a heart defect, and had to undergo three major operations before she was one year old. Nobody has really managed to find out whether the damage was done then, or whether it's an impairment she was born with.'

Karen smiled again and examined the photograph more closely. Looking at her old college friend reminded Johanne of how many years had passed. Karen had always been slim and fit, but now her face was thinner, more strained, and her black hair was streaked with grey. She had started wearing glasses. Johanne thought this must be recent, because she kept taking them off and putting them back on all the time, and she didn't really know what to do with them when she wasn't using them.

It was almost eighteen years since they last met, but they had recognized one another straight away. Johanne had been given the longest hug she could remember when Karen got out of the taxi outside Restaurant Victor on Sandaker, and as they walked inside she felt happy.

Almost exhilarated.

The waiter placed a glass of champagne in front of each of them.

'Would you like me to go through the menu with you right away?' he said with a smile.

'I think we'd prefer to wait a little while,' Johanne said quickly.

'Of course. I'll come back.'

Karen raised her glass.

'Here's to you,' she said, smiling. 'To think we've managed to meet up again. Fantastic.'

They sipped their champagne.

'Mmm. Wonderful. Tell me more about Kris ... Kristi ...'

'Kristiane. For a long time the experts insisted that it could be some form of autism. Asperger's perhaps. But it doesn't really fit. Admittedly, she does need fixed routines, and for long periods she can be highly dependent on order and clear systems. Sometimes she's almost reminiscent of a savant, someone who is autistic but has certain highly developed skills. But then, all of a sudden, without any clue as to what has brought about the change, she's just like an ordinary child with mild learning difficulties. And although she finds it difficult to make real friends, she shows great flexibility when it comes to relationships with other people. She's ...'

Johanne picked up her glass again, surprised at how good it felt to talk about her older daughter with someone who had never met her.

'... tremendously loving towards her family.'

'She really is absolutely adorable,' said Karen, handing back the photograph. 'You are so, so lucky to have her.'

Karen's comment made Johanne feel warm, almost embarrassed. Isak loved his daughter more than anything on earth, and Adam was the most loving stepfather in the world. Both sets of grandparents worshipped Kristiane, and she was as well integrated into the social environment surrounding the Vik and Stubo families as it was possible for a child like her to be. Occasionally someone would remark that Kristiane was lucky to have such a good family. Live Smith had given Johanne the feeling that she was happy to have Kristiane in her school.

But no one had ever said that Johanne was lucky to have a daughter like Kristiane.

'It's true,' said Johanne. 'I'm ... we're really lucky to have her.'

She quickly blinked back the tears. Karen reached across the table and placed her hand on Johanne's cheek. The gesture felt oddly welcome, in spite of all the years that lay between them.

'Children are God's greatest gift,' said Karen. 'They are always, always a blessing, wherever they come from, whoever they come to, and whatever they are like. They should be treated, loved and respected accordingly.'

A single tear escaped and trickled down Johanne's cheek.

Americans and their big words, she thought. Americans and their pompous, high-flown, beautiful choice of words. She smiled quickly and wiped the tear away with the back of her hand.

'Are you ready to order?'

The waiter reappeared, looking from one to the other.

'Yes,' said Johanne. 'It would be very helpful if you could go through the menu in English so that I don't have to translate for my friend.'

This was no problem for the waiter. He spent almost ten minutes explaining and describing each dish and answering all of Karen's interested questions. When they had finally agreed on food and wine, Johanne realized that Karen was far more worldly than she was. Even the waiter seemed impressed.

They began with oysters.

There were no oysters on the menu, and the waiter didn't mention them at all during his comprehensive account of what the restaurant had to offer. Karen shook her head when he had finished, smiled her dazzling white smile and suggested that every self-respecting master chef always has a few oysters tucked away.

Always, she insisted.

It was true.

The problem was that Johanne had never eaten oysters.

She was an academic with a PhD. Well-travelled and financially secure. She liked food. She had eaten dog in China and deep-fried spiders from a shack in Angkor Wat. But she had never dared to try oysters.

She looked at the plate. The half-shells lay there on a bed of ice, smelling faintly of the shoreline. Nobody could claim that the slimy, dirty white blobs looked appetizing. She glanced at Karen, who trickled a mixture of white wine and vinegar over each oyster from a small bowl, before picking up the first shell and sliding the contents into her mouth. She closed her eyes and rolled the oyster around in her mouth, then swallowed and exclaimed: 'Perfect!'

Johanne followed suit.

The oyster was the best thing she had ever tasted.

'Johanne,' said Karen when the dish was empty. 'Tell me more. Tell me everything. Absolutely everything!'

They talked their way through two more courses. They talked about their time at college and mutual friends from those days. About families and parents, about their joys and frustrations. About their children. They talked over each other, laughed and interrupted each other. The acoustics in the small restaurant were hopeless; Karen's loud laugh bounced off the bare walls, disturbing the other guests. However, the waiter remained friendly, discreetly topping up their glasses as soon as they were almost empty.

'Karen, I have to ask you about something.'

Johanne looked at the fourth course as it was placed in front of her: quail on a bed of artichoke purée. The little bird was surrounded by a circle of fine strips of Parma ham interspersed with pickled cherry tomatoes.

'Tell me about the APLC,' she said.

'How do you know I work there?' Karen carefully wiped her mouth with the thick fabric serviette before picking up her knife and fork again.

'I googled you,' said Johanne. 'At the moment I'm working on a project that—'

Karen laughed, making the glasses clink.

'We've been sitting here for over two hours, and we still haven't got round to telling each other what we do! You first – start talking!'

And Johanne talked. She talked about her job at the Institute of

Criminology, about the doctoral thesis she completed in 2000, about how she loved research but found the teaching obligations which went with her current position something of a trial, and about the joys and frustrations of having to combine her career with two demanding children. Gradually, she got around to talking about the project on which she was currently working. By the time she had finished, the quail were tiny skeletons on otherwise empty plates.

'You must come over and see us,' Karen said firmly. 'What we do is highly relevant to your research.'

'And now it's your turn,' said Johanne. 'Off you go.'

She asked the waiter if they could have a short pause before the next course. She could feel that she had had a little bit too much to drink, but it didn't matter. She couldn't remember when she had last eaten out, and she definitely couldn't remember when she had felt this good. So when the waiter refilled her glass, she smiled appreciatively at him.

'We started in 1971, and we're located in Montgomery, Alabama,' Karen began, holding her glass of red wine up to the light to assess the colour. 'The two founders – who are white by the way – were part of the civil rights movement. They founded the company mainly to work against racism. It doesn't make any money, of course.'

She paused, as if trying to work out how to tell a long story in the shortest possible time.

'From the start you could say we acted as an organization providing free legal aid. Not that I was there at the time!'

Once more her laughter echoed around the room, and an elderly couple two tables away glared in their direction.

'In those days I hadn't even finished elementary school. In 1981 the company set up an information department, simply to make it easier to reach our only real goal: an America that works in agreement with its once revolutionary constitution. For the first few years the struggle was mainly focused on white supremacy groups.'

'Ku Klux Klan,' Johanne said quietly.

'Among others. We've won a series of cases against members of the Klan. A couple of times we've even managed to close down their training camps and busted pretty big active cells. Of course the problem is ...'

She gave a little sigh and took a sip of her wine.

'KKK aren't the only ones in that particular arena. We've got the Imperial Klans of America, the Aryan Nations, the Church of the Creator ... You name it. Over the years our information service has become pretty comprehensive, and today I think we have an overview of 926 different hate groups distributed across the whole of the US. And they're extremely active.'

She emphasized the word *extremely*.

'I presume they're not all working against African-Americans?'

'No indeed. For example, we have black separatist movements that want to get rid of the rest of us. The Jews also have enemies every-where. In the US, too.'

Karen suddenly looked older. The lines around her eyes were not laughter lines, as Johanne had thought. Now that Karen was serious, they were much deeper.

'The Institute for Historical Review, Noontide Press ... way too many. On the other side, the Jews have the Jewish Defense League, which is most definitely a hate organization. So, there is enough hatred to go round in this world. We've got groups who are against South Americans, against Native Americans, for Native Americans, against all immigrants on more general and less prejudiced grounds ...'

An ironic smile ended the sentence. She was speaking more quietly now, but the married couple who had been sitting over by the wall still glared reproachfully at them as they got up to leave. As they passed behind Johanne she heard something about a ruined evening and the fact that there ought to be a limit, even for Americans.

'And then, of course, there are all those who hate gays,' said Karen.

Dessert arrived at their table.

'Strawberry carpaccio with a vanilla crust and a miniature cham-pagne sorbet,' said the waiter, placing the plates in front of them. 'I hope you enjoy it.'

'How big are these groups?' asked Johanne when they were alone again.

Karen stuck her spoon into the slices of strawberry. She rested her elbows on the table and gazed at her food as she answered slowly.

'That's not an easy question to answer, actually. As far as the purely racist organizations are concerned, they're bigger than you can imagine. Some of them are really old, and are run like military forces.

As for the others, particularly the anti-gay groups, it's much more difficult to ...'

She put the spoon in her mouth and closed her eyes in bliss as she chewed. She searched for the right words.

'How shall I put it? ... More difficult to define.'

Johanne nodded. She was also trying to find the right words, and asked: 'Because of strong links with church communities, which are actually legitimate?'

'Yes,' said Karen. 'That's one reason. Initially, we define a hate group as a more or less established organization that fosters hatred against groups, or promotes this hatred in some other way. They're not classified as criminal until they overstep the mark with regard to the rules on freedom of speech to which most countries subscribe, incite others to carry out actions punishable by law, or carry out such actions themselves, where the individual focus of this criminal action is targeted because they belong to a large group of people with specific, recognizable characteristics.'

She let out a long breath.

'That's not the first time you've said that,' smiled Johanne.

'I might have gone through it a few times.'

She was eating more slowly now. Johanne was full to bursting, and pushed her plate away.

'To give you one example,' said Karen. 'This happened in 2007. A young man, Satender Singh, was on holiday at Lake Natoma in California. He was from Fiji, and one day he was at a restaurant with some Indian friends. A group of people who spoke Russian decided that they could tell Satender was gay, and, to cut a long story short, they killed him.'

Johanne sat in silence.

'It does happen that homosexuals are killed just because they're homosexuals,' Karen went on. 'The particular thing about this case was that the murderers belonged to a very large group of Slavic religious immigrants in the Sacramento area. Their church communities are extreme in their condemnation of homosexuality. We're talking about almost a hundred thousand people, divided among seventy fundamentalist congregations in an area which used to be heavily populated by gays. To say that the relationship between these groups is now highly charged would be something of an understatement. The Christians are running an intensive anti-gay propaganda campaign, using both their own TV and radio stations and an enormous capacity to mobilize. At some protest meetings held by gay organizations, there are more anti-demonstrators than demonstrators.'

She took a deep breath and scraped up the remains of her sauce with her fork before going on.

'But when do they take that extra step and become criminals? On the one hand, it's clear they feel hatred. Their use of language and not least the disproportionate amount of attention they give to this whole issue makes it very clear that this is a question of pure, insane hatred. In addition, several of their spiritual leaders have refused to distance themselves from the murder of Satender, for example. On the other hand, freedom of speech is, and will remain, quite far-reaching, and many of those within such communities right across the US are very careful not to incite violence and murder directly.'

'They build the foundations for actions based on hatred, they refuse to condemn such actions when they occur, and afterwards they wash their hands of the whole thing because they didn't come straight out and say "kill them".'

'Exactly,' said Karen, nodding. 'And when a priest proclaims into the ether that homosexuals are wallowing in sin and will die an agonizing death, they will burn in hell, they will ... Well, he can simply say he was referring to the word and the will of God. If one of God's children took him literally, that's not his problem. And as you're well aware, religious freedom and the freedom of speech are ...'

'The very basis of America's existence,' Johanne concluded.

'More coffee?'

The waiter must have had a first-class degree in patience. They had been the only customers in the restaurant for more than half an hour. The staff were just waiting for them to finish. And yet the waiter took the time to top up their coffee cups and fetch more hot milk.

'None of this is good news,' said Karen when he'd gone. 'And apart from these extreme church groups, we have more established organizations in several parts of the US. Like the American Family Association. Of course, they don't incite murder either, but they make a hell of a lot of noise, and constantly create a bad atmosphere when it comes to public debate. A little while ago they started a boycott of McDonald's, of all things.'

'Actually, that sounds quite sensible,' said Johanne with a smile. 'But why?'

'Because the chain had bought advertising space at one of the Gay Pride festivals.'

'And how did it go?'

'The whole thing failed, of course. On that occasion. But some of these groups are powerful and influential; they have plenty of money, and they don't care what methods they use. They certainly express hatred, but you can't call them criminal. But the most frightening thing of all is that ...'

She raised her glass in a silent toast.

'Recently we've seen signs of a more systematic persecution. Six murders of gay men during the past year are still unsolved: three in New York, one in Seattle and two in Dallas. Each case was thoroughly investigated over a long period by the local police. The murders were all carried out using different methods, and other circumstances varied. However, our investigators gradually discovered that two of the victims were cousins; the third had been a school friend of the first; the fourth had travelled around Europe by train with the second; and the last two had had brief relationships with the fourth two years apart. The FBI has taken over the cases. Not that they've got any closer to finding the perpetrator. But our department isn't going to let this go until it's solved.'

'Bloody hell,' Johanne mumbled. 'What theories do you have?'

'Plenty.'

The noise from the kitchen had increased in volume. Whisks and ladles crashed down on metal worktops, and they could clearly hear the dishwasher. Johanne looked at her watch.

'I think we ought to make a move,' she said, hesitating briefly before she added: 'Do you still enjoy walking, Karen?'

'Me? I walk all the time!'

Johanne asked for the bill. It had been ready for a long time, and Karen grabbed it before Johanne had even realized the waiter was there.

'My treat.'

Johanne didn't have the energy to argue.

'Shall we walk back to my place and have a nightcap?' she asked as Karen got out her credit card. 'It's only about twenty minutes from here. Maybe a bit more in this weather.'

'Fantastic,' said Karen delightedly. She showered the waiter with compliments, picked up her coat and headed for the door.

'Oslo is a really quiet city,' she said in surprise when they got outside.

The traffic lights at the junction between Hans Nielsen Hauges Vei and Sandakerveien changed from amber to red with not a car in sight. The dirt and fumes from the day's traffic were concealed beneath a thin layer of fresh snow. There was hardly a footprint to be seen on the pavement. The clouds hung low over the city, and towards the south-west a pale yellow glow shone from the street lamps in the centre.

'This is mainly a residential area,' said Johanne. 'And in any case people don't go out much at night after Christmas. Norwegians party themselves to a standstill in December. January is the month of good intentions.'

They passed the video shop on the corner and set off along Sandakerveien.

'Where were we?' said Karen.

'Your theories,' Johanne reminded her. 'About those six murders.'

'Ah yes.'

Karen knotted her scarf more tightly as they walked. Johanne had forgotten how tall and long-legged her friend was; she had to hurry to keep up with Karen.

'As far as the anti-gay movement goes, we've seen some strange new alliances. Jews and Christians, Muslims and even extreme right-wing groups haven't been able to live in peace for hundreds and hundreds of years, but now they've found a common enemy: the gay community. We've just registered a group who call themselves "The 25'ers". The curious thing about them is that they work very quietly.'

'Quietly? Isn't the whole point of groups like that to make as much noise as possible?'

'As a rule. But these people are different. We think they originate from more traditional fundamentalist environments on both the Muslim and the Christian side. It's as if they think everything is moving too slowly. That it's time to do something radical. It's the same people as before, but

194

in a different combination, so to speak. They have the same goals, but are planning to use completely different methods to achieve them.'

They walked on for a while in silence. The conversation had taken an unpleasant turn, and Johanne wasn't sure she wanted to follow it to its conclusion.

'What methods?' she asked anyway as they reached the point where Sandakerveien levels out and curves towards the north-west.

Karen stopped so abruptly that Johanne had gone a couple of metres before she realized.

'Oslo isn't exactly a beautiful city,' said Karen, looking around.

Johanne smiled.

'I think the point where we're standing right now is the ugliest, most depressing place in the entire city,' she said. 'Not that I think our city is particularly beautiful, but don't judge it by what you see here.'

On the right-hand side lay several box-shaped warehouses, trying to hide beneath the snow as if out of sheer embarrassment. In front of them – where Nycoveien takes a couple of hundred metres to reach a desolate roundabout – half the wall of Storosentret had been torn down because the complex was being extended. The vast, patched-up shopping centre looked more like a ruin than a building site. From the roof a gigantic red O flashed in the darkness, an inflamed Cyclops eye. Between the two streets an office block with vertical turquoise stripes cast garish reflections on the snow. On the left-hand side stood a handful of yellow brick buildings at an angle. For some reason the architect had thought it a good idea to put all the pipes on the outside; it looked like the backdrop to a cheap sci-fi film.

'It'll be better when we get up to Nydalen,' said Johanne. 'Come on.'

They set off again, trudging along in the middle of the road.

'So far we don't know nearly enough about The 25'ers,' said Karen as they picked up speed. 'But we have reason to believe that an unholy alliance – to put it mildly – has been formed between fundamentalist Muslims and fundamentalist Christians. We have a theory that the name comes from the digit sum of the numbers 19, 24 and 27, the first number relating to the Koran and the other two referring to the Bible – St Paul's Epistle to the Romans. All very complicated. Of course we're not talking about some kind of church community here. Nor a political group.'

'So what are they?'

'A militant group. A paramilitary force. We think we've identified at least three of the members: two ultra-conservative Christians and one Muslim. All three have a military background. One was actually a Navy Seal. The problem is they know that we know who they are, and they've gone quiet. All they're doing at the moment is behaving perfectly normally. Unfortunately, we have reason to believe the group is quite large. Large and extremely well run. The FBI are banging their heads against a brick wall, and there's not much the APLC can do under the circumstances. But we're trying, of course. We're trying as hard as we can.'

'But what is it these people actually do?'

'They murder homosexuals and lesbians,' said Karen. 'The 25'ers is an organization for the discontented. Those who want action, not words.'

She paused as they moved to the side of the road to avoid an oncoming car.

'Fortunately, we make do with shouting at each other in Norway, thank God,' said Johanne.

Karen gave a wry smile as she stopped at the next roundabout. 'That's how it starts. That's exactly how it starts.'

There were no cars in sight, and they crossed the road.

'Is the anti-gay movement in Norway mainly religious?' asked Karen.

'To a certain extent. I'd say the element that can be defined as a movement is characterized by the Christian conservatives. Some individuals are trying to construct a more morally philosophical platform for their homophobic arguments. But when you examine their reasoning, you discover they all have a deep faith in God as their starting point.' She took a deep breath and sighed heavily. 'And then there's the constant whining from the caravans.'

'Caravans?'

'It's just an expression. I mean the masses. Not particularly Christian and most definitely not philosophical. They just don't like gays.'

They had reached the Congress Centre, and Karen stopped in front of one of G-sports windows. It obviously wasn't the January sales display of ski equipment she was interested in, because she was looking at the reflection of Johanne's face in the glass.

'I've always thought you were so far ahead when it came to equality. Anti-racism. Gay rights.'

She suddenly leaned closer to the window, mumbling something that sounded like a calculation.

'A thousand dollars? For those skis? I've got exactly the same ones, and they cost 450. I'm beginning to understand why the average wage is so high in this country.'

'Something happened here when gays started having children,' Johanne said thoughtfully, as if she'd suddenly been struck by a fresh insight. 'Before that, most things were running fairly smoothly. But this business with children has caused a real backlash.'

The cloud cover had broken up. Over Grefsenkollen three stars appeared on a strip of black. The wind had increased since they left the restaurant, and the temperature must have fallen. Johanne put her hands together and blew warm air into her woollen gloves. The wind carried with it a damp chill, and she pushed her hands in her pockets with her gloves on.

'More and more lesbians are having children,' she went on. 'At the beginning of this year a new gender-neutral law on marriage was brought in, guaranteeing the same rights to IVF as heterosexuals. In recent years gay men have also started on the same route, travelling to the US and using egg donors and surrogate mothers. All of which has led to ...'

They set off again.

'Do you know what they call those children?' she said angrily. 'Half-manufactured. Constructed children!'

Karen shrugged her shoulders.

'History repeats itself,' she said wearily. 'There's nothing new under the sun. When the first marriages between blacks and whites took place, some people claimed it went against God's commandments. That it was against the will of God and nature and customs and against everything we were used to. Their children were also given a nickname: half-castes. Which sounds quite a lot like your half-manufactured.'

She took a deep breath.

'It will pass, Johanne. In a few days a "half-caste" president will be inaugurated back home. Six years ago no one – but no one – would have thought that we would have a woman president, and now an

African-American. It's a pity about Helen Bentley, by the way. I was sorry she didn't want to stand for a further term. I've nothing but praise for Obama, but deep down ...'

It was half past eleven. A bus came chugging towards them. The driver was yawning as it passed, but he gave a start when a cat suddenly ran into the road, causing him to slam on the brakes.

'Deep down I think it was an even greater victory to get a woman president in the White House,' Karen said quietly, as if entrusting Johanne with a dangerous secret. 'And when the most powerful leader in the world says she's throwing in the towel for the sake of her family after only four years, I reserve the right not to believe her.'

Johanne tried to suppress a smile. She didn't often feel the need to share the story of the dramatic events that took place in May 2005. The twenty-four hours she had spent with Helen Bentley in an apartment in Frogner, while the whole world assumed the American president was dead, had over the years become a locked-in memory which she rarely opened in order to examine it more closely. She had been instructed to keep quiet in the interests of the security of both Norway and the United States, and had kept all the pledges she had signed. Now, for the first time, she was tempted to break her word.

'I've never heard of The 25'ers,' she said instead. 'Tell me more.'

They had reached Gullhaug Torg.

Karen moved her bag to the other shoulder. She opened her mouth a couple of times without saying anything, as if she didn't really know what words to choose.

'Rage,' she said eventually. 'While the rest of the hate groups grow strong on frenzy, prejudice and misdirected religious fervour, organizations like The 25'ers are built on holy rage. That's something different. Something much more dangerous.'

They stopped on the bridge over the Akerselva and leaned against the railing. The water level was low, and beautiful ice sculptures had formed along the edges.

'How ... how do all these organizations finance their activities?' asked Johanne.

'It varies,' Karen replied. 'When it comes to the extreme church groups, they finance themselves just like any other faith community. Rich members and generous donations. And they're not that expensive to run. The more militant groups also collect money from their members. But we think some of them are partly funded through serious crime.'

She paused and looked at a lovely arch of ice spanning three large rocks.

'The Ku Klux Klan and the Aryan Nations, for example. While KKK has traditionally directed its hatred against African-Americans – and they've killed God knows how many over the years – the Aryan Nations base their existence on a pseudo-theological belief that it's the Anglo-Saxons, not the Jews, who are God's chosen people. They hate the blacks as well, of course, but for them it's the Jews who are the real virus infecting the pure body of humanity. They rally an enormous amount of support in jails, something which has been a deliberate policy on the part of their leaders. Their money comes from ...'

She turned to Johanne and held up one finger at a time on her left hand.

'Fraud, larceny, narcotics, bank robberies.'

Four fingers stuck up in the air before her thumb joined them.

'And murder. Professional murderers. There are actually those who provide that service.'

Johanne didn't know much about the professional murder industry, and didn't reply.

'Someone orders a murder through an intermediary,' Karen explained. 'If the intended victim happens to be gay, you can hire a killer who thinks people like that should die anyway. If the victim is black you find an organization ...'

She raised her shoulders to make the point.

'You get the idea.'

A solitary duck had settled down for the night on the west bank of the river. It withdrew its beak from under its wing and stared at them in the hope that the two women on the bridge might have brought along some bread. When nothing happened it tucked its head down and became a round ball of feathers once again.

'When it comes to The 25'ers, we know far too little about them,' said Karen. 'However, we know enough to conclude that they remind us of The Order, who sprang up in the eighties as a splinter group from the KKK and AN. They were going to start a revolution and bring down the American government. The most striking difference between them and these new groups is the level of cooperation between different religions. And unfortunately they're not alone. For example, there's another splinter group from—'

'Stop,' Johanne said with a smile, putting her arm around Karen's shoulders. 'I can't cope with any more. I think we should say that's enough talk of hatred for tonight. I want to hear about your children, your husband, your brother! Is he still such a ladies' man?'

'You bet! He's on his third marriage!'

Johanne tucked her hand under Karen's arm as they set off again.

'Not far now,' she said, guiding her off to the right. 'Adam will be so pleased to see you.'

It was true. He would be pleased, however late it was.

By the time she had dealt with the children, her job, the house and the rest of the family, Johanne usually had no energy left. She and Adam sometimes went out to dinner, usually with old friends, but she always dreaded it. On very rare occasions they would invite someone round. It was always enjoyable, but took all of her strength for several days before and after. Adam, on the other hand, was good at pursuing his own interests as soon as he had an hour to spare. He devoted a lot of time to his grandson Amund, who had been a tiny baby when Adam's grown-up daughter and wife died in a tragic accident. He also met friends. And he had recently started saying that he wanted to have a horse again – as if he had ten or twelve hours a week he didn't know how to fill.

And he was always on at her. Go out. Ask somebody round. Ring a friend and go and see a film.

'Kristiane will be fine without you for a couple of hours,' he would say, more often than Johanne would like to admit.

Adam would be delighted.

They had almost reached Maridalsveien. The clouds were scudding across the sky, and the soughing of the bare treetops almost drowned out the hum of the traffic on Ringveien to the north.

Three minutes and they'd be home.

She was almost tempted to wake up Kristiane.

Just to show her off.

And When You Get There

'First of all I have to show you this,' said Kjetil Berggren, placing four items in front of her on a white cloth. 'Take all the time you need.'

His voice was quiet and almost overflowing with empathy, as if they were already at Marianne's funeral. In which case they would both have been inappropriately dressed. It was Saturday 10 January and Kjetil Berggren's scruffy anorak was hanging on a hook by the door. As he walked around the table to sit down again, he had to pull up one of his knee socks.

'I'd been expecting a skin suit and skates,' Synnøve said.

The detective didn't reply.

'I'm feeling better now,' she said tonelessly. 'It's fine.'

For the first time in exactly two week she had slept. Really slept. As soon as Berggren and the priest had dared to leave her in peace the previous evening, she had fed the dogs and fallen into bed. Fourteen hours later, she woke up. She had lain there for a few seconds not really knowing where she was or what she was feeling. When the realization that Marianne was dead suddenly hit her, she had started crying again. But this was different, in spite of everything. There was no longer anything to worry about. Marianne was dead, and the search was over. At some point in the future it would be possible to live with her grief. She realized this now, after fourteen days in hell. What had been a painful inertia had gradually turned into movement. Towards something. And when she arrived there, everything would be better.

This morning she had really noticed how tense she had been over the past two weeks. Her back was aching and it was difficult to move her head from side to side. Her jaws almost felt locked when she tried to eat a little porridge as a late breakfast. In the end she gave up and ran herself a scalding hot bath. She had lain there until the water grew cold and the skin on the tips of her fingers started to crinkle.

Synnøve Hessel had wandered around the empty house. She had brought Kaja inside for company and consolation, for the first time ever. Marianne had made it a condition of keeping huskies that they had to stay outside. Kaja had hesitated on the doorstep, before eventually allowing herself to be enticed inside and up on to the sofa. They had grieved there together, Synnøve and the dog, until Kjetil Berggren came to pick her up at three o'clock, as agreed.

She was sitting in the same room as before. An officer from Oslo had been there when she arrived, but she didn't want to talk to anyone but Kjetil. Not yet.

'I realize this has all been very difficult for you, Synnøve, and I—'

'Kjetil,' she broke in. 'I mean it. If you had any idea how I've been feeling since Marianne disappeared, you'd realize it's much easier to ...'

She stopped and closed her eyes.

'If we could just get this over and done with.'

'Have you had those cuts on your face looked at?' he asked.

'They're just superficial.'

Kjetil Berggren looked as if he were about to protest. Instead, he nodded at the objects between them on the desk.

'Can I touch them?' she asked.

'I'm afraid not.'

The white gold wedding ring was slightly bigger than her own. The inlaid diamond was dull, and might have gone unnoticed had she not known it was there. It was Marianne who had wanted diamonds. Synnøve had preferred a perfectly ordinary ring made of ordinary gold, without embellishments – a traditional wedding ring. She wanted to be married to Marianne in the same way everybody else is married, so the ring should be plain and gold.

'We didn't have time to get married,' she said.

'I thought you were—'

'We were registered partners – as if we were running a business together or something. But with the new law and everything, we were planning to get married properly in the summer.'

The tears made the cuts on her face smart.

'Anyway, the ring looks like hers.'

She held up her right hand limply to show its twin. Then she took a deep breath and went on much too quickly: 'The necklace too. The keys are definitely hers. I've never seen that USB stick before, but we must have about thirty lying around the house. Can you take them away now? *Can you take them away?!*' She hid her face in her hands. 'I assume,' she said, her voice muffled, 'that I have to identify these things because you don't want me to see Marianne.'

Kjetil Berggren didn't reply. Quickly, without touching the four objects, he slipped each one into a plastic bag and carefully folded the cloth around them.

'Of course, we'll have a DNA analysis done as well,' he said. 'But unfortunately there seems to be little doubt that the deceased is Marianne.'

'They said she'd paid,' said Synnøve, placing her hands on her knee at last. 'At the hotel, they said Marianne had paid for the room!'

'Yes, the bill had been paid. But not by her.'

'By whom, then? If someone else paid it must be the murderer, and in that case it should be easy to ... Haven't they got CCTV? Guest lists? It must be the simplest thing in the world to ...'

She fell silent when she saw the expression on Kjetil's face.

'The Continental has video surveillance in certain parts of the building,' he said slowly. 'In reception, among other places. Unfortunately, the tapes are erased after seven days. Next week they're switching to digital recordings, and then everything will be saved for much longer. Up to now they've been using old-fashioned equipment. Videotapes. It's not possible to keep them for ever.'

'Videotapes,' she whispered in disbelief. 'In a luxury hotel?'

He nodded and went on: 'The bill was paid on the evening of the nineteenth. We can tell that from the till. The receptionist insists it was a man who paid for the room. In cash. He can't really give us anything in the way of a more detailed description. There were a hell of a lot of people there that evening, bang in the middle of the Christmas party season. The Theatre Café was packed, and you can go straight from there into the foyer, where there's another bar. You pass reception on the way.'

'Does that mean ... ?'

Synnøve didn't know herself what that was supposed to mean.

'There was also a wedding reception that evening,' Kjetil went on. 'Lots of activity and noise. And apparently there was some kind of dramatic incident involving a child who went outside and almost got run over by a bus. No, hang on, a tram. Anyway, there was a huge commotion, and for the life of him the receptionist can't remember much about the actual payment.'

'But who ... who in the world would do all this? I just can't understand ... To murder her, hide her, pay the bill ... It's so absurd that ... Who on earth would think of doing such a thing?!'

'That's what we're trying to work out,' Kjetil said calmly. 'The key question is *why* Marianne was murdered. If you have any information whatsoever that might help us to—'

'Of course I haven't,' she snapped. 'Of course I haven't a clue why anyone would want to kill Marianne! Apart from her bloody parents!'

He didn't bother to comment on that.

Synnøve tugged at her sweater. She picked up the glass of water and put it down again without having a drink. Fiddled with her wedding ring. Ran her fingers through her hair.

Tried to make the time pass.

That was what she must focus on in the days to come. Making the time pass. Time heals all wounds, but whenever she glanced at the clock only half a minute had passed since the last time.

And no wounds had healed.

'Can I go?' she mumbled.

'Of course. I'll drive you. We're going to have to trouble you with more questions before too long, but—'

'Who?'

'Sorry?'

'Who's going to trouble me with more questions?'

'Since the body was found in Oslo, and all the indications are that the crime took place there, this is a case for the Oslo police. Naturally, we'll be assisting them as necessary, but—'

'I'd like to go now.'

She stood up. Kjetil Berggren noticed that her sweater was too big, and her shoulders were drooping. She must have lost five or six kilos in just a couple of weeks. Six kilos she couldn't afford to lose.

'You must eat,' he said. 'Are you eating?'

Without replying she picked up her quilted jacket from the back of the chair.

'You don't need to drive me,' she said. 'I'll walk.'

'But it'll only take me three minutes to—'

'I'll walk,' she broke in.

In the doorway she turned back and looked at him.

'You didn't believe me,' she said. 'You didn't believe me when I said something terrible had happened to Marianne.'

He examined his nails without saying a word.

'I hope that haunts you,' she said.

He nodded, still without looking up.

It doesn't haunt me at all, he thought. *It doesn't haunt me because Marianne was long dead by the time you came to us.*

But he didn't say anything.

*

She couldn't complain about the efficiency. The police sketch artist had produced not only a full-face picture but also a profile, a full-length picture from the front, and a detailed drawing of some kind of emblem or pin which Martin Setre claimed the man had been wearing on his lapel. Silje Sørensen leafed quickly through the drawings before laying all four out on the desk in front of her.

She was sceptical about sketches like these, even though she was the one who had requested them.

Most people made terrible witnesses. Exactly the same situation or exactly the same person could be described afterwards in completely different ways. Witnesses would talk about things that didn't exist, events that had never taken place. Animatedly and in detail. They weren't lying. They just remembered incorrectly and filled the gaps in their memory with their own experiences and fantasies.

At the same time, facial composites could sometimes be absolutely key. The artist had to be skilful and the witness particularly observant. There were advanced computer programs that could do the work more easily and in certain cases more precisely, but she preferred drawings done by hand.

And that was what she'd got.

She studied the portrait.

The man was white, and probably somewhere between thirty-five and fifty. From the notes in the file she could see that Martin Setre wasn't absolutely sure whether the man had shaved his head or had actually lost his hair. He was bald, at any rate. Round face. Dark eyes, no glasses. The nose was straight and the chin broad, almost angular. A narrow double chin framed the lower part of his face. He was heavily built, she could see that from the full-length drawing too, but not necessarily overweight. His height was estimated at around one metre seventy.

A short, stocky man who was smiling.

Silje presumed the picture had been drawn like that because the man had been smiling all the time. She glanced through the notes and her theory was confirmed.

Nice teeth.

His clothes were dark. A dark overcoat and a dark shirt. The tie was also dark, and the knot seemed loose. The drawing was in black and white, and all the monochrome tones made her feel pessimistic. When she held up the full-length picture and examined it more closely, it struck her that there must be thousands of men who looked more or less like this. Admittedly, Martin had said that the man spoke English or American, but using a different language from one's own was an old and well-established trick.

He had just a suspicion of dimples.

Knut Bork came in without knocking, and she gave a start.

'Sorry,' he said in surprise. 'I didn't know you were here. Haven't you got anything better to do on a Saturday afternoon?'

'If I hadn't been here, the door wouldn't have been open, would it?'

'I ...'

Knut Bork was tall and fair-skinned, almost pale, with red-blonde hair and ice-blue eyes. When he blushed he did it properly: he looked like a traffic light.

'It's fine,' said Silje, holding out her hand. 'What did you want to leave me?'

'This,' he said amiably, handing her a thin folder. 'It's to go in the Marianne Kleive file.'

She took the papers and put them down next to the sketches without looking at them more closely.

'Exactly what we needed right now,' she said. 'A spectacular murder at one of the city's best hotels. Have you seen the evening papers?'

He raised his eyebrows and let out a long, slow sigh.

'Anything new?' she asked, nodding at the folder.

'Only a couple of new witness statements. Half of Oslo seems to have been at that bloody hotel that night. And you know how it is – everybody thinks they have something interesting to pass on. The phones are red-hot with people wanting to talk.'

Silje picked up her cup of coffee.

'Sometimes no witnesses are better than a thousand witnesses,' she said. 'The worst thing is that we have to take them all seriously. Someone might actually have seen something relevant. Cheers!'

The coffee was bitter and lukewarm.

'Shouldn't you be going home soon?'

'The same applies to you,' he said. 'You got the drawings? Can I have a look?'

He came around the desk and leaned over the sketches.

'No particular distinguishing features,' he murmured.

'No. He's below average height, but the very word "average" tells you he's not the only one—'

'Do you think we're barking up the wrong tree here?'

He held one of the pictures up at eye level.

'Maybe,' she sighed. 'But it's the only tree we've got.'

'What's that?' he asked, pointing to the sketch of a lapel. 'A pin?'

'Something like that. Do you recognize it?'

'It's a clover leaf, isn't it?'

'Yes.'

'All the pictures are black and white, but the clover leaf is red.'

'Martin insisted he was absolutely certain. We generally prefer not to have any colour in these sketches, because it can be confusing. But this pin – or whatever it is – was evidently red, no doubt about it.'

'And these ... flourishes, what are they supposed to be?'

They both examined the picture. On each leaf was a shape that might possibly be a letter in an unfamiliar alphabet.

'Martin said there was a letter on each leaf,' said Silje. 'But he couldn't remember what they were.'

Knut Bork picked up a box of lozenges from the desk.

'Can I have one?' he asked, sticking his finger in the box before she had time to answer.

'Help yourself,' Silje mumbled. 'Have five. There's something familiar about that logo, isn't there?'

'Yes,' said Knut Bork, and suddenly he started to laugh. 'You're right there! My grandmother has one on every single jacket she owns!'

His laughter broke off abruptly. Silje looked up at him. His face was bright red once again, and he was gasping like a fish on dry land.

'Knut,' she said tentatively. 'Are you all right? Have you ...'

She got up so quickly that the desk chair rolled away and crashed into the wall behind her. Knut Bork was considerably taller than her. For a moment she thought about climbing up on to the desk, but dismissed the idea. She wrapped her arms around him from behind and linked her hands in front of him with her right thumb pointing in towards his body. Then she squeezed with every scrap of strength she could summon.

Three black projectiles flew out of his mouth.

He coughed and took a deep breath, and she let go.

'Thanks,' he panted. 'I couldn't get ... Look at that!'

He pointed to the wall opposite them. The throat lozenges had stuck to the wall in a triangle, with less than half a centimetre between them.

'Bang on target,' he puffed.

She looked at him, her eyebrows raised, and sat down again. 'Perhaps now you can tell me about this logo?'

His voice still sounded hoarse as he cleared his throat and said: '*Norske Kvinners Sanitetsforening.*'

'What?'

'The letters are N, K and S. *Norske Kvinners Sanitetsforening* – the Norwegian Women's Public Health Association.'

She pulled the drawing of the logo towards her, as if he had insulted her. A red clover leaf with a stalk, and a letter on each leaf.

'I need to check,' she muttered as she put down the sheet of paper and typed the name of the association into the search box on her computer.

'There you go,' said Knut Bork. 'What did I tell you?'

She was staring at the association's homepage.

The logo was a red clover leaf with the letters NKS in white. One on each leaf.

'What the … ?'

She couldn't marshal her thoughts.

'A punter who pays for sex, and a possible murderer,' she began, the words coming out in a staccato rhythm. 'Of the male gender. Going around. Pulling young lads. In the middle of Oslo.'

She swallowed and moistened her lips with her tongue.

'With a membership badge of the Norwegian Women's Public Health Association clearly visible on the lapel of his jacket. What the hell is going on? Is he taking the piss or what?'

Knut Bork picked up the drawing and walked over to the notice-board by the window. He pinned it up and took two steps back. He stood there for a while, his head tilted to one side, then he suddenly turned to Silje and nodded.

'Perhaps that's exactly what he's doing, Silje. Perhaps this guy is trying to take the piss.'

*

When the man on the phone said he was from the police, Marcus Koll Junior thought for a confused moment that someone was trying to play a joke on him. When he realized a few seconds later that he was mistaken, he got up and started pacing back and forth across the living room. To begin with he was concentrating so hard on sounding unconcerned that he didn't grasp what the man was actually saying.

They couldn't possibly know anything.

It was simply unthinkable, he tried to convince himself.

He stopped by the big windows looking south.

The sloping garden was lit up. Fir trees heavy with snow were an almost fluorescent ice-blue against the dense darkness beyond the fence. Low cloud hid the city and the fjord. From where he was standing, the world beyond his own domain did not exist.

Except on the telephone.

'I'm sorry,' said Marcus, trying to put a smile into his voice. 'I wonder if you could possibly go over that again? The connection isn't very good.'

'The information,' the voice said, clearly impatient. 'You called us on Monday with information about that series of break-ins.'

A faint puff of wind brought the snow cascading down from the nearest tree. The dry crystals sparkled in the lamplight. Right down at the bottom of the garden stood two tall pine trees with bare, erect trunks and rounded crowns, like soldiers standing to attention on sentry duty.

Marcus tried to absorb the feeling of relief.

He'd been right. Of course they didn't know anything

There was no cause for alarm.

'Oh,' was all he said, swallowing. 'I don't think that was me.'

'Aren't I speaking to Rolf Slettan?' said the voice at the other end of the phone. 'On 2307****?'

'No,' said Marcus, concentrating on breathing calmly. 'He's my husband. Rolf. He was the one who called you. My name is Marcus Koll. As I said when I answered the phone.'

There was silence for a couple of seconds.

That brief moment of silent confusion, thought Marcus. Or disgust. Or both. He was used to it, just as everyone grows used to a stigma when they have carried it for long enough. Before little Marcus started school, Marcus Koll Junior had persuaded *Dagens Næringsliv* to do a profile on him, pointing out that he was the only gay man with a husband and a child on the list of the hundred wealthiest people in the country. He hoped that little Marcus would be protected by the fact that everyone knew, and didn't need to whisper. That he wouldn't need to deal with it all later, when they found out.

It occurred to him several weeks later that not everyone read *Dagens Næringsliv*.

'Oh yes,' the voice at the other end of the line said eventually. 'Is … is he at home? Rolf Slettan?'

'Yes, but he's just putting our son to bed.'

This time the silence lasted so long that Marcus thought they'd been cut off.

'Hello?' he said loudly.

'Yes,' said the man. 'I'm here. Could you ask him to ring me? The information he gave has just been left lying around here, and I've got a couple of questions I'd like to—'

'Is it the number that came up on the display?' Marcus interrupted.

'Er … yes, that's fine. Tell him to ask for Constable Pettersen. Is he likely to ring this evening?'

'I wouldn't have thought so,' said Marcus. 'We have plans for this evening. But of course, if it's important I can ask him to call you. In half an hour or so.'

'That would be great, if you could. There was another break-in last night, and it would be—'

'Certainly. I'll tell him.'

He ended the conversation without any further farewell phrases, and put the phone down on the coffee table. It struck him that the room was too dark. He slowly walked around, from one source of light to the next, until the room was so well lit that the view of the garden almost disappeared in the sharp contrast between outside and inside.

Rolf had told him about the tyre tracks by the gate. To begin with Marcus had been surprised, almost annoyed that Rolf was getting so worked up about the fact that someone had pulled into the small area by the side of the road. It wasn't fenced off, and was a natural place to give way to oncoming traffic. Since the snow had started falling heavily after New Year, he had seen tracks there all the time.

It wasn't until Rolf had the chance to explain more clearly that Marcus was prepared to discuss the matter. He had to admit that it seemed strange for someone to stay there for a while, as the varying depth of the tracks and the number of cigarette butts seemed to indicate. When Rolf stubbornly maintained that the same car had been parked further up the road while he was examining the tracks by the gate, and had taken off as soon as he showed interest in it, Marcus fell silent.

Rolf's strong feeling that someone had been watching them fitted all too well with his own growing sense of unease. More and more often he caught himself looking over his shoulder for something, although he didn't know what it was. Or perhaps it would be more accurate to say he was looking for *someone*. Up to now he hadn't been able to put his finger on anything concrete, but ever since before Christmas the impression that he had a living shadow had grown stronger and stronger. Only after New Year had he realized that the panic attack that had almost brought him to his knees four days before

Christmas, after remaining at bay for many years, was not only due to the pangs of conscience with which he had been wrestling.

It was as if someone were keeping an eye on him.

The problem, as Marcus Koll Junior saw it, was that this surveillance presumably had nothing whatsoever to do with gangs of thieves and a spate of housebreaking.

If someone were spying on him, of course.

'No,' he said out loud, and sat down in the armchair again.

It was bound to be his imagination.

It had to be his imagination.

He was easily frightened at the moment, much too easily frightened, and Rolf's observations could just as easily be linked to a couple of young lovers who had stopped for a cuddle. A kiss and a smoke. Or perhaps a responsible driver who had stopped to answer his mobile.

The doorbell rang.

The babysitter, he thought, and closed his eyes.

It was ten o'clock, and he was really too tired to go out.

In three months and five days it would be ten years since his father's death.

Marcus Koll opened his eyes, stood up and tugged hard on both his earlobes to perk himself up. The doorbell rang again. As he crossed the living room he decided that 15 April would be the day when all his troubles would come to an end. Despite the fact that the date had lost its original significance, he would still use it as a milestone in his life: 15 April would be the turning point, and everything would be the way it had been before. If he could just get there. The house on the ridge would once again become a fortress; his secure framework around his family, far beyond his father's dominion.

It was a promise he made to himself, and for some reason it made him feel a little bit better.

Before the Day Dawns

Johanne felt remarkably contented when the alarm clock rang at the early hour of five-thirty on the morning of Monday, 12 January. At first she couldn't work out why she was being woken up so early, and lay there in that pleasant no-man's-land between dream and reality, while Adam hurled himself at the wretched thing and silenced it. The dry warmth beneath the covers made her draw them more closely around her. When Adam lay down again with a groan she wriggled up against his back.

'I've got to go,' he murmured. 'The plane to Bergen leaves in two hours.'

'Ragnhild's asleep,' she whispered. 'Kristiane and Jack are at Isak's. Can't you stay for quarter of an hour?'

It cost him his breakfast, and as he sat in the car on the way to Gardermoen just after six-thirty, late and with grumbling pains in his stomach, he almost regretted it.

Johanne, on the other hand, felt better than she had for a long time. The evening with Karen Winslow had gone on until three o'clock on Saturday morning. It would have been even later if Karen hadn't had to drive a good 200 kilometres to Lillesand the following day. Adam had taken Ragnhild to visit his son-in-law and his grandson Amund on Saturday morning, and stayed out all day. Johanne had slept for longer than she could ever remember. After a long breakfast and three hours with the Saturday papers, she had driven to Tøyenbadet and swum 1,500 metres. In the evening Sigmund Berli had called round. Uninvited. He had brought pizza and warm beer. The unwelcome guest gave Johanne a good excuse to go to bed before ten o'clock.

It had done her good.

She was still feeling happy after meeting up with her old friend.

Ragnhild had gone to bed too late on the Sunday, and she had finally reached the age where she caught up on some lost sleep the following day. Johanne ambled around in Adam's huge pyjamas, made a big pot of coffee and settled down on the sofa with the laptop on her knee. Her teaching commitments hadn't yet started post-Christmas, and she had decided to spend the day at home. She would leave Ragnhild to sleep until she woke up, despite the fact that the woman who ran the nursery got annoyed if she wasn't dropped off before ten.

Johanne checked her e-mail; she had nine new messages. Most of them were of no interest. One was from the police. She glanced through it quickly, and realized immediately that it was the same message Adam had received on Saturday morning about the murder of Marianne Kleive. The police had obtained a complete guest list from the wedding reception at the Continental, and were making routine enquiries as to whether any of the guests had noticed anything that might be relevant to the case. Johanne deleted the message straight away. Adam had already replied for both of them, besides which she wanted to devote as little thought as possible to that terrible evening when Kristiane had almost been hit by a tram.

Karen Winslow had already replied to the question Johanne had sent the previous day. She pulled the blanket more tightly around her and opened the message as she sipped the scalding hot coffee.

Dear Johanne,

It was so great to see you! A wonderful evening and an interesting(!) walk through the city! Meeting your husband was fantastic, and I have to say – my own man has one or two things to learn from him. His warmth and generosity when we showed up in the middle of the night exceeded all expectations.

I'm writing you from Oslo Airport. The wedding was unbelievable, but the drive to and from Lillesand a nightmare.

As we agreed, I'll fill you in on some of the most relevant parts of our research / intelligence as soon as I can. Just to respond to the questions in your message of this morning: the name 'The 25'ers' is based on the sum of the digits in 19, 24 and 27 (did I tell you that?). Our theory is that the numbers 24 and 27 point to St Paul's Epistle to the Romans, chapter 1 verses 24 and 27. Look it up yourself. The number 19 is claimed to have a somehow 'magical' significance in the Koran. It's too complicated to explain here, but if you google 'Rashad Khalifa' you'll figure it out. If our numerologists are correct, the name 'The 25'ers' is quite scary …

They're calling my flight now, so I'll have to run.

And don't you forget – you and your family have PROMISED to come visit us this summer!

All the best and a big hug,
Karen

Johanne read through the message again. She needed a printout to remember the strange references. The printer was in the bedroom. As she opened the door the closed-in smell of sheets, sleep and sex hit her. Adam refused to sleep with the window open when the mercury dropped below minus five. Quickly she linked the computer to the printer. When the rasping sound told her that the document was being printed, she went over to the window and threw it wide open.

She closed her eyes against the fresh, cold air.

The Bible, she thought.

She wasn't even sure if they had one, but she knew there was a copy of the Koran in Adam's bookcase. He insisted on having a bookcase of his own in the bedroom, five metres of shelving containing an absurd mixture of books. The Book Club's splendid series on holy scriptures stood alongside reference books on weapons, huge works on heraldry, almost twenty books about horses and bloodlines, an ancient edition of the *Encyclopaedia Britannica*, plus everything that had ever been drawn and published by Frode Øverli. Leaving the window open, she crouched down in front of the bookcase on Adam's side of the double bed. The Koran was easy to find: its spine was adorned with gold leaf and Oriental patterns. The book standing next to it was so worn that the spine was missing. When she carefully took it out, the covers felt soft with age.

The Bible.

Slowly she opened it. There was ornate handwriting on the flyleaf: *To Adam from Grandma and Granddad, 16 September 1956.* She quickly worked out that it must have been the day of his christening; Adam was born on Midsummer's Eve that same year.

She half-closed the window and tucked both books under her arm. With the printout in one hand and the laptop in the other, she went back to the sofa.

She saw that Adam's Bible was the old translation. She found Paul's Epistle to the Romans, and ran her finger down the page.

24. *Wherefore God gave them up to the desires of their heart, unto uncleanness: to dishonour their own bodies among themselves.*

She stopped.

... to dishonour their own bodies among themselves ...

'Presumably that means they had sex with one another,' she murmured, before her eyes found verse 27.

... And, in like manner, the men also, leaving the natural use of the women, have burned in their lusts, one towards another: men with men, working that which is filthy and receiving in themselves the recompense which was due to their error.

Even though she basically understood what it meant, she closed the tattered book and pulled the laptop on to her knee. She should have thought of this in the first place, instead of rooting around in Adam's bookcase. She had done something similar only once before, and he had been cross for hours afterwards.

It took her two minutes to find the same text on the Internet, but in the new translation.

Therefore God gave them over in the sinful desires of their hearts to sexual impurity for the degrading of their bodies with one another.

Much clearer, she thought, with a slight shake of her head.

Verse 27 was also clearer when clothed in more modern language.

In the same way the men also abandoned natural relations with women and were inflamed with lust for one another. Men committed shameful acts with other men, and received in themselves the due penalty for their error.

Johanne regarded herself as an agnostic. For her that was just a more elegant word for 'indifferent'. However, she had to deal with believers in her work and always tried to do so with due respect. Apart from a brief flirtation with religion in her teens, faith in God had never really interested her.

Until now.

Over the past few months she had been forced to develop a relationship with various religions on the most intense level. Texts such as the ones she had just read didn't frighten her in themselves. As a researcher and a non-believer, she looked at them within the historical context and found them quite interesting. However, taken literally with relevance to people living in 2009, she thought Paul's words were appalling.

If Karen and the APLC were right, and the name 'The 25ers' really could be traced back to these verses, then they must be an organization working directly against homosexuals and lesbians. Without paraphrasing. No church group. No religious community.

A pure hate group.

If ultra-conservative Christians really had joined up with radical Muslims in a new organization of their own, there was every reason to believe that their hatred was more violent than any she had spent the last few months examining more closely.

She read the last line again:

... received in themselves the due penalty for their error.

She shuddered and picked up the printout of Karen's e-mail.

The number 19. The Arabic-sounding name Rashad Khalifa. Her fingers flew over the keyboard: 4,400 hits on Google.

'Morning, Mummy. I need porridge.'

Ragnhild scurried across the living-room floor on bare feet. Johanne just had time to put the laptop on the coffee table before her daughter hurled herself into her arms.

'I'm not going to nursery today,' Ragnhild laughed. 'Today you and me are going to have a Teddy Bear Day!'

Johanne gently pushed her daughter away in order to make eye contact, then she said: 'No, sweetheart. You are going to nursery today. It's Monday.'

'Teddy Bear Day,' Ragnhild said mulishly, pushing out her lower lip.

'Another time, chicken. Mummy has to work today, and you have to go to nursery. Don't you remember? You're all going skiing in Solem Forest. You'll be cooking sausages over the fire and everything!'

The sulky face split into a big smile.

'Oh yes! And how many days is it till my birthday?'

'Nine days. It's only nine days until you're five!'

Ragnhild laughed happily.

'And I'm going to have the best birthday in the world, with bells on!'

'So to make sure you get to be such a big girl, we're going to make porridge. But first of all you and I are going to hop in the shower.'

'Yess!' her daughter replied, hopping off towards the bathroom like a rabbit.

Johanne smiled at the sight of her. It had been a lovely weekend, and she intended to enjoy an hour alone with her youngest daughter before she tackled a new week.

If only she could push away the thought of The 25'ers.

*

The last person to push open the door of the small chapel at Østre Crematorium was called Petter Just. He stood there for a moment, wondering if he was in the right place. It was three minutes to twelve, but there couldn't be more than twenty people in the chapel. Petter Just, a classmate of Niclas Winter's who hadn't seen his old friend for many years, had thought it would be packed. Niclas had done very well in life, from what he had read. Sold his work to museums and private collectors. A year ago the local paper had run a big article about Niclas and his work, and Petter Just had got the impression that he was on his way to a major international breakthrough.

A thin, elderly man wearing glasses that suggested he was almost blind pushed a folded sheet of paper into his hand. A photograph of Niclas adorned the front page, with his name and the dates of his birth and death printed in an old-fashioned typeface underneath.

Petter Just took the small leaflet and sat down quietly right at the back.

The clock struck its last four chimes, then fell silent as the organ took over.

The chapel was simple, almost plain: slate slabs on the floor and beige stone walls that turned into severe, rectangular windows for the last few metres. Instead of an altarpiece, the front wall was adorned with a fresco that Petter Just didn't understand at all. More than anything it reminded him of an old advertising poster for Senterpartiet, with trees and seeds, farmers and fields and a horse that looked an awful lot like a Norwegian fjord horse. At any rate, no animal like that had ever trotted around in the Middle East, he thought, as he tried to find an acceptable sitting position on the hard pew that was covered in red material with stains on it.

He really had thought that Niclas was famous. Not a celebrity like the people you see in magazines and on VG, of course, but fairly well known within his field. A real artist, kind of. When Petter decided to go to the funeral, it had been mainly because he had once had a lot of fun with Niclas. They'd had a pretty cool time for a while, in one way or another. Niclas had been completely crazy when it came to drugs and so on. He hadn't been all that particular about who he went to bed with, either.

Petter Just almost blushed at the thought.

At any rate, he didn't do that kind of thing any more. He had a girlfriend, a fantastic girl, and they were expecting their first child in July. He had never been like Niclas really, but when his mother happened to mention that his old friend was dead and the funeral was today, he wanted to pay his respects.

Hardly anyone was singing.

He didn't even bother miming, which he suspected the two men sitting on the other side of the aisle three pews ahead of him were doing. Some of the time, anyway.

There was only one woman in the chapel, and she didn't exactly seem crushed. Nor had she managed to dig something black out of her wardrobe. Her suit was elegant, fair enough, but red wasn't really appropriate for a funeral. She was sitting there looking bored stiff.

The music came to an end. The priest stepped up to the pulpit, directly in front of the central aisle, which resembled an oversized bar stool that might fall over at any moment.

The two men in front of Petter started a whispered conversation.

At first he was annoyed. It wasn't right to talk during a sermon. Well, maybe 'sermon' wasn't the right word, but any rate it was rude not to keep quiet while the priest was talking.

'... found several works of art ... no children or siblings ...'

Petter Just could hear fragments of the conversation. Although he didn't really want to, he found himself concentrating on them.

'... in his studio ... no heirs ...'

The priest indicated that the congregation should stand. The two men were so absorbed that they didn't react until everyone else was on their feet. They kept quiet for a little while, then started whispering to each other again.

'... lots of smaller installations ... sketches ... a final masterpiece ... nobody knew that ...'

The bastards were ruining the entire service. Petter leaned forward.

'Shut up, for God's sake!' he hissed. 'Show a little respect!'

Both men turned to look at him in surprise. One was in his fifties with thinning hair, narrow glasses and a moustache. The other was somewhat younger.

'Sorry,' said the older man, and both of them smiled as they turned to face the front.

He must have given them a real fright, because they didn't say another word for the rest of the ceremony. It didn't last much longer anyway. No one spoke, apart from the priest. Not like when Lasse died in a car accident two years ago; he had been one of three little boys racketing around in Godlia in the eighties. His funeral had been held in the large chapel next door, and there still wasn't room for everyone who wanted to attend. There had been eight eulogies, and even a live band playing 'Imagine'. A sea of flowers and an ocean of tears.

Nobody here was crying, and there was just one wreath on the coffin.

The thought brought tears to his eyes.

He should have got in touch with Niclas long ago. If it hadn't been for the aspect of their relationship that he really wanted to forget, the aspect that had never really been his thing, he would have kept up the friendship.

Suddenly he didn't want to be there any more. Just before the final note died away, he got up. He pushed the old, short-sighted man out of the way and yanked open the heavy wooden door.

It had started snowing again.

He started to run, without really knowing what he was racing towards.

Or from.

*

'Changing the subject,' said Sigmund Berli, before kicking off his shoes and putting his feet up on the little table between the two armchairs in Adam's hotel room. 'I've got myself a girlfriend.'

Adam held his nose, pulled a face and stabbed his index finger several times in the direction of his colleague's feet.

'Congratulations,' he said, laughing behind his clenched fist, 'but your socks stink to high heaven. Take them away! Put your shoes back on!'

Sigmund leaned forward as far as he could towards his own feet. Sniffed hard and wrinkled his nose slightly.

'They're all right,' he said, settling down again. 'I haven't had any complaints from my girlfriend, anyway.'

'Who is she?' asked Adam, moving over to the bed, as far from Sigmund as possible. 'And how long has this been going on?'

'Herdis,' Sigmund said eagerly. 'She's ... Herdis is ... Guess! Guess what her job is!'

'No idea,' Adam said impatiently. 'Are you actually going to offer me a drink or what?'

Sigmund fished a plastic bottle of whisky out of his inside pocket. He picked up one of the glasses Adam had fetched from the bathroom and poured a generous measure before handing it to his friend.

'Thanks.'

Sigmund poured himself a drink.

'Herdis,' Sigmund repeated contentedly, as if just speaking her name was a pleasure. 'Herdis Vatne is a professor of astrophysics.'

'Hmff ... !' Adam sprayed whisky all over himself and the bed. 'What did you say? What the hell did you say?'

Sigmund straightened up, a suspicious look in his eyes.

'I suppose you thought I couldn't pull an academic? The trouble with you, Adam, is that you're always so bloody prejudiced. You defend those Negroes to the death. Despite the fact that they're over-represented in virtually all the crime statistics we have, you're always going on about how difficult things are for them, and—'

'Pack it in,' said Adam. 'And don't use that word.'

'That's a form of prejudice, too, you know! Always thinking the best of people just because they belong to a particular group! You never think the best of anyone else. You're sceptical about every white person we pick up, but if their skin's just a little bit darker than ours, you start pointing out how decent they probably are, and how—'

'Pack it in! I mean it!' Adam suddenly sat up straight on the bed.

Sigmund hesitated, then added sullenly: 'And you don't believe for a moment that I've got a girlfriend who works at the university. You think it's funny. That's definitely what I call having preconceived ideas. And it's actually quite hurtful, to be perfectly honest.'

'Sorry,' said Adam. 'I apologize, Sigmund. Of course I'm very happy for you. Have you ... ?' He pointed to Sigmund's mobile phone. 'Have you got a picture of her?'

'You bet!'

Sigmund fiddled with his phone and eventually found what he was looking for, then held it out to Adam with a broad grin.

'Not bad, eh? Beautiful as well as clever. Almost like Johanne.'

Adam took the phone and examined the picture. A fair-haired woman in her forties was looking back at him with a big smile. Her teeth were white and even, her nose upturned slightly in an attractive way. She must be quite slim, because even on the little display screen he could see deep laughter lines, with a furrow running from the corners of her mouth down to her chin on either side. Her eyes were blue and she was wearing just a little bit too much eye make-up.

She looked like just about any competent Norwegian woman in her forties.

'Not bad at all,' he mumbled, handing back the phone.

'I was going to tell you on Saturday, before Johanne suddenly went off to bed. But then I decided to wait, because yesterday Herdis was meeting my boys for the first time. Well, it wasn't really the first time, because her son plays hockey with Snorre. They've been good friends for ages. But I had to see how things went when we kind of ... met up privately. All of us. I mean, I can't have a girlfriend who doesn't like my boys. And vice versa.'

'So I gather it went well?'

'Couldn't have gone better. We went to the cinema, then back to her place for a meal afterwards. You should see her apartment! Stylish and spacious. In Frogner. I almost feel like a stranger in that part of town. But it's lovely there, I have to admit.'

He sipped contentedly at his whisky and leaned back in his armchair.

'Love is a beautiful thing,' he announced solemnly.

'Indeed it is.'

They sat in silence for a while as they worked their way through about half of their generous drinks. Adam could feel the tiredness creeping up on him as he lay there on the bed, three pillows providing a soft support for his back and neck. He closed his eyes, then gave a start as he almost dropped his glass.

'What do you think about our woman?' said Sigmund.

'What woman? Herdis?'

'Idiot. Eva Karin Lysgaard.'

Adam didn't reply. The two of them had spent the day trying to impose some kind of system on the vast amount of documents relating to the case. Nineteen days had passed since the Bishop was stabbed to death, and basically the Bergen police were no closer to a solution. You couldn't actually blame them, thought Adam. He was just as much at a loss. So far they and Sigmund had worked well together, with no friction. To begin with Adam had taken responsibility for interviewing the witnesses who were most central to the case, while Sigmund had acted as a link between Kripos and Hordaland police district. This was a role he fulfilled admirably. It was difficult to find a more jovial soul than Sigmund Berli. He was a strong all-rounder who could usually sort out any potential conflict before things turned serious. For the last week they had both worked in a slightly different capacity, evaluating the material gathered so far. The Bergen police were responsible for all aspects of the investigation and coordination. They operated entirely independently, while Adam and Sigmund tried to gain an overview of all the information that came pouring in.

'I think we've made a mistake,' Adam said suddenly. 'The opposite of the mistake we usually make.'

'What do you mean?'

'We've been looking at too wide an area.'

'Rule Number One, Adam: keep all doors open at all times!'

'I know,' said Adam with a grimace. 'But listen ...'

He picked up a notepad and pen from the bedside table.

'With regard to this theory about a madman, one of those ticking bombs that everybody is talking about all the time—'

'An asylum seeker,' Sigmund chipped in, and was about to expand on this theme when a crushing glance from Adam made him hold up his hands in a placatory gesture.

'If that were the case, we would have found him long ago,' said Adam. 'That type of murder is carried out by psychotic individuals who happily roam the streets after doing the deed, spattered with blood and tormented by inner demons until we find them a few hours later. It's been three weeks now, and we've seen no sign of any maniac. No one is missing from the psychiatric clinics, nothing suspicious has been discovered at the centres for asylum seekers, and I think it's actually ...'

He tapped the pad with his pen.

'... out of the question that we're looking for that kind of murderer.'

'I should imagine that's exactly what the Bergen police are thinking.'

'Yes. But they're still keeping the door open.'

Sigmund nodded.

'That door should just be closed,' said Adam. 'Along with several other doors that are just creating draughts and chaos with all their possibilities. These poison-pen letters, for example. Have you ever been involved in a case where the murderer was one of the people who'd sent that sort of thing?'

'Well,' Sigmund said hesitantly. 'In the Anna Lindh case the murderer was unhappy about—'

'The Swedish Minister for Foreign Affairs was murdered by a madman,' Adam interrupted. 'In every practical respect, if not in the legal sense. A misfit with a psychiatric background who suddenly caught sight of a focus for his hatred. He was arrested two weeks later, and he left so many clues that—'

'That you and I would have picked him up in less than twenty-four hours,' Sigmund smiled.

Adam grinned back.

'They've been really unlucky, the Swedes, in several really, really serious cases ...'

Once again they fell silent. From the room next door came the sound of a running shower and a toilet being flushed.

'I think that's a blind alley, too,' said Adam. 'Just like this abortion business the papers are making so much of at the moment. It's the anti-abortion lobby that sometimes commits murders in support of their point of view. In the US, anyway. Not the pro-abortionists. That's just too far-fetched.'

'So what are you thinking, then? You've gone through virtually every possibility we've got! What the hell are you sitting there pondering?'

'Where was she going?' said Adam, staring blankly into space. 'We have to find out where she was going when she was murdered.'

Sigmund emptied his glass and stared at it briefly before resolutely opening the plastic bottle of Famous Grouse and pouring himself another decent measure.

'Take it easy,' said Adam. 'We've got to make an early start.'

Sigmund ignored his warning.

'The problem is, of course, that we can't ask Eva Karin Lysgaard,' he said. 'And her husband is still flatly refusing to say anything about where she was heading. Our colleagues here have told him he has a duty to answer, and have even threatened him with a formal interrogation. With the consequences that could have—'

'They'll never subject Erik Lysgaard to a formal interrogation. It would be pointless. He has suffered enough – and is still suffering. We'll have to come up with something else.'

'Like what?'

Adam emptied his glass and shook his head when Sigmund lifted the bottle to offer him a top-up.

'Door-to-door enquiries,' Adam said tersely.

'Where? All over Bergen?'

'No. We need to ...' He opened the drawer of the bedside table and took out a map of the town. 'We need to concentrate on a limited area somewhere around here,' he said, drawing a circle with his index finger as he held the map up to show his colleague.

'But that's half of bloody Bergen,' Sigmund said wearily.

'No. It's the eastern part of the centre. The north-eastern part.'

Sigmund took the map.

'You know what, Adam? This is the stupidest suggestion you've ever come up with. It's been made absolutely crystal-clear in the media that there's a great deal of uncertainty about why the Bishop was out walking on Christmas Eve. If anyone out there knew where she was going, they would have contacted the police long ago. Unless, of course, they have something to hide, in which case there's still no bloody point in going around knocking on doors.'

He threw the map on the bed and took a large swig from his glass.

'Besides,' he went on, 'she might just have gone out for a walk. In which case we wouldn't be any closer to finding an answer.'

Adam's face took on the glassy expression Sigmund knew so well.

'Any more bright ideas?' he said, sipping his whisky. 'Ideas I can shoot down right now?'

'The photo,' said Adam firmly, before glancing at his watch.

'The photo. Right. What photo?'

'It's half past eleven. I need to get some sleep.'

'Which photo are you talking about?'

Sigmund showed no sign of heading off to his own room. On the contrary, he settled himself more comfortably in the armchair and rested his legs on the bed.

'The one that disappeared,' said Adam. 'I told you about the photo-graph that was in the "spare room" ...'

He drew quotation marks in the air.

'... where Eva Karin used to go when she couldn't sleep, according to the family. There were four photographs in there the first time I saw the room, and three when I went back two days later. The only thing I remember is that it was a portrait.'

'But Erik Lysgaard doesn't want to—'

'We'll just have to forget Erik. He's a lost cause. I've spent far too long thinking the key to finding out more about this mysterious walk lies with him. But we've reached stalemate there. Lukas, however—'

'Doesn't seem all that keen to cooperate either, if you ask me.'

'No, you could be right there. Which means we have to ask ourselves why a son who is obviously grieving – and who really wants to find out who murdered his mother – is so reluctant to help the police. There's usually only one explanation for that kind of thing.'

He looked at Sigmund with raised eyebrows, challenging him to follow his reasoning through to its conclusion.

'Family secrets,' said Sigmund in a dramatic tone of voice.

'Bingo. They often have nothing to do with the matter in hand, actually, but in this case we can't afford to make any assumptions. My impression of Lukas is that he's not really ...'

There was a long pause. Sigmund waited patiently; his glass wasn't empty yet.

'... he's not really sure of his father,' Adam said eventually.

'What do you mean?'

'They're obviously very fond of each other. There's a striking resemblance between them, both physically and in terms of personality, and I have no reason to believe there's any problem with the relationship between father and son. And yet there's something unresolved between them. Something new. You notice it as soon as you're in the same room with both of them. It's a long way from hostility, it's more a kind of ...'

Once again he had to search for the right words.

'... broken trust.'

'Do they suspect each other?'

'I don't think so. But there's something unspoken between them, some kind of deep scepticism that ...'

Once again, mostly as a reflex action, he looked at his watch.

'I mean it, Sigmund. I have to get to sleep. Clear off.'

'You always have to spoil the party,' mumbled his colleague, putting his feet on the floor. His room was two doors away, and he couldn't be bothered with his shoes. He picked them up with two fingers of his right hand, and carried the whisky bottle in the other.

'What time are you having breakfast?'

'Seven. Then I'm going out to Os. I want to catch Lukas before he goes to work. That's what we have to hope for – that Lukas will agree to help us.'

He yawned and weakly raised two fingers to his forehead in a farewell salute. In the doorway Sigmund turned back.

'I think I'll get up a bit later,' he said. 'Then I'll go straight down to the police station about nine. I'll let them know you've gone to talk to

Lukas again. They seem to think it's OK for you to go off on your own here in Bergen. You'd never get away with it back home!'

'Fine. Good night.'

Sigmund mumbled something inaudible as the door closed behind him with a muted bang.

As Adam undressed and got ready for bed, he realized he'd forgotten to ring Johanne. He swore and looked at his watch, even though it was only two minutes since he'd established that it was eleven thirty-six.

It was too late to call, so he went to bed.

And couldn't get to sleep.

*

It was the number 19 that was keeping Johanne awake. She had spent the entire evening reading about Rashad Khalifa and his theories about the divine origins of the Koran. Whatever she tried to think about in order to tempt sleep, that damned number 19 popped up again, and she was wide awake once more.

After an hour she gave up. She would find something mindless to watch on TV. A detective programme or a sitcom; something to make her sleepy. It was already after one o'clock, but TV3 was usually showing some kind of crap at this time of night.

The sofa was a complete mess. Papers everywhere, every single one a printout from the Internet.

Johanne threatened her own students with death and destruction if they ever used Wikipedia as a source in a piece of academic work. She used it all the time. The difference between Johanne and her students was that she had the sense to be critical, in her opinion. This evening it had been difficult. The story of Rashad Khalifa made riveting reading, and every link had led her deeper into this remarkable story.

It was so fascinating.

She padded silently into the kitchen and decided to follow her mother's advice. Milk in a pan, two large dessert spoonfuls of honey. Just before it boiled she added a dash of brandy. As a child she hadn't had a clue about the final ingredient. As an adult she had confronted her mother, telling her it was totally irresponsible to give a child alcohol to get her to sleep. Her mother had waved away her objections, pointing out that the alcohol evaporated, and that in any case alcohol could be regarded as medicine. At least in these circumstances. Besides which they were very rarely given her special milk mixture, she had added, when Johanne still didn't seem convinced.

She smiled and shook her head at the thought. Poured the milk into a big mug. It was almost too hot to hold.

She put it down on the coffee table and made some space on the sofa. Switched on the TV and flicked on to TV3. It was difficult to work out what the film was actually about. The pictures were dark, showing trees being blown down in a violent storm. When a vampire suddenly appeared among the tree trunks, she switched off.

Without really making a conscious decision, she reached for a pile of papers next to her mug of milk. Despite the fact that it was a stupid thing to do in view of the late hour, she settled down to read more about Rashad Khalifa and his peculiar theory about the number 19.

The Egyptian had emigrated to the United States as a young adult, and trained there as a biochemist. Since he found the English translation of the Koran unsatisfactory, he re-translated the whole thing himself. During the course of his work, towards the end of the Sixties, he got the idea that the book ought to be analyzed. From a purely mathematical point of view. The aim would be to prove that the Koran was a divine text. After several years and a great deal of work, he put forward his theory about the number 19 as a kind of pervading, divine key to the word of Allah.

Johanne didn't have the requisite knowledge to follow the strange Muslim's great leaps of thought. The whole thing seemed to be based on comparatively advanced mathematics, while in some parts it seemed utterly banal. For example, he noted that in the Koran, 'Basmalah' is mentioned 114 times, which is a number divisible by 19. In certain places he based his comments more directly on the text, such as when he referred to the fact that sura 74:30 said, 'Over it is nineteen.'

Tentatively, she took a sip of the hot milky drink. Her mother's theory didn't stand up; the alcohol burned on her tongue and prickled in her nose.

Rashad Khalifa carried out an inconceivable number of calculations, she noted once more. The most ridiculous was to add up all the numbers mentioned throughout the whole of the Koran, and to show that this total was also divisible by 19. At first she really couldn't understand what was special about that, but then she realized that 19 was a prime number, and therefore divisible only by itself, and that made things slightly easier to understand.

'But then there are a hell of a lot of prime numbers,' she muttered to herself.

The room was cold.

They had installed a thermostat with a timer on every radiator in an attempt to protect both their bank account and the environment. While Adam kept on turning up the radiators to maintain the heat overnight, she kept turning them down to allow the system to work as it was meant to. She regretted it now. For a moment she considered lighting a fire, but instead she went into the bedroom and fetched a blanket.

Her drink was beginning to cool down. She took a big gulp, then put the mug down again and started to read.

To begin with, the Muslim world had seemed delighted with the eccentric Khalifa's discoveries. At first his work was taken seriously. Muslims the world over accepted the idea of mathematical evidence for the existence of Allah. Even the well-known sceptic Martin Gardner referred to Khalifa's mathematical discoveries as interesting and sensational in one of his articles in *Scientific American*.

Then things went downhill for the Egyptian-American Rashad Khalifa.

He wrote himself into the Koran.

Not content with regarding himself as a prophet on the same level as the Prophet, he created his own religion. According to 'The Submitters', all other religions, including corrupt Islam, would simply die out when the prophet foretold in both the Koran and the Bible arrived, and Islam would rise again in a pure, unadulterated form.

She was going cross-eyed. Johanne put down the papers.

Perhaps she would be able to sleep on the sofa.

She wasn't going to think about Rashad Khalifa any more.

Still, it was hardly surprising that he gained supporters, she thought, trying to get comfortable. Many modern Muslims welcomed his attack on the Muslim priesthood. On the other hand, numerology would always tempt those with a weakness for fanaticism – extremists of all kinds. Khalifa's theories were still accepted, in spite of the fact that the man himself had been murdered in 1990.

By a fanatical Muslim, following a fatwa issued at the same meeting as the one against Salman Rushdie.

'Oh my God,' she mumbled, trying to close her eyes. 'These religions!'

The number 19 was performing *Riverdance* on the inside of her eyelids.

It was ten past two.

Tomorrow would be terrible if she didn't get to sleep soon. She got up abruptly, and with the blanket tucked under her arm she padded into the bathroom to take a sleeping tablet. The very thought that they were there was usually enough, but this time she took one and a half tablets, swilled down with running water from the tap.

Fifteen minutes later she was fast asleep in her own bed, untroubled by dreams.

*

Lukas Lysgaard had waited until everyone was asleep. He left a note for Astrid saying that he was worried about his father and was going to check that everything was OK, but would be back later that night. He had left the car parked on the street so that the garage door wouldn't wake anyone.

The drive did him good. While his mother had always adored the light, Lukas was a man who felt comfortable at night. As a child he had always felt safe in the dark. The night was his friend, and had been ever since he was little and lived in the big house on Nubbebakken. From the age of six or seven he had often woken up and been fascinated by the shadows dancing on his bedroom wall. The big oak tree whose branches scraped against the window pane was illuminated from behind by a single yellow street lamp, making the most beautiful patterns on his bed. All of a sudden, when he could no longer sleep, he would tiptoe out of his room and up the steep stairs leading to the attic. In the semi-darkness, among trunks and old furniture, moth-eaten clothes and toys that were so old nobody knew who had owned them originally, he could sit for hours, lost in dreams.

Lukas Lysgaard drove from Os through the damp winter darkness into a Bergen that was heavy with sleep; he had finally made a decision.

When he thought back to his own childhood, he didn't have much to complain about.

He was a much-loved child, and he knew it. His parents' faith had been good for him when he was little. He accepted their God just as easily as all children accept their parents' ideals until they are old enough to rebel. His rebellion had taken place in silence. From seeing the Lord as a comforting father figure – forgiving, watchful and omnipresent – he had begun to have his doubts at the age of twelve.

There was no room for doubt in the house on Nubbebakken.

His mother's faith in God had been absolute. Her kindness towards others, regardless of their faith or conviction, her generosity and tolerance towards even the weakest among the fallen, all of this was firmly anchored in her certainty that the Redeemer was the Son of God. When Lukas became a teenager he discovered that his mother wasn't a believer. She knew. Eva Karin Lysgaard was absolutely sure about her religion, and he never dared confront her with his own doubts. God stopped answering his prayers. Christianity became more and more of a closed book to him, and he started to seek the answers to the mysteries of life elsewhere.

After completing his military service he began to study physics, and abandoned his religion. Still without saying a word. He and Astrid had been married in church – what else would they do? Their children had been baptized. He was pleased about that now; his mother had been so happy each time she held up one of her grandchildren before the congregation, after administering the sacrament herself.

It had always been different at home with his parents, he thought, as he drew closer to his father's house.

When he was a boy he had never noticed it. Since his mother's death he had been trying to remember when it first arose, this vague feeling that she was hiding something. Perhaps it had happened gradually, alongside his own dwindling faith. Although she had always been there as a mother, always spiritually and often physically, as he grew older it had become increasingly clear to him that he was sharing her with someone else. It was like a shadow hanging over her. Something missing.

He had a sister. That must be the answer.

It was difficult to work out how and why, but it had to be connected in some way to his mother's salvation as a sixteen-year-old. Perhaps she had been pregnant. Perhaps Jesus had spoken to her when she was thinking of having an abortion. That would explain the one area in which she was immovable and sometimes almost fanatical: it was not given to man to end a life created by God.

He quickly worked out that his mother had been sixteen in 1962.

It wasn't easy to be pregnant and unmarried in 1962, and most definitely not for a young girl.

The woman in the photo was so like him; he remembered that, despite the fact that on the few occasions when he had paid any real attention to the picture he had felt an antipathy, almost a sense of loathing towards this nameless woman with the attractive, slightly crooked teeth.

Lukas was going to find that photograph. Then he was going to find his sister.

On Nubbebakken he parked a short distance from his father's house. When he reached the front door, he tried not to rattle the bunch of keys.

Once inside, he stopped and listened.

It was never really silent in his parents' house. The wood creaked, the hinges squealed. Branches scraped against the window panes when it was breezy. The ticking of the grandfather clock was usually so loud that you could hear it more or less anywhere on the ground floor. The pipes sighed at irregular intervals; his childhood home had always been a living house. The floors were old, and he still remembered where to put his feet so that he wouldn't wake anyone.

Now everything was dead.

There wasn't a breath of wind outside, and even when he stood on a floorboard that usually protested beneath his weight, he could hear nothing but his own pulse beating against his eardrums.

He walked towards the narrow staircase, holding his breath until he reached the top. The door of his father's bedroom was ajar. The slow, regular breathing indicated that he was asleep. Lukas moved cautiously over to the door leading up to the attic. As usual the old wrought-iron key was in the lock, and he lifted the handle up and towards him while turning the key at the same time, which he knew was the trick. The click as the door unlocked made him hold his breath once more.

His father was still asleep.

With infinite slowness he opened the door.

Eventually he was able to slip through.

He placed his feet as close to the wall as possible on each step, as he had learned to do when he was only six years old. Silently he made his way up to the big, dusty room. He slipped the torch out of his waistband and began to search.

It was a reunion with his own childhood.

In the boxes piled up by the little round window in one gable he found clothes and shoes that had belonged to him when he was a little boy. Next to them were several boxes containing more clothes; his mother had thrown nothing away. He tried to remember when he had last been up here, and worked out that it must have been before they moved away for the first time, when he was twelve, and he had cried himself to sleep for two months at the thought of leaving Bergen.

And yet everything seemed so strangely familiar.

The smell was still the same. Dust, mothballs and rusty metal mixed with shoe polish and indefinable, comforting scents.

Suddenly he turned away from the boxes by the window and moved silently back to the staircase. He swept the beam of the torch over the floor at the top of the stairs. In the thick dust he could clearly see his own footprints. He could also see another impression, with no pattern on the sole, like the marks left by slippers. There were several when he looked more closely, and they went in both directions. Someone had been here recently.

Lukas couldn't help smiling. His father had always thought the attic was a safe place. Every Christmas Eve when he was a little boy, Lukas had pretended to be surprised at his presents. His father had hidden them up here until Christmas Eve, but he had no idea that Lukas had become an expert at opening presents and sealing them up again without anyone being able to tell.

He stretched and looked around.

The attic was large, covering the same area as the ground floor of the house. A hundred square metres, if he remembered rightly. His courage almost failed at the thought of how long it would take to search through all this rubbish – all these memories – for something as small as a photograph.

Once again the beam of the torch danced across the footprints by the stairs.

The impressions left by the slippers– almost invisible – were pointing in the opposite direction from where Lukas had been. They led over to the western end of the attic, where the little window was nailed shut. He traced them carefully.

A sound from downstairs made him stiffen.

The sound of footsteps. The footsteps stopped.

Lukas held his breath.

His father was awake. He could almost hear him breathing, even though there must be more than fifteen metres between them. It sounded as if he was standing by the attic door.

Shit. Lukas's lips silently formed the word. He hadn't closed the door, simply because he was afraid of making a noise later, when he came down from the attic. Presumably his father was going to the toilet, and, of course, he had noticed that the attic door was open.

Sometimes, if they had forgotten to lock the door, it would open by itself. Lukas closed his eyes and prayed to God for the first time in living memory.

Let Dad believe the door opened by itself.

This time his prayer was answered.

He heard his father muttering to himself, then the door closed.

And the key was turned.

God hadn't answered his prayer after all. Now he was locked in, and how the hell was he supposed to explain that? A stream of quiet curses poured out of his mouth before it occurred to him that he could use the roof light. He was only six years old when he climbed out of the little window in the roof for the first time; it was right next to the chimney, and he clambered down the sweep's ladder, scrambled along the guttering and across to the big oak tree just outside his old bedroom.

From there getting down to the ground was a simple matter.

But first he must find the photo of his sister.

He waited for ten minutes to make sure his father had gone back to sleep. Then he crept quietly across the floor.

It was all so simple that he couldn't really believe it. Underneath a banana box full of old newspapers – on top of a footstool he thought he remembered from when they lived in Stavanger – lay the photograph. The frame shone when the beam of the torch caught it. Only now did it occur to him that it was made of silver. The metal had oxidized over the years, but the weight and the quality of the chased frame convinced him.

A pang shot through him as he let the beam rest on her smiling face.

The woman was possibly in her twenties, although it was hard to tell. The only part of her clothing that was visible was a blouse with a small collar and something that might be flowers embroidered on the point at each side, white on white. On top of the blouse she was wearing a darker jacket – it looked like a thin, knitted jacket. One single colour.

Not particularly modern, he thought.

Quickly, he took the photograph out of the frame. He wanted to look for the name of the photographer or some other clue that might take him further in the hunt for the sister in whose existence he had believed for so long; now he had no intention of giving up until he found her.

Nothing.

The photograph was completely anonymous. He put down the frame and went over to an old armchair standing by the long wall on the southern side of the house. He sat down and balanced the torch on his shoulder so that the light was shining directly on the photograph.

If his mother had been pregnant in 1962, then this woman must be forty-six now, perhaps forty-seven; he had never known what time of year his mother had had her alleged revelation.

So the photograph must have been taken at least twenty-five years ago: 1984.

He had been five years old then. He didn't know much about the fashion in those days, apart from the fact that his best friend's older brother had worn pastel-coloured mohair jumpers which he tucked into his trousers, and his hair had been permed into fantastic curls.

His ran his fingertips over the woman's face.

She didn't have a perm, and although it was difficult to guess colours from a black-and-white photograph, he thought the jacket might be red.

Lukas had never missed having siblings. He grew up with a sense of being unique, the only child with whom his parents had been blessed. He found it easy to make friends, and they had always been welcome at home. His friends envied him: Lukas had his parents' undivided attention, and he often had the latest thing before other parents had even had time to consider whether they could afford it.

He felt as if the woman in the photograph was talking to him. There was something between them, a mutual love.

Quickly, he tucked the photograph inside his shirt and secured it in the waistband of his trousers. He put the frame back where he had found it, then moved over to the roof light, hoping it would still open after all these years.

It did.

Cold, damp air poured in, and he closed his eyes for a moment. When he opened them again he began to wonder if it would still be possible for him to squeeze out through the narrow opening. He looked around for something to stand on, and caught sight of a small stepladder, which he remembered from the kitchen in Stavanger. He carefully unhooked it from the wall, opened it out and placed it directly under the roof light. He just about managed to squeeze his shoulders through the gap. Once his upper body was through, the rest wouldn't be a problem.

However, there were other challenges.

He immediately realized that it would be madness to attempt to get over the roof and down the big oak tree in the dark. There was only a faint glow from the solitary street lamp, which didn't provide enough light to see what he was doing. Since he needed both hands to make his way over the roof and into the tree, the torch wouldn't be much use. Of course, he could fix it in his belt, but it wouldn't be enough.

Lukas Lysgaard was a 29-year-old father of three, and no longer a boy with no fear and no sense. Carefully, he wriggled back down and managed to get back inside without making too much noise.

He sat down in the armchair again, fished out his mobile and keyed in a message to Astrid.

Spending the night at Dad's. Will ring in the morning. Lukas.

Then he switched the phone to silent.

He would wait for daylight, even if the dawn came late at this time of year. Once again he took out the photograph of the person he now knew was his sister and studied it for a long time in the blue-white glow of the Maglite.

Perhaps he had nieces and nephews.

At least he had a sister.

The very thought made him dizzy, and suddenly tiredness crept up on him. His limbs were as heavy as lead, and he was no longer capable of holding the photograph steady. He tucked it back inside his shirt, switched off the torch and leaned back in the lovely, comfortable armchair.

In the small hours of the morning, he fell asleep.

Child Missing

Adam Stubo had been so tired when he woke up that he had wondered for a while whether he ought to be driving. He wasn't under the influence of alcohol, having restricted himself to just one decent drink. And yet he felt a heaviness in his body, a stubborn sleepiness that made it difficult to get out of bed. Perhaps he was coming down with something.

But after three cups of coffee, two portions of scrambled eggs and bacon and a freshly baked croissant, everything felt much easier.

He had almost reached Os.

He had decided against warning the family in advance. It was a risk, of course, since there was no guarantee Lukas Lysgaard would be at home, but Adam wanted to maintain the psychological upper hand by making an unannounced visit. He had never been to Lukas's house, and when the mechanical voice of the satnav kept on telling him to turn right when he was passing a field with not so much as a logging track visible, he decided it would be better to ask the way. A woman in her sixties hurrying along a cycle track looked as if she knew where she was going.

'Excuse me,' he said, pressing the button to open the side window. 'Do you know this area?'

She nodded, her expression dubious.

He mentioned the address, but this didn't make her any more inclined to talk.

'Lukas Lysgaard,' he said quickly as she was about to set off again. 'I'm looking for Lukas Lysgaard!'

'Oh, I see,' said the woman, with a sad smile. 'Poor boy. Third street on the right. Carry on for about three hundred metres. Turn left by a dilapidated little red house, then go straight on. When you see a white house on a bend, carry straight on up to the top of the hill, and there you are. It's a yellow house with a double garage.'

Adam repeated the directions, and received a nod of confirmation. He thanked the woman politely and put the car into gear.

As he approached the house he glanced at the clock on the dashboard: 8.10. Perhaps he was too late.

Lukas worked in Bergen, so he probably left home early. Adam didn't know much about the infrastructure in this part of the country, but when he was here after Christmas he had realized that the rush-hour traffic heading into Bergen from the south could lead to a complete standstill all the way from Flesland into the centre. Admittedly, Flesland lay to the north-west of Os, but as far as he could tell, you ended up in the same stationary queue as you drew closer to the city.

He stopped in front of a typical eighties house, large and painted yellow, with bay windows, small panes and every other characteristic of a practical and utterly unattractive dwelling.

He parked by the gate and walked up to the front door.

From inside he could hear the sound of a child crying, followed by an exhausted groan from someone he assumed to be Lukas's wife. A pathetic little miaow made him move back at the bottom of the stone steps and look up. On the porch roof sat a small tabby. When he met its green eyes, the cat crept silently over to the drainpipe, down the wall, and managed to slide into the house just as the door opened.

'Good morning,' said Adam, holding out his hand as he climbed the three steps.

Astrid Tomte Lysgaard stared at him in surprise.

'Morning,' she said uncertainly, shaking his hand.

'Adam Stubo. From NCIS. I'm working on the investigation into your mother-in-law's murder and—'

'I know who you are,' said Astrid, making no move to let him in. 'But Lukas isn't here.'

'Oh. Has he already left for work?'

'Possibly. He spent the night at his father's house.'

'I see.'

Adam smiled. Astrid Tomte Lysgaard wasn't yet dressed for the day. Her dressing gown was too big, and the milk-white legs revealed that she was as thin as a rake. Her eyes were surrounded by dry wrinkles, and the bags under her eyes were all too evident for a woman of her age.

'I'm sorry,' she said, spreading her hands wide in a weary gesture. 'We're running a bit late this morning, so if there's nothing else ...'

A three-year-old stuck his head out from behind her.

'Hello,' the boy said in a friendly tone of voice. 'My name is William, and Grandma is all dead.'

'My name is Adam. I'm a policeman. Was that your cat I saw just now?'

'Yes. Her name is Borghild.'

The boy couldn't pronounce the name properly, and said 'Boygil'.

Adam's smile grew even wider.

'That's a good name for a beautiful fat cat,' he nodded. 'I think you'd better go and get dressed now. You'll be off to nursery soon, won't you?'

'Did you hear that?' Astrid gave a wan smile and ruffled her son's hair. 'The policeman says you have to go and get dressed. We have to do what a policeman tells us, don't we?'

The boy turned and scampered away at once.

'How are you doing?' Adam asked quietly.

She still made no move to let him in, but nor did she close the door.

'Oh, you know.' The tears were threatening to spill over. 'It's hard for Lukas,' she said, wiping her left eye with a rapid movement. 'Losing Eva Karin is one thing. But it's almost as bad seeing Erik so ...'

Her hands were slender, with long, thin fingers. Her arms were wrapped around her upper body, and she kept tucking her hair behind one ear over and over again with a nervous movement.

'And Lukas has got it into his head that ...'

A car sounded its horn on the street. Adam turned and saw a car pulling out of next-door's drive with the back seat full of children; the driver was waving to Astrid, who raised her hand slightly in response.

'What has Lukas got into his head?' Adam asked when she didn't go on.

'I ... I don't really know.'

Borghild appeared in the doorway, rubbing around her bare legs.

'I really do have to go,' she said, taking a step back. 'I've got to get the kids ready for school and nursery. I'm sorry you've come all the way out here for nothing.'

'It's not your fault!' Adam walked backwards down the steps. 'Sorry to have disturbed you,' he said. 'I know exactly what these mornings are like.'

Astrid closed the door without another word. Adam walked back to the hire car and unlocked it with the remote. He got in and fiddled with the idiotic card Renault had decided was better than an ignition key. He inserted it into the slot and pressed the start button. Nothing happened.

Work, you bastard!

He snatched out the card and banged it hard against the dashboard before repeating the entire procedure. The engine started.

After he had been driving for five minutes with the intention of going back to Bergen, he changed his mind and decided to head over to Nubbebakken instead. Seeking Lukas out at the university would seem too dramatic. Astrid had made it clear that Erik's condition was deteriorating, so Lukas might have decided to stay with his father rather than go to work.

He increased his speed.

It had started to rain, and behind the heavy cloud cover the sun had just started to colour the world grey.

*

Lukas was woken by the fact that the roof light was no longer black, but a sooty grey. His right arm was completely numb. He had twisted and turned in the armchair and fallen asleep on it. When the circulation returned it was as if he had stuck his hand in a wasps' nest. It stung and ached, and he pulled a face as he stood up and started to shake his arm so violently that his shoulder protested.

It was already ten past nine in the morning, on Tuesday 13 January.

He should have been at a departmental meeting at nine o'clock. When he checked the display on his mobile, there were five missed calls: three from a colleague who would be at the same meeting, and two from Astrid.

He just hoped she hadn't tried calling his father's landline as well. It was unlikely; she couldn't stand talking to her father-in-law at the moment.

He quickly stretched his body from side to side to shake off the aches and pains of the night.

There wasn't a sound from downstairs. Perhaps his father was still asleep.

The photograph of his sister was still safe inside his shirt. It was bent, but not creased. He tightened his belt in order to keep the photograph in place before climbing the ladder and opening the roof light.

It was a miserable January morning.

Everything was wet. All the colours were in hibernation. The oak tree stood out, a black relief against the grey. Lukas wriggled through the narrow opening and pulled the rest of his body up using his arms. Once he was on the roof, he sat there for a few moments gasping for breath. He pushed his heels well in between the rungs of the chimney sweep's ladder and felt significantly more frightened than he had done when he was a boy. When he was halfway down to the gutter, he heard a car approaching. He stiffened.

The engine was switched off and a car door opened and closed.

The gate squealed and Lukas could clearly hear footsteps approaching his father's front door.

Someone rang the bell. He heard the sound from below, muted and distorted through two floors, but still clear. So far he hadn't even dared to move his eyes, but eventually he looked down. From where he was sitting he could just see the little porch and the stone steps, with the metal grille at the bottom for wiping shoes.

He immediately saw who it was.

At last the door opened.

Lukas held his breath, his eyes firmly fixed on the man down below. If Adam Stubo should look up, he would see him at once.

The voices were crystal-clear.

'Good morning,' said the police officer. 'I'm sorry to disturb you, but I'm trying to get hold of Lukas. I just wanted to go over a couple of points with him. Is he here?'

As usual his father's voice was expressionless and uninterested.

'No.'

'No? It's just that I spoke to his wife and ...'

Stubo took a step back. Lukas closed his eyes.

'I do apologize,' said the big man down below. 'I could have phoned, of course. How are you? Is there anything we can—?'

'I'm fine,' his father interrupted, then the door slammed shut.

Lukas was already soaked to the skin. He had left his outdoor clothes in the car, and the ice-cold rain was hitting the nape of his neck and running down his back. Instinctively, he leaned forward to protect the photograph. He opened his eyes again.

Adam Stubo was standing five metres from the wall with his head tilted to one side. When their eyes met he beckoned several times with his right index finger. He smiled and shook his head, then pointed to the gate.

Lukas swallowed, then went hot and cold.

It would take him three minutes to get down from the roof, during which time he was going to have to come up with a bloody good explanation. He must also make sure his father didn't see him. Having to explain himself to Adam Stubo was more than enough.

When he reached the ground after jumping two metres from a thick branch, he still hadn't come up with anything to say.

The truth, perhaps, he thought for a moment before dismissing the idea. He crept around the house to meet Stubo, who was waiting by the gate.

*

Johanne had realized long ago that the truth was the first victim of every war. And yet it was still difficult to accept that reality could be distorted to the degree that was evident in the article she was trying to read as Ragnhild gave her teddy bear his breakfast.

'Look,' her daughter said delightedly, pointing at the bear's nose, which was covered in a sticky mess. 'Bamse loves his porridge!'

'Don't do that,' Johanne mumbled. 'Eat your breakfast.'

She took a sip of coffee. Her body still felt heavy and sluggish from the sleeping tablets, and she was short of time, yet she couldn't tear herself away from the newspaper.

'What are you reading, Mummy?'

Ragnhild had pushed the bear's nose into the bowl of porridge, milk and strawberry jam. Johanne didn't even look up. She didn't know how to explain the war over the Gaza strip to a five-year-old.

'I'm reading about some silly people,' she said vaguely.

'Silly people go to prison,' Ragnhild said cheerfully. 'Daddy takes them and puts them in the slammer!'

'The slammer?' Johanne peered at her daughter over the newspaper. 'Where did you get that word from?'

'Slammer, clink, jail, prison. They all mean the same thing. And then there's something called custard.'

'Custody,' Johanne corrected her. 'Did Kristiane teach you that?'

'Mm,' said Ragnhild, licking the bear's nose. 'Why are the silly people in the paper?'

'It's an interview,' said Johanne. 'With a man called ...'

She looked at the picture of Ehud Olmert, and quickly turned the page.

'We haven't got time for this,' she said with a smile. 'Can you go and start cleaning your teeth, please? Then I'll come and finish off.'

Ragnhild tucked her teddy bear under her arm and disappeared into the bathroom. Johanne was just about to fold up the newspaper when a brief item on the front page caught her eye; reluctantly she turned to page five.

MARIANNE CASE STILL A MYSTERY – OVER 300 WITNESSES INTER-VIEWED SO FAR.

If there was one thing she didn't need at this time in the morning, it was yet another terrible murder to think about, but she couldn't help skimming through the article. The police still had no firm leads in the case, or at least nothing they wanted to reveal at this stage, but they were able to confirm that the murder had taken place at the hotel. There was nothing to indicate the body had been moved. Detective Inspector Silje Sørensen assured the public that the murder of the 42-year-old nursery school teacher Marianne Kleive was being treated as a matter of the highest priority, and that the investigation would be stepped up over the next few days. She had every confidence that the case would be solved, but she wanted to make it clear that this could take time. A long time.

Johanne had consciously avoided reading about the murder. Since the discovery of the body she had quickly flicked past the sensational headlines in the tabloid press and the more measured articles in *Aftenposten*. Her sister's wedding reception had been bad enough without the burden of knowing that a murder had been committed in close proximity to Kristiane.

She didn't really know what had made her turn to the article today. Crossly she tossed the paper aside.

A thought, a tiny little thought crossed her mind. She didn't want anything to do with it.

Suddenly she got to her feet.

'No,' she said, clenching her fists. 'No.'

Without clearing the table she marched into the bathroom, as if the sound of her footsteps on the parquet floor might chase away the terrifying seed of awareness that was making its presence felt.

'Right, let's get these teeth cleaned,' she said unnecessarily loudly, and grabbed the toothbrush so briskly that Ragnhild burst into tears. 'There's no need to start crying, Ragnhild. Open wide.'

The lady was dead.

Johanne could hear Kristiane's voice as clearly as if she were standing next to her.

'Albertine,' Johanne said out loud. 'She meant Albertine.'

'I don't want a babysitter!' Ragnhild yelled, clamping her teeth around the toothbrush.

The lady was dead, Mummy.

That's what Kristiane had said, several times, when she was brought in from Stortingsgaten during her aunt's wedding reception, frozen and confused.

'Mummy!' Ragnhild complained through clenched teeth. 'You're hurting me!'

'Sorry,' said Johanne, letting go of the toothbrush as if it were red-hot. 'Sorry, sweetheart. Silly Mummy!'

She dropped to her knees and flung her arms around her daughter, then pressed her face against Ragnhild's neck and hugged her tightly.

'Now you're suffocating me! I can't breathe, Mummy!'

Johanne let go and took hold of Ragnhild's shoulders with both hands. She looked her right in the eye and forced a smile.

'I need you to help me,' she said, swallowing hard. 'Do you think you can help Mummy?'

'Yeees ...' Ragnhild frowned, as if someone were about to trick her into doing something she wasn't going to like.

'Who does Kristiane call "the lady"?' Johanne asked, trying to smile even more broadly.

'Everybody she doesn't know,' said Ragnhild. 'Unless they're men, of course.'

'And people she doesn't know all that well?'

'No ...'

'Yes – people like Albertine, for example. She's only looked after you five or six times. Kristiane might call Albertine "the lady" some-times, mightn't she?'

Ragnhild laughed out loud. The tears on her eyelashes sparkled in the bright light in the bathroom.

'Silly Mummy! Kristiane calls Albertine Albertine, of course. But we don't need a babysitter today, do we Mummy? You're going to be here and—'

The lady was dead.

'Yes, of course,' said Johanne. 'I'm going to look after you today.'

She was no longer there.

It wasn't Johanne who took out a fluoride tablet and popped it in Ragnhild's mouth. It wasn't Johanne Vik who walked calmly into the kitchen to pick up the lunch boxes without even glancing at the news-paper. As she approached the stairs leading down to the outside door, she could hardly feel the soft little hand in hers.

The soul. You can't see it leaving.

Christmas dinner.

Kristiane's words when they were talking about death.

'Mummy,' said Ragnhild when she had put her boots on. 'I think you're being really, really funny.'

Johanne couldn't bring herself to reply.

Couldn't even manage a smile.

*

Adam had always thought of Lukas Lysgaard as an extremely serious young man. Perhaps that wasn't so strange; after all they had met in tragic circumstances. And yet he still thought he could detect something brooding, almost melancholy in Lukas's demeanour. Something not necessarily related to his mother's death.

He had never seen Lukas smile.

At the moment the man looked like a drowned cat, and the crooked smile seemed foolish.

'Morning,' he said, holding out his hand before changing his mind and withdrawing it. 'Cold and soaking wet. I do apologize.'

'We can go and sit in my car. It's warm in there.'

Lukas obediently followed.

'So,' said Adam, sliding into the driver's seat and placing his hands on the wheel without starting the car. 'What was all that about?'

Lukas was still wearing the same expression, a silly teenager's grin which suggested he hadn't a clue what he was going to say.

'Well,' he said, taking his time. 'I just wanted to ... When I was little ... before we moved to Stavanger, I used to do that sometimes. Climb across the roof. Playing the tough guy, perhaps. My mother was terrified when she caught me once. It was ... cool.'

'Mm,' Adam nodded. 'I'm sure it was.' He drummed his fingers on the steering wheel. 'And that's why you decided to do the same thing again just before you turn thirty, in the pouring rain in January, a couple of weeks after your mother's death, while your father is in the process of having some kind of breakdown?'

A sudden burst of hail rattled against the roof of the car. The noise was deafening. Adam took advantage of the pause in the conversation to start the car and turn the heating on full. He hadn't really paid much attention to how the handbrake worked when the man at Avis was trying to explain, so he sat there with his foot on the brake pedal and the car in neutral.

'Lukas, I have no intention of ...'

Lukas snivelled and half-turned in the cramped seat.

'I have no intention of handling you with kid gloves any more, OK?' He looked the other man straight in the eye. 'You're an adult, a well-educated father of three children. It's a little while now since your mother died. To be perfectly honest, I'm getting rather tired of the fact that you won't answer my questions.'

'But I've answered everything you've—'

'Shut up!' Adam snapped, leaning towards him. 'A great deal has been said about my patience, Lukas. Some people say I'm too nice. Too nice for my own good, they sometimes maintain. But if you think for one moment that I'm going to let you leave here before you've explained to me what that performance up on the roof was all about, then you're wrong. Completely, totally and utterly bloody wrong.'

The windows steamed up. Lukas didn't speak.

'What were you doing on the roof?' Adam persisted.

'I was coming down from the attic.'

Adam banged his fists on the steering wheel so hard that it shook.

What the hell were you doing in the attic, and why couldn't you come down the stairs like a normal person?

'This has nothing to do with my mother's death,' Lukas mumbled, looking away. 'It's to do with something else. Something ... personal.'

His teeth had begun to chatter, and he wrapped his arms around his body.

'I'll decide whether it's personal or not,' Adam hissed. 'And you have exactly twenty seconds from now to come up with some satisfactory answers. Otherwise I promise you I'll bloody well lock you up until you start cooperating.'

Lukas stared at him with a mixture of disbelief and something that was beginning to resemble fear.

'I was looking for something,' he whispered almost inaudibly.

'What?'

'Something quite ... something that ...'

He put his face in his hands.

'A photo,' said Adam. It was more of a statement than a question. 'A photograph.'

Lukas stopped breathing.

'The one that was in your mother's bedroom,' said Adam. 'The one that was there when I came to see you the day after the murder, but then disappeared.'

The shower of hail had turned into torrential rain, huge drops exploding against the windscreen. The world outside the car was blurred and undefined. It was as if they were sitting inside a cocoon, and Adam could feel the unfamiliar, peculiar fury ebbing away as quickly as it had come.

'How did you know?' asked Lukas, his hands dropping to his knee.

'I didn't know. I guessed. Did you find it?'

'No.'

Adam sighed and tried once more to find a comfortable sitting position in which he could relax.

'Who is the photo of?'

'I don't know. Honestly. I really don't know.'

'But you have a theory,' said Adam.

Once again silence fell. A car came towards them, its headlights transforming the windscreen into a kaleidoscope of yellow and pale grey, before leaving the interior in semi-darkness once more.

Lukas didn't speak.

'I'm perfectly serious,' Adam said quietly. 'I will do everything in my power to make life difficult for you unless you start communicating right now.'

'I think I might have a sister somewhere. The photograph might be of my sister. My older sister.'

A child, thought Adam. The same idea had occurred to him several days ago.

A child that had disappeared. A child that perhaps hadn't disappeared after all.

'Thank you,' he said almost inaudibly. 'I just wish you'd found the photo.'

'But I didn't. Presumably my father got rid of it. What would you have done with it? If I'd found it, I mean?'

Adam smiled for the first time since Lukas came down from the roof. He ran his fingers through his hair and shook his head slightly.

'If we had a photograph, Lukas, we'd find your sister in no time. If she's still alive, and doesn't live too far from Norway. If she is your sister, that is. We don't know. We don't know whether that photograph has anything whatsoever to do with the murder of your mother. But I can assure you that I would have devoted some time to finding out!'

'But what would you ... ? How could you use an anonymous photograph to ... ?'

'We have huge databases. Comprehensive computer programs. And if all the technology in the world wasn't enough, then ...'

The foot on the brake pedal was going to sleep, so he put the car in first gear and switched off the engine.

'If I had to knock on every door in Bergen myself, if I had to put up posters with my own hands all over the country, ring round every single TV station and newspaper, I would find her. You can rest assured of that.'

Lukas nodded.

'That's what I thought,' he said. 'That's exactly what I thought you'd say. Can I go now? My car's parked just up the road.'

Adam's eyes narrowed as he looked at Lukas.

'Yes. But don't forget what I've said to you today. From now on it's zero tolerance as far as I'm concerned when it comes to keeping secrets. OK?'

'OK,' Lukas nodded, opening the door. 'I'll be in touch.'

Once outside the car, he turned and leaned in.

'Thank you for not saying anything to my father,' he said.

'No problem,' said Adam, waving as he started the engine, indicated and pulled away.

Lukas scurried to his own car, keeping one hand on his stomach where he could feel the outline of a photograph he had no intention of sharing with anyone.

Not yet, anyway.

*

'School isn't over yet,' said Kristiane for at least the fiftieth time when they eventually got home. 'School isn't over yet.'

'No,' Johanne said calmly. 'But I want to talk to you about something really important, sweetheart. That's why I had to pick you up early today.'

'School isn't over yet,' Kristiane repeated, walking up the stairs like a mechanical doll. 'School finishes at four o'clock, and then I'm going to Daddy's. I'm staying at Daddy's today. School finishes at four o'clock.'

Johanne followed her without saying any more. Only when they were in the living room did she spread her hands encouragingly and confess: 'We're going to have a duvet day today, Kristiane! Just the two of us! Would you like some hot chocolate with whipped cream?'

'Dam-di-rum-ram,' said Kristiane as she slowly began rocking from side to side on the sofa.

Johanne went over to her daughter and sat down beside her. She pulled Kristiane's sweater and vest out of the waistband of her trousers and allowed her fingers to dance gently over her daughter's slender young back. Kristiane smiled and lay down across her knee. They sat there for several minutes until Kristiane began to sing a folk song.

'Bind deg ein blomekrans, kom so til leik og dans, fela ho let no så vakkert i lund.'

'That's a lovely song,' whispered Johanne.

'Sit ikkje stur og tung, syn at du óg er ung ...'

Kristiane stopped singing.

'A lovely spring song,' Johanne said. 'A spring song in January. What a clever girl you are.'

'If you sing about the spring, it will come.'

Kristiane's laughter was as fragile as glass. Johanne ran her forefinger along the contours of her spine, all the way down from the nape of her neck.

'That tickles,' Kristiane smiled. 'Do it again.'

'Do you remember Aunt Marie's wedding?'

'Of course. Where's Sulamit, anyway?'

'Sulamit was worn out, sweetheart. You remember that, don't you?'

When she was one year old, Kristiane had been given a little red fire engine. She decided it was actually a cat, and called it Sulamit. It had been her faithful companion for more than eight years. The wheels had fallen off one by one, the colours had faded. The ladder on the roof was long gone. The eyes on the headlights were blind, and little Sulamit looked like neither a fire engine nor a cat when Adam reversed over it by mistake on the drive one day.

Kristiane had been inconsolable.

'Sulamit was a wonderful cat,' she said now. 'Can I have another cat, Mum?'

'But we've got Jack,' said Johanne. 'He's not all that keen on cats, as you well know.'

'I am the invisible child,' said Kristiane.

Johanne's fingers hovered like butterflies over the thin skin on her back.

'Sometimes no one can see me.'

'When?' whispered Johanne.

'Sulamit, sulamat, sulatullamit on the mat.'

'Was it at Marie's wedding that no one could see you?'

'More. Tickle more, Mum.'

'Did you see anyone? Even if they couldn't see you?'

Johanne was desperately trying to remember what Kristiane had actually said that night at the hotel, when she herself had been terrified, furious and in no state to take in anything at all.

'A lady was murdered there,' said Kristiane, suddenly sitting up next to her mother. 'Marianne Kleive. Nursery school teacher. Married to the noted award-winning documentary film-maker Synnøve Hessel! Women can marry each other in Norway. So can men.'

Her voice had suddenly reverted to a monotonous chant.

'You read too many newspapers,' smiled Johanne, putting her arm around her daughter and drawing her close.

'Dearly loved, sadly missed.'

'Have you started reading the death notices?'

'A cross means the dead person was a Christian. A Star of David means the deceased was Jewish. What does the bird mean, Mum?'

At last Kristiane's eyes met her mother's gaze for a fleeting moment.

'That you hope the dead person will rest in peace,' Johanne whispered.

'I want a bird in my death notice.'

'You're not going to die.'

'I'm going to die one day.'

'We're all going to die one day.'

'You too, Mum.'

'Yes, me too. But not for a long time.'

'You can't know that.'

Silence. They were only whispering, sitting close together on the sofa, Johanne with her arm around the slender fourteen-year-old like a safety belt as the daylight poured in across the living-room floor, almost dazzling them. She could feel the budding breasts, the unavoidable signs that Kristiane, too, would become an adult, even if puberty had come late.

'No,' Johanne said eventually. 'I can't know that. But I don't think it will happen for a long time. I'm healthy, Kristiane, and not so very old. Have you ever seen a dead person?'

'You'll die before me, Mum.'

'I hope I do. No parent wants their child to die before them.'

'Who will look after me when you die?'

Johanne had been asking herself that same question, over and over again, ever since Kristiane was just a few hours old, and Johanne was the only one who realized there was something wrong with her child.

'You'll be an adult by then, sweetheart. You'll be able to look after yourself.'

'I'll never be able to look after myself. I'm not like other children. I go to a special school. I'm autistic.'

'You're not autistic, you're ...'

Johanne quickly sat up straight and placed her hand beneath Kristiane's chin.

'You're not like other children. That's quite true. You are just yourself. And I love you so much, just for being you. And you know what, Kristiane?'

Kristiane responded to her smile, her eyes focusing on Johanne.

'I'm not exactly like other people either. Actually, I think we all feel that way. None of us feels exactly like other people. And there will always be someone to look after you. Ragnhild, for example. And Amund, too. He's your nephew, after all!'

Kristiane's laughter was brittle and as clear as a bell.

'They're younger than me!'

'Yes, but by the time I die they'll be grown up. And then they can look after you.'

'I've seen a dead person. The soul weighs twenty-one grams. But you can't see it leaving.'

Johanne said nothing. She still had her hand under Kristiane's chin, but her daughter's gaze was turned inward again, focused on a place no one else could reach, and her voice was expressionless and mechanical once more as she went on: 'Marianne Kleive, forty-two years old, died 19 December 2008. Bishop Eva Karin Lysgaard, dearly loved, sadly missed, unexpectedly taken from us on Christmas Eve 2008. Funeral arrangements to be notified at a later date. The cross means she was a Christian.'

'Stop,' Johanne whispered, quickly drawing the girl close. 'Stop now.'

It was exactly twelve o'clock, and a cloud drifted across the unforgiving January sun. A pleasant darkness filled the living room. Johanne closed her eyes as she held her daughter tightly, rocking her from side to side.

'I am the invisible child,' Kristiane whispered.

Fear

Perhaps he should never have had children.

The very thought made the acid in his stomach eat away at his duodenum. He drew up his knees and placed both hands on the spot where in his younger days he had been able to feel the end of his ribs and the beginning of his stomach. Now it was all just one soft mass, in spite of the fact that he was lying on his back: a flabby belly that was far too big, with a stabbing pain deep inside a layer of fat.

Marcus Koll's entire life revolved around his son.

His work, his company, his extended family – it was all meaningless without little Marcus. When Rolf came into their lives they were already a twosome, but the three of them soon became a family, and Marcus would do anything to protect that family. But the boy remained the very hub of Marcus Koll's family wheel.

Little Marcus quickly accepted Rolf, and the love was mutual. After a while Rolf had tentatively raised the question of whether he might adopt his stepson.

As time went by, he dropped the subject.

Marcus had never told anyone about the dreams he used to have when he was young.

He wanted children.

He had been a strong boy; breaking with his father had taken real courage. It had cost him surprisingly little to come out as what and who he was. As a teenager his wilfulness could sometimes make him appear stubborn, but as an adult he became cleverer and more skilful. His obstinacy turned into purposefulness. Arrogance turned into pride. He took the sting out of his unconventional inclination with self-irony, and had never felt the need to seek out the gay haunts he knew existed in both Bergen, where he attended business college, and in Oslo when he returned home after completing his studies. On the contrary, he had always regarded seduction as a challenge. Until he met Rolf, he had seduced only heterosexual men. He was quietly proud of the fact that before him they had slept only with women. He wasn't quite so thrilled when they then returned to their straight lives.

Marcus Koll Junior hadn't exactly been a typical gay man of his time.

In addition, he wanted a child more than anything. His only sorrow – when, aged sixteen or seventeen, he had decided to stop pretending to be something he was not – was that the future would not bring him any offspring. He had never shared this sorrow with anyone, although his mother had been aware of it in the way that mothers can sometimes read their child better than the child himself. But they had never talked about that little empty space in Marcus's heart: the lack of a child of his own to love.

However, for many years Marcus Koll had been a contented young man anyway.

Things went well for him, and he never felt that his sexuality was being used against him, neither professionally nor among friends and colleagues. For a long time he served as their politically correct alibi. During the late eighties and early nineties, open homosexuality was not at all common, and his presence in the lives of other people somehow gave them something to show off about.

He was so happy with his life that he didn't even notice he was starting to burn out. He became so popular that he didn't realize he was putting too much energy into dealing with his status as an outsider. In the entirely heterosexual life he was leading – with the minor difference that he went to bed with men without lying about it – his soul slowly crumbled until he collapsed with exhaustion; he hadn't even seen it coming.

Then his friends started to have children.

Marcus Koll wanted children, too.

He had always wanted children.

He made the decision.

When he travelled to California to sign a contract with a surrogate mother and egg donor, he had recently taken over the running of his father's old company. The future lay before him. He had been blessed with money, and was able to explain away his frequent visits to America over the following year as essential business trips.

One evening in late January 2001 he had simply turned up at his mother's apartment with the boy in his arms. As soon as she opened the door she understood everything, and burst into tears. Gently, she took her new grandchild, held him close to her breast and carried him into the spacious apartment which her children had bought her when they suddenly became wealthy. She had never quite got used to the apartment, but when Marcus arrived with the child she sat down right in the middle of the sumptuous sofa that no one had ever used. With her nose against the boy's cheek she whispered almost inaudibly: 'Grandma's home, little one. Grandma's home at last. And you're at home with Grandma.'

'His name is Marcus,' Marcus said, and his mother had wept and wept. 'Not after me, after Grandfather.'

The idea of losing little Marcus was unthinkable.

Perhaps he should never have had him.

'Are you awake?' Rolf murmured, turning over in bed. 'What time is it?'

'Go back to sleep,' Marcus whispered.

'But why aren't you sleeping?' He turned on his side, resting his head on his hand. 'You lie awake almost every night,' said Rolf with a big yawn.

'No I don't. Go back to sleep.'

Only the glow from the digital alarm clock made it possible to see anything in the room. Marcus stared at his own hands. They looked green in the darkness. He tried to smile.

The fear had arrived with his son. The fact that he was different; the incontrovertible fact that he wasn't like everybody else and never could be became much clearer. He had always believed it was easy to protect himself. When his son came into his life, he realized how helpless he sometimes felt when he encountered prejudices that he would have ignored in the past and dismissed as the attitudes of a bygone age. He had always thought the world was moving forwards, but when little Marcus arrived he sometimes had the feeling that the development of society was actually describing an unpredictable, asymmetric curve, and that it was difficult to keep up. The joy and love he felt for his son were all-encompassing. The fear of not being able to protect him from the evils and prejudices of the world tore him apart. Then Rolf came along, and many things became much better. Never perfect. Marcus still felt like a marked man in every sense. But Rolf brought strength and happiness, and little Marcus had a fantastic life. That was the most important thing, and as time went by Marcus chose to keep the periods of helplessness and depression to himself. They became more and more infrequent.

Until Georg Koll, his own deceased, accursed father, had played one last trick on him.

'What is it?' said Rolf, more fully awake now.

The duvet had partly slipped off his body. He was naked, still lying on his side with one knee drawn up and the other leg stretched out. Even in the faint light the contours of his stomach muscles were clearly visible.

'Nothing.'

'Come on, I can tell there's something wrong!'

The duvet rustled as Rolf impatiently pulled it over his athletic body.

'Surely you can tell me! You just haven't been yourself recently. If it's to do with work, if it's something you can't talk about, then at least tell me that's what it is! We can't—'

'There's really nothing wrong,' said Marcus, turning over. 'Let's get back to sleep.'

He could hear that Rolf wasn't moving, and he could feel Rolf's eyes burning into his back.

He should have talked to Rolf as soon as the problem arose. Now, so many months and so many worries later, it struck him that he hadn't even considered the possibility of sharing his troubles with his husband. That frightened him. Rolf was one of the most sensible people he knew. Rolf would surely have found a way out. Rolf would have calmly analysed the situation and talked things over until he came up with a solution. Rolf was a positive person, an optimist with an indomitable belief that everything – even the darkest tragedy – has a silver lining if you just take the time to find it.

Of course he should have talked to Rolf.

That was the first thing he should have done.

Together they could cope with anything.

Rolf was still lying there in silence. Marcus kept his eyes fixed firmly on the clock. He blinked when the numbers changed from 3.07 to 3.08. Suddenly, he took a quick breath and searched for the words that could support the weight of the painful story they should have shared long ago.

Before he could find the words, Rolf turned over.

They were lying back to back.

Just a few minutes later, Rolf's breathing was once again heavy and even.

Suddenly, Marcus realized why it was too late to say anything to Rolf: he would never forgive him.

Never.

If he confided in his partner, their life as Marcus knew and loved it would be over. He wouldn't just lose Rolf; he would lose little Marcus. The fear shot through him, and he lay there wide awake until the numbers switched from 06.59 to 07.00.

*

When Johanne woke with a start, she was soaked in sweat. The bedclothes were sticking to her body. She tried to escape from their damp embrace, but merely succeeded in getting her feet caught in the opening of the duvet cover. She felt trapped, and kicked desperately to free them. The duvet fought back. In the end she was free. She tried to remember what kind of nightmare she might have had.

Her head was completely empty.

Her hands were shaking as she reached for the glass of water on her bedside table and emptied it. As she was putting it back, it fell on the floor. She screwed up her eyes and pulled a face until she remembered that Kristiane was at Isak's. Ragnhild never woke up this early.

She was still having some difficulty breathing as she flopped back against the pillow and tried to relax.

Despite the fact that she had spent more than twenty minutes talking to Adam on the phone the previous evening, she hadn't mentioned the conversation with Kristiane. Nor had she said anything to Isak when he turned up after school, feeling rather annoyed. She had forgotten to tell him that she had picked Kristiane up, contravening all their plans and agreements. When he came up the stairs with an uncharacteristically angry expression on his face, she simply said that she had taken some time off work and for once had seized the opportunity to spend some time alone with Kristiane.

She naturally apologized for forgetting to let him know.

As usual Isak accepted everything, and when he set off home with his daughter he was just as good-humoured as always.

Kristiane had witnessed something in connection with the murder of Marianne Kleive. That much was certain. She must at least have seen the dead woman on the evening she was murdered. But still Johanne hadn't really known what to say to Isak and Adam. Her daughter hadn't actually told her what had happened. It was her body language and facial expression, her choice of words and the tone of her voice that had been crucial.

Exactly the kind of thing that made Isak laugh at Johanne, and made Adam try to hide how exhausted he was.

And if either of them had believed – against all expectation – that she might be right, then Adam, at least, would have insisted on contacting the police straight away. Isak, too, probably. He was a good father in many ways, but he had never understood how infinitely vulnerable Kristiane was.

If there was one thing she wouldn't be able to cope with it was strangers trampling about in her own little sphere, asking her questions about something she had obviously managed to lock away, somehow. Clearing up a murder was important, of course, but Kristiane was more important.

This was something Johanne would have to tackle by herself.

Her pulse was steadier now. She was beginning to feel cold because of her night sweat, and decided to change the bed. She got out clean sheets and a duvet cover, and with practised hands she had a dry, cool bed in just four minutes. She hadn't the energy to change Adam's duvet. The bed looked odd with covers that didn't match, but it could wait until tomorrow.

She settled down and closed her eyes.

She was wide awake. Turned over. Tried to think about something else.

Kristiane had seen something terrible. A crime, or the result of a crime.

Someone was watching Kristiane.

She flung herself on to her other side. Her pulse rate increased.

Suddenly she sat bolt upright. Things couldn't go on like this. Right now there was nothing she could do. She couldn't ring anyone at this time of the day, besides which Kristiane was perfectly safe with Isak. Somehow she had to get through the night.

Tomorrow she would talk to Adam.

The decision made her feel calmer.

She would ask him to come home. She didn't have to say why. He would know from the sound of her voice that he had to come. Adam would return from Bergen, and she would tell him everything.

She couldn't tell him anything.

If he believed she was right, it would destroy Kristiane.

This was impossible. She grabbed Adam's pillow, placed it on her stomach and hugged it close, as if it were some part of her child.

She could get up and do some work.

No.

There were three books on the bedside table. She selected one of them. Turned to the page with the corner folded down and began to read. *The Road* by Cormac McCarthy didn't make her feel one jot calmer. After three pages she closed both the book and her eyes.

Her mind was racing, and she felt physically ill.

For a long time Adam had wanted to have a television in the bedroom. Now she regretted not giving in. She was incapable of watching anything attentively, but she had an intense need to hear voices. For a moment she was tempted to wake Ragnhild. Instead, she switched on the clock radio. It was tuned to NRK P2 and classical music filled the room – music that was every bit as melancholy as McCarthy's post-apocalyptic novel. She moved the dial until she found a local station that played chart music all night, then turned the volume up as loud as she dared; the neighbour's bedroom was directly below theirs.

Dagens Næringsliv had fallen on the floor.

She bent down and picked it up. It was the current edition, and she hadn't read it. Not that there was a great deal to read; the leading article and every other headline on the front page was about the financial crisis. Up to now the collapse of the world's financial markets had felt largely irrelevant to her, even if she was reluctant to admit it. Both she and Adam were employed within the public sector, neither of them was in danger of losing their jobs, and interest rates were in free fall. They were already noticing that they had more disposable income than they'd had for a long time.

She started reading from the back as usual.

The main news on the stock market page was to do with the death of the installation artist Niclas Winter. Johanne had seen several of his pieces, and *Vanity Fair, reconstruction* in particular had made an impression when the whole family went into the city one day and spent an hour among Winter's three installations on Rådhuskaia. Kristiane had been completely fascinated; Ragnhild had been more interested in the seagulls and the fountain; and Adam had snorted and shaken his head at the idea that this kind of thing was regarded as art.

It seemed Winter had no heirs.

His mother and maternal grandparents were dead. He had no siblings, and his mother had also been an only child. There was quite simply no one to inherit the small fortune Niclas Winter had unknowingly left behind. Apart from the completed piece *I was thinking of something blue and maybe grey, darling*, it turned out there were four more large installations in the deceased artist's studio.

Connoisseurs in the art world were expressing themselves in particularly high-flown terms about *CockPitt*, a homo-erotic homage to Angelina Jolie's husband. Evidently there had already been an anonymous bid of four million kroner for the work. *Dagens Næringsliv*'s sources claimed that the actor himself wanted to buy it.

In spite of the financial crisis, it seemed there was no shortage of money when it came to Niclas Winter's art now that he was dead. Statoil-Hydro had already put in a claim for the installation that they had ordered then cancelled, and only gave up when the administrator of the estate was able to produce the relevant documentation. His approximate and preliminary valuation of the sculptures was around 15 to 20 million kroner. Maybe more. The article mentioned that, ironically, Niclas had lived on a small income and the goodwill of various patrons of the arts, and only became a wealthy man after his death. A not uncommon fate among artists, as the businessman and art collector Christen Sveaas pointed out. He had two smaller installations by Niclas Winter in his extensive collection in Kistefos, and was able to confirm that the value of both pieces had risen dramatically.

A background article made it clear that Niclas certainly had his demons. He was HIV positive, but the condition was kept in check with the help of medication. Since the age of eighteen he had ended up in rehab three times. His last stay, four years ago, had been a success. His best work had been created since then, and two of his collaborators expressed great surprise at the fact that Niclas had started using heroin again. He was on the brink of a major international breakthrough, and particularly in the last few weeks before his death he had seemed contented, almost happy. Previous relapses had occurred as a result of artistic setbacks, so it was difficult to understand why he would have sought refuge in drugs at this point.

Johanne was aware that she was breathing more calmly, and was actually starting to feel tired. Reading about the misfortunes of others could sometimes provide a new perspective on things. She allowed the newspaper to drop on to the bed, and her eyes closed.

Kristiane is safe, she thought, feeling that sleep was on its way at last.

She didn't even dare to lie down and turn out the light. She just wanted to slip into the darkness inside her eyelids. Sleep. Just wanted to sleep.

Kristiane is safe with Isak and tomorrow I will speak to Adam. Everything will be fine, we'll all be fine.

When she woke up four hours later the newspaper was still lying in front of her on the bed, open at the article about the dead installation artist Niclas Winter.

*

'Have you seen this article?'

Kristen Faber looked up reluctantly from his documents and took the newspaper his secretary was holding out to him.

'What's it about?' he mumbled, trying to cram the rest of the Danish pastry in his mouth without making too many crumbs.

A fine shower of greasy dough and almond paste landed on his shirt front and he leaned forward in an attempt to brush it off without leaving a stain.

'Isn't that yesterday's paper?'

'Yes,' said his secretary. 'I took it home after work, as usual, and I found this. It's hardly surprising that your client didn't turn up! He's dead.'

'Who?'

He carried on chewing and held the paper up in front of him with one hand.

'Oh,' he said with his mouth full. 'Him. Jesus. Wasn't he quite young?'

'If you read the article,' said his secretary with an indulgent smile, 'then—'

'I never read the stock market page. Let's see. Niclas Winter. Aha. An overdose, eh? Poor sod. It looks as if ...'

He stopped chewing now.

'Bloody hell. He was famous. I've never heard of the bloke. Except as a potential client, I mean.'

As he put the newspaper down on the desk, his secretary went off to find a dustpan and brush. He carried on reading as she swept the floor around him, and he was still reading when she went away and returned with a Thermos of freshly brewed coffee.

'Your breakfast isn't particularly nutritious,' she said gently, filling his cup. 'You ought to eat before you leave home. Wholemeal bread or cereal. Not Danish pastries, for heaven's sake! When did you last drink a glass of milk, for example?'

'If I needed a mother around here I'd employ my own. Where are those bloody documents?'

He had started shuffling through the heaps of current material. He was certain he'd placed the sealed brown envelope in the pile on his desk before he went home for a shower, after an eventful return flight from Barbados. Now it was nowhere to be seen.

'Shit. I'm due in court in fifteen minutes. Can you try and find his papers? They're in a sealed envelope with *Property of Niclas Winter* and his date of birth on it.'

He stood up, pulled on his jacket and grabbed his briefcase on the way to the door.

'And Vera! Don't open it! I want to have that pleasure myself!'

The door slammed behind him, and once again silence descended on the office of Kristen Faber, solicitor.

*

Astrid Tomte Lysgaard didn't really know if she liked the depth of silence in the house when Lukas had gone to work and the children had been dropped off at school and nursery. None of her friends were housewives, apart from the obligatory year after each birth, but she had the impression that most of them envied her the peace they assumed must descend on the house each day between 8.30 and 4.15.

For a long time she had felt the same way.

The daily housework rarely took more than three hours, often less. Although she took the children each morning and picked them up each afternoon, and did all the family shopping, there was still a lot of time left over. She read. She enjoyed going for walks. Twice a week she went to the Nautilus gym on Idrettsveien. Occasionally, she would feel a pang of unhappiness, but it never lasted long.

The fact that everything was done and dinner was on the table when Lukas got home made the afternoons calm. Made their life together more enjoyable. Family life much better. They could spend time with the children instead of worrying about the housework, and Lukas showed her every single day how grateful he was that she had chosen to stay at home.

Since her mother-in-law's death, everything had changed.

Lukas was grieving in a way that frightened her.

He seemed so distant.

Mechanical.

He said very little, and was prone to losing his temper, even with the children. Under normal circumstances he was the one who sat down and helped their eldest son with his schoolwork, but at the moment he was clearly unable to concentrate on the complexities of Year 2 homework. Instead, he had started clearing out the garage, where he was intending to to build new shelves along one wall. It must be freezing cold out there every evening, and when he finally did come in he would eat his evening meal in silence, then go to bed without even touching her.

It was so quiet in the house, and she didn't like it.

She set down the iron and went over to the window to switch on the radio. Another miserable day was pressing itself against the wet glass. Surely it had to stop raining soon. January was always a desolate month, but this one was worse than usual. The low pressure was actually having a physical effect on her; for several days she had been troubled by a slight headache, and now it had got worse. Her temples were pounding, and she tried massaging them gently. It didn't help at all. She would go to the bathroom and take a couple of Alvedon before finishing the ironing.

There were no painkillers in the locked medicine cabinet. She searched in despair among Asterix plasters and Flux, bottles of Pyrisept and Vademecum. Not a painkiller in sight, apart from suppositories for children.

It was as if not being able to find any tablets had made the headache worse.

Lukas's migraine tablets, she thought.

They would help.

The problem was that they weren't in the medicine cabinet. Lukas thought the lock was too easy to force, and strong medication could be dangerous for a curious eight-year-old. Instead, he kept the box locked in the drawer of the big desk in his study. Astrid knew where the key was: behind a first edition of *Around the World in Eighty Days*, which his parents had given him on his twenty-first birthday.

She had never opened the drawer, and hesitated before inserting the key in the lock.

They had no secrets from one another, she and Lukas.

Perhaps she ought to ring and ask him first.

He was her husband, she thought wearily, and she only wanted one tablet. Lukas had never told her not to look in the drawer. The very idea of telling each other not to do something was completely alien to them.

The lock opened with an almost inaudible click. She pulled out the drawer and found herself staring down at a photograph. A woman, and the photograph must be quite old. For a while she just stood there looking down at it, then eventually she picked it up, cautiously, and held it under the brighter light of the desk lamp.

There was something familiar about the face, but Astrid couldn't quite place it. In a way the shape of the face and the straight nose reminded her of Lukas, but that had to be a coincidence. The woman in the photograph also had the same funny teeth, one front tooth lying slightly on top of the other, but after all lots of people had teeth like that. The singer Lill Lindfors, for example, as Astrid had often pointed out when they were young and she was besotted with everything about Lukas.

Despite the fact that she had no idea who the woman was, it struck her in some odd way that she had seen this photograph before. She just couldn't remember where. As she stared at the woman she realized her headache had disappeared. Quickly, she put the photograph back, closed and locked the drawer and returned the key to its hiding place.

When she left Lukas's study she closed the door carefully behind her, as if she really had done something forbidden.

*

The depressing piles of unsolved crimes in Silje Sørensen's office were getting her down. There was barely room for a coffee cup on her crowded desk, even though everything was in neatly sorted files. She sat down on her chair, pushed aside a bundle of newspaper cuttings and put down the cup, before starting to go through the whole lot.

She had to reprioritize.

Her list of things to do was growing.

The Police Officers' Association's more or less legal actions and protests against terrible working conditions, low pay, inadequate staffing and the threat to pension entitlement had led to a somewhat acerbic tone in any dealings between the government and the police. Officers were no longer so willing to work overtime. Things didn't get done as quickly nowadays. The organization's 11,000-plus members were gradually beginning to take a fresh look at their priorities. Although the statistics hadn't yet been processed, it looked as if the clear-up rate for 2008 had fallen dramatically in comparison with previous years – and it was only January. Employees were demanding their right to free time, and were off sick more frequently. Sometimes this coincided noticeably with public holidays and weekends, when major challenges awaited those who were charged with maintaining law and order.

The criminals were having an easier time all round.

People felt less and less safe. The police had always scored highly when it came to credibility and trustworthiness, but now they were losing the sympathy of the public. More and more frequently the papers were running stories about victims of violent crime who had been unable to report the offence because their local police station wasn't manned, rural stations that were closed at weekends, and victims of crime who had to wait several days for the police to turn up and look for any clues. If they turned up at all, that is.

Silje Sørensen was a member of the union, but she had long since abandoned any attempt to keep a record of her overtime. The only yardstick she used was the reaction at home. When her sons became too much of a handful and her husband became more and more taciturn, she tried to spend more time at home. Otherwise, she sneaked off to work outside normal working hours as often as she could.

As the only child of a shipping owner, her decision to train as a police officer hadn't exactly been expected. Her mother had gone into a state of shock and hysteria when she learned of her daughter's career choice. This lasted throughout Silje's first year in college. We've wasted a fortune on boarding schools in Switzerland and England, her mother wailed, and now my daughter is going to throw away her future working in the public sector! If she must get her hands dirty dealing with violent criminals and the like, then why on earth couldn't she become a solicitor instead? Or a legal advisor within the police service, if the worst came to the worst?

That was exactly the reaction Silje had wanted.

Her father had beamed and kissed her on the forehead when she told him she had got into the Police Training Academy. That wasn't exactly the idea.

Silje Sørensen had never rebelled as a child or a teenager. Never protested. Not when she was forced to move abroad at the age of ten, only seeing her parents during the holidays. Not when she had to spend two months at a French language school in Switzerland at the age of fifteen, where the working day began at 6.30 in the morning and the Catholic nuns had no qualms about using punishments that were probably forbidden under the Geneva Convention. Silje didn't even argue with her father when he decided that she should squeeze five school years into two and a half; she gained a degree in English by the time she was nineteen. By then she had come of age, and as a reward for her silent patience and remarkable hard work, her father had transferred more than half of his fortune to his only daughter.

Training as a police officer was Silje Sørensen's first deliberate act of rebellion.

When she was allocated to work with the legendary Hanne Wilhelmsen during her first year, she quickly realized that this stubborn, rebellious choice of career was going to make her happy. She loved it. The majority of what she knew about police work she had learned from her reluctant, uncommunicative mentor. Although Hanne Wilhelmsen had made herself more and more unpopular through her own headstrong approach, Silje had never ceased to admire her. When Inspector Wilhelmsen was shot during a dramatic incident in Nordmarka and paralysed from the waist down, Silje had grieved as if it had happened to a sister. She never really got over the fact that Hanne had then turned her back on the few remaining friends she had in the big shabby police headquarters on Grønlandsleiret.

Silje Sørensen was proud of her profession, but accepted with resignation the parameters within which she was forced to operate.

She decided to sort the cases in order of seriousness. Minor knife crimes and pub brawls with no life-threatening injuries she placed in a separate pile.

You'll probably get away with it, she thought wearily, and tried to forget that several of the cases involved known perpetrators. Their victims would regard any attempt to abandon these investigations as highly provocative. However, that was the way it was, and according to every directive from both the public prosecutor and the National Police Board, she was perfectly justified in prioritizing more serious cases. The public might have some difficulty in understanding the police definition of serious, but that couldn't be helped.

After about an hour the files had been sorted into five piles.

Silje finished off the dregs of her tepid coffee, then picked up three of the piles and placed them in the cupboard behind her.

Two left.

The smallest contained murders. Three files. The first very thin, the second almost as slim. The third was so fat that she had put two rubber bands around it to keep everything together.

Suddenly, she got up and went over to the noticeboard on the wall opposite her desk. She quickly scanned every piece of paper before placing one on the desk and dropping the rest into the large waste-paper basket beside it. She took three sheets of A4 out of the cupboard. They fitted next to each other perfectly at the top of the noticeboard.

Runar Hansen, she wrote with a red felt-tip on the first sheet.
19/11/08.

On the next sheet she wrote *Hawre Ghani*.
24/11/08.

She chewed the cap of the pen and thought for a moment before adding a question mark.

24/11/08?

It wasn't possible at this stage to say exactly when Hawre Ghani had been murdered, but at least they had confirmation that he had, in fact, been murdered. The pathologist had found clear signs of garrotting. It was hardly likely that the boy had hanged himself with a steel wire until his head almost came away from his body, then thrown himself in the sea. They were only able to hint at the time of death, but so far the investigation had found no evidence to suggest that the boy had been alive after he went off with a client outside Oslo's central station on Monday 24 November. All the CCTV cameras had, of course, been checked. No joy. This matched Martin Setre's story: the man had approached them just outside the entrance.

Clever bastard, thought Silje with a sigh.

Marianne Kleive, she wrote on the last sheet of paper.
19/12/08.

She put the cap back on the pen and took two steps back. She felt the edge of the desk behind her legs and sat down.

Three murders. All unsolved.

Runar Hansen was her guilty conscience. She couldn't even bring herself to look through the thin file. Instead, she stared at the name, the anonymous name of a drug addict who had been beaten and abused in Sofienberg Park, apparently without anyone taking much notice. All

Runar Hansen had merited was a quick examination of the crime scene some hours after his body had been found, a post-mortem report, and a brief mention in the evening paper. Plus two interviews with witnesses, whose only contribution was that Runar Hansen had no fixed abode and was unemployed, and that he had a sister called Trude.

At least something was happening in the investigation into the murder of Hawre Ghani. The sketch by the police artist had been distributed internally. It had been decided not to make it public yet, because experience indicated this would lead to a flood of calls. The man's appearance was so ordinary that there would be a deluge of callers insisting that they recognized him. Instead, Knut Bork was still working on the prostitution angle. Silje had ordered a new and extensive investigation into the boy's life since he came to Norway. If possible, she was hoping to obtain a clearer picture of Hawre Ghani's tragic fate.

Work on the Marianne Kleive case was proceeding at full throttle.

The murder of the 42-year-old nursery school teacher had all the ingredients of a juicy media story. The private pictures obtained by *Verdens Gang* just two hours after the murder was made public showed an unusually attractive woman. Thick, wavy blonde hair, a slim figure with long legs and an athletic appearance. Exactly the kind of lesbian the media loved. There was something of Gro Hammerseng about her, Silje thought, as she pinned up the front page she had torn out of *VG* a few days earlier. And even if her wife, Synnøve Hessel, wasn't exactly a celebrity, she occupied such a central position in the Norwegian film world that the papers were able to use their favourite phrase 'the noted and award-winning' when writing about the victim's grieving widow – who also looked pretty good, incidentally, even wearing a padded jacket with her hair blowing all over the place at a height of 5,208 metres at North Base Camp in Nepal.

The fact that the murder had taken place in the respectable Hotel Continental also helped. Two days after the body had been found, *VG* dedicated an entire page to an 'at home with' report on a man named Fritiof Hansen, an insignificant individual who was some kind of caretaker at the hotel. He had found the body, and thanks to his passion for the TV series *CSI* he had managed to keep everyone away from the scene until the police arrived to secure any evidence. In the picture he was sitting in his best armchair with a glass of beer and a small packet of crisps, looking as if all the cares of the world were resting on his shoulders.

Sometimes Silje Sørensen wished the mass media didn't exist. Sometimes she would have liked to abolish the freedom of the press.

She reached for her coffee cup.

It was empty.

She frowned and looked from one name to the other. She groped for the felt-tip without taking her eyes off the noticeboard. Quickly, she pulled the cap off with her teeth, went over and wrote SOFIENBERG PARK beneath Runar Hansen's name and the date of his death. Under Hawre's name she wrote UNDERAGE MALE PROSTITUTION, and finally – across the top of the photo of Marianne Kleive on Gaustatoppen Mountain in the sunshine, wearing a bikini top, cut-off jeans and sturdy walking boots – she wrote CIVIL PARTNERSHIP.

As she was settling back on her desk, there was a knock on the door. She took the cap of the pen out of her mouth and shouted: 'Come in!'

Knut Bork did as he was told.

'Hi,' he said breathlessly. 'I thought I'd just—'

'Stand here,' said Silje Sørensen. 'Come and stand next to me.'

DC Bork shrugged his shoulders and obliged.

'What are you up to? What's that?' He nodded in the direction of the noticeboard.

'Those are the three murders I'm dealing with at the moment,' said Silje.

'Three is too many.'

'I had four. I turned one down. Does anything strike you about those three?'

'Does anything strike me? Well, I'd need to look through the files and—'

'No. You're familiar with the cases, Knut. Just look at what's up on the board.'

He frowned without saying anything.

'Look at what I've written underneath the names!'

'*Sofienberg Park*,' he read. '*Underage male prostitution. Civil partnership.*'

He still couldn't see any connection.

273

'What's Sofienberg Park famous for?' she asked.

'Well ... I know! Those ambulance drivers who—'.

'No. Well, that too, but what else? I'm not thinking about the area to the west of Sofienberg Church, but the part behind it. On the eastern side.'

'Gay sex,' he said immediately. 'Buying and selling and mutual exchanges. Not a place I'd want to go in the dark.'

'Exactly,' said Silje with a wan smile. 'That's where Runar Hansen was found. He was murdered on a raw, wet November night at some point between midnight and half past. That's about all we've managed to accomplish in his case. Establishing when he was killed, I mean.'

'Was he gay?'

'No idea. But for the time being, just focus on the reputation of the place. Do you see where I'm going with this?'

She looked at him. A shadow of surprise passed over his eyes as he suddenly got the point.

'Bloody hell,' he said, running a hand over his fair stubble. 'It's strange that LHH haven't started shouting the odds!'

For a long time, LHH – the gay and lesbian movement – had been trying to get the justice department to take violence against homosexuals seriously. The problem, Silje Sørensen had always thought, was that attacks on homosexuals rarely differed significantly from all the other attacks that happened when people had been drinking. Attacks on women. On men. On heterosexuals and homosexuals. People drank. Became aggressive. Fought, stabbed, raped and murdered. For every homosexual victim, Silje could come up with a hundred heterosexuals. She couldn't understand why they made such a fuss about it.

But this was striking.

'Runar Hansen is in a park where it's well known that homosexual services are bought, sold and exchanged,' she said slowly. 'Hawre Ghani disappears with a male punter. Marianne Kleive is married to a woman. They were all murdered in different ways, in different places, and none of them had any connection with each other while they were alive. As far as we know, that is. But ...'

Her eyes narrowed.

'I'm responsible for three completely independent murder investigations, and each one has a possible link to homosexuality. What are the odds on that?'

'Bloody long,' said Knut Bork, starting to chew on a thumbnail. 'What the fuck is going on? And seriously, Silje, why hasn't anybody noticed a possible link before?'

She didn't reply. They stood in silence gazing at the noticeboard. For a long time.

'Nobody cares about the first case,' she said suddenly. 'Nobody knows anything about the second case. People might have read in the paper about a body being found in the harbour, and there might have been a few lines saying that the dead man turned out to be a young asylum seeker. But that's all. As far as Marianne Kleive is concerned, that case is ...'

She hesitated for such a long time that he carried on for her: 'That case is so unusual and absurd that nobody has actually made a connection with the fact that the victim is a lesbian.'

Silje went over to the board, took down the sheets of paper and the newspaper article, screwed them up and threw them in the wastepaper basket. Knut Bork remained standing there with his arms folded as she walked around the desk and sat down.

'You and I,' she said firmly, 'are going to keep this to ourselves. For the time being. It could all be a coincidence, just as every connection can be pure chance; on the other hand it could be ...'

'Something very nasty indeed,' Knut Bork supplied; his thumb had started to bleed.

*

For the second time in three weeks Johanne was at home alone, and it felt almost frightening. The apartment always seemed so different without the familiar sounds of the children. She noticed that she was moving cautiously across the floor, so as not to make any noise.

'Pull yourself together,' she muttered to herself, putting on a CD that Lina Skytter had compiled, burned and given to her for Christmas. Kristiane was at Isak's until Friday, and every other Wednesday Ragnhild went to visit her maternal grandparents and stayed over.

She had been trying to get hold of Adam for several hours, but her calls went straight to voicemail. Presumably, he was in a meeting. When the day had finally dawned after the restless, fearful night, she had realized she had to talk to him. There was no more room for doubt – unlike last night when she kept changing her mind. She had made her decision now, and that very fact made her a little more optimistic about the whole thing.

If only she knew what Kristiane had actually seen.

Even though she realized there must be something, she was still unsure what it was. It didn't feel right to press her daughter any further. Later, perhaps, she thought, as she tiptoed around in her stocking feet, not really knowing what to do.

The music Lina had put together wasn't entirely to Johanne's taste. She went over to the CD player and turned down Kurt Nilsen's voice right in the middle of the chorus of one of his ballads.

She ought to eat something, but she wasn't hungry.

Adam's meeting must be taking a long time; it was three hours since she left the first message asking him to call her.

She could sit down and do some work, of course.

Or read.

Watch a film, perhaps.

She reached for the phone and keyed in Isak's number without even thinking about it. He answered right away.

'Hi, it's Johanne.'

'Hi.' She could hear him smiling on the other end of the line.

'I just rang to ...'

'To ask how Kristiane is,' he supplied. 'She's absolutely fine. We've been to the pool at Bislett, even though children aren't really allowed in except at weekends. She's so quiet that the lady in the ticket office lets her in.'

'Do you let her go into the women's changing room on her own?'

'Of course. She's too big to come into the men's with me! She's starting to develop breasts, in case you haven't noticed! And she's got a little bit of hair down below too! Our little girl is growing up, Johanne, and, of course, I let her go into the women's changing room on her own.'

She didn't reply.

'Johanne,' he said wearily. 'She's fine! We're making tacos, and she's fried the mince all on her own. She's chopping vegetables and doing a great job. When she's with me we always cook dinner together. She'll be fourteen this year, Johanne. You can't treat her like a child all her life.'

She is a child.

She's the most vulnerable child in the world.

'Hello?'

'Yes, yes,' Johanne mumbled. 'I'm here. I'm glad you're having a good time. I just wanted to check if—'

'Would you like to speak to her? She's standing right here.'

There was a terrible clatter in the background.

'Oops,' said Isak. 'Something just fell on the floor. Can I ask her to call you later on?'

'No, no. There's no need. Have a good time. See you Friday.'

'See you!'

He disappeared and she tossed the telephone down on the coffee table. As she walked over to the big window, Johanne was no longer tiptoeing. She stomped angrily across the floor, unsure whether her aggression was directed at herself or Isak.

She still hadn't bought any curtains.

The snow was so deep that the fence on Hauges Vei was no longer visible. The piles left by the snowploughs were enormous. People had nowhere to put the snow they had cleared from their drives. Not knowing what else to do, they spread it out in the middle of the road, which meant that a considerable amount ended up right back where it came from every time the snowplough rattled past.

There wasn't a soul in sight. The cold from the window pane made her shudder. The big snowman the children who lived opposite had made stared at her with his coal-black eyes. He had lost his nose. His birch-twig arms stuck out like witch's talons. He wore an old hat; a bright red scarf covered half his face.

He reminded her of the man by the fence.

She stepped to one side.

Tomorrow she would get some curtains.

It suddenly struck her that she had been completely wrong.

The anxiety that had tormented her since Christmas had not

started with the man by the fence. The feeling that someone was watching Kristiane had not started when a strange man came up and asked her what she'd had for Christmas. The reason why Johanne had reacted so strongly on that occasion was because the fear already had her in its grip. The search for those damned spare ribs and all the stress of organizing a Christmas Eve that would satisfy her mother had just temporarily pushed it aside.

It wasn't the man by the fence who had triggered her anxiety. It had been there since the wedding. Ever since Kristiane had stood on the tram lines and Johanne had been certain she was going to die, she had felt that her own despair was linked to something more, something greater than the fact that her daughter had been in mortal danger. It had all worked out in spite of everything, and even if she was worrying unnecessarily, she couldn't remember feeling like this since Wencke Bencke had threatened her in her subtle way almost five years ago.

Johanne hurried over to the computer and switched it on.

It seemed to take an eternity for the start page to appear, and when she keyed in the name of the world-famous crime writer, she got it wrong four times before she was finally able to google the name: 26,900 hits. She tried limiting her search. The only thing she wanted to know about the author was whether she was still living in New Zealand.

Wencke Bencke had got away with murder. She had cold-bloodedly taken the lives of a series of celebrities during the winter and spring of 2004; Johanne had never fully understood her motives. Johanne had helped Adam and Sigmund with the wide-ranging investigation, but the only result was that the three of them became convinced that Bencke was guilty. They couldn't prove a thing. The celebrated author had come to see her one beautiful spring day when it seemed clear that the murderer would never be caught. Johanne had been out pushing the newborn Ragnhild in her buggy when Wencke Bencke confessed, calmly and with a smile. Not that her confession would have stood up in a court of law, but it was clear enough to Johanne. The hidden threat she left hanging between them as she trudged away in the spring sunshine was also subtle, but it was sufficiently unambiguous to leave Johanne scared out of her wits. The fear didn't really go away until the following year, when Bencke married a Maori man fifteen years her junior and emigrated to New Zealand. She had been back to Norway in connection with book launches, which made Johanne avoid the arts section of the newspapers for most of the autumn.

There.

An article from *VG* in September.

Wencke Bencke in the sunshine, surrounded by sheep. She and her husband had bought a farm in Te Anau. She hadn't even come home last autumn when her latest book was published; *VG* had visited her instead.

'This is my home now,' says the world-famous writer, proudly showing off her enormous flock of sheep. 'I write better here. I live better here. This is where I'm going to stay.'

Johanne breathed a little more easily.

This had nothing to do with Wencke Bencke.

The fear that plagued her now had started on 19 December, the evening when Marianne Kleive was murdered. Johanne blinked and saw the number 19 etched on the inside of her eyelids, shimmering and green.

The accursed number 19.

She opened her eyes and stared into space. The telephone rang.

Eva Karin Lysgaard was murdered on 24 December.

Niclas Winter, the artist she had read about last night, died on 27 December.

He died. He wasn't murdered. He died from an overdose.

The phone kept on ringing. She reached out and picked it up. It was Adam.

19, 24 and 27.

The digital sum was 25.

Giving drug addicts an overdose was a well-known method of covering up a murder.

The phone fell silent. A few seconds later it rang again.

This time she answered it with a brief 'Hello'.

'Hi sweetheart. I see you've rung me loads of times. Sorry I couldn't get back to you until now; I've been stuck in meetings all afternoon. We're getting nowhere and—'

'It's absolutely fine,' she mumbled. 'It wasn't anything important.'

'Is everything OK? You sound a bit ... odd.'

'No, no. Yes. I mean, everything's fine. It's just ... I was asleep. The phone woke me up. I think I might just go to bed, actually.'

'At this time?'

'Lack of sleep. Do you mind if we hang up? Only I don't want to end up wide awake ...'

'Of course ...'

His disappointment was so tangible she almost changed her mind.

'Sleep well,' he said eventually.

'Bye darling. Speak to you tomorrow? Good night.'

She sat there for a long time with the silent telephone in her hand. Toni Braxton was emoting her way through *Un-Break My Heart* on the stereo. A car was revving its engine over on Hauges Vei. The wind must have changed direction, because the constant, distant roar from Maridalsveien and the heavy traffic on Ringveien was so clearly audible that it sounded as if a pipe had sprung a leak in the bathroom.

Even if there had been nothing about Niclas Winter's proclivities in the article in *Dagens Næringsliv*, it was possible to read a great deal between the lines. The man was HIV positive. That could be a result of heroin abuse, but it could also be a consequence of unprotected sex with other men. The *CockPitt* installation certainly pointed in that direction.

Eva Karin Lysgaard was certainly a heterosexual woman, married and with children, but she had come out as a passionate defender of the rights of homosexuals.

Marianne Kleive was married to another woman.

Johanne got up from the sofa, suddenly ravenous.

But she was no longer afraid.

Clues

'**I**'m afraid Niclas Winter's envelope has simply disappeared,' said Kristen Faber's secretary as she came into his office on the morning of Thursday 15 January. 'I've looked everywhere, but I just can't find it.'

'Disappeared? You've lost a client's file?'

Kristen Faber was talking with his mouth full of a chocolate croissant, from which he had acquired a brown moustache along his upper lip.

'I haven't actually touched the file since last Monday,' she replied calmly. 'And that was when I gave it to you. In this room.'

'For fuck's sake,' said Kristen Faber. 'How difficult can it be to find a big envelope?'

'I haven't looked in your drawers, of course,' she said, equally unperturbed. 'You can check those yourself.'

Crossly, he started yanking out one drawer after another.

'I put the envelope on that pile on the corner of my desk,' he mumbled. 'You must have lost it.'

She didn't bother to reply; she simply picked up the plate and left.

'Hang on!' he shouted before she reached the door. 'This drawer's stuck! Have you been messing with my desk?'

'No,' she said. 'As I told you, I haven't touched your drawers. But I can try to help you.'

She put down the plate and tried to help him. Instead of tugging at the drawer as he had done, she attempted to work it free. When that didn't work, she suggested they should pick the lock.

'With a letter opener,' she said, thinking for a moment. 'Or a screwdriver. We've got a toolbox in the filing cabinet.'

'Are you mad?'

He pushed her aside and tried once again to open the uncooperative drawer.

'Have you any idea how much this desk cost? Get hold of a carpenter. Or a locksmith. I've no idea who we need to call to sort this out, but I want it fixed by the time I get back this afternoon, OK?'

Without looking at her he started stuffing files into his briefcase. He grabbed his winter coat and barrister's gown from a hook by the door.

'I don't suppose we'll finish today, but the judge might want to go on a bit longer, so it might get late. You'll still be here, won't you? I'll have a lot of things for you to check after today's proceedings, and you should have plenty to get on with until then.'

His secretary smiled and gave a brief nod.

The door closed, and she settled down to take her time over her morning coffee and the day's newspapers. When she had finished she logged on to the Internet version of *Passing Your Driving Test the Easy Way*. Her husband was beginning to have problems with his eyes, and it was time to get herself a driving licence before her faithful chauffeur lost his sight completely.

You're never too old for anything, she thought, and she had oceans of time.

*

Johanne was waiting impatiently for eight o'clock. The last half-hour had crawled by, and she couldn't settle to read the papers. But she couldn't ring any earlier. She had been wide awake at five, after seven hours of deep, continuous sleep. On a sudden whim she had taken out her skis and driven to Grinda for a little early morning skiing. She turned back after 500 metres. The illuminated track was snowed in, and the narrow super-skis Adam had given her for Christmas were useless on that kind of surface. She had asked for cross-country skis, but the shop assistant had convinced Adam that skating was the in-thing in Nordmarka right now. When Johanne finally got back to the car she was wondering if it was possible to take these bloody chopsticks back and exchange them. Not to mention the trousers; they felt tight around her ankles, and seemed more like slalom pants. She had never learned how to skate and had no desire to do so.

But at least the adventure had done her good.

She had eggs and bacon when she got back, and couldn't remember a breakfast ever tasting better. With a cup of coffee in her hand she went over to the sofa. The telephone was on the floor, on charge. She reached down and pulled out the cable, then scrolled through her address book until she found the number.

The call was answered after just one ring.

'Wilhelmsen,' said an expressionless voice.

'Hi Hanne. It's Johanne. How are you?'

Of all the ridiculous ways to start a conversation with Hanne Wilhelmsen, asking how she was had to be top of the list.

'Fine,' the voice said, and Johanne almost choked on her coffee.

'What?' she coughed.

'I'm absolutely fine. And thank you for Ida's Christmas present – much appreciated. And how about you? How are you?'

Hanne Wilhelmsen must have been given a crash course in normal good manners for Christmas, Johanne thought.

'OK, more or less. But you know how it is. I've got my hands full. Adam's in Bergen practically all week at the moment, so most of the stuff involving the kids lands on my shoulders.'

There was complete silence at the other end of the line. Hanne evidently hadn't got very far in her course.

'I won't take up too much of your time,' Johanne said quickly. 'I just wondered if you could help me with something.'

'Like what?'

'I need ... I need to talk to a reliable person in the Oslo police. Preferably someone who works in violent crime and vice. Someone with a bit of authority.'

'Me six years ago, in other words.'

'You could say that, but I—'

'Why are you asking me? Surely Adam can help you?'

Johanne gained some time by taking a sip of coffee.

'As I mentioned, he's in Bergen,' she said eventually.

'There are telephones.'

'Yes, but—'

'Is it something to do with Kristiane?'

Hanne laughed. She actually laughed, Johanne thought with increasing amazement.

'Not really, but ...'

Yes, she thought.

I don't want to talk to Adam yet. I don't want any critical questions. I refuse to answer all his objections, all his counter-arguments. Kristiane must be protected if it's at all possible. I want to find out about this for myself first.

'He just has this tendency to assume I'm ...'

'Moderately hysterical?'

Once again that same light, unaccustomed laugh.

'A bit too quick to assume that something's wrong,' Hanne clarified. 'Is that the problem?'

'Maybe.'

'Silje Sørensen.'

'What? Who?'

'Talk to Silje Sørensen. If anyone can help you, it's Silje. I have to go now. I've got a lot to do.'

'A lot to do?'

The thought that Hanne Wilhelmsen had a lot to do in her self-imposed exile in her luxury apartment was absurd.

'I've started doing a bit of work,' she explained.

'Work?'

'You have a very odd way of speaking on the telephone, Johanne. You keep coming out with individual words followed by a question mark. Yes, I've started working. For myself. On a small scale.'

'Doing ... doing what?'

'Call round one day and we'll have a chat. But now I really do have to go. Ring Silje Sørensen. Bye.'

Silence. Johanne couldn't quite believe what she'd heard.

Her friendship with Hanne Wilhelmsen had come about by chance. Johanne had needed help with one of her projects, and had sought out the retired, taciturn inspector. In some strange way she had felt welcome. They didn't meet often, but over the years they had developed an unassuming, careful friendship, completely free of any demands or obligations.

Johanne had never heard Hanne like this.

She was so taken aback that she hadn't even asked who this Silje Sørensen was. She was annoyed with herself, until she remembered reading about her in the paper. She was responsible for the investigation into the murder of Marianne Kleive.

Perfect.

It was probably still too early to get hold of her. Adam was rarely at work before 8.30, and she presumed the same applied to senior officers in the Oslo police district.

And so she stayed where she was, cradling her coffee cup in her hands as she waited for the daylight, wondering what on earth had happened to Hanne Wilhemsen.

*

'What's happened?' Astrid Tomte Lysgaard whispered as she opened the door and saw Lukas standing outside.

It was only eleven o'clock and he should have been at work. He looked as if he'd just found out that someone else had died.

'I'm really ill,' said Lukas, almost tottering into the hallway. 'Throat. Temperature. I need to lie down.'

'You scared me,' said Astrid, clutching at her chest with her slender hands before reaching out to stroke his cheek. 'You look as if you've seen a ghost.'

'I'm just ill,' he said curtly, turning away. 'I feel rotten.'

'That's what happens when you spend all evening out there in the garage. Obviously, you're bound to come down with something.'

He didn't even look at her as he headed for the living room. It suited him perfectly if she blamed his evenings working in the damp garage. He wasn't particularly keen on telling her about his idiotic scramble over the roof of his father's house in the ice-cold January rain. He was even less keen to explain that he'd spent more than fifteen minutes sitting in a barely warm car, soaking wet and frozen to the marrow while Adam Stubo told him off.

'Have we got any Alvedon?' he said pathetically. 'And Coke? Have we got any Coke?'

'Yes to both. I bought some Alvedon yesterday after I—'

She broke off.

'The Coke's in the fridge,' she said instead. 'And there's some Alvedon in the medicine cabinet in the bathroom. Would you like a hot-water bottle?'

'Yes please. I feel absolutely ...'

It wasn't necessary for him to go into any more detail about his condition. His eyes were red and his skin paler than the time of year warranted. His nostrils were inflamed and caked in snot, and his lips were dry and flaky. There was a thick white coating at the corners of his mouth, and when she moved towards him to get out a glass, Astrid was struck by a sour, tainted smell coming from his mouth.

'You're not very good at coping with illness, Lukas.'

She ventured a smile.

His back radiated self-pity as he shambled towards the stairs.

She followed him into the bathroom. As he fumbled with the lock of the medicine cabinet she let the water run for a while, so that it was really hot by the time she filled the hot-water bottle.

'To be perfectly honest, Lukas,' she said, 'you're not actually dying. You need to pull yourself together.'

Without replying he pushed three tablets out of their foil packaging, placed them in his mouth and swilled them down with half a bottle of Coke. His face contorted in a grimace of pain as he swallowed. He started to undress as he walked, leaving a trail of clothes behind him along the landing and into the cool bedroom. He sank down on the bed as if he had used up the very last of his strength, pulled the covers right up to his chin and rolled over on his side.

'Here's your hot-water bottle,' she said. 'Where would you like it?'

He didn't answer.

'Lukas,' she said hesitantly. 'There's something I want to talk to you about.'

Yesterday she had refrained from asking who the woman in the photograph in the drawer was. She had been on the point of asking several times, but other things kept on coming up. All the time. The kids. Dinner. Homework. That eternal bloody garage. When the two of them were alone at last and it was gone half past ten, Lukas insisted on watching a TV programme about a tattoo parlour in Los Angeles. Astrid had gone up to bed and fallen asleep before he joined her.

Today it had struck her that she should have asked him anyway. She had allowed everything else to get in the way, because she was ashamed at having opened his drawer without permission. She was annoyed with herself. She had nothing to be ashamed of; looking for tablets that were responsibly locked away lay well within the parameters of the permissible.

'I feel absolutely terrible,' came a whimper from beneath the covers.

'I just want to ask you something,' she said firmly.

'Oh, Astrid ... I'm losing my voice! Can I have some warm milk with honey in it? Please?'

For a while she stood there, trying to work out what she actually felt.

Exhaustion, she thought. Irritation, perhaps.

Anxiety.

'Of course,' she said wearily. 'I'll go and get you some milk and honey.'

She closed the door quietly behind her and went down to the kitchen. By the time she got back with the drink, Lukas had fallen asleep.

*

'There you go,' said Silje Sørensen, handing Johanne a cup of hot chocolate. 'I get a bit boss-eyed from all the coffee I drink, so I keep some of this in reserve.'

'Thanks,' said Johanne. 'And thank you for seeing me at such short notice.'

'I was curious!'

Silje Sørensen's laugh was somehow out of proportion with her slender body.

'I've heard of you and read about you,' she continued, 'but I'm also happy to see anyone Hanne Wilhelmsen sends in my direction. How is she, by the way?'

Johanne opened her mouth to reply, then changed her mind. Hanne wouldn't like being talked about.

'Oh, you know,' she said with a shrug, hoping that the non-committal response would make Silje Sørensen change the subject. Actually, she ought to be doing that.

'The thing is,' she said, clearing her throat, 'I don't really know where to start.'

'No?'

'I'm a criminologist and I work—'

'As I said,' Silje interrupted her, 'I know who you are. Is it OK if I call you Johanne?'

'Of course. I'm working on a research project on hatred at the moment.'

'Interesting.'

It almost looked as if she meant it. Her gaze was direct and she shook her head as if to clear her mind.

'Hate crime,' Johanne corrected herself. 'The National Police Board has asked me to undertake a major investigation into hate crime.'

Silje Sørensen blinked. She put her cup down on the desk and slowly pushed it away. Her eyes narrowed and the tip of a pink tongue flicked across her lips.

'I see.'

'Attacks on individuals where the crime is motivated by—'

'I'm well aware of what hate crime is.'

Silje Sørensen had a bad habit of interrupting, Johanne thought.

'Of course,' she nodded. 'Of course you are.'

They sat like that for a surprisingly long time. In silence, each waiting for the other to say something. Johanne tried to guess how old Silje Sørensen might be. She must be younger than her, but not much. Thirty-five, perhaps. Maybe even younger. She was well-groomed and smartly dressed without seeming out of place in this environment.

Dainty, thought Johanne. She had never felt dainty in her entire life.

Silje's hands were slender and her nails so perfectly manicured that Johanne hid her own by putting down her cup and sliding her hands under her bottom.

'Are you looking at hate crimes directed against one particular group, or are you looking at the bigger picture?'

Silje was leaning forward, her elbows resting on the desk.

'The thing is,' Johanne said, taking a deep breath. 'I think I need to start from the beginning. Can you spare half an hour to listen to a very strange story?'

A large diamond on the ring finger of Silje Sørensen's left hand sparkled in the bright light as she made a generous and inviting gesture.

'Fire away,' she said. 'I'm all ears.'

Johanne knocked back the rest of her hot chocolate and started to tell her story, unaware that she now had a large, brown, seriously unflattering milk moustache.

*

Adam still hadn't heard anything from Johanne, and it worried him. He was back in his hotel room picking up some notes he had forgotten when the temptation to lie down for a few minutes grew too much. Deep down he suspected he had left the papers behind on purpose. Lunch at the hotel was significantly better than anything the Bergen police had to offer, and since it was included in his full board he didn't even feel guilty.

Except when it came to the chocolate pudding.

He had eaten two helpings, and a slight feeling of nausea persuaded him that he really did need just a tiny little rest. He kicked off his shoes and threw himself on the bed. It was a bit too soft, particularly lying on top of the covers, but if he could just find the right position he would fall asleep.

He didn't want to sleep.

He wanted to get hold of Lukas.

Ever since the episode on the roof it was as if the guy was playing cat and mouse with him. Adam had decided not to disturb Astrid unnecessarily after their melancholy encounter out in Os. Therefore he had only called Lukas on his mobile, but it always went straight to voicemail. Lukas never called him back. In the end Adam had rung the university, but they seemed to have virtually no idea where Lukas might be. He was clearly being given considerable leeway after his mother's tragic death.

Adam's eyes closed.

The fact that Johanne hadn't called worried him. She had sounded so peculiar on the phone last night.

He sat up abruptly.

He didn't have time for this.

His irritation over the Bishop's uncooperative son made him feel wide awake.

'You might not want to, but you're going to have to,' he mumbled crossly as he searched for the number of the house in Os. He keyed it in. The phone rang for so long that he was on the point of giving up when a subdued female voice eventually answered.

'Lysgaard.'

'Good afternoon, it's Adam Stubo. I apologize for disturbing you on Tuesday. I hope you—'

'It's fine. No need to apologize. I assume you found Lukas eventually.'

'I did, yes. But now I need to talk to him again, actually. There's no answer on his mobile, and I wondered if you'd have any idea where he might be?'

'He's here.'

'At home? At this time of day?'

'Yes. He's ill. It's only a sore throat, but he's got a temperature and ... he's really not very well at all.'

'Oh.'

In a flash Adam saw the drenched, shivering figure of Lukas Lysgaard from two days ago in his mind's eye.

'Anything I can help you with?' said Astrid.

'No, I don't think so.'

He could hear running water and the slamming of a cupboard door.

'Then again, there might be,' he said suddenly. 'It's just one small detail. Nothing important, really, but perhaps you could help me, then I won't need to disturb a sick man. It's about your mother-in-law's ... sanctuary.'

He laughed. There was silence at the other end of the line.

'You know, the room on the ground floor where she used to go when she couldn't sleep. The room where—'

'I know the room you mean. I've hardly ever been in there. A few times, maybe. What's this about?'

'There are four photographs in there,' Adam said, keeping his tone casual. 'Two or three family photos and a portrait, as far as I remember. I just wondered who the portrait might be?'

'The woman with ...'

Her voice disappeared abruptly, as if it had been snipped off with a pair of scissors.

'Hello?' said Adam. 'Are you still there?'

'Yes. I don't know who she is. I can ask Lukas when he wakes up.'

'No, no, there's no need. Don't bother him with details. I'll give him a call in a couple of days.'

'Was there anything else?'

'No. Say hello from me and tell him to get well soon.'

'Thank you, I will. Bye.'

The connection was broken before he had time to say goodbye. He put down the phone and lay back on the bed, his hands linked behind his head.

At least now he knew the photograph was of a woman.

He felt slightly guilty at having deceived Astrid, but the feeling quickly disappeared when it struck him that she had probably lied to him in return. The way she had suddenly broken off in the mid-sentence suggested something had occurred to her.

Something she didn't want to share with him.

If nothing else, it suggested he was on the right track.

The Reluctant Detective

His underpants were lying on the floor. The skid marks showed up with revolting clarity, even against the dark green cotton fabric. She grabbed the waistband between her thumb and forefinger and went into the bathroom to drop them in the laundry basket. Since he had obviously had a bad stomach, his trousers could go in there, too. They were lying just outside the closed bedroom door. She had picked up his socks on the way. With the clothes bundled underneath her arm, she quietly opened the door and went in.

The room smelled of a sick person.

Bad breath, sleep and flatulence combined to produce a stench that made her fling the balcony door wide open. She filled her lungs with fresh air a couple of times before turning to look back at him.

He was so deeply asleep he didn't even notice the racket as she struggled with the awkward door, nor the blast of freezing cold air. The covers were moving slowly and evenly up and down, and she could see just the top of his head. He was starting to lose his hair. The lines on his face had grown deeper in the last few years, but this was the first time she had noticed he was getting a bald patch. It touched her; he looked so vulnerable lying there.

'Lukas,' she said quietly, moving over to the bed.

He didn't wake up.

She sat down on the edge of the bed and stroked his hair gently.

'Lukas,' she said again, louder this time. 'You have to wake up.'

He grunted and tried to pull the covers over his head.

'I want to sleep,' he mumbled, smacking his lips. 'Go away.'

'No, Lukas. I'm going to pick the children up soon, and there's something I have to talk to you about while we're on our own. Something important.'

'It can wait. My throat is ...'

He swallowed loudly and whimpered.

'... really, really sore!'

'Adam Stubo rang.'

The covers were no longer moving up and down. She noticed that his body was suddenly tense, and she stroked his head once more.

'He had a very strange question,' she said. 'And there's something I want to ask you.'

'My throat. It hurts.'

'Yesterday,' she began, and cleared her throat. 'Yesterday morning I had a headache. We'd run out of Alvedon, so I thought I'd take one of your migraine tablets.'

He sat up quickly.

'Are you mad?' he snapped. 'Those tablets are on prescription, and they're meant for me and me alone. I don't even know if they're any good for headaches that aren't migraine!'

'Calm down,' she said quietly. 'I didn't take one. But I have to confess that I opened the drawer of your desk and—'

'You did what?'

His voice shot up to a falsetto.

'I was just going to—'

'We do everything we can in this house to teach the children to respect other people's property,' he said, his voice beginning to fail him. 'We tell them not to open other people's letters. Not to look in other people's drawers. And then you ... you go and ...'

His fists thudded dully against the bedclothes.

'Lukas,' Astrid said calmly. 'Lukas, look at me.'

When he finally looked up, she was shocked.

'We have to talk to each other,' she whispered. 'You've started keeping secrets from me, Lukas.'

'I have no choice.'

'That's not true. We always have a choice. Who's the woman in the photograph from your mother's room? And why have you taken the picture out of the frame and locked it in your drawer?'

She placed her hand on his. It felt cold and damp, even on the back. He didn't pull away, but neither did he open his hand to take hers.

'I think I've got a sister,' he whispered.

Astrid couldn't grasp what he was saying.

'I think I might have a sister,' he repeated, his voice hoarse. 'An older sister who was my mother's child, at least. Perhaps my father's, too. From when they were really young.'

'I think you've gone completely mad,' Astrid said gently.

'No, I mean it. That photo has been there for so long, and I've never known who the woman was. I once asked my mother ...'

A coughing attack made him bend forward. Astrid let go of his hand, but didn't get up.

'I asked her who it was. She didn't tell me. She just said it was a friend I didn't know.'

'Then I expect that was true.'

'Why would my mother have a photograph by her bed of someone I've never met, unless she's my sister? The other photos are of me and my father.'

'I knew your mother for twelve years, Lukas. Eva Karin was the most honest, most beautiful and utterly decent person I've ever met. She would never, ever have kept a child secret. Never.'

'She could have had her adopted! There's nothing wrong with that! On the contrary, it would explain her intractable attitude on the issue of abortion, and ...'

His voice gave way completely, and he rubbed his throat.

'What did Stubo want?' he whispered.

'He wanted to know who was in the photo.'

'And what did you tell him?'

'Nothing.'

'Nothing?'

'I said I didn't know. It's true. I don't know who she is. But if this might have any significance for the investigation, you have to talk to Stubo.'

'It can't possibly have anything to do with my mother's death! I don't want any publicity about this. That's the last thing she would have wanted.'

'But Lukas,' she said, pressing his hand once more, 'why do you think Stubo is so interested in that photograph? He obviously thinks it's important. And we do want this cleared up, don't we Lukas? Don't we?'

He didn't reply. His stubborn expression and lowered eyes reminded her so strongly of their eldest son that she couldn't help smiling.

'Dad put it away,' he mumbled.

'When?'

'The day after the murder. It was there when Stubo came round the first time. He wheedled his way into Mum's room a few days later, and evidently noticed it had gone.'

He grabbed a handful of tissues out of a box she had placed on the bedside table, and blew his nose thoroughly and for a long time.

'So how did you get hold of it?' she asked. 'If Erik had put it away?'

'It's a long story,' he said, waving dirty tissues around. 'And now I have to go back to sleep, Astrid. I mean it. I really do feel terrible.'

She stayed where she was. There was such a strong draught from the open balcony door that the newspaper on the bedside table was flapping. It had started raining again, and the patter of heavy raindrops on the balcony floor made her raise her voice as she patted the covers twice and said: 'OK. But we're not done with this.'

He shuffled back under the covers and turned his back on her.

'Any chance you could close the door?'

'Yes,' she replied.

The wood had warped during the constant rain, and it was impossible to close the door completely. She left it slightly ajar and went out of the room with Lukas's dirty trousers and socks under her arm.

Downstairs the telephone was ringing.

She almost hoped it was Adam Stubo.

*

'Have you spoken to your husband about ... Does Adam Stubo know about this?'

Silje Sørensen had been listening to Johanne for almost three quarters of an hour. From time to time she had jotted something down, and once or twice she had interjected a question. The rest of the time she had listened, her body language becoming increasingly tense. A few moments into Johanne's cogent and incredible story, a faint flush had begun to spread up the inspector's throat. Johanne could clearly see the pulse beating in the hollow at the base of her neck.

'No,' she admitted. 'He's in Bergen at the moment.'

'I realize that, but this is ...'

Silje ran her fingers through her medium-length hair. The diamond sparkled.

'Let's see if I can summarize this correctly.'

She was balancing a blue pen between her index and middle fingers.

'So The 25'ers,' she began, 'are an organization we know very little about. You think they've come to Norway, for reasons of which you are unaware, and have started to murder homosexuals or sympathizers according to a more or less fixed calendar based on the numbers 19, 24 and 27. Which are supposed to be cryptic numbers relating to the Koran and to two Bible verses from St Paul's Epistle to the Romans, respectively.'

She looked up from her notes.

'Yes,' Johanne said calmly.

'You realize how crazy this sounds?'

'Yes.'

'Aren't you wondering why I've sat here listening to this for almost ...'

She glanced at her Omega watch made of gold and steel.

'... an hour?'

'Yes.'

Johanne sat on her hands again. She was bitterly regretting coming here. It was Adam she should have spoken to, naturally. Adam, who knew her and how she reasoned and what she knew. Now she was sweating and feeling grubbier than she had for a long time, sitting here with the detective inspector with the long nails and hair that must have been styled by a hairdresser this morning.

Silje Sørensen was on her feet.

She opened a drawer in her desk. She was so short she hardly needed to bend down. It struck Johanne that it must have been difficult for her to fulfil the physical criteria for acceptance into the Police Training Academy. She stood in silence for a while, staring at something. Johanne couldn't see what it was from where she was sitting. Then the drawer slammed shut, and Silje Sørensen went over to the window.

'And there wasn't actually a murder on 27 December,' she said, her back to Johanne. 'That's just a guess, the idea that this ...'

The pause lasted such a long time that Johanne mumbled: 'Niclas Winter.'

'That this Niclas Winter was murdered rather than died of an overdose.'

Johanne wondered if she should just say goodbye and leave. Her shoulder bag was lying at her feet, half-open, and she could see that she had three missed calls on her mobile.

'Besides which,' Silje Sørensen said so suddenly and loudly that Johanne jumped, 'the experience of the Americans suggests that they murder only homosexuals, not sympathizers. Isn't that right?'

'But so little is known about them, and they've—'

'Do you actually know if they feel constrained by those dates?'

'Yes!'

Johanne almost screamed the answer.

'I rang my ...'

She changed her mind. She had enough problems when it came to credibility without referring to a friend.

'I rang Karen Winslow, a solicitor at APLC,' she corrected herself. 'That's the centre I mentioned.'

It was true. On her way to police headquarters she had felt the need to put a little more flesh on the bones of her meagre story, and had called Karen in the States. It wasn't until her friend answered that Johanne realized it was still night in Alabama. Karen had assured her it really didn't matter, as she was still suffering from jet lag anyway.

'As I said, it was numerologists who worked out the background to the name The 25'ers,' Johanne continued. 'Naturally, they had something to build on. Something around which to base their theories. All six murders currently linked to the organization were committed on the 19th, 24th or 27th. According to Karen Winslow.'

She wiped her nose and added with a touch of embarrassment.

'Today. This morning.'

Silje Sørensen went back to her desk. Opened the drawer, looked down.

Suddenly she sat down, leaving the drawer open.

'If you'd come here a week ago,' she said, 'I would have politely got rid of you after five minutes. I didn't do that today because ...'

They looked at each other. Johanne bit her lip.

'I don't know whether I ought to tell you this,' said Silje, holding her gaze. 'You're not attached to the police. In a purely formal sense, I mean.'

Johanne didn't speak.

'On the other hand, I'm aware that you have a kind of general approved status from the relevant authorities in connection with your research project. I presume you must have been given extensive sanctions regarding access to our cases, at least in those instances where we suspect hate crime is involved.'

Johanne opened her mouth to protest, but Silje held up a hand to stop her.

'I presume, I said! I'm not asking you. I'm simply telling you what I presume. So that I can show you this.'

She took a single sheet of paper out of the open drawer and looked at it for a moment before passing it across the crowded but well-organized desk to Johanne.

She took the piece of paper and adjusted her glasses.

Three names and three dates.

'I recognize the name Marianne Kleive,' she said. 'But I have no idea who the other two—'

'Runar Hansen,' Silje interrupted. 'Beaten and killed in Sofienberg Park on 19 November. Hawre Ghani. Underage asylum seeker who—'

'Sofienberg Park?' Johanne broke in. 'The east or west side?'

'East,' said Silje with an almost imperceptible smile. 'And you might have heard of Hawre Ghani as the body we pulled out of the harbour on the last Sunday in Advent.'

Johanne's mouth was dry. She looked around for something to drink, but all that was left of her chocolate was a brown, congealed mass in the bottom of her cup.

'Among many other things,' Silje said, holding her breath as she paused for effect, 'he was a prostitute.'

'I need a drink of water,' said Johanne.

'We don't know exactly when he was murdered, but there is every indication that the murder took place on 24 November. We have a confirmed sighting on that date when he went off with a punter. No one saw him after that. It fits in with the estimate from the pathologist.'

'I'm just going to the loo,' said Johanne. 'I really do need a drink.'

'Here,' said Silje, passing her a bottle of mineral water from the cupboard behind her. 'I can understand how you feel. You put two and two together more quickly than we did. This is all to do with—'

'There's a murder missing for 27 November,' said Johanne. She was getting hotter and hotter. She couldn't get the bottle open.

'This could all be coincidence,' she went on, her voice almost breaking.

'You don't believe that. And you're wrong. There isn't a murder missing for 27 November. Last Tuesday, when my colleague and I spotted a clear connection between the three cases I'm working on at the moment ...'

She quickly leaned across the desk, waving her fingers at the bottle. Johanne passed it to her and Silje opened it with one quick movement. She passed it back and went on.

'It's tricky when one inspector is responsible for three murder investigations. I actually had four, but I passed one over to a colleague. I hadn't done very much work on that particular case before I handed it over. It's to do with suspected sabotage on a car. It came off the road in Maridalen, and since nobody sticks to the speed limit on what is an extremely dangerous stretch of road, the driver died. At first the case was treated as an ordinary road traffic accident. Then it turned out that someone might have ... tampered with the brakes. I knew this before, of course, but what I didn't know was that the victim, a Swedish woman by the name of Sophie Eklund, lived with Katie Rasmussen.'

Johanne needed a few seconds. She had already drunk half the mineral water.

'The MP,' she said eventually. 'The spokesman on homosexual issues for Arbeiderpartiet.'

'I think she prefers "spokeswoman".'

'Do you think ... was the sabotage aimed at her? Was ... was her partner murdered by mistake?'

'I don't know, and I have no opinion on that. I'm just telling you that your absurd theory seems a little too close to the mark for me to sit here and dismiss it.'

'It could be someone else, of course,' said Johanne. 'Another organization. Or a copycat. Or—'

'Listen to me,' said the inspector. 'I want you to listen very carefully.'

She rested her elbows on the desk and interlaced her fingers.

'You have a good reputation, Johanne. A lot of people in this building are aware of the work you've done for NCIS, without taking any credit for it. I noticed you in particular when NCIS solved the case of those murdered children a few years ago. It's no secret around here that it was your input that saved the life of at least one girl who had been kidnapped.'

Johanne stared at her, her face expressionless. She couldn't work out where the inspector was going with this.

'But people also say you can be quite ...'

She straightened her back and her eyes narrowed before she found a word she liked.

'... reluctant,' she said. 'Do you know what they call you inside NCIS?'

Johanne put the bottle to her mouth and took a drink. A long drink.

'The reluctant detective.'

Silje's laugh was big, warm and infectious.

Johanne smiled and put the top back on the bottle.

'I didn't know that,' she said candidly. 'Adam never mentioned it.'

'Perhaps he doesn't know. Anyway, my point is that you're sitting here, living proof that your nickname is well-earned. First of all you come out with a theory that's like something out of an American B-movie, then you try to distance yourself from the whole idea when I tell you there could be something in it. So it's hardly surprising that—'

Loud voices out in the corridor. A male voice bellowed, then a woman screamed, followed by the sound of running footsteps. Johanne looked in horror at the closed door.

'Someone trying to do a runner,' Silje said calmly. 'Unlikely to succeed.'

'Shouldn't we help? Or—'

'You and me? I don't think so!'

Someone must have caught the would-be runaway and rendered them harmless, because suddenly everything went quiet. Johanne was fiddling with the cuffs of her sweater when she caught sight of a calendar just behind Silje. There was a red magnetic ring around Thursday 15 January.

'Irrespective of my theory,' she said slowly, 'the fact is that during November and December we have six murders with ... some kind of homosexual link, I think we could call it. 19, 24 and 27 November. The same dates in December. And today is 15 January.'

Johanne kept her eyes fixed on the red ring. When she blinked it had etched itself firmly on her mind's eye as a green O.

'Yes,' said Silje Sørensen. 'In four days it will be 19 January. We may not have much time.'

The thought hadn't struck Johanne until now. It gave her goose-flesh on her arms, and she pulled down her sleeves.

'Do you have anything to go on? Anything at all? From what Adam says it sounds as if they're not really getting anywhere over in Bergen.'

Silje Sørensen pushed out her lower lip and shook her head slightly, as if she didn't really know whether what she was searching for could really be called a clue. She opened three drawers before she found the right one and took out a pile of drawings. The drawer slammed shut as she stood up. She went to the empty noticeboard.

'We've got this,' she said. 'Sketches of the man who was trying to buy sex from Hawre Ghani when he was last seen alive.'

She fixed the images to the board with bright red drawing pins. Johanne stood up and waited until all four sheets were in place: a full-length picture, a full-face portrait, a profile and a peculiar drawing of something that looked like a pin with an emblem on it.

'Is everything all right?'

Silje's voice sounded as if it was coming from a long way off.

'Johanne!'

Someone grabbed hold of her arm. Her head felt so light that she thought it might come loose and float up to the ceiling like a helium balloon unless she pulled herself together.

'Sit down! For God's sake sit down!'

'No. I want to stand here.'

Even her own voice sounded distant.

'Have you ... ? Do you know who this man is, Johanne?'

'Who did these?'

'Our usual artist, his name is—'

'No, that's not what I mean. Which witness helped to produce these sketches?'

'A boy. Homeless. A prostitute. Do you know the man in the drawings?'

She was still holding Johanne's arm. Her grip tightened.

'I slapped this man across the face,' said Johanne.

'What?'

'Either your witness is playing games, or he's the most observant person in the world. I'll never forget this man. He ...'

The blood had returned to her head. Her brain felt clearer than for a long time. A remarkable sense of calm came over her, as if she had finally decided what she wanted and what she believed in.

'He saved my daughter's life,' she said. 'He saved Kristiane from being hit by a tram, and I slapped him across the face by way of thanks.'

*

Kristen Faber's secretary had finally found the time to open the drawer in her boss's desk. There had been no need to call a locksmith or a carpenter, of course. All it took was a little skilful poking at the lock with an ornamental penknife that she kept on her own desk. Click went the drawer and it was open.

And there was the envelope. Large and brown, with Niclas Winter's name written on it just above his ID number. The envelope had an old-fashioned wax seal and, as an additional security measure, someone had scrawled an illegible signature diagonally across the flap where the envelope was stuck down.

When Kristen Faber took over the practice from old Skrøder, there had been a lot to deal with. Ulrik Skrøder had been completely senile for the last six months before his son finally managed to have the poor old soul declared incapable of managing his affairs, and the firm could be sold. At least that was what everyone said. Kristen Faber's secretary, having taken on the task of going through all the papers and following up every case where the time limit had elapsed or was about to do so, had the impression that Skrøder must have been confused for many years. There was no order to anything, and it took her months to sort out the worst of it.

When everything was finally finished, Kristen realized he had paid too much for the practice. The ongoing cases were far fewer in number than he had been led to believe, and most of the clients turned out to be around the same age as their solicitor. They simply died, one after the other, ancient and advanced in years, with their affairs in pristine order and with absolutely no need of the assistance of a solicitor. Eighteen months later Kristen managed to get back half the money he had paid out.

The secretary could well understand his frustration at having bought a pig in a poke. However, she couldn't help reminding him from time to time about all the sealed envelopes in a heavy oak cupboard in the archives. Some of them looked positively antique, and Skrøder's son had maintained that they could be extremely valuable. They had been handed over for safe keeping by some of the city's oldest and wealthiest families, he told them. His father had always said that the oak cupboard containing these documents provided proof of his good judgement. Every envelope was sealed, with the name of the owner of the contents neatly written on the front, and when he was in deep despair at having bought a portfolio that offered him little profit Kristen Faber had restricted himself to opening a dozen or so.

He found shares in companies that no longer existed, marriage settlements between couples long dead, a wad of banknotes that was no longer legal tender, and the outline of a novel by an unknown author, which, after reading just ten pages, he realized was completely worthless. After that he had closed the cupboard, decided to forget his crippling losses and build up the practice himself.

Since then the cupboard had just stood there.

The secretary had opened it for the first time in almost nine years when young Niclas Winter rang. He seemed frustrated and was quite rude when he asked if they might possibly have an envelope with his name on it in their archives. As she had little to do, and curious by nature, she had gone to have a look. And there it was. On closer inspection it looked newer than the rest.

Now she was holding the envelope up to the light.

It was impossible to see what was inside. Nor had Niclas Winter said anything about the contents as he showered her with noisy kisses over the phone before Christmas, when she rang to tell him she had found it.

The temptation to break the seal was almost too much for her. She placed the palm of her hand on the thick paper. It was usually possible to steam open envelopes like this, but the seal presented a problem.

With a small sigh she placed the envelope on Kristen Faber's desk and went back to her own office.

She would at least make sure she was there when he opened it.

*

'We can't go public on this,' said Silje Sørensen, covering the image of the mystery man with the palm of her hand. 'Not yet, anyway. If we publish the picture it will lose a significant amount of its value. Everybody will form their own opinions. People will start calling in with sightings, and experience suggests that we'll be completely stuffed before that approach turns up anything useful. Now, however ...'

She contemplated the picture for a few more seconds before going back to her seat.

'Now we have an ace up our sleeve. We've got something nobody knows about.'

Johanne nodded. When she had managed to pull herself together after recognizing the man in the sketch, they had gone through the case point by point one more time. She was halfway through a second bottle of mineral water, trying to suppress a belch.

'And you're absolutely certain?'

It was at least the third time Silje had asked.

'I'm absolutely certain that the man in that drawing looks amazingly like the man who saved Kristiane, yes. It's as if he'd posed for the picture. But as I said, I can't guarantee that it's actually the same man. The point is ...'

Air forced its way up her oesophagus and she belched.

'Sorry,' she said, her hand to her mouth. 'The point is that there are starting to be so many links here that it just can't be a matter of pure coincidence. Placing the man who was the last person Hawre Ghani was seen with at the location where Marianne Kleive was murdered has to be a breakthrough, surely. In both cases, I might add.'

'We could find you a job here.' Silje smiled, then a new furrow appeared between her fine eyebrows and she said: 'And since you're firing on all cylinders, perhaps you can explain this emblem?' She pointed at the drawing. 'It's really foxed us.'

'I should think that was exactly the intention,' said Johanne. 'We've moved on from false beards and dyed hair. Have you seen Hitchcock's *Strangers on a Train*?'

The furrow deepened.

'The one with the two strangers who meet on a train,' Johanne reminded Silje. 'Both of them want another person dead. One of them suggests they should swap murders, so that they can create watertight alibis. The murderer will have no motive whatsoever, and as we know the motive is one of the very first things the police try to establish.'

For the second time in just a few hours the thought of Wencke Bencke passed through her mind. She pushed it aside and tried to smile.

'I ... I don't really watch that kind of thing,' said Silje.

'You should. Anyway – the emblem is there because it has nothing at all to do with the matter. Look at what else he's wearing: dark, neutral clothes without a single distinguishing mark. Anyone who's even vaguely observant will fix on that bright red logo. Which means you expend enormous amounts of energy on—'

'But where did he get it from?'

'Anywhere. And it could be anything at all. Something he found somewhere. If our assumptions are correct, this is a highly professional killer. His hair, for example. Is he bald, or has he shaved his head? I would assume the latter.'

'It's as if you've read this,' said Silje, waving the sketch artist's accompanying notes. 'Martin Setre wasn't sure.'

'But he did think about it? I didn't. I assume this man ...'

She nodded in the direction of the noticeboard.

'... actually has perfectly normal hair. Instead of going for a wig or dying his hair, neither of which ever really looks natural, he shaves it off.'

Silje gave a slight shake of her head.

'We wondered if he was taking the piss,' she said.

They both sat in silence for a moment. Johanne's fingers were going to sleep, and she slid her hands from under her bottom. A quick glance revealed that they were no longer merely neglected, but also chalk-white with red blotches.

'He can't be acting entirely alone,' said Silje. It was more of a question than a statement.

'No. I don't think he is. This is a group, and they operate as a group. But nothing is certain.'

She shrugged her shoulders.

'I need to get going,' said Silje loudly, bringing the palms of her hands down on the desk. 'We need to set up a formal collaboration with NCIS as soon as possible. And with the Bergen police. And ...'

She took a breath and exhaled between lips that were almost compressed together.

'This is so fucking difficult I hardly know where to start.'

Johanne was surprised when this slender, feminine individual swore.

'I could be wrong,' she said quietly.

'Yes. But we can't take the risk.'

They stood up simultaneously, as if responding to a command. Johanne picked up her capacious bag, heaved it over her shoulder, then grabbed her duffel coat and headed for the door.

She hadn't said anything about her feeling that Kristiane was being watched. As she stood there shaking hands with Silje to say goodbye, it struck her that she should have mentioned it. Silje Sørensen was a stranger. Unlike Isak and Adam, she wouldn't instinctively assume that Johanne's anxiety was exaggerated. Silje was a mother herself, as far as Johanne could tell from the attractive family photos in the room.

Perhaps she should trust her.

It could be significant for the case.

'Thank you for listening to me,' she said, letting go of Silje's hand.

'We should be thanking you,' said Silje with a joyless smile. 'And I'm sure we'll talk again soon.'

As Johanne got into her car two minutes later she realized why she hadn't said anything about the missing file, the man by the fence and an indefinable, frightening feeling that there was someone out there who didn't necessarily wish her daughter well.

It would be a betrayal if she didn't speak to Adam first.

Now the Oslo police were taking her seriously, he would be more prepared to listen.

She hoped.

*

Astrid Tomte Lysgaard really, really wished Lukas had given her a different answer. She didn't doubt that he was telling the truth; they knew each other too well. And yet something had come over him that she didn't understand. She had admired Lukas ever since they got together in their first year at secondary school, initially because he was attractive, hard-working and kind. With the years came financial obligations, everyday life, and three children. Lukas took everything seriously. Bills were never left unpaid. He had attended every single parents' evening since their eldest son started nursery, and volunteered as a member of the PTA as soon as the boy started school. Lukas was skilful and industrious, and had built both the extension and the garage himself. It would never occur to him to do anything underhand when it came to money. He always clamped down on any form of racism or gossip.

However, her friends sometimes mentioned that they found Lukas boring.

They didn't know him as well as she did.

Lukas was anything but boring, but right now she didn't understand him at all.

The shock of Eva Karin's murder must have done something to him, something worse than plunging him into grief. The fact that he wasn't doing all he could to help the police was incomprehensible.

Lukas never did anything wrong.

Not helping the police was wrong.

She poured herself another cup of coffee and sat down on the sofa. She held the cup up to her face, feeling the dampness of the steam as it touched her skin and cooled.

Lukas didn't have a sister. Of course he didn't. If Eva Karin had had a daughter from a previous life – whether Erik was the father or not – she would have acknowledged her. If the child had been adopted, she would have told her family. Admittedly, Eva Karin could appear reserved in certain circumstances, almost unapproachable. Astrid had always put this temporary distance down to the fact that, as a priest, Eva Karin carried the secrets of so many other people. She inspired trust. Her voice was quiet, even in the pulpit, with a melodious, considered way of speaking that in itself invited confidences. And Astrid had never known Eva Karin to make a thoughtless remark, not once in all these years.

When it came to herself, on the other hand, Eva Karin was a generous person. She talked openly about things she had done wrong and mistakes she had made. She had an immense respect for life, which sometimes manifested itself in strange ways, making life difficult for others. Her deep faith in Jesus bordered on the fanatical, but never crossed the line. Some years ago she had shed tears of joy after spending a small fortune on the picture of the Messiah that was now hanging on the living-room wall in the house on Nubbebakken. It was said to be the sketch of an altarpiece from a church somewhere in the east of the country, but Eva Karin had explained that only in this particular image did the artist make the Saviour's eyes ice-blue. Once or twice Astrid thought she might have caught her mother-in-law talking to the figure in the picture, with his short, blonde, tousled hair. Eva Karin had smiled and laughed at herself, before brushing the matter aside and making small talk about the weather.

As far as Astrid knew, the real Jesus must have been dark, with brown eyes and long hair.

Jesus was forgiveness, her mother-in-law used to say.

Jesus holds all life sacred.

Keeping a child secret would have meant showing a lack of respect for life.

Abruptly, Astrid put down her cup.

If Eva Karin had given up a daughter for adoption, then surely she would have a photograph of her as a baby.

Lukas wasn't himself. He was usually the one who sorted things out for her when the world was a mess and everything got a bit too much. Now it was Astrid's turn. She had to do the right thing for him.

She took her cup into the kitchen and put it in the dishwasher. If she waited, she might change her mind. As she picked up the telephone she noticed that her hands were shaking. Stubo's number was still there, at the top of the list of incoming calls.

'Hello,' she said when he picked up almost at once. 'It's Astrid, Lukas's wife. I think you should come over right away.'

*

'You should have told me right away!'

If Rolf wasn't furious, then he was unusually cross. In the background Marcus could hear a dog barking and a woman's voice trying to calm it down.

'I forgot,' Marcus said wearily. 'We were going out for something to eat and I just forgot about it.'

'The police asked me to ring on a serious matter almost a week ago – and it puts me in a fucking bad light if it looks as if I didn't bother.'

'I understand that, Rolf. As I said, I'm sorry.'

'That's not enough. What the hell's got into you lately?'

Rolf's voice had acquired an aggressive tone that Marcus had never heard before. He took a deep breath and was about to embark on another apologetic tirade when Rolf got in first.

'You're not really with us,' he muttered angrily. 'You forget the most routine things. Yesterday you hadn't even done little Marcus's lunch box when it was time for him to go to school, even though it was your turn. I found out by chance and just had time to make him a couple of sandwiches.'

'All I can do is apologize. There's ... a lot to do. The financial crisis, you know, and ...'

Marcus could hear rapid footsteps at the other end of the line.

'Hang on,' Rolf mumbled. 'I'm just moving so I can talk freely.'

Scraping. A door slamming. Marcus closed his eyes and tried to breathe calmly.

'It's only three weeks ago since you told me how happy you were about the financial crisis,' Rolf said eventually, just as angrily as before. 'You said you were the only person you knew who was making money out of it! You said the company was on the up and up, for fuck's sake!'

'But you know that—'

'I know nothing, Marcus! I have no idea why you lie awake at night. I have no idea why you've become so short-tempered. Not only with me, but with Marcus and your mother and—'

'I've said I'm sorry!'

By now Marcus, too, was raising his voice. He got up and went over to the window. The sun was glowing fiery red as it lay low on the horizon. The ice on the fjord was criss-crossed with furrows made by ships. The harbour directly in front of him was covered with slushy ice on top of the black water. The Nesodden ferry had just heaved to at the quayside, and a handful of shivering people poured out into the beautiful, ice-cold afternoon.

'This can't go on,' Rolf said in a resigned tone of voice. 'You're at work virtually all the time. It can't possibly be necessary to ...'

He was right.

Marcus had always been proud of the fact that he worked more or less normal office hours. His philosophy was that if you couldn't get everything done between eight and four, then the fault lay with your own inefficiency. Of course, he had to work late occasionally, just like everyone else. However, since nothing was more important than his family, he still tried to be home at the normal time every day, and to keep his weekends free.

These days he was staying at the office until late in the afternoon and into the evening more and more often. The office at Aker Brygge had become a refuge. A sanctuary from Rolf's searching looks and accusations. When everyone had gone home and he was left alone, he sat down in the comfortable armchair by the window and watched the evening creep across the city. He listened to music. He read a little – or at least he tried to, but it was difficult to concentrate.

'For fuck's sake,' Rolf went on wearily. 'You're not one of those capitalists, Marcus! You've always said that the money was there for us, and not vice versa! If the firm is going to take up all our time, then we'd be better getting rid of the whole bloody lot and living a simpler life.'

'It's 15 January,' Marcus protested feebly. 'A couple of weeks' stress at work isn't enough for you to start drawing drastic conclusions, in my opinion. I also think, to be perfectly honest, that you're being completely unreasonable. I can't even begin to count all the evenings when you've suddenly had to dash off to splint the broken leg of some animal or help some over-bred bitch to pup when she's not even capable of feeding her own offspring.'

There was silence at the other end of the phone.

'That's completely different,' Rolf said eventually. 'That's about living creatures, Marcus, and my profession is very important to me. I've never said that animals don't mean anything. You're constantly insisting that money means nothing to you. And what's more, we've always agreed that precisely because I sometimes get called out, you'll be at home with little Marcus. I mean, we've ... We agree on this,

Marcus. But to be honest I don't think we're going to get much further. At least not on the phone.'

The coldness in his voice frightened Marcus.

'I'll be home early tonight,' he said quickly. 'And did you manage to sort things out with the police?'

'Just now. They're sending a patrol car to pick up the cigarette butts this evening. I've already e-mailed them the photos of the tyre tracks. Not that I think they'll be any use, but still ... See you later.'

He didn't even say goodbye.

Marcus stared at the silent telephone, then slowly walked over to the armchair and sat down. He stayed there until the sky had turned black and the lights of the city had come on, one by one, transforming the view from the enormous window into a picture-postcard image of a wintry city night.

The worst thing of all was that Rolf had accused him of being a capitalist.

If only he knew, thought Marcus, wondering how he was going to summon up the strength to get to his feet.

*

'Do you know what's in it?' Kristen Faber said pointlessly to his secretary.

The seal was unbroken.

'Of course not,' she said blithely. 'You told me to leave it until you could open it yourself. But ... isn't that actually illegal? I mean, the name of the addressee is written clearly on the envelope, and even if he's dead—'

'Illegal,' Kristen Faber mumbled contemptuously as he rummaged around in the mess on his desk, searching for a letter opener. 'It's hardly illegal to open an envelope I found in my own office, for which I paid a fortune! How did you get the drawer open anyway?'

'Here,' she said, handing him a long, sharp knife. 'I used my womanly wiles.'

He slit the envelope open, stuck two fingers into the gaping hole and fished out a document. It consisted of only two pages, and at the top of the first sheet it said LAST WILL AND TESTAMENT in capital letters.

'It's a will,' he said, disappointed and once again completely superfluously, because the secretary was standing right next to him. He turned away irritably and demanded a cup of tea. She nodded stiffly and went into the outer office.

The name of the testator seemed familiar to Kristen Faber, even if he couldn't quite place it. Niclas Winter was the sole heir. A quick glance suggested an extensive estate, even if phrases such as 'the entire portfolio' and 'all property' didn't actually say very much.

The document met all the legal requirements. The pages were numbered and it had been signed by both the testator and two witnesses who did not stand to benefit from the contents. When the solicitor saw the date the will had been drawn up, he frowned for a moment before making a brief note on a Post-it.

The secretary was back with a cup of tea. Irritating, thought Faber. It must have been ready before he even asked. Quickly, he slipped the will back in the envelope and sealed it with a wide strip of sticky tape. He put the yellow Post-it note on the front.

'Put this in the safe,' he said. 'I need to work out what to do with it. Niclas Winter is dead, but he might have heirs.'

'No,' said the secretary. 'It said in the paper that he hasn't got a single heir. As far as I understood, the state will get the lot.'

'Right,' said Kristen Faber, shrugging his shoulders. 'Well, that's not such a bad thing. The state bloody well takes enough from most people. But anyway, I think this document ought to be handed over to the State Inheritance Fund. I'll look into it tomorrow.'

'Tomorrow you're in court with a new case,' she reminded him. 'Perhaps I could—?'

'Yes,' he said curtly. 'You do it. Ring the inheritance fund and ask what we should do.'

'Of course,' she said with a smile. 'I'll do it first thing in the morning. Is your tea all right?'

He couldn't even bring himself to answer.

*

'Thank you so much for taking the trouble to come all the way out here again,' she said, smiling uncertainly at the tall police officer. 'I've sent the two older ones across to the neighbour's, and William is just about to fall asleep. Lukas, poor soul, has slept all day.'

Adam Stubo kicked off his shoes and handed her his jacket, then went into the light, comfortable living room. There were toys and children's books lying around, and a woollen sweater had been draped over the back of a dining chair to dry, and yet the room gave the impression of being tidy. Very pleasant, thought Adam, noticing the enormous framed child's drawing hanging above a beige sofa piled high with brightly coloured cushions.

'Who's the artist?' he smiled, nodding at the picture.

'The middle one,' she said. 'Andrea.'

'How old is she?'

'Six.'

'Six? Goodness, she's talented!'

Astrid waved in the direction of the sofa.

'Please sit down. Would you like a coffee?'

'No, thank you. Not this late in the day.'

She glanced at a wall clock above the worktop in the open-plan kitchen. It was just after seven.

'Water? Something else?'

'No thanks.'

He moved a couple of cushions before sitting down. There was a faint smell of lemon and freshly baked bread, and the tinder-dry wood was burning brightly in the open fireplace. There was something very special about this home. The atmosphere was somehow more peaceful than he was used to in families with small children, and in spite of the slight untidiness everything seemed to be under control. He looked up when she put a cup of coffee, a jug of milk and a plate of buns in front of them, in spite of the fact that he had said no.

'This sort of thing isn't good for me,' he said, taking one of the buns.

She smiled and went over to a shelf by the window looking out over the garden. When she came back she hesitated for a moment before sitting down next to him on the big, deep sofa. Adam was already halfway through his bun.

'Absolutely delicious,' he mumbled with his mouth full. 'What's inside?'

'Ordinary jam,' she said. 'Strawberry jam. Here.'

She was holding out a photograph. Confused, he put the rest of the bun down on the plate and wiped his fingers assiduously on his trouser legs before taking the photograph and carefully placing it on his right knee.

The paper was thick and slightly yellowed, and the photograph had been taken at quite close quarters.

'I hope I'm doing the right thing,' she said almost inaudibly.

'You are.'

He studied the picture in detail. Even if the woman wasn't exactly beautiful, there was something appealing about the young face. She had big eyes, which he guessed were probably blue. She had a lovely smile, with the hint of a dimple in one cheek. One upper front tooth lay slightly on top of the other, and for a moment he frowned, deep in concentration.

'I feel as if I've seen her before,' he murmured.

Astrid didn't reply. Instead, she looked at him with her mouth half-open, not breathing, as if she were about to say something, but couldn't quite bring herself to.

He pre-empted her.

'She looks a bit like Lukas, doesn't she?'

She nodded.

'Lukas thinks she's his sister,' she said. 'That's why he didn't want to show you the photo. He wants to find her himself, and he doesn't want any publicity about this. He thinks the family has had a hard enough time without this being plastered all over the papers. I'm sure he's thinking mainly of his father, but also his mother's reputation. And himself, to a certain extent.'

'A sister,' Adam said thoughtfully. 'An unknown sister would definitely fit in with this story, but she's—'

'It's just not possible,' Astrid interrupted, sitting up very straight.

She sat like a queen beside him, erect and with no support for her back, legs close together.

'Eva Karin would never have kept the existence of a sister secret from Lukas.'

'I believe you,' said Adam, without taking his eyes off the photograph. 'Because if this woman is still alive, she's too old to be Lukas's sister.'

'Too old? How do you know? There's no date on the photo, and—'

It was Adam's turn to interrupt.

'In fact, we've already considered the possibility there might be a child. The story about meeting Jesus when she was sixteen was clearly crucial in Eva Karin's life. It's easy to imagine that she might have been pregnant at the time, and that she was saved in that context. The usual practice in those days was for young, unmarried mothers to give up their child for adoption. But ...'

He grimaced and shook his head slightly.

'I've formed a pretty good picture of the Bishop over the past few weeks. And I have to say I agree with you. If there was a child from those days, she would presumably have told Lukas. When he was grown up, at least. Today nobody would criticize her in any way. On the contrary, a story like that would back up everything she says ... everything she said about abortion.'

Astrid took the photograph and held it up in front of her.

'The resemblance could be pure coincidence,' she said. 'I've always thought Lukas looked like Lill Lindfors, and they're definitely not related.'

'Lill Lindfors?' Adam grinned and shook his head as he examined the photograph once more. 'She looks like her, too,' he said in surprise. 'And now you come to mention it, I can see the resemblance with Lukas. A dark-haired, male version of Lill Lindfors.'

'And you look like Brian Dennehy,' said Astrid with a smile. 'You know, the American actor. Even though I'm sure he's not your brother.'

'You're not the first person to say that,' grinned Adam, sitting up a little straighter. 'But he's a bit fatter than me, don't you think?'

She didn't answer. He took another bun.

'How do you know she's too old?' she asked.

'A woman born in 1962 or 1963 would be ...'

He did a quick calculation.

'Somewhere around forty-six today. Forty-six years old. How old do you think she was when this photograph was taken?'

Astrid held it up once again.

'I don't really know,' she said dubiously. 'Twenty-three? Twenty-five?'

'Younger, probably. Perhaps only eighteen. People looked a little bit older in those days when they had a professional portrait taken.

Something to do with clothes and hairstyles and so on, I should think. I was born in 1956 and I'd put money on the fact that the woman in that photograph is older than me.'

'But how ... ? You can't—'

'To begin with, there's the quality of the paper,' he said, gently holding one corner of the photo. 'If this woman really was born at the beginning of the sixties, then the picture would have been taken ...'

Once again he did a rapid calculation in his head.

'Around 1980. Is there anything about this photo that suggests it was taken so late?'

Astrid slowly shook her head.

'No,' said Adam. 'I think it was taken somewhere around the early sixties. Perhaps as late as 1965, but no later. Look at the clothes! The hairstyle!'

'I was born in 1980,' she said feebly. 'I don't know much about fashion in the sixties. But that means this woman ... this lady ... she must be the same age as Eva Karin!'

'Yes,' said Adam, stopping himself as he was about to take another bun. 'And that means ...'

He placed the photograph on his knee again. He leaned forward, examining the facial features. The straight, slender nose. The forehead, high and curved and completely unlined. The cheeks were smooth, and the hair looked as if it could have been painted on her head, in neat waves with a curl over the temple.

'Could it be a sister?' he murmured as he straightened up at last. 'She doesn't look like Eva Karin, but in a way it could explain the resemblance to Lukas. Sometimes our genes follow a strange, round-about route, and—'

Astrid was staring at him in horror.

'A sister? Eva Karin has two siblings, both younger than her. Einar Olav, who must be around forty-five, and Anne Turid, who turned fifty last year – no, the year before. That isn't her!'

They heard a noise in the hallway. High, childish voices. Someone laughed and the front door banged shut.

Astrid quickly slipped the photograph back in its envelope. She hesitated only for a second before handing it to Adam.

'Calm down, both of you!'

She didn't take her eyes off him.

'Daddy and William are asleep. Quiet, please.'

Adam got up. He headed for the hallway, and was almost bowled over as two children came racing in. They looked at him with curiosity.

'Who are you?' asked the younger child.

'My name is Adam. And you're Andrea, the new Picasso.'

The girl laughed. 'No, I put the ears and the feet in the right places.'

'That's good,' said Adam, ruffling her hair. 'It's always good to have those in the right place.'

'Thank you for coming,' said Astrid.

She was leaning on the door frame, her arms folded. She seemed somehow relieved. Her smile was no longer quite as guarded as it had been when he arrived, and she laughed when the eight-year-old showed her a pretend tattoo covering the whole of her lower arm

'I'm the one who should be thanking you,' he said, raising the envelope in a gesture of farewell as he stepped outside.

The door closed behind him and he hurried to the car. Before he had time to start the engine, Astrid came running after him. He rolled down the window and looked up.

'I thought you might like these,' she said, handing him a plastic bag containing the rest of the buns. 'They're really best eaten fresh, and you seemed to like them.'

He didn't even manage to say thank you before she was hurrying back up the drive. He sat there for a moment, then opened the bag and took out one of the delicious buns. As he was about to sink his teeth into it, he felt a pang of guilt.

But there was something very special about freshly baked buns.

And the strawberry jam was the best he'd ever tasted.

Shame

Marcus was trying to think about the good things in life. Everything that was beautiful and wonderful and had made his existence worth the effort so far. Everything that had existed before – before the brutal realization that his life was built on a mistake. A misunderstanding.

A theft.

The whole thing was stolen, and it overshadowed everything he was trying to think about and made it impossible to sleep.

Rolf was snoring gently.

Marcus sat up slowly in bed, pausing briefly between movements. Eventually, he was on his feet and padded cautiously towards the bathroom. The door leading from the landing creaked, so his plan was to go through the spa next door to the bedroom. He made it and managed to close the door behind him without waking Rolf.

A faint light was still burning. Little Marcus had his own bathroom, but preferred to use his parents' if he needed to get up during the night.

Even in the dimness Marcus looked terrible. He gave a start when he saw himself in the mirror. The dark shadows under his eyes were turning into thick folds of flesh, and his skin was so pale it looked almost blue. He was getting heavier and heavier, and hadn't kept to his New Year resolution for even one of the fifteen days of 2009 that had passed so far. His own body odour made him recoil: night sweat, unwashed pyjamas and fear. He turned away from the ghostly reflection and went out on to the landing.

The door to little Marcus's room was ajar. Marcus could move more easily out here. The house could fall down around the boy's ears at this time of night, and he still wouldn't wake up. Marcus stood in the doorway, watching the sleeping child.

The room rested in the faint blue chilly glow of the night light above the bed, a spaceship on its way through the galaxy. The shelves along one wall were packed with books and toys, and the computer monitor glimmered with stars on a screensaver the boy himself had downloaded. The shabby teddy bear Marcus still had to have with him in bed in order to get to sleep lay helpless on the floor. It had lost one eye long ago. The other stared blindly up at the ceiling. Marcus tiptoed across the floor without treading on any of the numerous items lying around, and picked up the bear. He held it to his nose for a moment, inhaling the smell of everything that meant something.

Silently, he bent over his son, placed Freddie in the crook of his arm and adjusted the covers. The child grunted, smacked his lips and suddenly turned over, hugging the bear tightly.

An almost irresistible urge to crawl into bed with him overcame Marcus so suddenly that he gasped for breath. He wanted to be strong again. He wanted to be the daddy who comforted his son when he was occasionally woken by a nightmare and needed him. He wanted to lie down with his arm around little Marcus, quietly telling him stories about the olden days or outer space. The boy would snuggle up close and smile, his hair tickling Marcus's nose. There would be nobody in the whole world except the two of them, just like it had been before Rolf came, before they became three.

The way it had been before the terrible thing crept up on him.

Slowly, he backed out of the room.

He had no idea what he was going to do.

Not with his life, and not with the nights. Not with this night. The darkness grinned scornfully at him out of the corners, and he could feel his pulse rate increasing. Quickly, he began to move towards the stairs. He would go down to his study. Close the door. Watch TV. Switch on all the lights and pretend it was daytime.

He stopped himself just as he was about to slam the door behind him when he finally arrived safely in his study. Breathlessly, he smacked the panel that controlled the lighting. Nothing happened. He pulled himself together and pressed all the sensors firmly with one finger. At last the room was bathed in light, and the television came on. It was pre-programmed to NRK, which was showing *Dansefot Jukeboks*. He picked up the remote from his desk and turned down the sound, then switched over to CNN. He sank down on the broad, heavy desk chair and leaned his head back. His stomach ulcer was painful and he had a bitter, acrid taste in his mouth. Pain radiated from below his breastbone, and his whole body hurt. His mind was racing, and he was so frightened that his bladder felt full to bursting, even though he'd been less than half an hour ago.

This was no kind of life any more.

Suddenly, he sat up straight and found the key to the heavy corner cupboard that had come with the house. As time went by he had learned to like the Kurbits-style painting, which at first he had thought bizarre and somewhat vulgar. It helped that the cupboard was eighteenth-century, in excellent condition and worth a fortune. Now it was as if the ranks of fat, grotesque flowers were reaching out to grasp him as he put the antique key in the lock and turned it.

Inside were five small drawers. He opened the top one. There lay the tablets he had never mentioned to Rolf. It hadn't been necessary. Both these and the box in his office had remained untouched for many years. He tipped them into the palm of his hand and went back to his chair, where he let them trickle on to the calf-skin desk mat.

He still didn't know if drugs lost their effect once the use-by date had passed. Hardly. At least, not completely. If he took the lot, it would probably do the job. He placed one tablet experimentally on his tongue.

The taste was the same. Insipid, slightly salty.

Things would be better for little Marcus if he wasn't around any more.

Rolf would look after him.

Rolf was a better father than he was. Through his actions Marcus had not only committed a crime; he was no longer worthy of being a father. His whole life was being a father, and his life as a father was over.

The tears poured silently down his cheeks as he placed another tablet in his mouth.

And another.

A slight feeling of sleepiness made him lean back in the chair and close his eyes. He moistened the tip of his index finger with saliva and pressed it down on the desk without looking. Another tablet stuck to his finger, and he placed it on the tip of his tongue.

The last thing he did before he fell asleep was to open the desk drawer and sweep the rest of the tablets inside with the back of his hand.

You can't even manage to kill yourself, he thought listlessly before blessed sleep finally overcame him.

*

Adam Stubo woke up on Friday 16 January at 7.40 feeling as if he hadn't slept at all. Every time he had been on the point of dropping off, he had seen the picture of the woman from Eva Karin's bedroom in his mind's eye. The idea that their theory about a child who had disappeared or been disowned might have been correct, but with the proviso that all the circumstances had to be moved back a generation, had left him wide awake over and over again. The theory seemed more and more credible as the hours went by. The idea that the Bishop wanted to protect the memory of her parents was considerably more likely than the idea that she had wanted to avoid the shame of having a child as an unmarried sixteen-year-old.

Leaving aside the fact that there was no longer any shame attached, and that the photograph couldn't possibly be of a woman born in the early sixties.

It must be a sister, Adam thought as he swung his leg over the side of the bed. The last time he looked at the clock it had been just after five, so he must have had two and a half hours' sleep in spite of everything.

Another thing that had kept him awake was the fact that Johanne hadn't called. They hadn't spoken for a day and a half. He had tried to ring her three times yesterday evening, but all he got was the mechanical sound of her voicemail asking him to leave a message after the tone. The first time he called he had left a message, but she still hadn't called back. He felt a mixture of intense irritation and anxiety as he plodded into the bathroom.

He was tired of living in this hotel.

The bed was too soft.

The soap made his hands dry, and he had lost his appetite.

Adam wanted to go home.

Someone was banging on the door. With a stab of annoyance he flushed the toilet, wound a towel around his waist and went to see who it was. The acrid smell of morning urine surrounded him. He opened the door a fraction and put his face to the gap.

'What the fuck's wrong with your phone?' said Sigmund Berli, trying to push the door open and holding up a newspaper in the other hand. 'Have you seen this? We're going home, by the way, on the first available plane. Get your clothes on and start packing.'

'Good morning to you, too,' Adam said sourly, letting his colleague in. 'Do you think you could possibly take one thing at a time? Start with the phone.'

'I've called you five times since yesterday evening. You know perfectly well you're not supposed to make yourself unavailable.'

'I haven't,' said Adam. 'Try again now.'

He picked up his mobile from the bedside table as Sigmund keyed in his number on his own phone.

'It's ringing,' said Sigmund with the phone to his ear. 'Have you got it on silent?'

'No.'

Adam stared at the display. Nothing was happening. So Johanne might have tried after all.

'Why didn't you ring me on that?' said Adam, pointing to the hotel phone on the small desk by the window.

'Never occurred to me,' Sigmund said blithely. 'But forget that. We're going home. Now. Just take a look at this and you'll see why!'

Adam took the copy of *VG* as if the newspaper might suddenly bite him.

HATE GROUP BEHIND SIX MURDERS, screamed the front page. The subheading read: *Police horror theory – Bishop Lysgaard one of victims.*

'What the hell?' said Adam, raising his voice by several decibels. *'What the fuck is this?'*

'Read it,' said Sigmund. 'And you will discover that the Oslo police have found a possible link between the murders of Marianne Kleive and some Kurdish kid who was floating around in the harbour just before Christmas, as dead as a doornail and badly disintegrated.'

'What? But what's this got to do with Eva Karin?'

Adam sank down on the bed and turned to pages five and six. He was finding it hard to focus. His eyes flew across the article. After a minute and a half he looked up, flung the newspaper at the wall and bellowed:

'*How the hell did* VG *get hold of this before me?* I mean, I've learned to live with the fact that they know way too much way too soon, but this is ...'

He got up so quickly that the towel slipped off. He ignored the fact that he was stark bollock-naked and hissed at Sigmund, his fists clenched: 'Are we supposed to start reading the paper every morning just to find out what's fucking going on? This is ... this is ... For fuck's sake, Sigmund, this is fucking scandalous!'

Sigmund grinned.

'You're stark naked, Adam. You're getting fat, boy!'

'*I couldn't give a fuck!*'

He marched into the bathroom. Sigmund sat down on the chair by the desk and switched on the TV. He turned to TV2 as he listened to Adam banging about behind the closed door. Thirty seconds later Adam emerged, grabbed some clean clothes out of his suitcase and got dressed with surprising speed.

'The news is on in five minutes,' Sigmund said. 'We'll watch it before we go.'

'A gang from the US,' Adam growled as he tried to knot his tie. 'That's the most ridiculous fucking thing I've ever heard.'

'Not a gang,' Sigmund corrected him. 'A group. A hate group.'

'That's even more insane. Who the hell came up with something so utterly ... idiotic!'

He picked up a bag of dirty laundry and stuffed it in his suitcase, having given up on his tie.

'Johanne,' said Sigmund with a laugh. 'It's Johanne's theory!'

'What? *What are you saying?*'

Adam stormed over to the newspaper, which was lying in a crumpled heap on the bed. Once again his eyes flew over the article.

'It doesn't say anything about her here,' he said without looking up from the report, which was illustrated with pictures of Marianne Kleive and Bishop Lysgaard. 'It doesn't mention Johanne at all.'

He exhaled and dropped the paper on the floor.

'I spoke to a ... Silje Sørensen,' said Sigmund. 'She's with the Oslo police. She rang me at six o'clock. She'd tried to get hold of you, but with no luck.'

'Has everybody gone mad or what? I'm staying in a hotel for fuck's sake! This ...'

He reached the white, old-fashioned telephone in three strides. He picked up the receiver in one hand and the body of the phone in the other, and held it five centimetres from Sigmund's face.

'This is a telephone!'

'Calm down, Adam. Take it easy.'

'Take it easy! I don't want to fucking take it easy! I want to know what all this crap is about, and why—?'

'Well, listen to me then! Listen to what I have to say instead of rushing around like a lunatic. We'll get thrown out in a minute if you don't calm down.'

Adam took a deep breath, nodded and sat down heavily on the bed.

'Start talking,' he mumbled.

Sigmund clapped his hands almost silently.

'That's better. I don't know a great deal. Silje Sørensen was just as furious as you about the fact that *VG* has got hold of this, and they've turned the whole of Grønlandsleiret upside down to try and find the leak. She did tell me that this does, in fact, involve six murders. Some artist who died around Christmas, apparently from a heroin overdose, turns out to have minute traces of curacit in his blood. We were lucky. Curacit is broken down incredibly fast, and the guy had already been cremated. However, because it was routinely regarded as a suspicious death, they had some of his frozen blood in the lab, and the curacit—'

'What?'

'Curacit. You know, it's a poison, a muscle relaxant that paralyzes the breathing—'

'I know perfectly well what curacit is! What I'm wondering is—'

'Just hang on, Adam. Listen to me. So this artist had been murdered. And he's also ... he was also gay. And then there was a young man who was killed in Sofienberg Park some time in November, and we all know what people get up to in Sofienberg Park at night, don't we?'

Without giving Adam time to respond, he went on.

'Then there was a woman everybody thought had died in an RTA, but on closer inspection it turned out that someone had tampered with the brakes of her car. And I'm sure you can guess what her preferences in the bedroom were!'

Adam merely stared at him with a resigned expression.

'That Silje Sørensen really is paranoid,' Sigmund continued, unabashed. 'She called me from home. On her son's mobile. But whether those journalists have reliable sources or are bugging the police or whatever it is they might be doing, *VG* has named only three of the victims. The Bishop, Marianne Kleive and the kid in the water. I can never remember those Hottentot names.'

Adam felt so floored by the whole thing that he didn't even protest at this expression.

'Anyway, Sørensen told me Johanne had come to see her with some questions and a theory relating to her research. That stuff she's doing on hate crime. Something that ... I don't know, actually. Anyway, her theory fitted in so well with the material Oslo are sitting on that they've now put together a team to work on a major investigation, with the Oslo police and NCIS collaborating. That's where we're going. And that's more or less all I know. Ssh! News!'

'Ssh?' Adam repeatedly sourly. 'I haven't said a word!'

Sigmund turned up the volume.

TV2 led with the newspaper story.

They had obviously been short of time, because the report was illustrated with archive clips. They hadn't even managed to find winter pictures; police HQ was bathed in sunshine, with people dressed in summer clothing going in and out of the main entrance. The reporter had nothing more to add to what had been in the newspaper.

'Ssh!' Sigmund said again as the camera showed a slim woman in uniform with gold stripes and two stars on her shoulders.

'We are unable to comment on the case at this stage,' she said firmly, turning away from the microphone.

It followed her.

'Can you confirm the information in today's edition of *VG*?' asked the journalist.

'As I said, I have no further comment on this matter.'

'When will you be informing the public about this story, which seems to be particularly serious and far-reaching?'

'As I said, I am unable to comment on—'

Sigmund switched off.

'Let's go,' he said, getting to his feet. 'I'm starting to get really curious about this whole thing. I'll fetch my bags and see you downstairs in two minutes. What's that, by the way?'

He nodded in the direction of the bedside table, where Adam had placed the photograph of the unknown woman.

'That's the photo I told you about,' he said.

'What photo?'

'The one that was in Eva Karin's room. We need to call in at the police station with it. I want to know who she is. They're probably best placed to find out.'

'How did you find it?' Sigmund asked.

'Long story.'

'Spare me the details. See you downstairs?'

Adam nodded. He remained sitting on the bed. He was finding it hard to digest everything he had heard in the past half-hour, and felt slightly dizzy. He couldn't remember ever being caught so off-guard. When he did eventually stand up, exhaustion forced him to take a step to one side to keep his balance.

The fact that *VG* knew significantly more than he did in a case he was investigating was a blow. Far worse was the knowledge that Johanne had gone to the Oslo police with information he didn't even know about.

Adam picked up his small suitcase and his coat and headed for the door. As it closed behind him he realized that the gnawing pain in his stomach wasn't due to hunger.

He felt humiliated by his own wife, and he couldn't even manage to feel angry any longer. He just had a pain in his stomach.

Just like when he was a little boy, ashamed of something he'd done.

*

Kristen Faber's secretary wasn't in the least ashamed of the fact that she occasionally made copies of documents to take home. Her husband loved to hear about the cases she came into contact with, and sometimes they had great fun with a police interrogation where the suspect tried to wriggle out of things even when it was obvious he or she was guilty, or with a hopeless performance in court by some poor sod who couldn't afford a brief. She never kept the documents for very long. They ended up on the fire as soon as the case was no longer exciting.

As far as the will from the big oak cupboard in the archive was concerned, it wasn't exactly for fun that she made a copy and popped it in her bag. On the contrary, her husband had grown very serious when she told him about the case during dinner the previous evening. He didn't know anything about poor Niclas Winter, but he had heard of the testator. He was very keen to take a look at the will, so this morning she had made two copies. Only one was placed in Kristen Faber's archive.

It couldn't do any harm if her husband took a little look.

She fastened the accompanying letter to the original will and slipped them both in an envelope. It had taken less than two minutes to establish that the inheritance fund was the right destination for such a document, and to make sure nothing went wrong she was going to take it to the post office and send it by registered mail. Best to be on the safe side in such matters. The court had once claimed that Faber had been late lodging an appeal, even though she was 100 per cent certain she had posted the papers in time.

Not that the will was as important as an appeal, but the dressing-down from her boss on that occasion had made an impression. There was going to be no doubt that this letter had been posted. She pulled on her coat, put the envelope in her bag and hummed a little tune as she locked the door and set off in the bright morning sunshine.

Sense and Sensibility

FOLDER FOUND *this morning. Had been borrowed by Special Needs teacher and put back in the wrong place. Sorry to have bothered you* ☺ *Live Smith*

Johanne read the text twice, not knowing whether to feel relieved or angry. On the one hand it was obviously a good thing that Kristiane's file had been found. On the other, it frightened her that the school had such inadequate routines when it came to handling sensitive material. As she locked the door of her office behind her it struck her that she ought to be delighted. If Kristiane's file really had simply been put in the wrong place, it ought to ease her anxiety that someone was watching her daughter.

She pushed her mobile into her bag and crept out of the building without being seen. It was only two o'clock and she couldn't concentrate on anything but trying to get hold of Adam. She still hadn't heard a thing, and he wasn't answering his phone.

She had lost count of how many times she had tried to call him.

*

Kristen Faber's secretary decided to ring through an order just to be on the safe side. Laksen's Delicatessen in Bjølsen was the best place for calves' liver, and her husband set great store by a good liver casserole for Sunday lunch. It had to be calves' liver, otherwise the flavour was too strong. They might still have dried stockfish, too, even if the season was over. Fish on Saturday and beef on Sunday, she thought contentedly. The phone rang just as she was about to pick it up. She grabbed it quickly and reeled off the usual formula: 'Mr Faber's office, how may I help you?'

'Hello, sweetheart!'

'Hello yourself,' she said amiably. 'I was just about to ring Laksen's to order some stockfish and calves' liver, so we can have a lovely weekend.'

'Fantastic,' her husband said on the other end of the phone. 'I'm looking forward to it. Is Mr Faber there?'

'Kristen? You want to speak to Kristen?'

She couldn't have been more surprised if he'd suddenly appeared in front of her. Her husband had never set foot in the office, nor had he ever met Kristen Faber. The office was her domain. Since her husband's sight began to deteriorate and he took early retirement, he had suggested a couple of times that he might take a stroll down to the city centre to see what she got up to during the day. Out of the question, she said. Home was home, work was work. Admittedly, she enjoyed telling him what she'd been doing, and they laughed together at the documents she sometimes took the liberty of showing him, but she didn't want any link between her husband and her rude, self-righteous boss.

'What for?'

'Well, it's ... There's something not quite right about that will you brought home yesterday.'

'Not quite right? What do you mean by that?'

She had read it aloud to him last night. He could still read, but the tunnel vision meant that he asked her to read to him more and more often these days. It was quite nice, actually. After the evening news she would read him bits and pieces from the newspaper, with pauses for major and minor discussions on the day's events.

'There's something ...'

Kristen Faber burst in through the door leading to the lobby.

'I need something to eat,' he puffed. 'The lunch break will be over in half an hour, and I've got to sort out some documents. A baguette or something, OK?'

The secretary nodded, keeping her hand over the mouthpiece.

'I'll nip out right away,' she said.

As soon as his office door closed, she went back to her conversation.

'There's absolutely no need to speak to Kristen, darling.'

'But I have to—'

'Look, we'll talk about this when I get home, all right? I'm up to my eyes in work today. We'll have a chat this afternoon.'

329

She hung up without waiting for an answer.

As she pulled on her coat as quickly as possible, she felt a pang of guilt for once. Perhaps taking confidential papers home wasn't entirely legal. She had never really looked at it that way; after all, she had unrestricted access to all the papers here, and her husband could almost be regarded as a part of her after all these years.

However, it probably wasn't quite the right thing to do, she thought, picking up her bag before dashing off to Hansen's bread shop. At any rate, she didn't want any contact whatsoever between her husband and Kristen Faber.

Bjarne had a habit of letting his tongue run away with him.

*

'Have you been running, sweetheart? You're all sweaty!'

Johanne hugged her daughter, who flung her arms around her and didn't want to let go.

'All the way from Tåsensenteret,' she said. 'And I had a really good week at Dad's. Did you manage OK without me?'

'I did,' nodded Johanne, kissing the top of her head. 'And how are you?'

The last remark was directed at Isak. He had put Kristiane's bag down on the hall floor and was standing with his hands in his pockets. He looked tired. His smile didn't quite reach his eyes, and he looked as if he couldn't decide whether to stay around or leave straight away.

'Not too bad,' he said hesitantly.

'Do you want to come in for a while?'

'Thanks, but ...'

He took his hands out of his pockets and gave Kristiane a hug. 'Could you pop up and see Ragnhild, chicken? I just want a word with Mum. Love you. Thanks for coming.'

Kristiane smiled, picked up her bag and dragged it up the steep staircase.

'I'm going out on the mountains at the weekend,' said Isak. 'Is it OK if I hang on to Jack?'

'Of course.'

The yellow mongrel sat down on the steps and shook his head.

'What is it?' asked Johanne. 'Is something wrong?'

'No, but ...'

He took a deep breath and started again.

'I really don't want to worry you, but ...'

Johanne took his hand. It was ice cold.

'Is it something to do with Kristiane?' she asked sharply.

'No,' he said. 'Well ... not really. She's had a really good time. It's just that ...'

He shifted his body weight from his right to his left foot, and leaned against the opposite side of the door frame.

'It's so cold with the door open,' Johanne said. 'Come inside. Stay there, Jack. Stay.'

Both the dog and Isak did as they were told. He leaned against the wall, and Johanne sat down on the stairs opposite him.

'What is it?' she said anxiously. 'Tell me.'

'I think ...'

He broke off again.

'Tell me,' Johanne whispered.

'I've had a strange feeling that somebody is watching me. Or rather ... that someone is watching ...'

He looked like a little boy, standing there. His jacket was too big for him and he couldn't stand still. His gaze flickered here and there before he looked her in the eye. She was just waiting for him to start scraping one foot on the floor.

'You're not going anywhere,' she said calmly, getting up.

He took his hands out of his pockets again and spread them helplessly.

'I can't really explain it,' he said in a subdued voice. 'It's so kind of—'

'You're staying here,' she said, letting Jack in and locking the door.

She pushed the handle to double-check that the lock had clicked into place.

'You need to speak to Adam.'

'Johanne,' he said, reaching out to grab her arm. 'Does that mean I'm right? Do you know something that—?'

'It means exactly what I say,' she said, without trying to free herself from his grasp. 'You need to tell Adam about this, because he wouldn't believe me.'

He let go, and she turned and led the way up the stairs.

Not that I've ever given him the chance, she thought, and decided to try calling him for the sixth time in three hours.

He was probably furious.

She was so frightened she was having difficulty walking in a straight line.

*

The man in the dark-coloured hire car had had no difficulty finding his way. It was actually just a matter of following the same road all the way from Oslo to Malmö, then taking a right turn across the sound to Denmark.

Even though it got dark at such an ungodly hour in this country, and in spite of the fact that the snow had been coming down thick and fast ever since Christmas, it was easy to maintain a good speed. Not too fast, of course; a couple of kilometres over the speed limit aroused the least suspicion. The traffic had been heavy coming out of Oslo, even at three o'clock, but as soon as he had travelled a few kilometres along the E6, it eased off. The map showed that he was essentially following the coastline, so he assumed that Friday afternoons brought traffic chaos on this particular road in the spring and summer. Evidently, the sea wasn't quite so appealing at minus eight and in a howling gale.

He was approaching Svinesund, and the time was ten to five.

He would drive to Copenhagen and leave the car with Avis on Kampmannsgade. Then he would walk a few blocks before asking a taxi driver to take him to a decent hotel on the outskirts of the city centre. He was too late to catch the last flight to London anyway. He had got rid of the dark clothes. It had taken him more than two hours to cut them into strips, which he divided into small piles and stuffed in the pockets of the capacious red anorak. It made him look fatter, which was good. In the space of just over an hour he had got rid of a bundle here and a bundle there in the public rubbish bins he passed on his stroll through Oslo.

He had had to leave at short notice.

He didn't speak much Norwegian, just enough to send simple text messages. However, a passing glance at the newspaper stand next to the small reception desk this morning had made him realize there was no time to lose. Not that he rushed anything, but the instructions were clear.

No doubt the others were also on their way out of the country. He didn't know how they were travelling, but purely to pass the time in the evenings he had come up with a number of alternative routes. Only in his head, of course; there wasn't a single scrap of paper with his handwriting on it in Norway. Apart from the distorted signatures when he had used the Visa cards, which were actually genuine but issued under false names. The cold weather in Norway had been a blessing. He had made sure he signed only when he was wearing his outdoor clothes, so that it didn't seem odd when he kept the tight pigskin gloves on.

For example, the individual or individuals who had been in Bergen should drive to Stavanger, in his opinion, and fly from there directly to Amsterdam. But it wasn't his business to speculate on the travel plans of others, any more than it was his business to know who they were.

He operated alone, but knew he was not alone.

He was trained to lay a false trail and hide his own. He avoided surveillance cameras as far as possible. On the odd occasion when he had no choice but to pass through an area covered by cameras, he made a point of altering his gait, pushing his lips out slightly, flaring his nostrils. And looking down.

In addition, his appearance was perfectly ordinary.

It was as if he had never been in Norway.

The Svinesund Bridge lay ahead of him. There was no barrier, no checkpoint. There was a customs post on the other side of the road where a truck was just being checked over, but no one asked him for any documentation. When he passed the imaginary line separating Norway and Sweden in the middle of the high bridge, he couldn't help smiling.

Naive Scandinavians. Stupid, naive Europeans. One reason why he had been allocated this task was because he had studied Scandinavian languages during his military training, but he had never actually been here before. Nor was he tempted to make a return visit.

He drove on for about fifteen minutes, then turned off at a suitable point. The road was narrow with very little traffic, and it wasn't long before he spotted a small forest track leading off to the right. Slowly, he drove a hundred metres or so in among the fir trees, then stopped and switched off the engine. The snow was deep in spite of the dense forest, and only the day-old tyre tracks left by a tractor made it possible for him to drive here.

He got out of the car.

It was cold, but there was barely a breath of wind.

He drank in the clear, pure air and smiled. When he looked up he could see stars, and part of the waning moon between two gently swaying treetops.

He closed his eyes and leaned his upper arms on the car roof, then rested his head on his joined hands.

'Dear Lord,' he whispered, 'thank you for all your blessings.'

The familiar warmth rose in his body like a feeling of intoxication as he whispered his prayer.

'Thank you for giving me the strength to follow your word, dear Lord. Thank you for giving me the energy and courage to fulfil your commands. Thank you for allowing me to be a tool in the battle against the darkness of Satan. Thank you for giving me the ability to distinguish right from wrong, good from evil, true from false. Thank you for punishing me when I deserve it, and for rewarding me when I have earned it. Thank you for ...'

He hesitated, then clasped his hands even more tightly and closed his eyes once more, his words sincere.

'Thank you for allowing me to spare that beautiful young girl, that innocent angel. Thank you, O Lord, for enabling me to recognize the presence of Jesus. For everything is yours, and purity is the goal. Amen.'

Slowly he turned his face up to the sky. The strength that poured through him made him shudder; it was almost as if he had become weightless. A bird took off from a snow-laden branch hanging over the track, screeching eerily as it disappeared into the dark sky. The man stretched, breathed in the fresh smell of cold and fir needles, and fished a small red clover leaf in enamelled metal out of his pocket. He pushed his hands in a pair of gloves he had found in the underground station at the National Theatre, and rubbed the emblem thoroughly before drawing back his arm and hurling it in among the trees. As he got back in the car he felt happy.

He had to reverse the hundred metres back to the main road, but it wasn't a problem. Fifteen minutes later he was back on the E6, heading towards Gothenburg. In two days he would be back in the States, and there wouldn't be a single clue that he had ever been in Norway.

He was absolutely sure of that.

*

'This is the best clue we have.'

Adam leaned back on the sofa and held the picture of Kristiane's saviour up in front of him.

'But that's worth having.'

Johanne shuffled closer to him. He smelled of a long working day, and she pressed her nose against his arm and inhaled deeply.

'Thank you for not being so cross any more,' she mumbled.

He didn't reply.

'Or are you?' She smiled and looked up at him.

'No, no. I suppose I'm just ... disappointed. Mostly disappointed.'

'Now you sound as if you're telling a child off.'

'I expect that's what I am doing, in a way.'

She sat up abruptly.

'OK, Adam, that's enough! I've said I'm sorry. I should have come to you first. It's just that you ... you're so bloody ... *sceptical* all the time! I knew you'd have doubts about my entire theory and I—'

'Stop,' he interrupted, waving his hand vehemently. 'What's done is done.'

'And in any case, contacting Silje Sørensen turned out to be a lucky break.'

She forced an encouraging smile in the hope of evoking a smile in return.

It didn't happen. Adam scratched his scalp with both hands and sighed wearily. Then he picked up the picture of the bald man in the dark clothes once again.

He examined it for a long time, then suddenly said: 'You know, I have a good relationship with Isak. I'm perfectly happy for him to be here. However, I can't accept the fact that you're using him as a shield to protect yourself from me, that he's sitting here waiting when I get

335

home after working in another city for several days, when we haven't spoken to one another for more than thirty hours, and we have a great deal that is ... unresolved, to put it mildly. It must never, ever happen again.'

'But you wouldn't have believed me! I've had this horrible feeling ever since 19 December, and I haven't dared say anything, either to you or to Isak! The conversation I had with Kristiane last Monday when I realized she was a key witness was so vague, with so little in terms of ... concrete information that I ... When Isak told me he also had the feeling that ... You wouldn't have believed me, Adam!'

'It isn't a question of believing or not believing, Johanne. Of course I have no problem believing that you – and subsequently Isak – had a feeling someone was watching Kristiane. Or that you believe she saw something significant with regard to the person or persons who murdered Marianne Kleive. But just because you have that kind of feeling, it *doesn't necessarily mean it's actually happened*. Particularly when neither of you can come up with anything more concrete than "a feeling".'

He was sitting up straight and drew quotation marks with his fingers on her cheeks.

'The file was missing, and the man by the—'

'The file is back, you said so yourself. It was just carelessness.'

'But—'

'OK, let's just drop this, shall we? I've asked a patrol car to drive past a couple of times a day, just to be on the safe side. Beyond that, there's not much we can do if you don't want us to subject Kristiane to a formal interview, with the stress that would mean for her. So can we forget it? At least for the moment. Please?'

His hand grasped the wine glass.

'No,' she said. 'I can't do that. I realize you're hurt. I realize I should have come to you with all this right from the start. But listen, Adam, I've been thinking about—'

'No,' he broke in harshly. 'Listen to me! If Kristiane really did witness something to do with the murder of Marianne Kleive, *then why the hell didn't they just kill her?*'

His last few words were so loud that they both gave a start, then instinctively sat still as they listened for signs that Kristiane might have woken up. The only thing they could hear was the sound of

Mamma Mia on DVD coming from the apartment below. For the tenth time since Christmas – or so it seemed to Johanne.

'Because they believe,' she said. 'Because they believe in God.'

'What?'

'Or Allah.'

'Because they believe – so what?'

He seemed more interested now. Or perhaps just confused.

'Because they believe, they don't kill blindly,' Johanne said. 'They believe with a sincerity which is probably alien to most people. They're fanatical, but they have a deep faith. Taking the lives of adults who in their view are sinners who must be punished with death in accordance with a God-given imperative is something completely different from killing an innocent child.'

She spoke very slowly, as if these thoughts were new to her, and she therefore had to choose her words with the greatest care.

Adam's expression was no longer so dismissive when he asked: 'But these people, these groups, are they really ... are they really religious? Aren't they just lost souls using God and Allah as some kind of ... pretext?'

'No,' said Johanne, shaking her head. 'Never underestimate the power of faith. And in some ways my theory is made more credible because ...'

She lifted her feet on to the sofa and grabbed hold of one of them, as if she were cold.

'... because Kristiane did actually see something. The man who murdered Marianne Kleive presumably realized straight away that Kristiane isn't like everyone else. If the man who saved her from the tram really is the murderer, at least that incident proved to him that she's ... different. And if there's one thing that's more striking about my daughter than anything else, it's ...'

The tears almost spilled over as she looked at Adam.

'Her innocence,' she said. 'She is innocence personified. One of God's little angels.'

'The lady helped me,' Kristiane said quietly from the doorway.

Adam stiffened. Johanne turned her head slowly and looked at her daughter.

'Did she?' she whispered.

'Albertine was asleep,' said Kristiane. 'And I wanted to find you, Mum.'

Adam hardly dared breathe.

'I had to hide from all the people, because I didn't want to go to bed without you. And then suddenly I came to a door that was open. There were some stairs. I went down the stairs, because I thought you might have been there, and at least there was nobody else around. It was so quiet when I got to the bottom. It was really a cellar, and it wasn't at all posh. And then the lady was standing at the top of the stairs. "Hello," said the lady.'

Kristiane was wearing new pyjamas. They were too big and the sleeves came down over her hands. She started tugging at them.

'I think I'd better go to sleep,' she said.

'What did you do when the lady said hello?' Johanne asked with a smile.

'I think I'd better go to sleep. Dam-di-rum-ram.'

'Come over here and be my little girl.' Adam turned to her at last and gave her a little wave.

'I'm Daddy's girl,' she said. 'And actually, I'm not a girl any more. I'm a young woman. That's what Daddy says.'

'You can be my girl and Daddy's girl,' Adam said with a laugh. 'You always will be. However old you are. Haven't you heard Grandpa calling Mum his little girl?'

'Grandpa calls all women his little girl. It's one of his bad habits. That's what Granny says.'

'Come here,' Johanne whispered. 'Come to Mum.'

Kristiane walked hesitantly across the floor.

'She called to me,' she said, settling down on the sofa between them. 'She didn't know my name, because of course she didn't know me. She just called out "Come here" and then she smiled.'

'And what happened next?' said Johanne.

'Adam,' Kristiane said in a serious tone of voice. 'You must weigh ...' She thought quickly.

'About 230 per cent more than me.'

'I think that's exactly what I weigh,' replied Adam, with an embarrassed glance in Johanne's direction. 'But I kind of wanted to keep that as my little secret.'

'I weigh thirty-one kilos, Mum. So you can work it out.'

'I'd rather hear what happened, sweetheart.'

'The lady called me and I went back up the stairs. She had really warm hands. But I'd lost one of my slippers.'

'Slippers?' said Adam. 'I thought you weren't wearing any—'

'Did the lady go back to fetch it?' Johanne quickly interrupted.

'Yes.'

'And where were you in the meantime?'

'Dam-di-rum-ram. Where's Sulamit?'

'Sulamit died, sweetheart. You know that.'

'The lady was dead, too. Dam-di-rum-ram.'

Adam held her close, resting his cheek on the top of her head.

'I'm so sorry I ran over Sulamit,' he whispered. 'But it was a long time ago.'

'Dam-di-rum-ram.'

She had drawn her knees up to her chin and wrapped her arms around her legs as she slowly rocked from side to side. She bumped into Johanne, paused for a moment, bumped into Adam. Over and over again.

'Let's get you to bed,' Johanne said eventually.

'Dam-di-rum-ram.'

'Off we go.'

She got up and took her daughter's hand. Kristiane happily went with her. Adam reached out to her, but she didn't see him. He sat there listening to Johanne's patient small talk and Kristiane's strange chatter.

It struck him that realizing Johanne was right was almost worse than the fact that Kristiane had witnessed something traumatic. Overcome with fatigue, he sank back against the cushions.

He had believed what Johanne told him, but not what she thought it implied. Once upon a time he had cynically drawn her to him precisely because of her judgement. Because he needed it. He had drawn her into an investigation she really didn't want to get involved in by forcing her to imagine every parent's nightmare. Children were being kidnapped and murdered, and he was completely at a loss. It was Johanne's unique experiences with the FBI and her sharp eye for human behaviour that solved the case and saved a little girl's life. He had fallen in love with Johanne for many reasons, but whenever he thought back to the time after the dramatic search for the missing child, it was Johanne's ability to combine intellect and intuition, rationality and emotion that had attracted him with a power he had never experienced before.

Johanne was the perfect blend of sense and sensibility.

But this time – so many difficult years later – he just hadn't believed in her.

The feeling of shame made him close his eyes.

'Now do you believe me?'

Her tone wasn't aggressive. It wasn't even reproachful. On the contrary, she sounded relieved. It made him feel even smaller.

'I believed you all along,' he mumbled. 'I just thought that—'

'Let's forget it,' said Johanne, sitting down beside him. 'What do we do now?'

'I don't know. I have no idea. The best thing might be to wait. She talked to you on Monday, and to us just now. We should probably wait until she decides to tell us more.'

'There's no guarantee she ever will.'

'No. But do you want to put her through an interview?'

She placed one hand on his thigh and picked up his wine glass with the other.

'Not yet. Not unless it becomes absolutely necessary.'

'Then we're agreed.'

She felt a wave of tenderness for him that was unusual these days, a deep gratitude for the fact that his immediate instinct was to protect his stepdaughter, even though she might have vital information in an ongoing murder enquiry.

'Thank you,' she said simply.

'Why are they here?' Adam said, so quietly that she almost didn't hear.

'What?'

'Why are they here?' he repeated. 'The 25'ers. Here. In Norway.'

She swirled the wine around the glass. The beat of *Money, Money, Money* thumped up through the floor from down below. For a moment she considered thumping back. If Kristiane didn't fall asleep properly now, it was going to be a long night.

'I don't know,' she said. 'But of course, they could be in other places as well.'

'No.'

He took the glass from her and had a sip.

'Interpol has no information on similar cases anywhere else in Europe. In the US, however, the FBI is working on a case where—'

'Six gay men have been murdered and it turns out there's a connection between all of them,' she finished off for him. 'And that particular case is a hard nut to crack.'

He laughed.

'Do you know everything that's going on in that bloody country?'

'America is not a bloody country. It's a wonderful, wonderful country, the USA.'

His laughter grew louder, positively hearty. He pulled her close. She was smiling, too. It was a long time since she'd heard him laugh like that.

'It could be just a coincidence, of course,' she said.

When he didn't reply, she added: 'But I don't believe that for a second.'

'Why not?' Adam asked. 'If they've decided to ... export their hatred, I suppose we're as good a country to start in as any. In fact, if you think about it ...'

He tried to get more comfortable.

'... perhaps we're better than any other country. We've got the most liberal laws in the world when it comes to gay rights, we've got—'

'Along with several other countries,' she broke in. 'And a number of states in the US. So they've got no real reason to come here, in fact. I just don't believe ...'

Adam was shifting about so much that she sat up and undid his belt.

'I love you however much you weigh,' she said. 'But it does look a little bit ridiculous when you start literally tightening your belt. Couldn't you perhaps buy yourself some bigger clothes, sweetheart?'

She could have sworn he was blushing. But he left the belt hanging open.

'I think they're here for a very definite reason,' she said.

'Which is?'

'If only we knew. But there's something.'

'Shit,' said Adam, lumbering to his feet.

'What are you going to do?'

He mumbled something she didn't catch and headed towards the hallway. She could hear *Super Trouper* coming from below, and realized she was humming along. In order to get the enervating melody out of her head, she picked up a pen from the coffee table and took a newspaper out of the basket on the floor. She jotted down a few notes in the margin of the front page of *Aftenposten*. When she had finished she sat there brooding so intently that she didn't even notice Adam until he flopped down beside her. He was wearing generous pyjama bottoms and a big American football shirt.

'Look at this,' she said, tapping the paper with her pen.

'I can't make head or tail of it,' he said, wrinkling his nose at her incomprehensible scrawl.

'The methods,' she said succinctly.

'Yes?'

'Sophie Eklund was killed after someone sabotaged her car. So there was an attempt to cover up a murder.'

'Yes ...'

'Niclas Winter was written off as the victim of an overdose. Which he was – to be fair – but all the indications are that he was killed with curacit. In other words, another attempt to cover up a murder.'

'How do you actually inject curacit into an adult, relatively healthy man?' Adam muttered, still trying to decipher what she had written down. 'I would have fought like the devil.'

'The first thing that occurs to me is that he might have been fooled into thinking it was something else. Heroin, for example.'

'Yes ...'

'Or he was taken by surprise. Curacit works incredibly fast. If you inject into the mouth where there are a lot of blood vessels, it's only a matter of seconds before the effect kicks in.'

'Into the mouth? But you can't force someone to open wide so you can inject a little curacit, surely?'

'I'm afraid we'll never know the answer to that. He's been cremated. But listen to me, Adam. Pay attention. The point is there was an attempt to cover up the next two murders, exactly like the ones I've just mentioned.'

She chewed her pen.

'Runar Hansen, poor soul – nobody really bothered too much about him. Drug addicts who get beaten up and die as a result of their injuries don't attract much attention these days. And as far as Hawre Ghani is concerned, he was thrown in the water and was virtually unrecognizable by the time they pulled him out. To be perfectly honest, I think his case would have ended up well down the pile at police headquarters if Silje Sørensen hadn't ... felt something for the boy.'

'Where are you going with this, Johanne?'

'I want my own wine. Can't you go and get me a glass?'

He got up without a word.

Johanne stared at her scribbles. Six murders. Two covered up, two almost ignored, simply because the victims were right at the bottom of the scale of humanity in every way. She suddenly drew a thick ring around the last two names.

'There you go,' said Adam, handing her a half-full glass. 'Not exactly the usual Friday night. Apart from the wine, I mean.'

'What we can almost definitely say,' said Johanne, taking the glass without looking up, 'is that something unforeseen happened when Marianne Kleive was murdered. The killer was surprised by Kristiane. In other words, we can't actually be certain whether this murder would also have been covered up. As an accident. An illness. Something. To make sure the alarm wasn't sounded straight away, the murderer sent text messages from her mobile. That gave him a whole week.'

'Does this just mean they don't want to get caught, that they just want to buy themselves time, or that they want—?'

'But let's look at the Bishop,' said Johanne, suddenly realizing that the page she was writing on had a picture of Eva Karin in the right-hand column.

She turned the old paper ninety degrees and drew a square around the small portrait on the front page.

'There was no attempt to disguise this murder,' she said, mostly to herself.

Adam was sensible enough to keep quiet.

'Quite the reverse,' she went on. 'Stabbed out in the street. True, it happened on the only day of the year when you can be fairly sure nobody is out and about, but still ... The intention was that she should be found quickly. The intention was that the murder of ...'

She held her breath for so long that Adam wondered if something was wrong.

'Of course!' she said suddenly in a loud voice, turning to look at Adam. 'Let's assume that my theory is correct. The other murders are perceived as something else. The objective was quite simply ...'

She stared at him as if she had only just noticed that he was sitting there.

'... that they should die,' she said in surprise. 'The only objective was that they should die! Death itself was the goal!'

Adam thought it was fairly obvious that a person was murdered because someone wanted them dead, but he kept quiet.

'They're sinners,' said Johanne, waxing almost enthusiastic. 'And they must be punished for their sins! It doesn't matter to The 25'ers whether the rest of us can see a link, or whether we even realize a crime lies behind their deaths. The most important thing is that they must die, and then that the murderers – God's instruments, so to speak – are not subject to our worldly legislation.'

'Yes,' Adam ventured tentatively.

'Only one of these victims is known to the public,' Johanne went on. 'Eva Karin Lysgaard. And she was the only one who was murdered in a way that positively cries out for attention. Why would that be, Adam?'

She knelt on the sofa and turned towards him. Her face was glowing. Her eyes were shining, her mouth half-open. She took his hand and squeezed it so hard it almost hurt.

'Why, Adam?'

'Because,' he said. 'Because ...'

'Because they want us to start digging into her life! The investigation into the murder of Eva Karin Lysgaard is an investigation they *wanted* to happen, Adam! The whole *point* was for us to turn her life upside down, just as all murder victims have their lives turned inside out in the hope that something will turn up!'

'In the hope that something will turn up,' he repeated quietly. 'Hang on a minute.'

Johanne followed him with her eyes as he padded into the hallway.

She was out of breath, and her palms prickled when he came back and handed her a photograph before sitting down again.

'Who's this?' she asked.

'I don't know who she is,' he said. 'But this is a copy of a photograph that went astray.'

He told her about the room that had been Eva Karin's sanctuary at night. About the photograph that had been there the day after the murder, but had disappeared when he went back a couple of days later. When he got to the part about Lukas scrambling across the roof in the January rain, he started to laugh. At the end he took back the photograph and laid it on his knee.

'Lukas thought she might be his sister,' he said. 'But you can tell from both the quality of the picture and the clothes she's wearing that it's hardly likely it was taken around 1980. And her hairstyle isn't exactly typical of the eighties either.'

'So what do you think?' said Johanne, without taking her eyes off the photograph.

'I've been wondering whether she might be an unknown aunt rather than sister to Lukas. Eva Karin's illegitimate sister. That would explain the fact that she looks a bit like Lukas.'

'Does she? I think she looks like Lill Lindfors.'

Adam grinned. 'You're not the only one. Anyway, it won't be long until we know who she is. Both the Bergen police and NCIS are working on it. If this woman is still alive, we'll know who she is in a few days. If not sooner.'

'And where will that lead?'

'What? Finding out who she is?'

'Yes. How can you be sure she's got something to do with the case?'

'I suppose I can't be sure,' Adam said hesitantly. 'But you have to admit it's weird that Erik Lysgaard put it away as soon as he had the chance.'

'Have you asked him about it?'

'No ... It gives me the upper hand if he doesn't even know I've discovered the photograph, and I want to keep it that way.'

In the apartment below the film had reached *Knowing Me, Knowing You*. The neighbours had turned down the volume at last, but the bass still vibrated through the floor. Johanne took back the photograph.

'What an exciting face,' she murmured. 'Strong, somehow.'

Adam leaned forward and grabbed a handful of crisps. So far he'd managed to resist temptation.

'Can you move those out of the way, please,' he mumbled as he crunched away. 'Crisps are the work of the devil.'

Instead of doing as he asked, she got up and started to walk around the room with the photograph in her hand.

'Adam,' she said expressionlessly, almost absent-mindedly. 'Eva Karin's murder is different from the others in terms of the method. What else distinguishes this case from the rest?'

'I ... I don't really know.'

'There's reason to believe that all the other victims were gay. Or at any rate that they had a direct link to homosexual or lesbian activities.'

Adam stopped chewing. The crisps suddenly felt like an unappetizing, sticky calorie bomb in his mouth. He picked up a used serviette from the table, spat the revolting, yellowish-brown mass into it and tried to screw it up. A little bit fell on the floor, and he bent down sheepishly to retrieve it.

Johanne took no notice whatsoever. She had stopped by the window. She stood with her back to him for a long time before turning around and pointing at the photograph.

'Eva Karin is the only heterosexual,' she said. 'At least, she's the only one who is *apparently* heterosexual.'

'What do you mean by ... ? What do you mean by "apparently"?'

'This,' said Johanne, holding the photograph up to face him. 'This is neither Lukas's nor Eva Karin's sister. This is the Bishop's lover.'

There was complete silence in the building. The film must have finished in the apartment below. The wind had dropped. The floorboards didn't even creak as she walked back to the sofa and carefully – as if she didn't want to lose a complex chain of thought – sat down beside him.

'It's not possible,' Adam said eventually. 'We haven't heard a single rumour. That kind of thing leads to gossip, Johanne. People talk about that kind of thing. It's not possible for ...'

He grabbed the photograph, a little more roughly than he had intended.

'In that case, why does she look so much like Lukas?'

'Pure coincidence. Besides which, both you and no doubt Lukas have studied this photograph so intently to try and find a clue that even the slightest resemblance would strike you. It happens. People look like one another sometimes. For example, you look a lot like—'

'But if it hasn't occurred to us that Eva Karin might have been living a double life, then how could The 25'ers know about it? If you're right about this completely absurd ... If you're right about ...'

He swallowed and ran his fingers through his hair in an uncertain, resigned gesture.

'Nobody knew about it! How can The 25'ers have known about a ... a lesbian lover ...'

He spat out the words as if they had a bitter taste.

'... when nobody else knew?'

'Somebody knew. One person knew.'

'Who?'

'Erik Lysgaard. Her husband. He must have known. You don't live together for forty years without knowing that sort of thing. They must have had ... some kind of agreement.'

'And then he would have ... told ... he would have ... if he had any idea that ...'

It almost seemed as if the big man was about to burst into tears. Johanne still hadn't noticed a thing.

'He must have told someone,' she said. 'Not The 25'ers, obviously, but someone close to them. That's why they wanted this case investigated, Adam. They wanted us to discover Eva Karin's ... sin. And that's what we've just done.'

Adam put his hands to his face. His breath was coming in short gasps. Johanne had never noticed it before, but his wedding ring was digging so deep into his finger that he probably wouldn't be able to get it off.

'You have to find this woman,' she whispered, moving so close to him that her lips brushed his ear. 'And then you have to get Erik to tell you the name of the person to whom he revealed this great secret.'

'The first part will be easy,' he said from behind his hands, his voice muffled. 'I think the second part will be impossible.'

'But you have to try,' said Johanne. 'At least you have to make an attempt to talk to Erik Lysgaard.'

*

The Bishop's widower was sitting in his usual old armchair staring blankly out into the living room, which was almost in darkness. Only a lamp next to the TV and a candle on the coffee table cast a soft, yellow glow over the room. Lukas was sitting in his mother's armchair. It was as if he could feel the warmth of her on his back, the contours of the mother he missed with an intensity he couldn't possibly have imagined before she died.

'So at least we know the reason,' he said quietly. 'Mum died because she took a stand. She died for her generosity, Dad. For her faith in Jesus.'

Erik still didn't answer. He had barely said a word since his son had arrived three hours ago, and he had refused to eat any of the food Lukas had brought with him. A cup of tea was all he had managed to get down, and that had taken some persuasion.

He had, however, agreed to read the newspaper. In a way that was a sign of life, Lukas thought.

'Why hasn't anybody contacted me?' his father said, so unexpectedly that Lukas spilt a little of his own tea. 'I don't think I should have to read about this in the paper.'

'They rang me. I had Inspector Stubo on the phone this morning, from Flesland. He had to go back to Oslo, and I didn't think it was a good idea for them to send somebody else to talk to you. You've kind of ... got used to him. I knew you wouldn't be listening to the radio or watching TV, and you don't answer the phone either, so I thought it was best if I came myself. I came as soon as I could, Dad.'

Erik gave him a long, lingering look. His eyes were red-rimmed, and from the corners of his mouth a deep, dark furrow ran down either side of his chin. His nose was narrower now, and seemed bigger. In the flickering candlelight he looked half-dead.

'You don't sound very well,' he said. 'You sound as if you've got a cold.'

'Yes.' Lukas smiled wearily. 'I'm not on top form. But it's good to

348

know this, Dad. To know there was a particular reason why she was murdered. We should be proud of the fact that she ...'

His father gasped. Snorted, snivelled audibly and covered his eyes with the back of his hand.

'I don't want to talk about it,' he said in a loud voice.

'But Dad, things will be easier now. Stubo thinks this is a major breakthrough, and they're almost bound to clear up the case. It'll be easier for both of us to move on when we know what—'

'Did you hear me? Did you hear what I said?'

His father was trying to shout, but his voice wouldn't hold.

'I don't want to talk about this! Not now. Not ever!'

Lukas took a deep breath and was about to say something, but changed his mind. There was nothing more to say.

Sooner or later his father would reach a turning point in his grief. Lukas was sure of it. Just as he himself had felt a strange sense of relief when Stubo rang while they were getting William dressed, in time his father would also find comfort in the knowledge that Eva Karin had died for something she believed in.

There was no longer any point in going on at his father about the photograph.

When Astrid told him late last night that she had given the photograph to Adam Stubo, he had yelled, ranted and sworn at her. In the middle of his outburst he had hurled a glass vase on to the kitchen floor. It exploded into a thousand pieces, and only when he saw her terrified expression and realized she was afraid he was going to attack her did he manage to calm down.

It didn't matter so much any more.

His mother's murder would be cleared up, and it evidently had nothing to do with a missing sister. Adam Stubo had promised him over the phone that the photo would be returned as soon as they had made copies, and had said it was probably less central to the murder than he had first thought. The body would be released and the funeral could take place in just five days.

That would help all of them.

His father, too, he thought. It was more important for his father than for any of them to be able to draw a line under this before too much longer.

When all this was over, Lukas could look for his sister in peace. Whatever Astrid thought. At any rate, there was no need to bother his father about why the photograph had been moved from his mother's room and hidden in the attic.

He still had a sore throat. The tea tasted bitter, and he put down the cup.

His father was asleep. At least it looked that way: his eyes were closed, and his scrawny chest was moving up and down with a slow, even rhythm.

Lukas decided to stay. He closed his eyes, pulled his mother's old tartan blanket over him and fell asleep.

Long Day's Journey into Night

When the telephone rang it was as if someone were tugging at him. Adam grunted, turned over and tried to get whoever was holding his calf to let go. He kicked out at thin air, pulled the covers over him and groaned again. The sound of the mobile grew louder, and Johanne put the pillow over her head.

'It's yours,' she said sleepily. 'Answer the bloody thing. Or switch it off.'

Adam sat up abruptly and tried to work out where he was.

He fumbled around on the bedside table in confusion. His old mobile had turned out to be beyond repair, and he wasn't used to the ringtone of the new one.

'Hello,' he mumbled, and noticed that the glowing numbers on the clock were showing 05:24.

'Good morning, it's Sigmund! Were you asleep? Have you read *VG* yet?'

'Of course I haven't read the bloody paper, it's the middle of the night.'

'Do you know what's in it?'

'Of course I don't,' Adam growled. 'But I assume you're intending to tell me.'

'Go away,' Johanne groaned.

Adam swung his legs around and rubbed his face with one hand to wake himself up.

'Hang on,' he said, pushing his feet into a pair of dark blue slippers.

Johanne and Adam had sat up until three. When they finally stopped discussing the case, they decided to wind down with an old episode of *NYPD Blue*. Detective series always made him sleepy.

Now he was practically unconscious.

He stumbled into the bathroom and the stream of urine splashed against the bowl of the toilet as he held the phone up to his ear and said: 'Right, I'm listening now.'

'Are you pissing? *Are you pissing while you're talking to me?*'

'What's going on with *VG*?'

'They've got every single bloody name. Of the victims.'

Adam closed his eyes and swore, silently and with feeling.

'I can't get my head round this at all,' said Sigmund. 'But all hell has broken loose here, as you can imagine! There are journalists everywhere, Adam! They're calling me and everybody else non-stop, and—'

'Nobody's called me.'

'They will!'

Adam shambled into the kitchen, trying not to make a noise as he picked up the kettle with one hand.

'I realize we're in deep shit when it comes to leaks,' he said with a yawn. 'But did you really have to wake me before half past five on a Saturday morning to tell me?'

'That's not the main reason why I'm calling. I'm calling because ...'

The cafetière was full of coffee grounds. As he rinsed it out under the tap, the water made such a noise splashing against the glass that he couldn't really hear what Sigmund was saying.

'I didn't quite get that,' he muttered, the telephone clamped between his shoulder and ear. He pushed the measuring spoon down into the coffee tin.

'We've found the woman in the photo,' said Sigmund.

It was as if the very aroma of the coffee suddenly made Adam feel wide awake.

'What did you say?'

'The Bergen police have found the woman in your photograph. It probably doesn't mean as much as you'd like to think, but you've been so keen to—'

'How did they find her?' Adam interrupted him. 'In such a short time?'

'Somebody who works there actually recognized her! Here we are with our databases and our international collaboration and Lord knows what else, and it's actually the old methods that—'

'Who knows about this?' said Adam.

'Who knows about what?'

'That we've found her, for fuck's sake!'

'A couple of people in Bergen, I presume. And me. And now you.'

'Let's keep it that way,' Adam said decisively. 'For God's sake don't let anybody at headquarters know! And nobody with NCIS either. Ring your man in Bergen and tell him to keep his mouth shut!'

'It's a woman, actually. You've got so many preconceptions that I—'

'I couldn't give a toss about that! I just don't want this to end up in the paper, OK?'

The water was boiling; Adam measured out four spoonfuls of coffee, hesitated, then chucked in a fifth. He poured in the hot water and headed back towards the bathroom.

'So who is she?' he asked.

'Her name is ...'

Adam could hear papers rustling.

'Martine Brække,' said Sigmund. 'Her name is Martine Brække, and she's alive. Lives in Bergen.'

Adam stopped in the middle of the living room. The almost empty wine bottle from the previous night was still on the table. The newspaper with Johanne's scribbles was lying on the floor, the bowl of crisps tipped over beside it.

'How old is she?' he asked, feeling his pulse rate increase.

'I don't know,' said Sigmund. 'Oh yes, there it is! Born in 1947, it says here. She lives in—'

'Sixty-two this year. Johanne was right. Johanne might be bloody well right!'

'About what?'

'I have to go to Bergen,' said Adam. 'Are you coming?'

'Now? Today?'

'As soon as possible. Come and pick me up, Sigmund. Straight away. We have to go to Bergen.'

He rang off before Sigmund had time to reply.

Adam managed to shower, get dressed and drink a pitch-black cup of coffee without waking either Johanne or the children. When Sigmund's car obediently drove along Hauges Vei and parked outside the apartment block half an hour later, Adam was waiting by the gate.

It was Saturday 17 January, and he was standing there with no luggage.

*

The man who had saved a girl from being hit by a tram on Stortingsgaten in Oslo twenty-nine days earlier was drinking expensive mineral water from a long-stemmed glass and wondering if his suitcase had made it on to the plane. He had been late arriving. Now he was sitting on board British Airways flight BA 0117 from Heathrow to JFK in New York, one of only three passengers in first class. The other two were already well into their third glass of champagne, but he politely refused when the flight attendant offered him more water.

He was enjoying the generous amount of space he had, and the calm atmosphere in the front section of the plane. The curtain separating them from the other passengers transformed the racket from behind into a low murmur, which combined with the even hum of the engines to make him sleepy.

On this final section of the journey home he was travelling under his own name. The high-level security measures within US air travel and border controls following 9/11 made entering the country under false papers a risky business. Since he hadn't booked in advance, and everything but first class was sold out, he had had to pay out more than $7,000 for a single ticket to the United States. It couldn't be helped. He was going home now. He had to go home, and he was travelling under his real name: Richard Anthony Forrester.

During the two months he had spent in Norway, he hadn't called the United States once. The National Security Agency monitored all electronic traffic in and out of the country, and it was unnecessary to take such a risk. The instructions were clear from the start. If he needed to contact the organization for some unexpected reason, he could ring an emergency number in Switzerland. He hadn't needed to.

However, during Richard A. Forrester's stay in Norway, there had been a considerable amount of lively activity on his laptop. It was in Britain, being looked after by a short, stocky man with chalk-white teeth and a dark, close crewcut, who was visiting various rural communities presenting a new holiday offer from Forrester Travel. The company belonged to Richard. He had set it up two years after his wife and young son had been killed by a drunk driver, who had left the scene of the accident and killed himself in another crash four kilometres down the road.

As far as it was possible to check in practical terms, Richard A. Forrester had been in England since 15 November. It was only a safety measure, of course; no one would ever ask.

He lowered the back of his seat and covered himself with the soft blanket. It was only nine o'clock in the morning, but he hadn't slept much the previous night. It felt good to close his eyes.

When Susan and little Anthony died, his life had ended.

He had tried to follow them to heaven in a suicide attempt. It achieved nothing, apart from the fact that he could no longer count himself a US Marine. They had no use for suicidal soldiers, and Richard had to face the future without work as well as without his wife and child. All he had was a small pension, a suitcase full of clothes, and an insurance payout which he didn't really want from the accident.

'Can I get you anything else?' asked the attractive flight attendant. She leaned across the empty seat beside him and smiled. 'Coffee? Tea? Something to eat?'

He returned her smile and shook his head.

In the three months after the accident he had more or less become a tramp, usually drunk and constantly possessed by a blind, white-hot rage. One night he had quite rightly been thrown out of a bar in Dallas. He lay semi-conscious on the ground in some back street until a man appeared out of nowhere and offered him a meeting with God. Since Richard wasn't due to meet anyone else, he allowed himself to be helped up and led to a little chapel just two blocks away.

He met the Lord that night, just as the stranger had promised.

Richard Forrester ran a hand over his hair. It was nice to let it grow again, but he still had only a few millimetres of stubble covering his scalp. He was blessed with thick hair with no sign of bald patches yet, and he always kept it short. However, when he shaved his head his appearance changed considerably.

He settled down more comfortably, turned off the light above his head and pulled down the blind.

The God he had met in Dallas that November night in 2002 was completely different from the one he knew from home. His parents were Methodists, as were most people in the neighbourhood of the small town where he grew up. As a child Richard had thought of his religion as a kind of social participation in a closed community more than as a personal relationship with God. There was a service every Sunday, and the odd church bazaar. There was the football team and the Mothers' Union, barbecues and Christmas parties. Richard had mainly grown up with a *pleasant* God who made little impression on him.

When the stranger took Richard along to the chapel, he met the omnipotent God. He had a revelation that night. God came to him with a violence that made him think he was going to die at first, but eventually he passed into a state of peace and total surrender. That night in the chapel was Richard Forrester's catharsis. By the time the new day dawned, he was reborn.

His life as a soldier for his country, as a married man and a father, was over.

His life as a soldier of God had begun.

He never touched alcohol again.

Richard Forrester listened to the low hum of the engines, and saw the pretty girl in his mind's eye.

She had seen him. When the woman who was going to die went down into the cellar on her own, it provided him with a chance he just had to take. When the child appeared he was in despair for a moment, because of what he knew he must do.

Then he realized that this was a pure and honest child.

Just like Anthony, who had been born prematurely and with brain damage, which would have prevented him from ever maturing mentally. The girl was the same kind of child. Richard had understood that after just a few seconds.

He allowed her to run away, up the cellar steps.

In order to be completely sure, he had kept an eye on her. After he had saved her from being hit by the tram, it was easy to get one of the agitated observers dressed in his party clothes to tell him who she was. Richard had simply stood there on the opposite side of the street until the mother had carried the child inside. A man who was busy entertaining the constant stream of smokers with a dramatic eyewitness account had willingly given Richard the mother's name when he said he wanted to send her some flowers. He had found the address on the Internet.

Unfortunately, the girl had prevented him from killing the woman in the way he had originally intended, camouflaged as an accident. But it wasn't the child's fault. Fortunately, he had had the presence of mind to search through the woman's pockets and her bag; he had found the ticket to Australia and taken her mobile phone. Then he had gone into her room, collected her luggage and paid the bill. The chaos in reception suited him perfectly; he virtually disappeared among the crowd of partying guests and drunks. He had hidden her suitcase right at the back of an unlocked storeroom full of rubbish, underneath a big cardboard box that was so dusty it couldn't have been touched for years. He had to prevent her disappearance from being discovered immediately, and by sending a couple of short, nondescript texts over the next few days he had bought himself a decent interval. Every minute that elapsed between the murder and the start of an investigation reduced the chances of the case being solved.

'Can I get you a pillow?' he suddenly heard the flight attendant whisper.

Without opening his eyes he shook his head almost imperceptibly.

The child's mother had been hysterical. First of all she had slapped him across the face, once the girl was safe. In the period between Christmas and New Year he had once stood just a few hundred metres from the white building where the family lived. A man had come out of a neighbouring property and stopped by the fence to chat with the two girls playing in the garden. The mother was standing at the window, watching them. She was frightened out of her wits, and seemed beside herself when she came out to fetch them inside.

A bit like Susan, he thought, although he didn't allow himself to think about Susan very often. She was always anxious about Anthony, too.

It wasn't the first time he had noticed how the people he observed had a horrible feeling they were being watched. They never saw him, of course, just as the mother of the pretty girl hadn't seen him when he followed her to school in his neutral hire car, where he finally found confirmation that the child was different. He was too well trained ever to be seen. But she sensed his presence. It had taken Richard a little while to identify the girl's father, but he had become uneasy the very first time. Richard had wanted to find out if the child behaved differently away from her mother, and had observed them together on three separate occasions. The man started looking over his shoulder at an early stage.

The man who lived on a hill high above the city in a twisted caricature of a family had reacted in much the same way. Felt persecuted. His lover had been completely hysterical, rushing around photographing tyre tracks on the Monday almost two weeks ago. Richard had been standing at a safe distance, watching the whole thing. Two dark-skinned lads had driven up in a big BMW. Pakistanis, he guessed. Oslo was crawling with them. They obviously had something to sort out between themselves, because they had driven into the little pull-in outside the gate of the house where the so-called family lived and stayed there for a good while, gesticulating violently and smoking countless cigarettes before they drove off.

The sodomite had sensed Richard's presence, but hadn't seen him. Just like the others.

They didn't see him and, come to think of it, they didn't sense his presence either.

What they sensed was the presence of the Lord, Richard Forrester thought. And even if that perverted travesty of a father had escaped on this occasion, his time would come.

Richard Forrester smiled and fell asleep.

*

The house looked as if it was lying at rest on the steep hillside. The windows were small and divided into four panes. The wooden building was tucked in between two similar but larger houses, and was a modest dwelling. Almost shy. A narrow opening led into a little back garden. A lady's bike was propped up against a stone wall, and a collection of brightly coloured ceramic pots had been piled up in one corner for the winter. Stone steps led up to a small green door, beside which hung a porcelain nameplate. The name, and the meadow flowers surrounding it, had faded to pale blue in the wind and rain and sunshine over the years.

M. Brække, it said in ornate letters.

Adam Stubo hesitated. He stood on the stone steps with his back to the simple, wrought-iron fence and tried to think the whole thing through one more time.

He was about to deprive this woman of a secret she had kept for almost half a century, as far as he could tell. By placing his finger on the brass bell below the nameplate he would intrude upon a life that had been difficult enough already. The woman who lived in the little white house had made her choice and lived her whole life in the shadow of another's marriage.

The female employee at Bergen police station who had recognized the woman in the photograph had briefed him during the drive from Flesland. Martine Brække was a tutor at Bergen's cathedral school, unmarried and childless. She lived a quiet life, cut off from most things, but she was a respected teacher and also gave private piano lessons. She had once been a promising concert pianist herself, but at the age of nineteen she had been struck by a form of rheumatism which put an end to the brilliant career she had envisaged.

Fragile, tentative music could suddenly be heard from somewhere inside. Adam shook his head and listened to the piece being played on the piano. He didn't recognize it. It was light, dancing, and it made him think of the spring.

He lifted his hand and rang the doorbell.

The music stopped.

When the door opened, he recognized her at once. She was still beautiful, but her eyes were red-rimmed and the area around her mouth was puffy from crying.

'My name is Adam Stubo,' he said, holding out his hand. 'I'm a police officer. I'm afraid I need to talk to you about Eva Karin Lysgaard.'

The fear in her eyes made him glance to the side, as if he could still change his mind and leave.

'I'm alone,' he said. 'As you can see, I'm completely alone.'

She let him in.

*

'I really don't want to hear any more about that will, thank you,' Kristen Faber's secretary said to her husband as she was making sandwiches for lunch. 'It has absolutely nothing to do with you.'

Bjarne was sitting at the kitchen table with the photocopy in his hand, peering short-sightedly at the small writing.

'But you have to understand,' he said crossly, which was unusual for him, 'that this could actually mean the man has been conned out of a considerable inheritance!'

'Niclas Winter is dead. There are no heirs. That's what it said in the paper. A dead man can't be conned out of anything. Except life, of course.'

She snorted decisively and placed a generous portion of salmon on top of the mountain of scrambled eggs.

'So that's the end of that. Lunchtime!'

'No, Vera, that's not the end of anything!'

He banged his fist down on the table.

'This could involve a crime! I mean, it says here ...'

He slapped his other hand down on that day's copy of *VG*, which was lying open at a double-page article about some terrible gang from America that had killed six people out of blind hatred for homosexuals and lesbians. Bjarne Isaksen was shocked. Admittedly, he wasn't too keen on the sordid things that kind of person got up to, but there had to be limits. You couldn't just go around killing people in the name of God just because you weren't a fan of their love lives.

'It says here that Niclas Winter was murdered!'

Vera turned to him, put her hands on her hips and cleared her throat, as if bracing herself for what she intended to say.

'That will has nothing to do with Niclas Winter's death. I've read the article to you three times now, and there is no mention of money, an inheritance or a will. Those lunatics from America have just been killing indiscriminately, Bjarne! They can't possibly have known anything about a document that was lying in a dusty old cupboard in Kristen Faber's office!'

She was getting more and more angry as she went on.

'I've never heard anything so stupid in my entire life,' she said crossly, turning back to the worktop.

'I'm going to call the police,' Bjarne said obstinately. 'I can call them without saying who I am, then I can suggest they get in touch with Faber and ask him about a will with Niclas Winter as the beneficiary. They have those information lines, where you can ring up without saying who you are. That's what I'm going to do, Vera. And I'm going to do it now.'

Vera groaned theatrically and ran her slender hand over her hair.

'You are *not* going to call the police. If anyone in this house is going to speak to the police, it's me. At least I can explain how I ...'

Another nervous adjustment of her well-groomed coiffure.

'... have legal access to the will,' she concluded.

'Go on, then, do it!' Bjarne said agitatedly. 'Ring them!'

She banged the butter knife down on the worktop and fixed him with the sternest look she could muster, but he wasn't giving in. He stared back like a stubborn little boy, refusing to back down.

'Right then,' she said, and went to fetch the telephone.

*

'That was Adam Stubo,' Lukas said, slightly surprised. He put the phone down on the coffee table. 'He's on his way over.'

'Why? I thought you said he'd gone back to Oslo.'

At least his father had started talking again. A little bit.

'Evidently he came back today.'

'Why did he phone?'

'He wanted to speak to you. In person.'

'To me? Why?'

'I ... I don't know. But he said it was important. He said he'd tried to call you. Have you unplugged the landline?'

Lukas bent down and peered behind his father's armchair.

'You mustn't do that. It's important that people can get hold of you.'

'I have a right to peace and quiet.'

Lukas didn't reply. A vague sense of unease made him start wandering around the room. Only now did he notice that the house hadn't been cleaned since before Christmas. Apart from the fact that the pile of newspapers by the television was about a metre high, the place was tidy. His father kept things in order, but nothing else. When Lukas ran his finger over the smooth surface of the sideboard, it left a shiny streak. The nativity crib was still on display. The bulb inside the big glass box was broken, and the once atmospheric tableau was reduced to a gloomy memory of a Christmas he just wanted to forget. As he walked quickly around the corner and went over to the sofa in the L-shaped living room, the dust bunnies swirled silently across the floor. He stopped just outside his father's field of vision and sniffed the air.

It smelled of old man. Old house. Not exactly unpleasant, but stuffy and stale.

Lukas decided to do some cleaning, and went into the hallway to fetch a bucket and detergent from the cupboard. As far as he recalled, the vacuum cleaner was in there as well. When he remembered that Adam Stubo was on his way, he changed his mind.

'I think we could do with a bit of air in here,' he said loudly, walking over to the living-room window.

He fought with the catch and cut his thumb when it finally opened.

'Shit,' he said, sticking his thumb in his mouth.

The fact that Adam Stubo was already back in Bergen could be a good sign. Obviously, the investigation had picked up speed. Lukas hadn't heard any news bulletins or read the papers yet today, but Stubo had sounded optimistic on the phone.

There was a sweet, metallic taste on his tongue, and he examined his injured thumb. He was on his way to fetch a plaster from his mother's bathroom cabinet when the doorbell rang.

With his thumb in his mouth he went to open the door.

*

'Come in,' Silje Sørensen said loudly, looking over towards the door.

Johanne pushed it open hesitantly and poked her head in.

'Come in,' the inspector repeated, waving at her. 'I'm so glad you were able to come over. These stories in the papers are making me totally paranoid, and Adam thought you could give me an update. I daren't even trust my own mobile.'

'That's probably the last thing you should trust,' said Johanne, sitting down on the visitor's chair. 'Have you any idea who the leak is?'

'No. The press knowing too much has always been a problem for us, but this is the worst example I can remember. Sometimes I wonder if the journalists are blackmailing someone. If they've got something on one of us, I mean.'

She gave a fleeting smile and placed a bottle of mineral water and a glass in front of Johanne.

'You're usually thirsty,' she said. 'Right, I'm curious. Adam said the case in Bergen seems to have taken a completely fresh turn.'

'Well, I'm not ...'

The telephone rang.

Silje hesitated for a moment, then made an apologetic gesture as she answered it.

'Sørensen,' she said quickly.

Someone had a lot to say. Johanne felt more and more bewildered. The inspector didn't say much; she just stared at her from time to time, her gaze expressionless, almost preoccupied. Eventually, Johanne decided to go out into the corridor. The unpleasant experience of listening to a conversation not intended for her ears was making her sweaty. She was just getting up when Silje Sørensen shook her head violently and held up her hand.

'Is she bringing it over here?' she asked. 'Now?'

There was a brief silence.

'Good. Straight away, please. I'll stay in my office until you get here.'

She hung up, a furrow of surprise appearing across the top of her straight, slender nose from her left eyebrow.

'A will,' she said thoughtfully.

'What?'

'A woman who is evidently the secretary at a legal practice here in the city called the information line to say that she's sitting on a will that has Niclas Winter as the beneficiary, and that it could have some relevance to the investigation into his murder.'

'I see ... so ...'

'Fortunately the information was picked up relatively quickly, and one of my team has got hold of this woman. She's on her way over with the will right now.'

'But what ... ? If the theory about The 25'ers is correct, what would a will have to do with anything?'

Silje shrugged her shoulders.

'No idea. But it's on its way here, so we can have a look at it. Now, what was it you were going to tell me? Adam made me really curious, I have to admit.'

Johanne opened the bottle and poured herself a drink. The carbon dioxide hissed gently, tickling her upper lip as she drank.

'Eva Karin Lysgaard wasn't just sympathetic towards gays,' she said eventually, putting down the glass. 'She was, it appears, a lesbian herself. Which strengthens our theory about The 25'ers.'

Judging from the expression on Silje Sørensen's face, Johanne might as well have said that Jesus had come back to earth and sat down on the bed in Kristiane's room.

*

Marcus Koll sat up in bed in confusion, mumbling something that neither Rolf nor little Marcus could make out.

'Lazybones,' Rolf grinned, placing a tray of coffee, juice and two slices of toast topped with ham and cheese on the bedside table. 'It's gone one o'clock!'

'Why did you let me sleep so late?'

Marcus moved to avoid their hugs; he was sweaty, and smacked his lips to try to get rid of the sour taste of sleep.

'I don't think you got a wink of sleep last night,' said Rolf. 'So when you finally dropped off, I didn't have the heart to wake you.'

'We've been flying the helicopter,' little Marcus said excitedly. 'It's so cool!'

'In this weather?' Marcus groaned. 'It says in the instructions that the temperature is supposed to be above zero when you fly it. Otherwise the oil freezes.'

'But we couldn't wait until spring,' Rolf smiled. 'And it was brilliant. I had full control, Marcus.'

'And me!' said the boy. 'I can fly it all by myself!'

'At least when it's up in the air,' Rolf added. 'Here you go: today's tabloids. That's a terrible story – the one about that gang who've been murdering people! We've been shopping, too. Lots of good food for this evening. You haven't forgotten we're having guests?'

Marcus didn't remember anything about any guests. He reached for *VG*. The front page made him gasp out loud.

'Are you ill, Dad? Is that why you slept so late?'

'No, no. It's just a bit of a cold. Thank you so much for breakfast. Maybe I can enjoy it and have a look at the papers, then I'll come down in a little while?'

He didn't even look at Rolf.

'OK,' said the boy, and headed off.

'Is everything all right?' asked Rolf. 'Anything else you need?'

'Everything's fine. This is really kind of you both. I'll be down in half an hour, OK?'

Rolf hesitated. Looked at him. Marcus forced himself to adopt an unconcerned expression and licked his finger demonstratively as he prepared to turn the page.

'Enjoy,' said Rolf as he left the room.

It didn't sound as if he meant it.

*

'I was really intending to speak to you alone,' said Adam Stubo, looking from Erik to Lukas and back again. 'To be perfectly honest, I'd be much happier with that arrangement.'

'To be perfectly honest,' Erik replied, 'what makes you happy isn't the most important thing right now.'

'Jesus Christ,' Adam mumbled.

Erik had certainly perked up. In their earlier encounters his indifference had bordered on apathy. This time the scrawny widower had something aggressive, almost hostile about him. Adam hesitated. He had prepared himself for a conversation with a man in a completely different frame of mind from the one Erik was clearly in at the moment.

'I'm rather tired,' said Erik. 'Tired of you constantly turning up here with nothing to tell us. From what Lukas tells me, there has been a breakthrough in the investigation, in which case I would have thought you might have better things to do than coming out here yet again. If you're going to start on about where my wife was going so late at night, then ...'

It was as if he had suddenly used up all his reserves of energy. He literally collapsed; his shoulders slumped and his head drooped down towards his flat, bony chest.

'I'm not going to say anything I haven't said already. Just so we're clear.'

'There's no need,' Adam said calmly. 'I know where Eva Karin was going.'

Erik slowly lifted his head. His eyes had lost their colour. The whites had taken on a bluish tinge, and it was as if all the tears had washed away the blue from the irises. Adam had never seen an emptier gaze. He had no idea what he was going to say.

'Lukas,' Erik said, his voice steady. 'I would like you to leave now.'

*

At last time could begin to move again, thought Martine Brække as she struck a match.

The portrait of Eva Karin, which normally stood in the bedroom where no one ever saw it, had been moved into the living room. It had been the police officer's suggestion. He had asked her if she had a photograph. She had fetched it without a word, and the big man had held it in his hands. For a long time. He almost seemed to be on the point of bursting into tears.

She held the match to the wick of the tall white candle. The flame was pale, almost invisible, and she went and switched off the main light. She stood for a moment before picking up a little red poinsettia and placing it next to the photograph in the window. The glitter on the leaves sparkled in the candlelight.

Eva Karin was smiling at her.

Martine moved a chair over to the window and sat down.

A great sense of relief came over her. It was as if she had finally, after all these years, received a kind of acknowledgement. Until now she had borne her grief over Eva Karin's death all alone, in the same way as she had borne her life with Eva Karin for almost fifty years all alone. When Erik turned up the day after the murder, she had let him in. She had regretted it immediately. He had come for company. He wanted to grieve with the only other person who knew Eva Karin as she really was, but she had quickly realized they had nothing in common. They had shared Eva Karin, but she was indifferent to him now, and had sent him away without shedding a tear.

The big police officer had been another matter.

He treated her with respect – admiration almost – as he walked around the small living room talking to her quietly, occasionally stopping at some item he found fascinating. The only thing he really wanted to ask her about, and the reason for his visit, was whether she had ever told anyone else about her relationship with Eva Karin Lysgaard.

Of course she hadn't. That was the promise she had once made, that sunny day in May 1962 when Eva Karin promised never to leave her again – with the proviso that their love be a secret, a secret only the two of them knew.

Martine would never break a promise.

The policeman believed her.

When he told her that the funeral was to be held on Wednesday and she replied that she didn't want to go, he had offered to call in when the ceremony was over. To tell her about it. To be with her.

She had said no, but it was a kind thought.

Martine moved her chair closer to the window and ran her finger gently over Eva Karin's mouth. The glass felt cold against her fingertips. Eva Karin's skin had always been so soft, so unbelievably soft and sensitive.

They would do all they could to keep the story out of the public eye, Adam Stubo had said. As far as the investigation was concerned, there was probably nothing to be gained by publicizing details of this kind, he added, although of course he couldn't guarantee anything.

As she sat here by her own window looking out over the city beyond the portrait of the only love of her life, she felt as if it wasn't really important. Naturally, it would be best for Erik if their secret was never revealed. And for Lukas, too. It struck her that as far as she was concerned, it didn't matter at all. She was surprised. She straightened her back and took a deep breath.

She felt no shame.

She had loved Eva Karin in the purest way.

Her, and her alone.

Slowly she got up and blew out the candle.

She picked up the photograph.

Martine was almost sixty-two years old. Her life as it had been up to this point was over. And yet there could be more waiting for her – a whole new life as a wise old woman.

She smiled at the thought.

Wise, old and free.

Martine was free at last, and she put the photograph back on the bedside table. Adam Stubo had told her about his own grief when he found his wife and child dead after a terrible accident, an accident for which he felt he was to blame. His voice shook as he quietly explained how life had begun to go round in circles, a constantly rotating dance of pain from which he could see no escape.

She closed the bedroom door.

Time could begin to move again, and she said a quiet prayer for the kind police officer who had made her realize that it was never, ever too late to start afresh.

*

DC Knut Bork shook hands with Johanne before passing a document over to Silje Sørensen.

'There you go,' he said. 'I haven't had time to look at it yet.'

Silje opened a drawer and took out a pair of reading glasses.

'According to the woman who brought it in, we're talking about a considerable amount of money here,' Bork went on. 'Apparently, the testator died a long time ago, and Niclas Winter hasn't seen any of the inheritance to which he's entitled under the terms of this will.'

'May I see?' Johanne asked tentatively.

'We need a lawyer,' said Silje without looking up. 'This is sensational, to put it mildly.'

'I'm a lawyer.'

Both Knut Bork and his boss looked at her in amazement.

'I'm a lawyer,' Johanne repeated. 'Although I did my doctorate in criminology, I have a law degree. I don't remember much about inheritance law, but if you've got a statute book I'm sure we can work out the general gist.'

'You never cease to impress me,' said Silje Sørensen. She passed her the will, then went over to the shelf by the window and picked up the thick red statute book. 'But if you know as much as I do about this particular testator, then I'm sure you'll agree that we're going to need a whole heap of lawyers.'

Johanne glanced through the first page, then turned to the last.

'No,' she said. 'The name rings a bell, but I don't know who it is. However, what I can see is that this will becomes invalid in ...'

She looked up.

'In three months,' she said. 'In three months it won't be worth the paper it's written on. I think so, anyway.'

'Bloody hell,' said Silje, putting her hands on her hips. 'Now I don't understand anything. Not a bloody thing.'

*

Richard Forrester realized another meal must be on the way. The aroma of hot food had woken him. Perfect. Even though he was still a little befuddled after his deep sleep, he was hungry. The menu, which the attendant had thoughtfully left on the empty seat next to him rather than waking him up, looked appealing. He studied it carefully and decided on duck with orange sauce, wild rice and salad. When the fair-haired woman leaned over to take the menu, he asked for fresh asparagus as his starter.

He held up his hand to refuse the white wine she was offering.

'Water, please.'

When he opened the little blind, an intense light poured in through the window. It was half past twelve, Norwegian time. He half stood up to look down at the Atlantic, but the view below was made flat and uninteresting by dirty white cloud cover like an endless carpet. Only another plane, away to the south and heading in the opposite direction, broke the monotonous whiteness. The light bothered him, and he pulled the blind halfway down again.

He felt a blessed sense of peace.

It was always like that after a mission.

He hated those who were perverted with an intensity that had led him back to life, when he was hell-bent on drinking himself to death. He had come across a few of them in the military, cowardly curs who tried to hide the fact they did unmentionable things to each other, while somehow imagining they were good enough to defend their country. Back then – before he was saved – he had contented himself with reporting their activities. Three cases had disappeared into the bureaucratic machinery of the military, but he didn't lose any sleep over them. He had at least inflicted on them the unpleasant experience of coming under scrutiny. The fourth sodomite did not escape. He received a dishonourable discharge. Admittedly, the reason was that he had approached a young private, who threatened to sue the entire US Marine Corps, but Richard Forrester's report on immoral pornography had certainly not done any harm.

The aroma of food was getting stronger.

He dug the Bible out of his shoulder bag.

It was soft and shabby, with countless small notes in the margins on the thin paper. Here and there the text was marked with a yellow highlighter. In certain places the words were so unclear they were difficult to read, but it didn't matter. Richard Forrester knew his Bible, and he knew the most important passages off by heart.

When he was twelve years old, one of them had tried it on with him.

He closed his eyes, allowing his hand to rest on the book.

Life since his redemption had convinced him that Susan and Anthony had died for a reason. They had to be taken home to God, so that the Lord could reach him. With a wife and child he was deaf to His call. Richard had to be tested before he could become a worthy servant in the struggle for what was right.

When the man who had picked him up in that Dallas back street introduced him to Jacob a few months later, Richard was ready. Jacob was called only Jacob, nothing more, and Richard had never met anyone else in The 25'ers. As far as he knew, there could be several individuals like him on board this plane, and he caught himself stealing a glance at the woman across the aisle.

In fact, he had had to wait a couple more years before he was told the name of the organization, and its significance. At first he was furious when he realized he was working with Muslims in a common cause. Jacob had tried to convince him that this collaboration was right and necessary. They had common goals, and the Muslims had experience vital to the organization. This argument cut no ice with Richard. Nor did it help when he learned that The 25'ers received significant financial support from Muslim extremist groups. Richard Forrester knew they were practically self-financing, and couldn't grasp the idea that they were accepting money from terrorists. By that time he had killed two people in God's name, but he could never countenance taking innocent lives. He had been just as shocked as everyone else when two planes hit the World Trade Center, and he hated Muslims almost as vehemently as he hated sodomites. He had only conceded when he was woken one night by the intense presence of God, and was given an order by the Lord Himself.

After each mission a considerable sum of money was paid into his bank account. This was supposed to cover travel and accommodation, and was reported to the tax authorities as such. In the beginning he felt slightly uncomfortable. The generous payments made him feel like a contract killer.

Quickly, he put the Bible on his knee.

The flight attendant folded down his table and served the starter.

He got paid, he thought as he watched her quick, practised hands. But that wasn't why he killed.

Richard Forrester killed because the Lord commanded him to do so. The money was necessary only to carry out the missions he was given. Like now, when it was impossible to get home quickly enough unless he travelled first class.

Occasionally, he wondered where the money came from. It had kept him awake for a while during the odd night, but his trust in God was infinite. He quickly got over the slightly unpleasant feeling in his stomach when he realized with surprise from time to time how much was in his bank account.

'Thanks,' he said as the flight attendant refilled his glass.

He started to eat, and decided to think about something completely different.

*

'You need to think carefully, Erik. This is absolutely crucial.'

Adam had chosen to sit in Eva Karin's armchair this time. A faint scent lingered in the yellowish-brown upholstery, a half-erased memory of a woman who no longer existed. The fabric was soft, and a few fine strands of dark grey hair had stuck to the antimacassar. Adam had never called the widower by his first name before, but in view of the circumstances it seemed inappropriate to use a more formal form of address. Almost disrespectful, he thought, as he tried to get the man to look up.

'Eva Karin believed she had Jesus's blessing,' Erik wept. 'I've never really been able to come to terms with the idea that this was right, but—'

'You have to listen to me, Erik,' said Adam, leaning towards the other man. 'I have no desire, no need and no right to sit in judgement on the life you and Eva Karin shared. I don't even need to know anything about it. My job is to find out who killed her. Which means I have to ask you once again: who else knew about this ... relationship, apart from you, Martine and Eva Karin?'

Erik suddenly got to his feet. He clutched at his head and swayed.

Adam was halfway out of his chair to help him when Erik kicked out at him, making him lean back.

'Don't touch me! It couldn't be right! She wouldn't listen. I allowed myself to be persuaded that time, it was so ...'

It was thirty-two years since Adam Stubo started at the Police College, as the Training Academy was called in those days. In all those years he had seen and heard most things – experiences he thought he would never get over. His personal tragedy had almost broken him – and yet in many ways telling other parents that their child had been killed, that a husband or wife had been murdered, or parents mown down by a police car during a car chase was far worse. His own suffering was manageable, in spite of everything. Faced with other people's grief, Adam all too often felt completely helpless. However, over the years he had come up with a kind of strategy when he encountered bottomless despair, a method that made it possible for him to do the job he had to do.

But he wasn't up to this.

Over half an hour ago he had told Erik Lysgaard that he knew. He had tried to explain why he had come. Over and over again he had interrupted the widower's long, disjointed story of a life built on a secret so big that he had never really had room for it. It was Eva Karin's secret, Eva Karin's decision.

Erik Lysgaard was yelling at the top of his voice. He stood there in the middle of the floor wearing clothes that were too big and not very clean, bellowing out accusations. Against God. Against Eva Karin. Against Martine.

But most of all against himself.

'How could I believe in that?' he wailed, gasping for breath. 'How could I ... ? I didn't want to be like them ... not like that teacher, Berstad, not like ... You have to understand that ...'

Suddenly he fell silent. He took two steps towards Adam's armchair. His greasy, grey hair was sticking out in all directions and his lips were blood-red. Moist. His eyes were sunken and his chin trembled.

'Berstad killed himself,' he whispered hoarsely. 'In the spring of 1962. Eva Karin and I were in the third form. I couldn't be like him. *I couldn't live like him!*'

Heavy, viscous drops of saliva spurted out of his mouth; some trickled down his chin, but he took no notice.

'I'd seen the looks. I'd heard the ugly words, it was like ... like being lashed with a whip!'

He had foam all around his mouth. Adam held his breath. Erik looked like a troll, scrawny and bent, and he was gasping for breath.

'We came to an agreement,' he panted. 'We agreed to get married. Neither of us could live with the shame, with our parents' shame, with ... I was fond of Eva Karin. She gradually became my life. My ... sister. She was fond of me, too. She loved me, she said, as recently as the evening when she ... While I chose to live ... alone, for ever, she wanted to keep Martine. That was the agreement. Martine and Eva Karin.'

Slowly he went back to his armchair. Sat down. Wept silently without hiding his face in his hands.

'There had to be a punishment,' he said. 'There had to be a punishment eventually.'

'Who did you tell?'

'I'm the one who has to bear the punishment,' Erik whispered. 'I'm the one who is living in hell. All the time, every day. Every night, every second.'

'I have to know who you told, Erik.'

'Here.'

Erik's outstretched hand was holding a book with a worn leather cover. It had been lying on the coffee table when Adam came in, shabby and stained and without a title. Adam hesitated, but took it when Erik insisted.

'Take it! *Take it!* It's my diary. If you read the last twenty pages, you'll understand. You'll find what you want to know in there. Read it all, in fact. Try to understand.'

'But I can't, I mean I can't just—'

'I'd like you to leave now. Take the diary and go.'

Adam just stood there with the book in his hand, the book containing all of Erik Lysgaard's thoughts. He had no idea what to do, and still hadn't come to terms with the chaotic impressions crowding in on him after the grieving widower's outburst. Just as he was about to ask if there was anything he could do for him, he finally understood: there was nothing anyone in the whole world could do for Erik Lysgaard.

He tucked Erik's life under his arm and slipped silently out of the house on Nubbebakken for the very last time.

*

Rolf had crept along the landing as quietly as possible. Perhaps Marcus had fallen asleep again, it was so quiet in there. With all the sleepless nights he had suffered, it would be fantastic if he could get some rest. Rolf slowly pushed down the door handle. Too late he remembered the hinges squeaked, and he pulled a face at the harsh sound as the door opened.

Marcus was awake. He was sitting up in bed staring into space, the newspapers in a neat pile beside him. The food was untouched, the glass still full of orange juice.

'Weren't you hungry?' asked Rolf, surprised.

'No. I have to talk to you.'

'Talk away!' Rolf smiled and sat down on the bed. 'What is it, my love?'

'I want you to send little Marcus away. To my mother or to a friend. It doesn't matter which, but when he's safe and sound I would like you to come back here. I have to talk to you. Alone. Without anyone else in the house.'

'Good heavens,' said Rolf, with a strained smile. 'What's wrong, Marcus? Are you ill? Is it something serious?'

'Please do as I ask. And I would very much appreciate it if you could do it straight away. Please.'

His voice was so different. Not hard, exactly, thought Rolf, but mechanical, as if it wasn't actually Marcus who was talking.

'Please,' Marcus said again, more loudly this time. 'Please get my son out of the house and come back.'

Rolf got up hesitantly. For a moment he considered protesting, but when he saw the unfamiliar look in Marcus's eyes, he headed for the door.

'I'll try Mathias or Johan,' he said, keeping his tone as casual as possible. 'A school friend will be easier than driving him all the way to your mother's.'

'Good,' said Marcus Koll Junior. 'And come back as soon as you can.'

*

'Georg Koll knew my father,' said Silje Sørensen. 'They were business acquaintances. Even though I only met him a couple of times when I was a child, it was enough to realize the man was a real shit. My parents didn't like him either. But you know how it is. In those circles.'

She looked at the others and shrugged her shoulders apologetically.

Neither Johanne nor Knut Bork had any idea what it was like to move in the circles of the wealthy. They exchanged a quick glance before Johanne once again immersed herself in the document the solicitor's secretary had brought in.

'As far as I can see, this is a completely valid will,' she said. 'Unless a new will was made at a later date, then ...'

She gave a little shake of her head and held up the papers.

'... this is the one that applies.'

'But Georg Koll died years ago,' Silje said in bewilderment. 'His children inherited everything! The children from his marriage, that is. I had no idea Georg had another son. That is what it says, isn't it?'

Johanne nodded.

'*My son Niclas Winter*,' she quoted.

'Nobody must have known about him,' said Silje. 'I remember my father laughing up his sleeve when the inheritance was due to be paid out, because Georg lost touch with all his children after he left his wife when they were little. He really was a complete bastard, that man. His ex-wife and kids lived in poverty in Vålerenga, while Georg lived in luxury. It's Marcus Koll Junior, the eldest son, who runs the whole company now. I think they reorganized slightly, but ...'

She turned to the computer.

'Let's google Georg,' she murmured, staring expectantly at the screen. 'Bingo. He died ... on 18 August 1999.'

'Almost exactly four months after this was drawn up,' said Johanne, growing increasingly thoughtful. 'So it's hardly likely that he would have made a new will after that. I think our friend Niclas Winter was done out of his inheritance, simple as that!'

'But you can't just disinherit children born within a marriage in this country, surely?' Knut Bork exclaimed.

'If the estate is big enough ...'

Johanne leafed through the thick red book.

'The legitimate share to the children is one million kroner,' she said, searching for inheritance law. 'How many siblings does this Marcus Koll have?'

'Two,' said Silje. 'A sister and a brother, if I remember rightly.'

'According to this will,' Johanne said, 'the three of them should have received a million each, and Niclas should have inherited the rest.'

Silje gave a long drawn-out, shrill whistle.

'We're talking big money here,' she said. 'But surely there has to be ...'

Knut Bork leapt up and grabbed the document.

'Surely there has to be a statute of limitation,' he said agitatedly, as if it were his own fortune they were discussing. 'I mean, Niclas couldn't just turn up after all these years and start demanding ...'

He broke off and adopted a posture that made him look like a keen lecturer.

'Why the hell did I let that woman go?' he said. 'She mentioned something about Niclas Winter ringing around various solicitors more or less at random. He said his mother had just died, and she had told him on her deathbed that there was an important document addressed to him held by a legal practice in Oslo. It would secure his future. Perhaps he didn't ...'

They looked at each other. Johanne had found the section on inheritance law, and was sitting with her hand between the pages.

'There's a lot that needs checking, of course,' she said hesitantly. 'But at the moment it looks as if he didn't know about the will.'

'Why did his mother keep the fact that he was going to be rolling in money a secret from him? Shouldn't she have made sure that ... ?'

'Perhaps she didn't want him to find out his father's identity until after her death,' said Silje. 'There's so much we don't know. There's no point in speculating any further, really.'

'But we do know something,' Johanne interjected. 'There have been a couple of articles in *Dagens Næringsliv* about Niclas Winter since he died. His installations have shot up in price, at a time when sales of modern art are virtually non-existent. It said in the paper that he had no heirs, and that he was ... fatherless. His mother was an only child, and his maternal grandparents are dead.'

'So we can draw the conclusion that Niclas had no idea who his father was, or that he was the rightful heir,' said Knut Bork, perching on the windowsill with one foot on Johanne's chair.

'Not at the time, anyway,' she said. 'In which case the statute of limitation doesn't run out until ...'

The thin paper rustled faintly as she turned the pages.

'Paragraph 70,' she said vaguely. 'He's got six months. From when he finds out about the will, I mean. But I agree with you, Knut. As far as I know there is a definite statute of limitation ... I think it's ...'

The rest disappeared in an unintelligible mumble as she read. Knut waggled his foot impatiently, and leaned forwards to try and see the book for himself.

'Paragraph 75,' Johanne suddenly said loudly, following the text with her finger: *The right to claim an inheritance lapses when the heir does not validate such a claim within ten years of the death of the testator.* That's what I thought.'

'Fifteenth of April this year,' said Silje. 'That's when the statute of limitation would run out.'

The computer's screen saver suddenly burst into a silent firework display. Johanne stared at the red magnetic ring around Saturday 17 January. It had an almost hypnotic effect on her. In two days it would be the nineteenth once more, and she felt the hairs on her arms stand on end. Knut put his feet on the floor and stood up.

'But could Niclas come along and claim everything his siblings have owned for almost ten years?' he exclaimed. 'Isn't that bloody unjust, actually?'

Johanne was lost in thought.

'Why did he fall out with the children?' she said quietly, staring blankly into space.

'Georg Koll?'

'Yes.'

'As I said, he was an absolute shit most of the time. And I'm sure there was something about Marcus – he didn't like the fact that

Marcus was gay. The other two children sided with their brother. Marcus Koll was probably one of the first who really ... Well, he was the first person I knew who was openly gay. There was quite a bit of talk about it. In those circles. You know.'

Knut still knew very little about those circles, and Johanne looked as if she had barely heard what the inspector had said.

'Niclas was gay as well,' she said expressionlessly.

'Georg can't possibly have known that.'

'In the case in the US there's a link between ...'

Her eyes suddenly focused.

'So these two men are brothers,' she said, so quietly that Knut had difficulty hearing her. 'Half-brothers. In a similar case in the US it turned out there was a remarkable link between the victims. Could ... ?'

She looked from one to the other.

'Could Marcus Koll be the next victim?'

Her eyes slid from Knut to the calendar.

'The nineteenth of January is the day after tomorrow,' she said. 'Could it be ... ?'

'Do you believe in your own theory?' Knut broke in irritably. 'Or have you already dropped it? If The 25'ers really are behind these murders, I'm sure they'll have made sure they got their people out of the country long ago! *VG* gave away virtually everything we know, and the perpetrators must be idiots if they ... For fuck's sake, NCIS has been in constant contact with the FBI for the last twenty-four hours! The Americans might be bowing and scraping and thanking us for putting all our resources into the investigation, and sending people over tomorrow to help us, but they're making no effort to hide the fact that they think the perpetrators are on their way home!'

Johanne slammed the statute book shut with a dull thud.

'If we really do believe they intend to go on murdering people,' Knut said harshly, 'then we ought to do what they suggest in this rag ...'

He waved the newspaper around.

'... and warn every gay man and woman about next Monday. And the twenty-fourth. And the twenty-seventh. There'll be total—'

'It can't do any harm to send a patrol car,' Silje said reprovingly. 'An unmarked car. With plain-clothes officers. Nothing to attract attention. Marcus Koll ought to be informed about the fact that—'

'He ought to be informed about as little as possible,' Johanne interrupted. 'Or at least he shouldn't be told anything whatsoever about this will. I think he should be confronted with that particular piece of information under different circumstances and by different people, not during a visit by a couple of plain-clothes officers. We don't even know if he's aware he has a brother.'

'We'll send someone round anyway,' Silje said firmly. 'They're not going to say anything about the will, because so far we're the only ones who know about it. They can ... express a general concern for homosexuals with a public profile. Everyone knows about this case now. It should be fine.'

She smiled and stood up, signalling that the meeting was over.

Johanne remained seated, lost in her own thoughts, until Knut Bork had left the room and Silje was standing with her hand on the light switch.

'Are you thinking of staying here?' she asked. 'If so, it could get a bit lonely.'

*

Marcus Koll was all alone in the big house on Holmenkollen, apart from the dogs who were fast asleep in their basket next to the open fire. He had showered and put on clean clothes. Since he didn't know how long Rolf was going to be away, he had used the electric shaver instead of bothering with foam and a razor. When he was ready he had spent a few minutes in his study before sitting down in one of the soft, wing-backed armchairs in front of the picture window that looked out over the city and the fjord.

He was waiting.

He felt calm. Relieved, somehow. A faint tingling in his body reminded him more of being in love than of the sorrow he felt, and he breathed deeply through his nose.

It was the view he had fallen for once upon a time.

The garden sloped gently down towards the two tall pine trees by the fence right at the bottom. The other trees along the boundary provided privacy from the neighbouring house down below, but in no way detracted from the glorious panoramic view. Living up here was like living well outside the city, and it was this feeling of isolation combined with the view that had made him buy the house.

'Are you sitting here in the dark?' said a voice from behind him.

One by one the lamps in the living room were switched on.

'Marcus?' Rolf came and stood in front of him, a slightly puzzled expression on his face. 'You're ready. But it's only half-past two, and—'

'Come and sit down, please.'

'I can't make you out at all today, Marcus. I hope this won't take long, because we've got a lot to do. Marcus has decided to sleep over at Johan's, so that's—'

'Good. Sit down. Please.'

Rolf sat down in the matching armchair a metre away. They were half-facing the view, half-facing each other.

'What is it?'

'Do you remember that hard drive you found?' asked Marcus, coughing.

'What?'

'Do you remember finding a hard drive in the Maserati?'

'Yes. You said ... I can't remember what you said, but ... what about it?'

'It wasn't broken. I took it out of my computer so nobody would be able to see which websites I'd been surfing that night. If anyone happened to check, I mean.'

Rolf was perched on the edge of the chair, his mouth half-open. Marcus was leaning back with his feet on a matching footstool, both arms resting on the soft upholstery.

'Porn,' Rolf said with an uncertain smile, taking a guess. 'Did you ...? Have you downloaded something illegal that—?'

'No. I'd read an article in *Dagbladet*. It was quite harmless, in fact, but I wanted to be on the safe side. Absolutely on the safe side.' He snorted, a mixture of laughter and tears, then looked at Rolf and said: 'Could you possibly sit back a bit?'

'I'll sit how I want! What's the matter with you, Marcus? Your voice sounds strange and you're behaving ... oddly! Sitting here in your suit and tie early on a Saturday afternoon, talking about illegal surfing ... in *Dagbladet*! How the hell can it be illegal to—?'

Marcus got up abruptly. Rolf closed his mouth with an audible little click as his teeth banged together.

'I'm begging you,' said Marcus, running both hands over his head in an impotent gesture. 'I'm begging you to listen to what I have to say. Without interrupting. This is difficult enough, and at least I've found a way to begin now. Let me get through this.'

'Of course,' said Rolf. 'What's ... ? Of course. Carry on. Tell me.'

Marcus stared at the armchair for a few seconds, then sat down again.

'I came across a story about an artist called Niclas Winter. He was dead. The suggestion was that it was due to an overdose.'

'Niclas Winter,' said Rolf, clearly puzzled. 'He was one of the victims of—'

'Yes. He was one of the people murdered by the American hate group that *VG* has been writing about over the past few days. He was also my brother. Half-brother. My father's son.'

Rolf slowly got to his feet.

'Sit down,' said Marcus. *'Please sit down!'*

Rolf did as he asked, but once again he perched on the very edge of his seat, one hand on the armrest as if ready to leap up if necessary.

'I didn't know about him,' said Marcus. 'Not until last October. He came to see me. It was a shock, of course, but mostly I was pleased. A brother. Just like that. Out of the blue.'

Outside the sky was growing dark. In the west the sun had left a narrow strip of orange behind. In half an hour that, too, would be gone.

'I wasn't pleased for very long. He told me he was the rightful heir to everything. The whole lot.'

He took a quick, deep breath. There wasn't a sound.

'What do you mean the whole lot?' Rolf dared to whisper.

'All this,' said Marcus, with a sweeping gesture around the room. 'Everything that is mine. Ours. The entire estate left by his father and mine.'

Rolf started to laugh. A dry, peculiar laugh.

'But surely he can't just turn up and claim that he's a long-lost son who—'

'A will,' Marcus broke in. 'There was a will. Admittedly, he hadn't managed to get hold of it at that point, but his mother had told him such a document existed. All he had to do was find it. I thought he was a thoroughly unpleasant individual, and I didn't really believe him either, so I threw him out. He was furious, and swore he would have his revenge when he found the will. He seemed almost ...'

Marcus covered his eyes with his right hand.

'Crazy,' he murmured. 'He seemed crazy. I decided to forget about him, but after just a few hours I started to worry.'

He took his hand away and looked at Rolf.

'Niclas Winter was not unlike my father,' he said hoarsely. 'There was something about his appearance that made me check out his story. Just to be on the safe side.'

'And how did you do that?'

Rolf was still sitting in exactly the same position.

'By asking my mother.'

'Elsa? How the hell would she be able to—?'

Marcus held up his hand and shook his head.

'As soon as I told her I'd been visited by a man who not only insisted he was my brother, but also thought he had a claim on Georg's entire estate, she broke down completely. When I eventually got her to talk, she told me she had seen my father five days before he died. She had gone to see him to beg for ... to ask for money on behalf of Anine. My sister had split up with her partner, and she didn't want to lose her little apartment in Grünerløkka. She couldn't afford to keep it on the money she earns from working in a bookshop.'

'I think you should stop now,' said Rolf, swallowing audibly. 'You look like a living corpse, Marcus. You ought to go and lie down, you ought to—'

'*I ought to finish telling my story!*'

He banged the arm of the chair with his clenched fists. The dull thud made Rolf sink back in his own chair.

'*And you are going to listen!*' Marcus hissed.

Rolf nodded quickly.

'Georg threw my mother out,' said Marcus, taking a deep breath.

Keep calm, he thought. *Tell your story and do what you have to do.*

'But he did manage to tell her that he had made a will in favour of ... the bastard, as my mother refers to him. She had known about him all along. My father had no relationship with him either. He just wanted to punish us. Punish my mother, I assume.'

One of the setters stood up in its basket. The wicker creaked and the dog gave a long drawn-out yawn before padding over to Marcus and laying its head on his knee.

'When I realized the man was telling the truth, I didn't know which way to turn.'

He placed his hand on the soft head.

Rolf was breathing with his mouth open. A wheezing noise was coming from his throat, as if he were about to have an asthma attack.

'I'll cut a long story short,' said Marcus, pushing the dog away.

Slowly, as if he were an old man, he got up from his chair. He took a step forward and stopped, half-facing away from Rolf. The dog sat down beside him, as if both of them were looking for the same thing out there in the darkness.

'Three days later I was in the US,' said Marcus. His voice had acquired a metallic quality. 'It was business as usual, but I didn't feel too good. I got drunk one night with one of the directors of Lehman Brothers, who had just lost his job. I'd intended to ...'

The pause lasted for a long time.

'Forget it. The point is that I told him the story. He had a solution.'

An even longer pause.

The dog whimpered, and the very tip of his tail swept across the floor.

To the south the flashing light of a plane moved slowly across the sky.

'What kind of ... ?' Rolf had to clear his throat. 'What kind of solution?' he said.

'A contract killer,' said Marcus.

'A contract killer.'

'Yes. A contract killer. As I said, I was drunk.'

'And the following day you laughed it off, of course.'

The dog looked up at his owner and whimpered again, before getting up and ambling back to his basket.

'Marcus. Answer me. The next day you both had hangovers and laughed about it, the way you laugh at a joke. Didn't you? *Didn't you, Marcus?*'

Marcus didn't answer. He just stood there, shoulders slumped, arms hanging by his side, in his suit and tie and a state of total apathy.

'I set a monster free,' he whispered tonelessly. 'I couldn't have known I was setting a monster free.'

Rolf finally made his leap and grabbed Marcus by the arm.

'What are you telling me?' he roared, squeezing hard.

Marcus ignored both the pain in his arm and Rolf's violent outburst.

'*Tell me you didn't order a fucking murder, Marcus!*'

'He was going to take everything away from me. Niclas Winter was going to steal everything I deserved. Everything. Anine's money. And Mathias's. Ours. Everything that will go to little Marcus one day.'

His voice was nothing more than a monotone now, as if every word were being recorded individually on tape, to be edited into sentences at a later stage. Rolf raised his other hand, clenching his fist until the knuckles turned white. He was taller than Marcus. Stronger. Considerably fitter.

'If you're standing here telling me that you paid a contract killer, then I'll kill you! I'll kill you Marcus, I swear it! *Tell me you're lying!*'

'Two. Million. Dollars. For two million dollars, my problem would disappear. I paid. The man from Lehman Brothers organized the rest. The whole thing was so ... impersonal. A transfer to the Cayman Islands, and neither the money nor the ... order had anything to do with me any longer.'

Suddenly Rolf let go of his arm.

'That night,' Marcus went on, not even noticing that the dogs had started circling around them, yelping and whimpering, 'I got the confirmation I needed. A great deal is being written about The 25'ers at the moment, and doubtless quite a lot of it is unreliable. But the serious web pages gave me the confirmation I needed.'

'Of what?' Rolf sobbed, backing away slowly, as if he no longer wanted or dared to stand next to Marcus any longer. 'Confirmation of what?'

'The 25'ers commit murder for payment. Just like the Ku Klux Klan and The Order and ...'

He gasped for breath.

'They earn money by killing people they would like to eliminate anyway,' he whispered. 'I was the one who brought them here. My contact – or whoever he contacted – must have found out that the person I wanted killed was gay, and passed the job on to The 25'ers. So simple. So ... clinical. I'm the one who has financed the murders of six

Norwegians. I didn't even know that Niclas Winter ... my brother ... was gay too. I set a monster free. I ...'

He staggered backwards as the huge window exploded. A freezing cold wind rushed into the room. Shards of glass lay everywhere like fragments of ice. The dogs were howling. Rolf stood there with the heavy floor lamp in his hand, ready to strike again.

'You killed someone for this?' he yelled. 'You decided to buy a murderer? For a fucking Nazi place in Holmenkollen? For expensive cars and a bloody wine cellar? You've turned into one of them, Marcus! *You've turned into a fucking capitalist!*'

With a roar he braced himself, lifted the two-metre tall lamp with six kilos of lead in its base and smashed it into the next window with all his strength.

'*We would have managed without all this! I'm a vet, for fuck's sake! You're well educated! Things could have been just as good without ...*'

He was on the way to the next window when the doorbell rang.

He stood there, frozen to the spot.

It rang again.

Marcus heard nothing. He had sunk down into the armchair, among pieces of glass and broken lampshade. The dogs were running around barking. One of them had a badly cut paw, leaving a trail of blood across the floor as the terrified animal disappeared into the hallway.

'I set a monster free,' Marcus whispered, closing his eyes.

He registered voices from the hallway, but he didn't hear what they were saying.

'A monster,' he whispered again, then stood up and walked across the room.

'It's the police,' Rolf sobbed from the doorway. 'Marcus! The police are here.'

But Marcus was no longer there. He had gone into his study and sat down on his calfskin-covered desk chair behind the desk made of polished silver birch. The door was closed but not locked. When he heard Rolf call out again, he opened the top drawer, where he had placed the pistol from the gun cupboard in readiness.

He removed the safety catch and placed the barrel to his temple.

'Tell them the whole story,' he said, even though no one could hear him. 'And take good care of our son.'

The last thing Marcus Koll Junior heard was Rolf's scream and just a fraction of the short, sharp report.

*

A short man accompanied by a fat African-American came towards Richard Forrester as he approached passport control at John F. Kennedy International Airport. The queue looked endless, and for a brief moment it occurred to him that they were perhaps going to offer him special privileges as a first-class passenger, allowing him to go ahead of all the other travellers. He smiled encouragingly as the smaller of the two men looked at him and asked: 'Richard Forrester?'

'Yes?'

The man took out an ID card, which was very easy to recognize. He began to speak. Richard's voice disappeared. There was a rushing sound in his ears, and he felt so hot. Too hot. He tugged at his tie, he couldn't get his breath.

'... the right to remain silent. Anything you say can and will be used against you in ...'

Richard Forrester closed his eyes and listened to the drone of the Miranda warning that seemed to be coming from somewhere far, far away. Something had gone wrong, and for the life of him he couldn't work out what it was. There wasn't a trace of him anywhere. No prints. No photos. He had only been in England, on a business trip relating to his small but well-run travel company.

'Do you understand?'

He opened his eyes. It was the fat man who had asked. His voice was rough and deep, and he glared at Richard as he repeated: 'Do you understand?'

'No,' said Richard Forrester, holding out his hands as the smaller man requested. 'I don't understand a thing.'

*

'Adam,' Johanne said quietly, moving close to his sleeping body. 'Wasn't there anything we could have done to prevent that suicide?'

'No,' he mumbled, turning over. 'Like what?'

'I don't know.'

386

The time was 2.35 in the morning on Sunday 18 January 2009. Adam licked his lips and half sat up to have a drink of water.

'I can't sleep,' Johanne whispered.

'I've noticed,' he smiled. 'But it has been rather an eventful day, after all.'

'I'm so glad you caught the last flight home.'

'Me too.'

She kissed him on the cheek and wriggled into the crook of his arm. The worn old leather-bound diary was still lying on Adam's bedside table. He had shown it to her, but hadn't let her read any of it. No one else knew of its existence. The highly personal contents had affected him deeply. Religious musings, philosophical observations. Accounts of everyday life. The story of how a homosexual man had created a child with a lesbian woman, about the happiness and the pain of it, the shame. All in small, ornate handwriting that seemed almost feminine. As soon as Adam had landed at Gardermoen he had decided to write a report on the key elements relating to the murder of Eva Karin Lysgaard, and to make it look as if Erik had told him everything. No one else would ever see the diary.

'I'm sure he's not going to convert after this,' Adam said quietly.

As early as their second meeting, Lukas had mentioned Erik's fascination with Catholicism. The young man had actually smiled when he talked about his parents' trip to Boston the previous autumn. Eva Karin was a delegate attending a world ecumenical congress, and Erik had visited the city's Catholic churches. What neither Eva Karin nor Lukas knew was that he had gone to confession. He had a theological background, and could pass for a Catholic if he so wished. His conversation with the priest in the confessional was reproduced in detail in the brown leather-bound diary. It had been Erik's very first confidential discussion about the great lie of his life that was so difficult to bear.

'Do you think it's the priest? Is he something to do with The 25'ers?'

Johanne was whispering, even though she had let the children stay over with her parents. They had looked after them while she was with Silje Sørensen, and both children had flatly refused to come home when she eventually turned up to collect them, puffing and panting.

'Who knows? The priest or someone connected with him.

Catholics have a certain ... tradition when it comes to taking the law into their own hands, you could say. At any rate, it's clear Erik never spoke to anyone else about this, and I think it's out of the question that Eva Karin would have had another confidante apart from Martine. I've met Martine. Eva Karin didn't need anyone else, believe me. A really lovely woman. Very wise. Warm.'

He smiled in the darkness.

'Anyway, the Americans will clear things up now. It turns out the FBI had quite a lot of information already. They just needed this ... key. We've given them so much information they think they'll probably be able to blow the entire organization apart. Back here the investigation is firing on all cylinders. We'll be mapping the movements of all American citizens over the past few months. We can combine and compare information from all six murders now we know they're linked. We'll be—'

'The picture,' Johanne interrupted him. 'The artist's sketch, that was what led to the breakthrough. For the Americans and for us. Silje told me it took the FBI only nine hours to establish the identity of one of the perpetrators. The driving licence register combined with information about travel between Europe and the States over the past few months was enough to identify the man. That drawing solved the entire case.'

'True. It's quite frightening to think how surveillance actually works. This will be grist to the mill for those who want to see more of that kind of thing.'

Adam kissed the top of her head.

'The picture was important,' he went on. 'You're right there. But it was mostly down to you, sweetheart.'

They both fell silent.

'Adam ... ?'

'Yes.'

'If they do destroy The 25'ers, sooner or later a new organization will emerge that stands for the same thing. Thinks the same way. Does the same kind of thing.'

'Yes. I'm sure you're right.'

'Here in Norway, too?'

'In some ways that's in our hands, I suppose.'

The silence went on for so long that Adam's breathing fell into a slower, deeper rhythm.

'Adam ... ?'

'I think we should get some sleep now, sweetheart.'

'Have you never believed in God?'

She could hear that he was smiling.

'No.'

'Why not? Not even when Elisabeth and Trine died and—'

He carefully moved his arm and gently pushed her away.

'I really would like to go to sleep now. And you should do the same.'

The bed bounced as he turned on to his side with his back to her. She shuffled after him, feeling his body like a big, warm wall against her own nakedness. It took him less than a minute to get back to sleep.

'Adam,' she whispered, as quietly as she could. 'Sometimes I believe in God. A little bit, anyway.'

He laughed, but in his sleep.

EPILOGUE / PROLOGUE

May 1962

The Encounter

Eva Karin has just turned sixteen, and she has a dress made of pale blue polyester.

Her mother made it, just as she has made every single dress Eva Karin has ever owned. This is the best one of all, and the first with an adult cut – a Jackie Kennedy dress she didn't even get around to wishing for. She didn't get around to wishing for anything at all. She didn't give her birthday a thought.

There has been no room for anything apart from this one huge thing, this terrible thing that has to go away.

When she opened her present she had to pretend she was happy. As if it were possible for her to be happy. Her mother was so overjoyed with the beautiful material and her fine stitching that she didn't notice how Eva Karin was feeling.

No one can see how Eva Karin is feeling. Except God, if He exists.

She put on the dress when she got up this morning. Her mother was annoyed; she was supposed to save it until 17 May, Norway's National Day. Eva Karin said she didn't want to be late for school, and hadn't got time to change. Her mother gave in. She was also a little proud, Eva Karin could see that. Dark-eyed, black-haired Eva Karin with the ice-blue dress that made her look American.

She had hidden the ballerina pumps in her bag. She changed out of her sensible walking shoes as soon as she was out of sight.

Eva Karin has dressed up to die.

She doesn't want anyone she knows to find her body. She is heading up to Løvstakken, all the way up; her younger siblings are too little to go up there, and her mother and father never set foot there either.

The air is sharp and clear. It's chilly, and she pulls the golf jacket more tightly around her. She has to look where she's going. There are roots and stones on the track, and she doesn't want her ballerina pumps to get dirty.

Her father doesn't believe in God.

Eva Karin wants to believe in God.

She has prayed so hard.

She has read His book, which she has to hide in her underwear drawer so that her father won't find it. Religion is the opium of the people, he frequently growls, and Eva Karin and her siblings are the only children she knows who have not been baptized and confirmed. She has read and searched in the forbidden Bible, but all she finds is condemnation.

God and her father are in agreement on just one thing: people like her have no right to live.

People like her must be spoken about using a particular language. A particular language consisting of looks, gestures and words which actually mean something else, but when they are used about people like her, they acquire a dark meaning that she cannot live with.

She always thought it was only men who were like that.

They exist, she knows they exist, because they are the ones who become the object of those ambiguous words, those looks, those obscene gestures the boys make behind Mr Berstad's back, making the girls snigger. All except Eva Karin, who blushes.

She stops for a moment. The sun is shining down through the fresh new leaves. The ground looks as if it is covered with shimmering liquid gold. Dense carpets of wood anemones surround the trees, protecting the roots. The birds are singing, and high above the tree-tops, white fluffy clouds drift by.

She has been going out with Erik for six months now.

Erik is nice. He never touches her. Doesn't want to kiss and cuddle, doesn't grope her the way her friends tell her the other boys do. Erik reads books and works hard in school. They drink tea together, and Erik sometimes shows her a few of the poems he has written, which are not particularly good. Eva Karin enjoys Erik's company. She feels safe. She feels calm when she is with Erik. Not like when she sees Martine.

Suddenly she sets off again.

She mustn't think about Martine. She mustn't see Martine in her mind's eye, when they stay the night with each other and their mothers don't even knock on the door when they come in to say goodnight.

Eva Karin has prayed and prayed. That she might escape Martine. That she might find the strength to stop wanting her. Eva Karin has spent entire nights on her knees by her bed, with her hands clasped together and her eyes closed. No one has answered her, not even on those occasions when she placed shards of of glass beneath her knees. Martine is with Eva Karin whether she is there or not; she never goes away. Eva Karin prays until she faints with exhaustion, but no one ever answers her prayers. Perhaps her father is right after all, just as he is right when he says that people like her are an abomination.

Her father and mother must never know, thinks Eva Karin as she stumbles on up the track. Her father, who has sung to her, played with her, who made a wooden doll's pram for her in his workshop when she was five years old; her father who cheered and swung her up on to his shoulders and carried her along in the procession every year on 1 May until she got too heavy, and was allowed to carry the left-hand tassel on the trade union flag instead; her father must never find out that his daughter is one of those.

One of those.

Eva Karin is *one of those.*

Eva Karin wants to die, and she has one of her father's razor blades in her bag.

A boy is coming towards her through the trees. Not along the track, like her. He appears from the side, she turns away, no one must see her tears, and certainly not now, not when she is about to die. Eva Karin increases her speed.

Suddenly, he is standing in front of her.

He is smiling.

He is more of a man than a boy, she sees now, and his hair is unkempt. It can't have been cut for ages, and she recoils.

'Do not be afraid,' he says, holding out his arms with the palms facing her. 'I only want to talk to you.'

When he extends one hand towards her, she takes it.

She doesn't know why, but she takes the stranger's hand and goes with him into the forest. They walk among the trees, wading through the wood anemones to a little glade warmed by the sun. He sits down with his back resting against a tree trunk, and gently pats the ground beside him.

The man is wearing American blue jeans and a white collarless shirt. His feet are bare apart from a pair of sandals like the ones her father has; they never come out of the wardrobe until the summer holidays. The stranger speaks with a Bergen accent, but he is not like anyone she has ever met.

Eva Karin sits down. The sun pours its warmth over her, and the light is intense. She screws up her eyes as she looks at the sky.

'You are not to do this,' says the man with the ice-blue eyes.

'I have to,' says Eva Karin.

'You are not to do this,' he repeats, opening her bag.

She allows a strange man to open her bag and take out the razor blade, which she had tucked into a tear in the lining. He places it on top of a scar on his hand, then closes his hand.

'Look,' he says with a smile, slowly opening his hand with the palm upwards.

The razor blade has disappeared.

His laughter comes from all around, it is the soughing of the wind and the song of the birds. He laughs until she cannot help smiling, and when he sees her smile he claps his hands softly.

'I love my magic tricks,' he says.

Eva Karin rests. Almost summer.

'Life is sacred,' the man says. 'You must never forget that.'

'Not mine,' she says with her eyes closed. 'I am ... a sinner.'

She hesitates before using such a word. It is too high-flown. It feels wrong in her mouth, it is too big and grown-up and she is only sixteen years old.

'We are all sinners,' he says in a casual tone of voice. 'But I don't want the entire population of the city running around trying to kill themselves for that reason.'

'I ... I love another girl.'

Once again a word that is too big for her. 'Love' is a word for the darkness, a word to be whispered, almost inaudibly.

'And the greatest of these is love,' he smiles, and all around them the forest begins to laugh again. 'When I think about it, I have never said anything more true.'

His hand brushes against her knee. It is heavy and light at the same time. Warm and cold, and something else for which she does not have the words.

'You must listen to me,' he says, suddenly serious. 'Not to all those who think they know me.'

'I've read and read,' Eva Karin whispers. 'But I cannot find any comfort.'

'Listen to what I say. Not to the things people say I have said.'

He gets on his knees and turns to face her. His head hides the sun, and becomes a black silhouette surrounded by a light so strong that Eva Karin cannot look. Once again she feels that heavy lightness in his hands as he clasps them around hers.

'I am not harsh, Eva Karin. Admittedly, my father can be a little strange and thunderous from time to time, but I myself have experienced too much to sit in judgement on love.'

She cannot see him, but she can hear his smile.

'It is evil I condemn. Darkness. Never light and love.'

'But I—'

'Be true to yourself, and true to me.'

'How shall I—?'

'I don't give prescriptions for life, Eva Karin. But you will find a solution. And if you should stumble and fall, if you should have doubts and be afraid, then all you have to do is speak to me. I have been listening to you for a while, you see. I just had to wait for the right moment.'

He stands up and takes a step to the side. The warmth of the sun once again pours over Eva Karin. Shading her eyes with her right hand, she looks up.

'Do not fail your own ability to love,' he says, beginning to move away. 'And above all: do not judge your own life according to the standards of others.'

Halfway across the little glade he turns to her once more.

'There is only one thing that you must hold sacred and inviolate,' he says. 'And that is life itself.'

'Life itself,' she whispers, and he is gone.

But he never left her.

Author's Afterword

This book is a novel, and is therefore not true. To be a writer is to lie, to make things up, to invent. This means that you can describe a cellar at the Hotel Continental, for example, without even knowing whether or not it exists. I know nothing about the hotel's air-conditioning system, nor do I know whether the hotel has a system of CCTV cameras which is out of date. I hope I am forgiven for using the building as part of the backdrop for my story; it's just so perfect.

What is true, however, is that in many countries there are a number of groups united in particular by their hatred and contempt for certain sections of society. It is also true that some of these groups are fairly systematic in their use of violence against the people they hate. Some of them have demonstrably perpetrated the most serious crimes in order to finance their macabre projects. It is also true, unfortunately, that murder and acts of terrorism have been carried out in the name of various gods all over the world since time immemorial. All the hate groups mentioned in this novel actually exist, with the exception of The 25'ers.

APLC does not exist. It is, however, modelled on the Southern Poverty Law Center in Montgomery, Alabama. Their homepage (www.splcenter.org) with its links and suggestions for further reading has been extremely helpful in my work on this book.

Fear Not could not have been written without patience, loving encouragement and stubborn opposition from my spouse of ten years, Tina Kjær. Thanks to her, and to our daughter Iohanne, who cannot understand why I have to spend so much time in my office for four months of the year during the final phase of every new novel. We are heading for brighter days, my love.

Thanks also to Mariann Aalmo Fredin for valuable help along the way; to Berit Reiss-Andersen for everything she knows about the law, which I have long forgotten; and to my brother Even Holt, who always has piquant medical refinements to offer. A big thank you also to Kari Michelsen, who in May 2008 at a beach bar in France persuaded me to abandon a project which had been under way for a long time and to write this book instead.

Finally, a loving thank you to Picasso. She warms my feet while I write, forces me out in sunshine or rain, and gives me wholly undeserved, unconditional devotion.

ANNE HOLT
Nydalen, Oslo 2009

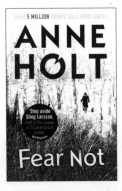
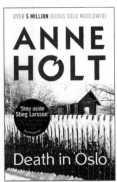

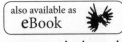